To M...
with love
Della Galton

PASSING SHADOWS

By

DELLA GALTON

Published by Accent Press Ltd – 2006
ISBN 1905170238
Copyright © Della Galton 2006

The right of Della Galton to be identified as the author of this work
has been asserted by her in accordance with the Copyright, Designs
and Patents Act 1988.

The story contained within this book is a work of fiction. Names
and characters are the product of the author's imagination and any
resemblance to actual persons, living or dead, is entirely
coincidental.

All rights reserved. No part of this book may be reproduced, stored
in a retrieval system, or transmitted in any form or by any means,
electronic, electrostatic, magnetic tape, mechanical, photocopying,
recording or otherwise, without the written permission of the
publishers: Accent Press Ltd, PO Box 50, Pembroke Dock,
Pembrokeshire SA72 6WY.

Printed and bound in the UK by
Clays PLC, St Ives

Cover Design by Emma Barnes

The publisher acknowledges the financial support
of the Welsh Books Council

To my dear friend, Jan, and to my darling Tony.

With love and thanks

Acknowledgements

This novel would never have been written were it not for two men, both named Ian. The late Ian Sommerville, who inspired me to write it, and Ian Burton, whose help and support has been invaluable.

I would also like to thank, Sharon Brook, Ann Caulfield, Su Cooke, Eileen Dredge, Barbara Featherstone, Nancy Henshaw, Adam Millward, Sandy Neville, Janine Pulford, Sue Sami, Carol Waterkyn, David Wass, the entire Wednesday night writing class and the Dunford Novelists.

And last, but by no means least, my editor, Catherine Merriman, for her help and advice, and my publisher, Hazel Cushion, for believing in me.

Chapter One

Maggie could feel the familiar tension coiling in her stomach as she locked her front door, the key slippery in her fingers. She wiped her hands on her jeans, picked up the cellophane-wrapped spray of white roses and was just turning when she heard the sound of running footsteps on the unmade road that fronted her cottage, followed by a woman's breathless voice.

The woman, grey-haired and with a vibrant yellow straw bag flapping from one arm, appeared, panting heavily, in her front garden.

"Oh, I'm so glad I caught you," she gasped. "You are the animal rescue woman, aren't you, dear? They said in the pub I'd find you here." She paused for breath and added in a bemused voice, "You don't look a bit like I expected."

Maggie smiled and wondered what she was supposed to look like. As well as the jeans, which had started off black, but were now faded to grey, she was wearing a cream tee-shirt – one of the few she owned that didn't have a flippant slogan on the back, in deference to where she was going. She'd meant to be smarter. She'd clipped back her unruly brown hair and sprayed it within an inch of its life, but she hadn't been able to find any more suitable clothes in her wardrobe. Probably because most of them were stuffed in the laundry basket and laundry was way down her priority list at the moment.

"I thought you'd be older," her visitor gasped. "And bigger – stronger – you know."

"I'm stronger than I look," Maggie murmured, wondering what she was letting herself in for. Lots of people who turned up at the sanctuary seemed surprised when they saw her. She wasn't sure what she was supposed to look like. Evidently not tall and slightly built – she hadn't been called beanpole for nothing at school – and most people were amazed when she told them she was twenty-seven, not seventeen.

"Are you all right?" she asked gently, because the woman's face was scarlet with exertion and there were beads of sweat below the silver rims of her glasses. "Where have you run from?"

"Oh, only a little way – my car's parked down on the main road. He flew straight at me, you see. I didn't have a hope of stopping."

"A bird?" Maggie said, concerned, because birds rarely survived run-ins with cars. "Do you know what sort of bird he was?"

"Blooming great thing – I was lucky my window wasn't open, he'd have been in the car then and I'd probably have crashed it. I don't know what kind he is, I don't know anything about birds, see. He's not dead though, he was fluttering about on the grass verge. I couldn't get anywhere near 'im. Tried to attack me, he did." She was already backing away down the path. "You will come, won't you?"

"Yes, of course I'll come. It was good of you to stop." Maggie caught up with her visitor, torn between not wanting to rush her – she was elderly and still out of breath – and worry about getting to the injured bird before a predator did. Mind you, not being able to get 'near 'im' sounded promising. The bird couldn't be too badly hurt if it was still trying to defend itself.

"I hope I'm not holding you up, dear. You were just on your way out, weren't you?"

"Yes, but it's okay, you're not holding me up. I was on my way to see someone, but we didn't have a set time." That was the understatement of the year, Maggie thought, swallowing down a mixture of regret and relief that she had an excuse to put off the confrontation for a little longer. She grabbed a small animal transporter and a net from an outbuilding on her way past and followed the woman back along the lane.

She'd been expecting a buzzard – there were dozens in the Wiltshire countryside – but as they got closer to the stricken bird, she realised it was bigger than a buzzard. A lot bigger and not the right colour, either. It had chestnut feathers and a pale-coloured head, almost white. Maggie frowned, racking her brains. She'd had a friend at vet school who was really into birds. They'd often spent nights chatting about wildlife and about how to recognise the different birds of prey. This bird had distinctive yellow legs and a yellow beak.

The memory of a photograph in Ellen's bird book slid into her mind and her face cleared. "I've never seen one of these before, but I think it might be a red kite," she told her companion, with growing excitement. "They're virtually extinct in England. You see them a lot in Wales, though."

"Well, if he was emigrating for the winter, Salisbury wouldn't be too far out of his way, would it? Perhaps he got blown off course." Maggie suppressed a smile, as the woman, whose geography was obviously a lot better than her knowledge of birds, eyed her anxiously. "You watch yourself, dear. Mind his claws. Poor little lamb's none too happy – not that I can blame 'im for that." She hung back. Maggie approached cautiously with the net.

'Poor little lamb' were the last words she'd have used to describe the kite. Proud and beautiful certainly, but this bird of prey was far from a 'little lamb'. Maggie felt a surge of admiration as the bird glared at her and tried to rise in flight, but only succeeded in toppling sideways on to the grass verge. Its wingspan must have been a couple of metres and she knew that netting it without injury to either of them was going to be tricky, if not impossible.

She contemplated heading back to the Red Lion and enlisting some help. On the other hand, the pub would have been open an hour by now, which was long enough for the die-hard drinkers to be on their fourth pints of real ale. The last thing she needed was a crowd of rowdy onlookers who fancied themselves as bird experts following her down here.

Deciding to have a go on her own, she edged forward. If she could restrain the bird with the net, she might be able to get close enough to immobilise it without frightening it into hurting itself further or injuring herself.

Luck was on Maggie's side for once. When the bird felt the net, it flapped angrily, tried to back its way out and ended up trapped against the fence that edged the fields of fat golden hay bales beyond the road. Taking care to avoid the lethal talons and wickedly hooked beak, Maggie tightened the net, and the bird, no longer trying to escape but shrieking furiously, let her get close enough to touch.

Sweat dripped into her eyes as she crouched on the grass verge and, talking softly all the time, let the bird get used to her presence. "All right, my sweetie, I'm not going to hurt you. I just want to check out that wing. You are a beauty, aren't you."

When a car door slammed close by, Maggie assumed the woman had decided to wait in her car, but then she heard a voice. She glanced up and saw a man in jeans and denim jacket heading her way.

Great, that was all she needed. An interfering passer-by.

"Can I help?" He paused a few feet away, which she supposed was better than blundering in and frightening her prospective patient.

4

"I'm fine," she muttered, wiping sweat out of her eyes. "Don't make any sudden movements, I don't want it scared. And please don't come any closer."

"I wasn't planning on it." His voice was wry and now she could see him properly she had an impression of a strong, angular face, fair hair that was slightly too long and cool, grey eyes.

He looked perfectly sober too, which was a relief.

"I thought you might have broken down," he added, hunkering down on the grass verge, his movements slow and controlled. "That's why I stopped."

The bird fluttered, aware of his presence, and, distracted, Maggie nodded. "You could do something to help, if you don't mind. You could open the door of that cage for me and pass it over very slowly."

"Sure." He did as she said and inched the transporter across the grass towards her.

There was one sticky moment when she was edging the bird into it and the woman, who Maggie had forgotten all about, clapped her hands in excitement and shouted out, "Well done, dear! Good for you!"

The bird fluttered wildly and extricated a leg from the net and Maggie was only just in time to snatch her fingers out of slicing distance of its talons. She drew the net gently back into place, latched the transporter with a sigh of relief, wiped her face once more with the back of her hand, and stood up slowly.

The man who'd stopped to help glanced at her. "Nice work. What will you do now – take it to a vet?"

"No need, I can sort it out myself. I think the wing's broken, but it's not irreparable. It just needs strapping up for a while. If it survives the shock of all the human contact, it'll be fine. I'm trained as a vet," she added, which was true. She'd expected raised eyebrows, which was how people usually reacted, but he just nodded thoughtfully.

"Good luck."

She smiled at him. "Thanks. And thanks for your help."

"Pleasure." He gave her a little nod and headed back to a white Toyota, which was parked behind the woman's car.

"He was a nice young man, wasn't he, dear? I'm Dorothy by the way. Dot to my friends." The woman's sunny smile told Maggie that she was now included in Dot's circle of friends. "I'll give you a lift back up the lane, shall I?"

"It's probably better if I walk," Maggie said. "Less stressful for our friend here than going in a car. It's not far."

"Well, if you're sure, dear." Dot's voice was dubious. "I think it's wonderful what you do. I'm so relieved, I can't tell you. I felt awful when I hit him. I wasn't going very fast. I never do around these country lanes."

"It's all right," Maggie reassured her. "There's not a lot you can do when they fly straight into you." She wondered if she should ask Dot back for a brandy – she could have done with one herself. And then she remembered she had a prior engagement. She'd been putting it off all day; she was amazed she'd managed to forget about it.

"Well, I'd like to give you a donation, dear. It's the least I can do after putting you to all this trouble."

Maggie shook her head, taking in for the first time her companion's appearance. Grey hair, which was coiled in a tight bun, kind, faded blue eyes, a face creased with years of worry and navy blue trousers shiny with age. Living on a pension, Maggie decided. "No, don't worry," she murmured. "Thanks again for coming to find me. Lots of people wouldn't have stopped."

She watched the woman drive away and then lifted the transporter, which wasn't much heavier with the bird in it than it had been when it was empty. She would settle her patient in more permanent accommodation and leave it alone for the night. Then she really should get going before dusk fell. She'd rather have dealt with a dozen birds of prey than go where she'd been heading before Dot had interrupted her, but there could be no more putting it off. Bracing her back slightly and feeling a little guilty that she even wanted to put it off, Maggie quickened her step until the lights she'd left on in her cottage came into view.

Chapter Two

Having settled the bird and left it water Maggie locked up the converted pigsty, which she referred to lightly as 'the hospital block', and went to collect the white roses she'd abandoned by her front door. Then she strolled along the quiet roads past untidy hedges that spilled out like overgrown mops of hair, revelling in the peace and enjoying the clear honey-coloured light that preceded sunset.

Ten minutes later, she was letting herself through the lichen-covered gate of the churchyard, aware of the small wooden thud as it swung shut behind her. She walked slowly along the mossy, cobbled path between the graves. It seemed rude to run through a cemetery, disrespectful somehow, and however much she longed for this visit to be over, she didn't want to offend anyone. These people, whose headstones rose higgledy-piggledy from the ground on either side of her, seemed almost like friends, their names were so familiar, and she'd often wondered about their lives.

Who was John Taverstock? Pillar of the community, respected councillor, father of seven, grandfather of eleven. Maggie pictured him in the Red Lion, which had been the heart of the village for a couple of hundred years. He'd probably have drunk real ale, Tanglefoot or Pilgrim's Pride, standing with his back to the open fire and a little frill of froth on his moustache. She was sure he'd have had a moustache, a black curly one like Agatha Christie's Hercule Poirot.

And was Renie happy to be reunited with her Bert, after twenty years of separation? Her family certainly seemed to think so. Maggie paused to trail her fingers over the twin cherubs on Renie Johnstone's final resting place.

She knew all she was really doing was putting off the moment of confrontation. Silly to still think of it as a confrontation, yet a year of coming here hadn't made things any more bearable than they'd been in the beginning.

Sighing, she continued on past the McTaggarts, Evie and Benjamin, whose grave was always decked out with carnations – pink ones, which seemed out of place somehow, more of a wedding flower. And then she was in one of the most peaceful parts of the cemetery, shaded as it was by a giant oak. Its leaves were caught halfway between summer and autumn. Soon they would fall, but for now they shone gloriously orange in the liquid golden light of the September sunset.

She halted, her heart pounding, by the gleaming milk-white headstone with its marble angel, wings folded peacefully and head bowed, eyes cast forever downwards.

Elizabeth Clarke
16 September 1948 – 21 September 2002
Rest In Peace

Such a simple epitaph for such a complex woman, Maggie had thought at the time, but she'd been unable to think of anything else to say. She'd always had trouble knowing what to say to her mother. And when she'd died so unexpectedly just after her fifty-fourth birthday, it had suddenly been too late for words.

"Hi, Mum," she whispered, pausing for a few moments and feeling a little shiver run across her bare arms. It still felt odd to be talking to a grave, as if her mother could somehow hear her from beneath six foot of soil. And why should she be listening in death, when she had never listened in life, Maggie wondered, as she knelt on the dusty earth.

She laid the white roses on the grave and stroked their petals, feeling their cool perfection beneath her fingertips. Silken and unscented, so perfect on the outside, but with something vital missing. Like Maggie's childhood had been. She'd had everything she'd ever wanted, in material terms. Her own pony, piano lessons, swimming lessons, ice-skating lessons and a string of childminders to take the place of her mother, whose hotel business paid for it all. On the outside she'd had an idyllic, rural upbringing, which she knew that her school friends, with the exception of her best friend, Sarah, who was far more perceptive than most, had envied madly. But she'd have swapped it all for the chance to have spent more time with her mother instead of being looked after by strangers.

She sat back on the warm ground and hugged her knees to her chest. Arleston Court Hotel had been a business, not a home. And the biggest regret of her life was that she'd never really known the woman who now lay beneath this Wiltshire soil, and now she never would.

"The sanctuary's coming along well," she murmured. "I rescued a red kite today, a bird of prey – beautiful..." She tailed off because even as she spoke, she could see the disappointment in her mother's dark eyes and hear her voice in her head, contemptuous and impatient. "Oh, for God's sake, Maggie. Most people grow out of wanting to save the world when they're about twelve."

Guilt washed over her. It left a deep uneasiness in her, even now, knowing that her mother would have been furious to know that she'd sold the family business and spent her money on the old farm cottage and its few acres of scrubby land. But she'd gone ahead and done it anyway, rebelling after her mother's death in a way she'd never quite dared to do while she was alive.

Which probably meant she was weak, she thought, swiping a stray tear from her eye, although she didn't really know if the hard knot of grief in her chest was down to guilt, or pain because she'd never been allowed to get close to her mother. Never been allowed inside the barriers her mother had erected.

"Your father would have stayed if it wasn't for you," she'd told Maggie once. "He never wanted kids. He had big plans. Thought kids would get in the way. Pity he didn't hang around to see how wrong he was." She'd smiled at the young Maggie as she'd spoken and with the benefit of hindsight Maggie knew her words were intended to be a comfort, not a rejection. But it hadn't felt like that at the time. Her parents would have stayed together if it hadn't been for her. That still hurt. It hurt desperately.

She let the tears fall for a while. She often cried here when she was alone, although strangely she'd shed no tears at the funeral. Perhaps she was still hoping for absolution, she thought, rising slowly to her feet, wanting desperately to be away from this place of shadows, which seemed to encapsulate all that had been wrong in her life for so long.

She hurried back through the churchyard, her eyes so blurred with tears that she didn't see the man until she'd collided with him.

"I'm so sorry," she mumbled, glancing up into startled grey eyes that softened immediately as he looked at her.

"No problem. Hey, are you all right? No, you're not, are you?"

It was him, the man who'd stopped to help her earlier. Recognition softened his voice and Maggie bit her lip, embarrassed to be caught in tears. She wanted to run past, but he was blocking the path so she stayed where she was, trying to sniff inconspicuously and wishing he'd leave her alone.

He looked vaguely familiar. She'd thought so earlier, but now she was less distracted it was more apparent. Perhaps he worked in the village. Perhaps he was one of the shop owners she'd approached about sponsorship for her sanctuary.

It was his eyes, she thought, frowning. His grey eyes were comfortingly familiar, yet she was almost sure they hadn't met before today.

"We must stop meeting like this," she muttered, trying to bring some levity into the situation, but spoiling it when she had to wipe more tears from her face with the back of her hand because she hadn't brought a hanky.

"People will talk." He finished the phrase for her, rummaged in his pocket and pulled out a white handkerchief. "I'm not following you – in case you were wondering – I've been visiting my grandparents. They're in that plot over there." He gestured with the hanky and then handed it to her. "Here, use this."

She took it, grateful that he hadn't claimed to know how she felt or offered any of the usual platitudes. Practical help she could deal with. Anything else would have felt like an intrusion.

He waited while she blew her nose, not looking at her, but not looking embarrassed either, as if he was quite used to dealing with sobbing women. Even through her distress she thought how kind he was. She racked her brain to work out why he was so familiar.

"What did you say your name was?" she asked, when she was in control of herself again.

"I didn't. But it's Finn. Finn McTaggart. I'm not local, although I did spend quite a bit of time down here when I was younger – my grandparents retired here – but Dad and

I still live in Nottingham. We're here to sort out their house and I thought I'd pop by, say hello to them. You know how it is."

She nodded. "I'm Maggie Clarke. I know your grandparents – well, what I mean is that I know their grave, I pass it every time I come. Pink carnations." She stumbled to a halt, aware of how inane she must sound. He put the carnations there, of course, and she had just trampled like an idiot over his feelings.

"I've been visiting my mum," she mumbled, feeling her face burn. "It's a year today since…" She tailed off, unsure what else to say to him. It felt slightly surreal, standing in the swiftly gathering mosquito-edged dusk crying in front of a stranger. She twined the damp handkerchief around her fingers and wondered whether she should offer to give it back. "Well, thanks for the use of this."

"Keep it," he said, his eyes sympathetic. "And believe me – it does get easier, Maggie. I promise."

"Right," Maggie said, touched by his kindness, but anxious to get away. She was beginning to feel supremely embarrassed that he'd seen her in such a state. He'd think she wasn't capable of looking after herself, let alone running an animal sanctuary. Annoyed with herself, she looked back into his eyes, her gaze steady.

"Well, thanks again," she muttered, relieved when he moved out of her path. "I'd better get going."

Finn watched her hurry back along the moss-covered path and reflected wryly that after two chance meetings he should have taken the opportunity to ask for her number so he could see her again. Except that at neither time would it have been appropriate.

Then he chided himself for assuming she'd be interested in him – whatever the circumstances. He'd thought she was lovely earlier and she was, even with her nose red from crying and the strands of her long dark hair that had escaped from their clips in a scatter around her face. Her eyes, almost black with pain, had looked haunted, and even though everyone was vulnerable when they were visiting their lost loved ones, he'd sensed that she didn't usually 'do' vulnerability.

He'd had to fight back the urge to put his arms around her slender shoulders and hold her tightly. He told himself he'd have felt the same towards any woman so obviously in need of comfort, but he suspected it wasn't true.

"Forget it," he muttered crossly. Why on earth would she take a second look at him? She'd barely taken a first look, he reminded himself, as he watched her fumbling with the latch on the gate and tear up the road. She'd been too preoccupied with rescuing the bird and this time she'd been too blinded with grief to see where she was going, poor kid. She was young to have lost her mother. He hoped she had a father back home, someone else who was supporting her through it. Losing a parent was terribly tough. He waited until she was out of sight, sensing her need for distance, and then strolled back to his grandparents' cottage, which was less than a quarter of a mile from the cemetery.

He still thought of it as theirs, even though they'd left it to his father when they'd died within weeks of each other, eight months earlier.

"You took your time, lad, thought you'd got lost," Albert greeted him from the front garden where he was puffing furiously on a roll-up, and Finn realised that his father must feel the same. His grandmother had never let anyone smoke in the house.

"I bumped into a girl in the churchyard. I saw her earlier too," he added, frowning, and deciding not to tell Albert about the bird rescue, as the only birds he was interested in came fully plucked, cooked and with gravy.

"Oh, aye – you were supposed to be sorting out graves, not chatting up women."

Finn watched him draw on the thin roll-up so deeply that the burning end shot towards his fingers and he had to drop it on the path.

"That stuff will kill you one day," he said mildly. "I wish you'd pack it in."

"Too late now. I reckon I've done all the damage I'm going to do."

Finn doubted that very much, but his dad could be a stubborn old fool where his health was concerned.

"And I wasn't chatting her up. She was upset. She was visiting her mother's grave."

"Ah," Albert said, and promptly shut up.

One nil to me, Finn thought without much satisfaction, as he pushed past his father and into the house. The mention of mothers worked every time. But he'd have given a lot for things to be different.

He was reading the paper when Albert came into the back room.

"Shall I do us some burnt sausage and chips again for tea or shall we risk the pub?"

"The pub, I think," Finn said, glancing up. "I could do with a pint of Guinness."

And he could ask the landlord about Maggie, too, he decided, as they strolled down to The Red Lion. Mike would know who she was. He knew everything that was going on in the village and was an incorrigible gossip.

He looked pleased to see them, too, Finn saw, as he pushed open the heavy oak door, lowering his head as they stepped into the dark beamed interior. They weren't here often enough to be classed as locals, but often enough for Mike to know what they drank.

"Usual, is it, gentlemen?" he queried, grinning through his salt and pepper beard and rubbing his hands together. He'd have looked more at home behind the bar of a seafaring pub strung with fish nets holding plastic lobsters, Finn had often thought. Captain Bird's Eye. Deciding against asking about the girl in the cemetery, he carried their pints to the table where his father sat. He didn't want it to get back to her that he'd been asking and it more than likely would if he said anything to Mike.

"Do you two want the wood burner on?" Mike called after him. "It's a bit chilly once the sun goes down, isn't it?"

"No, you're all right," Albert said, lighting another rollie, and blowing out a thin plume of smoke, as Finn settled opposite him.

It was a nice pub, he thought, trying to decide if it had changed since the last time they'd been down. No. The Red Lion probably hadn't changed much in the last couple of hundred years. It was a piece of English heritage, with its thick cob walls, ancient beams and big old fireplace. Not at all like their local, back home, which was a working man's club, with pitted tables and faded velveteen seats that you sank into when you sat down because the springs had long since gone.

The walls of the Sheaf of Arrows were dotted with black and white pictures of football teams that no one had ever heard of. The walls of the Red Lion sported ancient hunting prints and a couple of faded water colours. Above the bar hung a banner printed with the words *A good wine should be drunk and not worshipped. A good landlord should be worshipped and not drunk.* Finn decided this summed up this particular landlord perfectly.

"So, what's the verdict, son?" Albert said, blowing a smoke ring towards the fireplace and interrupting Finn's musings. "Do we let the place go to rack and ruin for lack of funds, or do we cut our losses and put it on the market?"

"It's yours. What do you want to do with it?" Finn murmured, even though he had a pretty good idea that he already knew. His father had never really taken to the countryside. He was much happier in his terraced two-up two-down in Nottingham, steeped in traffic fumes and noise and surrounded by tarmac. He'd never been one for open spaces and 'wild animals', as he called them – which covered everything from rabbits to cows.

"I think we should get it on the market," Albert said. "I could buy my place then. Might even get enough for you to put a deposit down on a little place yourself."

"Yes," Finn replied, without enthusiasm. As far as he could see, his grandparents had had the right idea. Who wanted to live in the city when they could be surrounded by clean air and rolling fields? Ever since they'd died and left his father the cottage, he'd harboured the faint hope that he could somehow raise the funds to buy it from him and move down here. He was sure he could get work locally – he could turn his hand to most things. And in his spare time he could paint.

It was a pipe dream, really. Cottages in Arleston, even tiny ones which needed a lot of money spending on them, didn't come cheap. He knew his dad couldn't afford to sell it to him for much less than the market value. Not unless he wanted to spend the rest of his life scrimping and saving, which Finn was determined he wasn't going to do. Consequently, he hadn't ever raised the subject.

17

"Course – you've probably got better memories of the place than me, eh, lad?" Albert said slyly, tapping his rollie over the ashtray and missing so that ash scattered over Finn's beer mat instead. "Wild, drunken Christmas parties, if my memory serves me right."

"I was young and foolish then. It was a one-off," Finn said, frowning, "Which is the reason Gran never forgot it."

"She never forgot it because you were sick all the way up her stairs." Albert drained his pint triumphantly, leaned forward and tapped his empty glass on the table. "Want another one? It's my round."

"I'll get them," Finn said, escaping to the bar because that was one night he particularly didn't want to remember and certainly didn't want to discuss. He'd had the worst hangover of his life the following morning. Being sick all up the stairs hadn't been good – but it had been a fairly minor crime in the scheme of things.

The Christmas party had been held in someone's house on the outskirts of the village. He'd been drinking with a group of lads in the Red Lion and when the pub had closed they'd invited him along. The alcohol had been flowing freely and Finn had drunk far more than he was used to. He vaguely remembered leaving the party with a really pretty blonde, who'd been younger than him. He wished he could blank out the rest of the evening, but he couldn't. He'd hated himself for weeks afterwards. Not because the girl hadn't been willing – she'd been just as keen as he was to find a field where they could 'get to know each other better'. But he'd known they were both too drunk to have really known what they were doing. And it wasn't Finn's style to have one-night stands.

What had made it worse was that he'd had to leave for Nottingham the following morning, which meant he hadn't had time to see her again. What would he have said if he

18

had, he wondered? 'Sorry' or 'thanks' or maybe even, 'what did you say your name was?' He doubted they'd have seen each other again. A few minutes of fumbled love-making in a freezing, muddy field wasn't the best start to a relationship.

He'd never seen her since, which he supposed wasn't all that surprising. Arleston wasn't a tiny village; there was no reason to bump into her even if she had been a local, which he'd doubted. Local girls probably didn't have one-night stands at parties. Unfair though it was, they'd probably end up the subject of nasty gossip. Like him, she'd probably been far from home and had simply done too much celebrating and got too full of Christmas spirit, quite literally.

He sighed and headed back to their table with the drinks. Maybe his father had a point about it being best to cut all ties with the place. Nottingham was home. It was where his mates were, where his roots were, and very probably where his future lay. Moving to the countryside, swapping his job at the factory and trying to paint for a living, were all pipe dreams. Fleetingly he thought about Maggie again and rationality kicked in. Another pipe dream. There were plenty of attractive women in Nottingham.

"I think you're right, Dad," he said, clunking their pints on to the knotted wooden table and watching a thin trail of froth spill down one of the glasses. "You should put it on the market – we don't get a lot of use out of it, do we? Do you want me to nip down the estate agents in the morning?"

"Aye, thanks, lad. You're better at all that malarkey than me."

Albert's grey eyes lit briefly with warmth and Finn thought with a mixture of regret and relief that it was probably for the best.

Chapter Three

Maggie shielded her eyes against the afternoon sun and watched the two people she loved most in the world heading up the yard towards her. Ben was only five, but already he was the image of his mother. It really hit her when she saw them side by side like this. He had the same honey-coloured hair with streaks that were bleached almost white from playing outside over the long summer holidays. A smattering of freckles curved across his cheekbones, and he had the same small nose as Sarah's and the same eyes. No, he didn't, she thought with a small frown. Ben's eyes weren't the same shape and they were grey, not summer blue.

His shorts and tee-shirt were a lot grubbier than her friend's, too, she saw, smiling as they got closer. Then Ben spotted her standing by the kennels, dragged his hand from his mother's and came hurtling up the dusty concrete yard.

"Can I see Sacha's puppies, Auntie Maggie? Have they grown any bigger? How's the little black one? I bet he's as fat as a piglet." The words tumbled out in one long, unbroken line. "Can I help give Sacha her dinner? Mum said you might let me if I was really good and quiet."

It was impossible to imagine him being quiet for long. Maggie smiled into his eyes, which were as wide and innocent as he could make them. "Of course you can, sweetheart." She bent to kiss his head, ignoring his screwed-up face as her lips brushed his hair. He was going through the 'kissing is for girls' stage, Sarah had told her last time they'd spoken.

"So how was school, Ben? Is it good to be back?"

"We did maths today. Boring. Double boring. Treble boring." Ben spun out the words dramatically. "I like art best. We did that yesterday. Mrs Benson said I'm really

21

good. I did a picture of a horse like Woena with brown hair and a white patch on her head."

"Did you now?" Maggie said, straightening and looking across to where Rowena grazed in the paddock, flicking away flies with her tail. "I'd love to have a look at that some time."

Then Sarah caught up with her son, puffing in the heat and flapping her pink tee-shirt with her hands to get some airflow.

"Still hard at it, I see," she muttered, looking at the half empty pot of creosote at Maggie's feet. "Did you realise you've got that stuff in your hair?"

"It washes out," Maggie said, pulling a section of her long dark hair in front of her face to look and wrinkling her nose. "Yuck. It doesn't make very good perfume, though. I should get this cut. It would be much more practical."

"It wouldn't suit you," Sarah said, grinning. "So how's it going? You look as though you're getting somewhere at last." She looked around the smallholding, narrowing her eyes approvingly. "You've transformed this place. It almost looks like an animal sanctuary. Which reminds me. The woman across the road from me can't keep her dog any more because her grandchildren are asthmatic. Would she be able to bring it here? It's only a mutt. It looks like a rug on legs. You'd have a right job re-homing it."

"There'll be someone out there who'll love him," Maggie said, feeling a stab of sadness, because she knew Sarah was right. When she'd been at vet school in Bristol she'd helped out at a local dog's home and people did seem to go for looks, passing over the mutts and the older dogs in their quest for cute. Still, at least she was in a position to do something about it now.

"And if I don't find a home for him, then he can stay here forever," she added, touching Sarah's arm. "That's

22

why I started this place. It feels so good to actually be able to do something. When I worked at the vets I used to feel so helpless when people brought their unwanted animals in for us to…" She didn't finish the sentence, but spread her arms wide to encompass the kennels and fields. "But now I can take them all in. I've decided to call this place The Ark. What do you think?"

Sarah shook her head. "I think you're barking mad," she said with affection. "But then I suppose that's pretty appropriate in the circumstances. These are kennels, too, aren't they? Why are there two lots?"

"This is the quarantine block. It's for when new dogs come in. You have to have somewhere to segregate them in case there's anything wrong with them. The block further down is the regular kennels and I've got the cattery sorted now, too. Someone brought a cat in last week. Poor little mite had hardly any fur left. He got trapped under the bonnet of a car and driven for miles before the owner realised he was there."

"Is he all right?" Sarah gasped in horror. "Did you sort him out?"

"It was touch and go, but yes, he'll be fine. I've called him Diesel because it seemed appropriate. I think I might keep him."

"You'll be overrun at this rate. I thought the idea was to re-home them, not keep them."

"I'll only keep the odd one. Did you see the chicken run I've just set up in the small field? I scrounged it from a farmer up the road, along with some of his ex-battery hens. I like chickens."

"Ben saw it. I had to drag him out of it by his ankles. That's how he got so filthy. He's almost as crazy as you are about animals."

Maggie laughed. "He'll clean up. I've got another bird he'd like to see, it's a red kite, a bird of prey. It ran into a woman's car out on the main road a couple of days ago and injured its wing."

"So you're taking in wildlife as well now, are you? Isn't that the council's responsibility? I hope the woman left a donation."

"She wanted to, but she didn't look like she could afford it so I didn't let her."

"You can't afford it either." Sarah shook her head. "Maggie, you're way too soft. Your mum's money isn't going to last forever."

All too aware of this, Maggie smiled and decided to change the subject. "It's really good to see you both. I've hardly seen you, lately. I take it the romance is still going strong?"

Colour crept across Sarah's freckled cheekbones. "You've been busy with this place. I didn't like to intrude while you were setting things up. But yes. Yes, it is. Jack's great. He adores Ben."

"Good." Maggie glanced at her friend's face, which looked hotter and more flushed than the sun warranted. "So, when do I get to meet him? Or are you going to keep him under wraps forever? I'm beginning to think there's something wrong with him. Or is it me you're ashamed of?" she added lightly. "Your mad friend with the animal sanctuary."

"Of course I'm not ashamed of you." Sarah sounded genuinely affronted. "I just didn't want to tempt fate. In case things didn't work out between me and Jack – you know."

"Hmm," Maggie said, deciding that there was probably an element of truth in that, although she had a feeling there was more to it. They'd been friends since infant school and there wasn't much they didn't know about each other. Maggie decided that Sarah was being cagey about Jack for reasons that had nothing to do with tempting fate.

"You can come round for tea one night if you like," Sarah said, picking a piece of straw out of Ben's hair. "How about Friday? I'll get Jack to cook us something. He's utterly gorgeous, Maggie, and he can cook, too. Very important, as I can't. Did I tell you his dad's a chef?"

"Once or twice." Maggie smiled and took a deep breath of the balmy Wiltshire air and turned her face up to the sun, which was still warm despite the fact that it was late afternoon. There was a part of her that still couldn't believe she was really here – doing what she'd wanted to do, all her life.

"So, what have you told Jack about Ben's father?" she asked casually, when Ben was out of earshot, running ahead of them to the newly installed cattery. She stole a glance at Sarah's face and could tell by her fleeting look of panic that she was right on target. That was why she hadn't been allowed to meet Jack yet – in case she inadvertently let something slip. Feeling a little put out that Sarah might not trust her, she added softly, "I am on your side, you know. I'd back up whatever you said."

"Yes, I know you would." Sarah glanced at her son, who'd paused just ahead and was crouched in the dust, staring intently at something on the ground. She hesitated and then, aware that Maggie wasn't going to let her get away with that, she added, "To be honest I haven't told Jack much. I just said that Ben's father was much older than me and that he did a runner before Ben was born."

Maggie suppressed a sigh. Not that she was surprised. Sarah was hardly going to admit that Ben's father was still blissfully unaware of his son's existence.

"Well, what did you expect me to say?" Sarah's voice was defensive, picking up on her friend's unsaid words. "I couldn't exactly tell him that Ben was the result of a one-night stand in a field, and I didn't get round to asking the bloke's name, could I?"

"No," Maggie said dryly. "I don't suppose you could have said that. But isn't it going to be difficult, Sarah, if it ever comes out? It sounds to me as though you're pretty serious about this guy."

"It won't come out. It can't. You're the only person who knows." Sarah flicked back her shaggy blonde perm and gave Maggie a sharp, sideways glance. "And you're not going to tell anyone, are you?"

"My lips are sealed," Maggie said, smiling to soften the seriousness of her voice, because it did worry her that Sarah was still living a lie. Not because she hadn't confessed to Jack – after all, they'd only been seeing each other a few weeks – but because Maggie knew her friend had never faced the truth herself. She'd somehow managed to disconnect the one-night stand from Ben, whom she adored, and in doing so she'd deprived him of ever knowing his father.

Maggie and Sarah were the same age, twenty-seven, and they'd been best friends forever, but in many ways they were worlds apart. It bothered Maggie a lot more than it seemed to bother Sarah that somewhere out there was a man who didn't know he had a son. But mainly she was concerned about Ben. She knew what it was like to grow up without a dad. One day, Ben was going to want to trace him. He was going to want to put a face to the man who'd helped to conceive him, and Maggie was worried about how Sarah would cope when he did.

"Enough of my love life, how's yours?" Sarah asked, fanning her face with her hand and pausing to check on

Ben who was now heading purposefully across the small field towards the chickens once more. "Is he all right in there, Maggie?"

"Yes, he's fine. It doesn't matter if he lets them out. I'll deal with them later."

"Has that hunky vet persuaded you to go out with him yet?"

"If you mean Gary Collins, then no – and he's not interested in me," Maggie said, although she wasn't a hundred per cent sure of this. Gary had said a couple of things lately that had made her wonder. Or he might just have been being friendly. He'd certainly never asked her out.

"I'm too busy for a relationship, so it's neither here nor there. And I've had enough of vets," she added, with a small frown.

"Not all vets are like Alex. Anyway, who said anything about a relationship? You could have some fun, couldn't you?"

"I am having fun, sorting this place out."

"Maggie, this is work, not fun." Sarah screwed up her face in exasperation and put her hands on Maggie's arms. "I know you've had a rough time of it lately. In more ways than one. And I know that's why you've buried yourself in deepest Wiltshire with a bunch of waifs and strays that no one else wants. I'm not completely blind, you know." Her blue eyes softened. "But you can't hide yourself away forever, there's a world out there."

"I'm not hiding," Maggie protested, gazing across the fields of long grass that surrounded her land. The grass, bleached yellow by the sun, flowed like a golden sea in the sultry breeze. "I'm fine now. Truly I am." She waved her hands in a careless gesture of dismissal, daring Sarah to argue with her. "I'm over everything. Alex, my old life,

Mum. All the stuff in Bristol – well, it all seems like it happened to someone else. Really, I'm fine." She rushed on before Sarah could contradict her. "If Ben wants to feed Sacha's pups I'm just about to do it. Do you want to give him a shout?"

Sarah shook her head in exasperation, and then put her fingers to her lips and gave an ear-splitting whistle.

Maggie breathed a sigh of relief and hurried ahead of her to unlatch the metal gate that led down to the lower part of the sanctuary. She'd had two stone outbuildings turned into a reception and a feed storage area, and in the old pigsty 'hospital block', quiet and out of bounds to the public, she kept the smaller more vulnerable animals until they were ready for re-homing. Dogs like Sacha and her litter of scraggy black Heinz 57 pups. Not that the fact they were scraggy bothered Maggie in the least.

In fact, sometimes she thought she cared about the ugly ones more than she cared about the sleek, expensive pedigrees that were guaranteed a loving home. They brought out all her protective instincts; she'd have kept them all if she'd had the money.

She tugged open the wooden door of the feed store, bashed her head on the low beam just inside, and swore under her breath. After years of living in houses with normal height ceilings she still hadn't got used to the low doorways of the farm buildings. Her cottage wasn't much better. When she'd first moved in six weeks ago she'd banged her head so many times that she'd found herself going around with a permanent stoop. She'd got used to the place now and only the odd doorway, like this one, still caught her out.

Standing for a moment in the dim coolness of old stone, she rubbed her head and then hauled down a sack of dog food ready for Ben to open. She wondered what Sarah would have said if she'd confessed the only man she'd felt completely comfortable around lately had been the one that she'd bumped into in the cemetery. Which was a bit of a contradiction, given that she'd spent most of their meeting blubbing. She'd have bet money on it that he hadn't been comfortable, however chivalrously he'd behaved. She'd never come across a man who'd been able to deal with a woman in tears. None of the vets in Bristol had been very good with tears, especially Alex, who should have been used to it, considering how many hearts he broke.

Perhaps Sarah was right, she conceded ruefully, perhaps she wasn't quite as recovered as she thought. Alex had hurt her badly and she'd still been reeling from his betrayal when she'd lost her mother. Two devastating body blows in a matter of months. It was bound to take time to recover. But the sanctuary was going to help her, not hinder.

Hard work was a cure-all, her mother had often told her. It cured everything from the pain of a broken love affair to the absolute full stop of bereavement.

Maggie had to admit that her mother had been right about that. She was too busy to hurt most of the time. She reached up for the plastic scoop and one of the pristine stainless steel dog bowls from the shelf and put them on the floor beside the sack of food.

As for Sarah's throwaway line about hiding away from the world, that was rubbish. She shook her head impatiently in an attempt to banish the shiver of unease that always accompanied thoughts of her mother. The clang of the gate heralded Ben and Sarah's approach. Maggie glanced up and smiled as they came into the feed room. Sarah might be a little right, she might not be a hundred per cent recovered, but she was healing, not hiding. There was a massive difference.

Chapter Four

Maggie felt oddly nervous as she pulled up outside Sarah's little semi on Friday evening. She reached for the bottle of her friend's favourite red wine that was rolling about in the passenger foot-well and wondered what Jack would be like.

All Sarah had told her was that he was a travelling salesman and they'd met when his minibus had broken down at the end of the lane. Maggie had just parked behind it and she wasn't a bit surprised it had broken down. It was pink and blue and looked like something from a hippie commune. She eyed its rusting wheel arches with horror as she climbed out of her Land Rover.

Edging past it, she breathed in the scent of jasmine that clambered up the front of the house while she waited for Sarah to answer the bell.

Then the door opened and Sarah was smiling, her face unusually shy, and behind her was Jack, who wasn't a bit like Maggie had expected.

He towered over Sarah and had a good four inches on Maggie. At least six foot three, he had flaming red hair and eyes the colour of amber and a gold hoop in one ear. He looked like a pirate from one of those swashbuckling films, and Maggie had a brief, vivid image of him forcing people to walk the plank.

"It's great to meet you, Maggie." He held out a giant hand, and she felt her own hand disappearing within his firm grip. She had an impression of warmth and strength and gentleness. "Sarah's told me so much about you." His voice was soft, with a faint Scottish accent and there was shyness behind his smile.

Another contradiction, Maggie thought, a little breathlessly, as the pirate image evaporated. "All good, I hope?"

"What do you think?" Sarah interrupted. "Come on, come through, Ben's refused to go to bed until he's seen you."

Ben, dressed in Thomas the Tank Engine pyjamas, was sitting on the settee watching television, but he leapt up when he spotted Maggie, hurtled across the room, and wrapped his arms around her legs.

"Steady on, you'll have me over," she said, hugging him. "So what are you doing up this late, young man?"

"Waiting to see you, lung lady."

Maggie giggled, as much at the seriousness in his grey eyes as his pronunciation. "You're a bundle of trouble, you are."

"You're a bundle of trouble!" Ben shrieked in delight.

"Don't call your Auntie Maggie names," Sarah chided. "Or she might not want to stay."

"I started it," Maggie said, smiling. "Come and sit on my lap then, Ben. You're not too big for laps, are you?"

He shook his head, put his thumb in his mouth and clambered up, a little more reticently than usual, which she put down to the fact that Jack was there. The balance in the room had changed – she supposed it was bound to with Jack around. But it was a nice change. Comfortable.

"Five minutes," Sarah told Ben. "And then it's bed for you."

"Can Auntie Maggie read me a story?"

"Auntie Maggie might be too tired, she's been working hard all day."

"I'm not too tired," Maggie said. "I'm never too tired for a story."

"Don't make it a very long one then," Sarah said, her eyes softening. "Jack's done us home-made burgers – he's even made veggie ones especially for you – and they'll be ready in about ten minutes."

                    *   *   *

"So, what do you think?" Sarah asked, putting her hands behind her head and leaning back against the settee with a smile of such utter satisfaction that it was obvious the question was rhetorical.

"I think he's awful. Big-headed, boring, ugly. Can't cook either, can he?"

Sarah's eyes widened in shock. Maggie giggled and poured more wine into their glasses from her position on the carpet beside the coffee table. "God, you're so easy to wind up. What do you think I think, you lucky cow. Has he got any brothers?"

"No, he's a one-off," Sarah said proudly, and unnecessarily, because Maggie couldn't imagine ever meeting anyone like Jack, who, half an hour ago, had said he couldn't stand any more of their girlie chat and had escaped up to bed. When Sarah had told her he was a salesman, she'd conjured up a smooth-talking charmer, probably blond, because Sarah usually went for blonds. She hadn't been expecting a Scottish flame-haired giant of a man who could cook like a top chef, which apparently he'd learned in his father's Dundee restaurant before he'd left home.

"What?" Sarah asked and Maggie jumped.

"I was just thinking that Jack wasn't what I expected. He's not your usual type. Why didn't he go into the family business, do you suppose?"

"Because he wanted to see the world – well, he wanted to see England anyway." Sarah giggled. "What did you think of his tattoo? He had that done in London."

Maggie smiled. Sarah had made Jack show her the wolf, which was emblazoned across his chest, halfway

32

through their second bottle of wine, and he'd blushed scarlet as he'd undone his shirt buttons.

"The poor guy looked as if he wanted the floor to swallow him up," she chided gently. "He's obviously not an exhibitionist like you. But seriously, Sarah, I'm really pleased for you. It's about time you met someone really nice."

Sarah's blue eyes were as contented as a Cheshire cat's. "You see, there are some good ones out there. You mustn't let one bad experience put you off men for life."

"I wasn't planning to," Maggie said, warmed by the wine and Sarah's almost tangible happiness. "I'm over Alex now. Seriously – I can't imagine what I ever saw in him in the first place."

An image of her ex-boyfriend flashed into her mind. Dark eyes, that he'd inherited from his Italian grandmother, a tangle of black hair, a sexy pouting mouth, which could transform instantly from sultry to sulky if he wasn't getting his own way, and a body that wouldn't have looked out of place in an upmarket porno film. If there was such a thing, she thought wryly.

It was hard to hold on to the image – dark eyes were fading to cool grey ones, and, disconcertingly, she saw Finn's face again. She hadn't told Sarah about their two chance meetings. Partly because if she had she'd also have had to confess she'd gone to pieces in front of a stranger, which would have meant admitting she wasn't as over everything as she wanted Sarah to think. Finn was an attractive stranger too; it was a shame he wasn't local. She'd half hoped she'd bump into him again, some time when she wasn't looking as if she'd just been dragged through a hedge backwards. But she hadn't, which probably meant he was back in Nottingham again. Pity.

She sighed and Sarah, who'd obviously misread her expression as regret that she and Alex were finished, threw a cushion at her.

"The bloke was sex on legs. I could see exactly what you saw in him. And he was a complete two-timing bastard as well," Sarah added with venom in her voice. "Don't you ever forget it. I bet he's doing the dirty on that bimbo receptionist, by now. He's not the type of bloke who can stay faithful for more than a few months."

"Six in my case," Maggie murmured, surprised to find it didn't hurt any more. At the time it had been pretty painful. But then Alex's betrayal had been overshadowed by her mother's sudden death. Everything had been overshadowed by her mother's death.

"I'm surprised he hasn't been sniffing around here, now you're a rich heiress."

"He wasn't exactly broke himself," Maggie chided, because whatever else Alex had been he'd never been a sponger. "Besides, I can't see him leaving Bristol. He always hated the countryside. He hates the smell and he doesn't like animals much. Strange," she mused, half to herself, "that he ever decided to be a vet. He was quite good at it, too."

Sarah ignored this diversionary tactic and went straight for the jugular. Still smiling sweetly, she added, "So, he was hardly a long term option, was he? For a woman who prefers animals to people."

For once, Maggie was far too relaxed to rise to the bait. She yawned and stretched her arms above her head and then rubbed her eyes. "I think it's about time I curled up on your sofa. Some of us have to get up at the crack of dawn. I may only have a handful of animals at the moment, but they still need looking after."

"You can help me finish this wine first," Sarah pressed, refilling their glasses. "I'm glad you're over Alex. You can do far better than him." She paused and sipped her wine. "Bugger, I've just remembered that Jack made us a lemon meringue pie, too, because I told him it was your favourite. I think I might have a bit to mop up some of this alcohol. He'll be disappointed if we don't eat it. Do you fancy some?"

"I'll get it," Maggie offered, escaping to Sarah's tiny kitchen and poking about in the fridge, which seemed to be filled mainly with cans of beer. The pie, tucked away at the back, was a beauty, all white curly peaks topped with golden brown, and she felt her mouth watering.

She cut them both a slice and it was as the lemon scent hit her nostrils that she was transported back to a long-ago day in her mother's kitchen.

She'd been about seven and had just come in from school when she'd discovered a whacking great lemon meringue pie cooling on the top shelf of the larder. She'd needed a chair to reach it and she'd struggled with her conscience because she knew it was for the guests' dessert that night and pinching a slice was going to end in trouble. Then again, the pie was massive. No one was going to miss a little slice, she'd reasoned. There'd be plenty left for the guests.

She'd reached up, pushed the giant-size coffee tin across, and, taking care not to knock the butter portions over, inched the plate towards her.

"Maggie Clarke, whatever do you think you're doing? Get out of there, this minute. Do you hear me?"

Maggie had jumped violently and after that everything seemed to happen in slow motion. Half on and half off the shelf, the plate tilted and then overbalanced and the lemon meringue pie slid between her hands and the whole lot went crashing on to the tiled floor.

Her mother was beside her in an instant. "You naughty, naughty, little girl! How many times have I told you not to come in here and help yourself?" Maggie felt her arm seized roughly and she was half lifted, half pulled from the chair, which also overbalanced. She scraped her knee on one of its wooden legs, felt the stinging hotness of the graze, and the hurt of her mother's digging fingers. Then, suddenly, the utility room was full of people. Through a red haze of tears she heard the angry voices.

"What's going on? Oh, good heavens, I am sorry, Elizabeth, I didn't realise she was in there." That had been Brian, the chef with his hideous red face and sharp eyes.

"It's not your fault. She knows she's not allowed. Christ, look at this mess. Get a mop, can you. And you, my girl, can go straight to your room. Go on."

"But... I only wanted... some pie... and, and..." Tears were getting in the way of her voice. She wasn't sure which was worse, the beautiful pie smashed to pieces on the larder floor, more lemony now it was broken, or everyone staring at her. Her mother's face was blotched and furious and her voice hot-edged with crossness.

"If I've told you once, I've told you a million times, you do not just help yourself to food. That's tonight's dessert you've ruined. What am I going to give the guests now?"

"I don't know."

"No, I don't know either. Go on, get out of my sight and stop snivelling. Or I'll really give you something to cry about."

Maggie stopped crying and ran. The unfairness of it all was bubbling into her throat, but there was no arguing with her mother when she was in this mood. She didn't go to her room, though. She raced out of the door at the other end of the kitchen and through the games room, past the darts board and the pool table and out of the side door, which led on to the little yard where they grew runner beans and tomatoes.

Felix, her cat, was lying on an upturned milk crate, flicking his tail in the sun. She wrapped her arms around his neck and cried into his warm, ginger fur. Someone would come in a minute and tell her off again, but she didn't care. She hated them both, Mum and Brian, but most of all she hated the guests.

"Bloody guests," she sobbed and Felix wriggled a bit, but he didn't move away. Felix was the only one who understood. No one else knew how she felt, what it was like to always come second to the guests. He began to purr and she buried her face in his soft body.

"Bloody guests, bloody guests, bloody guests," she'd whispered, her voice matching the rhythm of his purrs. "Bloody guests, bloody guests, bloody guests."

"Maggie, what are you doing? I thought you'd fallen asleep out there." Sarah's voice jolted her back to the present and she jumped.

"Sorry, I was daydreaming."

"Hey, you're not upset because I mentioned Alex, are you? That was a bit insensitive. I didn't mean to rub it in…"

"I wasn't thinking about Alex – and you haven't. Honestly."

"Wow, it does look good, doesn't it? There's some squirty cream in the fridge, shall we have that too?"

Maggie smiled. "You're not supposed to have midnight feasts when you're our age."

"I know. I'm going to be as fat as a pig soon. Jack loves cooking puddings." Sarah squirted cream liberally over their plates and rolled her eyes in ecstasy. "I definitely recommend a man who can cook. By the way, I thought I saw one of my exes the other day in the village."

Her eyes clouded and Maggie glanced at her curiously.

"Well, that's okay, isn't it? Jack knows you're not a virgin."

"Ha bloody ha. I'm not talking about any old ex. I'm talking about the one I met at the Christmas party."

"What Christmas party?" Maggie frowned, and then realisation slowly dawned. "Are you talking about Ben's father – the one you…?"

"Shagged in a field," Sarah finished quietly, moving across to shut the kitchen door. "Keep your voice down. Yes, I am, but that doesn't make him Ben's father."

"Why didn't you say so before?" Maggie gasped, coming very close to dropping this plate of pie, as well, and too shocked to argue with Sarah's illogical statement. "Where was he?"

"He was going into the Post Office in Arleston." Sarah sighed. "When I got closer I realised it couldn't be him. I mean he doesn't live round here, does he? I expect it was just someone with the same colour hair. To be honest, I doubt I'd recognise him anyway, after all this time, even if I did bump into him. I think I'm a bit paranoid. I probably only thought I saw him because we were talking about him the other day."

"Yes," Maggie said, blinking and swallowing a mouthful of lemon, which was exquisitely smooth – just the right balance between tangy and sweet. "I'm sure that's it."

"Have you seen that picture?" Sarah asked her, gesturing to the fridge door, where Ben's latest drawing was held up by two Thomas the Tank Engine fridge magnets.

Maggie gazed at the stick family. It showed two women, one blonde, one dark, a child, and a man with a blob of vibrant red hair. They were standing outside a house with a big smiley yellow sun in the sky. Underneath the picture, scrawled in loopy, childish writing were the words 'My Family'. Maggie felt a lump in her throat. She'd always thought of Ben as family, even though they weren't related. It was good to know he felt the same.

Sarah's eyes shadowed and she blinked a few times. "I know you think I was wrong not telling Ben who his dad was, but you can see why I did it, can't you? It wasn't just for me. Ben's happy, too. He loves you and he loves Jack. And the past is done with. Finished. A closed chapter." She underlined her words by drawing a swift line in the air with her hands.

Maggie nodded slowly. They'd had dozens of arguments about this when Ben was a baby. It was one of the few things they'd ever totally disagreed on. But Maggie understood her friend's decision, even if she didn't agree with it. Sarah had been brought up in a children's home where her parents had dumped her when she was six months old. Ben was the only family she'd ever had. Maggie knew that Sarah's reasons for not contacting his father stemmed mainly from fear. Sarah had been scared he might fight her for custody and, more worryingly, that he might even win. She hadn't dared risk it.

And now, as Maggie looked into Sarah's anxious eyes and then back at the picture, which summed up how Ben saw the world, she was almost certain that Sarah had been right. There was no guarantee that Ben's father would have wanted a child. He certainly hadn't bothered to contact Sarah again and distance was no excuse in Maggie's mind.

He knew roughly where Sarah lived. He could have made an effort, if she'd meant more to him than just a one-night stand.

"I'm so happy at the moment," Sarah went on, blinking rapidly. "I've never felt like this. I've never had a proper family before. And I don't want anything to spoil it."

"Nothing's going to spoil it," Maggie said firmly, abandoning her pie and going across to hug her friend and hoping that her words wouldn't come back to haunt her.

Chapter Five

Nearly five months later, Maggie was stamping the heel of her boot against an ice-plated puddle in the yard and wishing Gary would hurry up and get there. He wasn't usually late. Her opinion of the vet had gone up over the last few months. Unlike a couple of the vets she'd worked with in the city practice in Bristol, he seemed to care more about the welfare of his patients than in how much revenue they brought in. He was always prepared to go the extra mile, coming out uncomplainingly at odd hours if she was worried about any of her animals, and refusing to take extra payment.

Maggie had a feeling that Sarah had been right about Gary being interested in her. Even though he still hadn't asked her out she sensed he was building up to it, which was awkward because, much as she liked the guy, she didn't want anything other than a professional relationship with him.

So far she'd managed to avoid the issue, but it was getting more difficult. As she waited for him to arrive she tried to analyse her feelings. Gary was attractive in a slightly old-fashioned, gentleman-farmer sort of way. He always wore a tweed jacket with leather patches on the elbows and green wellington boots, which never looked dirty; she had no idea how he managed that when he spent so much time tramping around farmyards. He had neat brown hair, serious dark eyes, and a slightly intense way of looking at her, which she found a bit unnerving. Yet there was no doubt that he was kind and generous and shared her passion for animals, particularly dogs.

He let her have drugs at cost and regularly brought over batches of medicines that were close to their sell-by date, which he refused to let her pay for. They had masses in common, and, logically, she knew he'd be the perfect partner. Yet she couldn't summon any interest beyond friendship despite Sarah's regular jibes that she ought to get a life beyond the animals. Perhaps she just didn't fancy him, she thought wryly. Her experience with Alex had taught her that logic had nothing to do with attraction.

The crunch of tyres on gravel heralded Gary's arrival and his white van drew into the yard. Even that looked immaculate, she thought idly as she went to meet him. He must hose it down every night.

"Afternoon, Maggie, sorry I'm late, I got a bit held up with a sow at Jackson's – cold one today, isn't it?" He rubbed his hands together as he spoke, his breath clouding the winter air, his swarthy face wreathed in smiles.

"You're not late." She smiled back at him. "And I'm probably worrying about nothing. But I thought it was better to be safe than sorry."

"Always better to be safe than sorry." He leaned into the van to get his case. "And you know you're my favourite customer."

"Right," she said briskly, deciding it would be better not to say she was bound to be with all the work she put his way, in case he contradicted her. "Step this way and I'll show you your patient."

The hospital block, warmed by a pair of Calor gas stoves, felt cosy and inviting after the bitterness of the February afternoon and Maggie hurried ahead of Gary towards a pen inhabited by a thin lurcher bitch and her litter of pups.

"I'm just going to borrow one of your babies a second," she murmured, stroking the bitch's soft head. Then very gently she leaned into the pen and scooped up the smallest pup, who was a miniature version of his mother, brindle stripes running through his pale gold fur.

*   *   *

Gary frowned as he watched her bend over the pen, feeling both aroused and disconcerted. How could anyone who spent her life in sweatshirts and old jeans have such an instant and devastating effect on him?

Not that Maggie could have the faintest idea of how he felt about her, or ever would, the way things were going. He'd been her vet for the last six months, give or take a week, and he'd been meaning to ask her out for most of that time. But he'd never quite found the courage to cross the bridge between professional and personal.

"This is the pup I'm worried about," she said, straightening and handing him a scraggy lurcher pup. "Whoever tied his mum up to the gate last week must have known she was just about to whelp, but the poor love was far too thin. This little one only just made it. I've called him Tiny. He's got a slight infection and I'm worried."

Gary took the pup, which squeaked and snuffled blindly at his fingers. Forcing himself to concentrate, he examined it carefully.

"Yes, you're right. I'll give him something for that. He's a little dehydrated, too. Try and get more fluid into him and make sure he gets plenty of Mum."

She nodded, her eyes anxious, and he placed the pup gently back into the run. "He's tougher than he looks, Maggie. He's got this far, I'm sure he'll be fine."

She smiled at him and he was momentarily lost in her eyes. They changed colour according to her mood, going from soft brown to almost black. Today they were very dark.

"I'm so pleased." She touched his arm. "I know it sounds mad, since I'm not exactly short of dogs round

43

here, but Tiny's a bit special. Probably because he kept me up all night when he arrived. Does that make sense?"

"Perfect sense." Gary tried to give her a meaningful look. The sort of look he hoped would convey that he thought she was a bit special, too, and that he'd definitely like to keep her up all night, but if she noticed it she didn't react.

He cleared his throat. "How are the rest of the crew? Is there anything else you'd like me to take a look at while I'm here?"

"I had another horse come in the other day." She frowned. A strand of dark hair had come loose from the band she tied it back with and Gary had to suppress the urge to reach out and brush it back with his hand.

"A horse? That's unusual. Cruelty case, was it?"

"No. I was a bit surprised at the time, actually. The owners were very keen to get rid of him and he's not just some shaggy pony. He's part thoroughbred. The last sort of horse you'd expect to end up in a place like this. Come on, I'll show you."

They left the litter of puppies and went out into the small courtyard and on up towards the stables. Gary followed her, which gave him the opportunity to study her bottom again. "You've lost weight, Maggie. You are eating properly, aren't you?" Christ, why did he have to say such inane things? Why couldn't he just come straight out with it and ask her out to dinner?

"It's probably all the tearing about I've been doing lately," Maggie said, without glancing back. She never seemed particularly interested in her appearance. As far as he could tell, she didn't wear make-up, but her skin always looked perfect, and the most she ever did with her shoulder-length, dark hair was tie it back off her face. She had a strong face, an air of confidence that drew people to

44

her, but there was a touch of aloofness too that said, 'don't take liberties, don't get too close'. Or maybe that was just his paranoia. He'd never had much confidence with women.

She was different around animals, softer. It was people she kept at arm's length, well, men anyway, Gary thought. Or maybe it was just him.

He was no closer to working out what made Maggie tick than he'd been on the first day he'd met her.

"I'm Maggie Clarke," she'd said, when she'd called into his practice at the tail-end of the previous summer. "I've just opened an animal rescue place up at Home Farm. And I'd like to discuss your rates."

Gary's illusions about her being some romantic animal lover had swiftly dissolved as she'd negotiated payment periods and discounts with the skill of one of his drug reps.

When she finally got up to go, she'd shaken his hand again. "It's been a pleasure doing business with you, Mr Collins."

"Call me Gary, please," he'd said, but that was the closest he'd ever got to being personal with her. She was always pleasant, happy to talk about neutering programmes or treatments or her plans for the sanctuary, but on a personal level he was still at first base.

"Actually, Gary, I've decided to get some help with the place," Maggie said conversationally as they walked up towards the stables in the fading light. "Paid help, I mean. I've put a card up in the post office, and Mike, at the Red Lion, said he'll keep an eye out for me, too."

He looked at her, startled. There were dozens of volunteers who came in on an ad hoc basis to walk the dogs and help out in reception, mostly mothers from the surrounding villages, nagged by their offspring and the lure of animals.

"I've got enough on my plate with the fund-raising and looking after this lot," she went on. "I can't keep up with the heavier jobs. Most of the fencing in this place is rotten and the guttering is coming off the older kennel block. With hindsight it was a mistake to buy second-hand." She sighed. "Not to mention the drainage problem."

"Maybe I could help you out with some of that," he heard himself saying. "It would be a pleasure."

"That's very sweet of you, Gary, but you haven't got time." She smiled at him and he nodded and tried not to feel rebuffed.

Changing tack he said, "Can you afford to employ someone? I thought it was a bit touch and go on the financial side."

"I can afford someone for a while and I was thinking I could throw in somewhere to live. I thought they could share the cottage with me. I've got a spare room."

"Good idea," Gary said, although he wasn't at all sure that it was. His heart was thumping uncomfortably. Did she mean to share her cottage with a man?

They went past the paddock railings, which looked pretty solid to him, and Maggie switched on the stable lights. A chestnut horse stuck his head over the door of the middle stable and whinnied at them.

"This is Ashley," Maggie said, undoing a padlock before sliding back the bolt. "He can undo them," she explained, ushering Gary into the stable ahead of her. "So if I don't padlock him in he lets himself out and causes chaos."

"What sort of chaos?" Gary asked, still wondering if Maggie was seriously considering letting a man live in her cottage. Perhaps he should ask her out now before she got too set on the idea. If he was taking her out, then he could offer to pay for someone to come in and do the jobs she'd mentioned. He'd offered to do this once before, but she'd turned him down flat. She might feel differently if they were together. Spurred by the consequences of not acting and with his heart pumping madly in his chest, he said, "Maggie, there's something I've been meaning to ask you."

"I think the Hendersons may have got rid of him because he was – er – over-sexed."

They spoke at the same time and he gestured for her to go first.

"He keeps chasing after Rowena. He lets himself out, and then he lets her out and… Well… You don't need me to spell it out for you." She hesitated. "Rowena's in season at the moment and she's a terrible flirt, but this horse is supposed to be a gelding. He looks like a gelding – well, he does to me. Does he look like one to you?"

Gary looked and agreed that he did.

"I've tried keeping them apart, but it's tricky because he can get out of anywhere. Dawn caught them in the hay barn the other day. They'd bent the lid of one of the feed bins, but they certainly didn't have food on their minds. They…" She broke off and looked at him and he could feel her discomfort. "I've got enough to do without dealing with over-sexed males," she added briskly. "Sorry, what was it you wanted to ask me?"

"Oh, it was nothing important," Gary said, avoiding her eyes and glancing back at Ashley. There was an awkward pause.

"So what do you think his problem is?" Maggie asked. "Could it be hormonal?"

His was definitely hormonal, Gary thought, wishing that she'd change the subject, but she was obviously waiting for his expert opinion.

"Just because he looks like a gelding, it doesn't mean he is. Sometimes you get what's called a rig. He might

47

have been gelded when he was younger, but perhaps he had an un-descended testicle. Then he'd look like a gelding, but he'd still have all the normal urges."

"I see." She was nodding. She looked interested and was evidently completely unaware of the effect this conversation was having on him.

"There's a test that can be carried out. I'll look into it for you if you like. I can speak to one of my colleagues who's more of an equine specialist." In an attempt to disguise his embarrassment he knew he was talking far too quickly, but she didn't seem to notice.

"Thanks, Gary, I'd really appreciate it. It's embarrassing having two horses – well – mounting each other in the field when there are people walking about with kids. Talking of kids, I've got to go and get Ben from school. I'm baby-sitting for Sarah tonight. So I'm going to have to love you and leave you."

He nodded, wishing she would. Well, not the leaving part, but the love would be good. They came out of the stable together and he watched her hurry away from him, her hips swinging tantalisingly. He was going to have to ask her out soon. Either that or suggest she found herself another vet. There were only so many cold showers a man could take.

"We're going to the Red Lion for tea," she called back over her shoulder. "I want to see if Mike's found me a handyman yet and I promised Ben a pizza as it's Friday and there's no school tomorrow. Pop by if you've got any news about Ashley. It is quite urgent."

"I could give you and Ben a lift there if you like?" he said before he had time to think about her refusing. "To save you driving."

"Okay, great, thanks. About seven. That should see me done here." She gave him another quick smile and then she was gone, driving out of the front gate in her Land Rover in a spray of gravel.

Gary had an urge to punch the air, but restrained himself. It was hardly a date. She'd have Ben with her and much as he liked the youngster, he'd far rather have taken Maggie out on her own. Still, it was a start.

Maybe he could raise the idea of a proper date while they were there. Yes, he would, he would bloody well do it. Tonight he would ask her out, come what may. If she hadn't liked him she wouldn't have suggested he join them, would she?

Chapter Six

"I know you, don't I?" Mike said, his forehead wrinkling in puzzlement, as he pulled Finn a pint of Guinness and put it on the bar to settle.

Finn nodded. "My father's got a cottage in the village – the last time we were here was at the end of last summer. We came in quite a lot then, but we've not had the chance to get down again since. I'm only here now because we've just sold the place."

The landlord's face cleared and he clicked his fingers in the air. "Of course. It's Finn, isn't it? Good to see you again. Did you get a good price?"

Finn told him, knowing he could probably find out anyway if he was interested enough, and the big man nodded seriously. "Mmm, not bad. Not bad at all. So how long are you planning on staying? Just until the deal goes through?"

"Maybe a bit longer than that. I thought I might spend a couple of months here. I'm between jobs at the moment." 'Between jobs' sounded better than admitting he'd just been made redundant, along with several of his colleagues, after a management buy-out.

"What sort of work do you do?" Mike asked.

"I'm an engineer – lately I've been doing maintenance for a factory in Nottingham. Electrical work mostly, but I can do basic plumbing. A bit of an odd-job man, really. I can turn my hand to most things." He hesitated, not sure whether to divulge the rest of his plans, but Mike looked interested, so he cleared his throat and carried on.

"I can paint a bit, too. I thought I might do some painting while I'm here."

"Houses, you mean?"

"No, I'm an artist." The words felt strange. Probably because it was the first time he'd ever said them. He wasn't sure if he even meant them, but they were out now, and he was Mike's only customer so it wasn't as if there were any witnesses. "I do landscapes mostly – water colours."

"Are you any good?"

Finn sipped his pint for Dutch courage. "I've got some framed canvasses at the cottage – local views. My grandparents liked them, but as we're selling the place, they'll probably end up at Oxfam."

"Mmm. Tell you what. Why don't you let me have a look. That sort of thing can go down quite well with the tourists. If I like them, you can put a couple on the walls, stick a price on. I'd have to take commission, of course – if any were sold."

"Why not?" Finn said, smiling nervously, and wondering what on earth he'd let himself in for. "Yeah – go on then – I'll pop a couple in the car next time I'm in."

A few more customers began to drift in: an old boy in a flat cap, with a border collie at his heels; then a couple of teenagers, their mobile phones clamped to their ears.

Finn was on his second pint when the door opened and a couple came in with a child. The woman was Maggie, he realised with a little jolt.

It was true what he'd told Mike, he was here to sort out the house sale to save his father the hassle, and he liked the idea of spending some time painting – the scenery was beautiful in this part of the world. But he couldn't deny that the possibility of bumping into Maggie again had been appealing, too.

He just hadn't expected it to happen so soon.

Finn put down his pint and tried not to stare. She probably wouldn't remember him, anyway. He picked up a paper that was lying on the bar and withdrew to a table in the window, where he could watch the trio without being obvious. Perhaps the guy was her boyfriend, husband even.

He watched as the man, a burly, stocky guy, wearing a tweed jacket that made him look a bit like a gentleman farmer, took Maggie's coat and draped it awkwardly over the back of her chair. Then he fussed around her, his hands fluttering, as if he wanted to touch, but wasn't quite sure of his welcome.

Business acquaintances, Finn decided, or casual friends, at most. The body language was wrong for them to be anything more. He'd have laid bets on it that the boy wasn't hers, either. Well, not if looks were anything to go by. Maggie had dark hair and the child was fair and they had different-shaped faces, different colouring altogether.

He went back to his newspaper, feeling a surge of disappointment. He'd wanted to bump into her, but these circumstances were no more ideal than when they'd met before.

The idea of Mike selling his paintings also seemed suddenly ludicrous. He'd spouted off about being an artist, and it was true that he'd drawn and painted since he was a child. But he'd never been professionally trained, unless you counted the odd evening class, where he'd always felt out of place, being the only man.

Going to Art College hadn't been an option. He hadn't even bothered suggesting it to Albert, knowing what his reaction would be. "Don't be so bloody soft, lad, art's not a man's job."

Neither was factory work, in his father's opinion. Mind you, he'd probably got off lightly, Finn decided, feeling a surge of affection for his father despite their differences. Had there still been working mines in his home town when he'd left school, Albert would have had him down one at the first opportunity.

He supposed he should head back to the cottage. He had the last of the packing up to do, but it was still early and he didn't relish the prospect of spending the next twelve hours alone. Not that this place was exactly buzzing. Maggie and her companion had ordered food, which had just arrived, and the boy was tearing open sachets of tomato ketchup and squirting patterns with them on to his chips. The smell of the chips had Finn's stomach rumbling and he realised he hadn't eaten all day.

Packing up the last of his grandfather's suits for the charity shop had been sadder than he'd anticipated – the end of an era. It was a pity that Albert had decided to sell up, but Finn could see the sense in it. Albert would put the money to good use, he knew.

The next time he looked up, they'd finished eating and Maggie was chatting to the landlord. Every so often they glanced in his direction and he had the odd feeling they were talking about him. He was being paranoid. Why would they be?

He stared out at the velvet blackness beyond the dark wood-framed windows and decided to forget the chips and head back. If the truth be told, he was just as alone here as he'd be at the cottage.

He took his empty glass back to the bar, confident now that Maggie hadn't recognised him, and was about to head for the door when Mike called, "Hey, Finn. You got a sec? Maggie, here, has a proposition for you."

Finn jumped out of his skin. He was really going to have to get a grip on himself. He turned slowly.

"What sort of proposition?" He smiled as he met Maggie's direct gaze.

"Hello, Finn. I thought it might be you, but I wasn't sure until Mike told me your name. We met last year," she explained, turning to her companion, who looked none too happy about the turn events were taking.

"Back in September," Finn murmured. "Yes, I remember. How are you?"

"I'm fine, thanks." She gave him a quick, embarrassed smile and he knew she was remembering the circumstances of their meeting.

"You were right," she added, a faint flush colouring her cheeks. "It does get easier."

Finn nodded, aware that the man was watching him, his gaze cool. The little lad was fiddling with a beer mat, bending one corner of it backwards and forwards. Close up, Finn was even more certain that they weren't related – although he supposed the child could be adopted. No, that was unlikely – she was too young to have decided to adopt a child.

Realising that Maggie was still speaking to him, he looked back into her face.

"I've a job I think might interest you, Finn. Why don't you join us and we can have a chat?"

Frowning, he was about to protest that he wasn't looking for a job, but then caught the enthusiasm on Mike's face and, realising he'd misinterpreted his 'between jobs' as meaning, 'looking for a job', he nodded slowly.

"This is Ben, my godson," she went on, warmth threading through her voice as she glanced towards the boy, who gave Finn a gap-toothed grin. "And Gary Collins, my vet, and – er – friend."

Finn heard the edge of awkwardness in the word 'friend' and felt a little stab of relief. That was good news. There was nothing established there, then – at least not as far as Maggie was concerned.

Ben, obviously anxious to get back into the limelight again, drew his plate towards the edge of the table and began to fiddle with his knife and fork.

Out of the corner of his eye, Finn saw the plate begin to tip towards the boy's lap. He'd always had lightning reflexes. Before anyone else could move, he reached across in front of Gary, who was sitting next to Ben, and caught the plate just before it tipped completely and deposited its cargo of untouched peas and tomato-sauce-soaked chips into Ben's lap.

Unfortunately, he wasn't quite quick enough to prevent the sauce-smeared knife from landing in Gary's lap, pointy end down.

"Shit," Gary muttered, leaping out of his chair like a scalded cat and glaring at Finn as the knife clattered to the wooden floor.

"Sorry." Finn held up his hands in a gesture of contrition, aware that Maggie was frowning at Gary, presumably because she didn't approve of him swearing in front of her godson, who looked thrilled at the fuss he'd caused.

"Mum tells me off if I say shit," Ben said, slurping his orange squash and trying not to look too pleased that he'd managed to slip the word 'shit' into the conversation legitimately.

"I should think so, too," Maggie said, with mild reproof in her voice. Finn could see she was trying not to smile. It was only Gary who looked thunderous, as he dabbed at the red smear on his hitherto immaculate trousers with a green paper napkin. Oops, not a good start.

"Sorry," he said again, but to Maggie this time.

"Don't apologise, it's a good job you caught it. I've never believed those washing powder adverts that say their brand gets tomato sauce out of everything."

Gary coughed pointedly and her eyes widened as she glanced at him. "What I mean is when there's a lot of it – they're probably okay for small amounts. I'm sure they work absolutely fine for those."

"Shall we sit down?" Finn suggested before she dug herself in any deeper and she shot him a grateful glance.

Mike, looking pleased with himself at having made the introductions, hastily cleared away the empty plates.

"What's everyone drinking?" Gary muttered, presumably eager to get back into Maggie's good books, and Finn found himself being pressed into another pint of Guinness.

"Do you like animals?" Maggie asked while Gary was at the bar.

"We used to have a dog," he said puzzled. "My father reckons they're less trouble than people. They're always pleased to see you and they stay loyal."

She nodded in approval and went on without preamble. "I run an animal sanctuary, not far from here, and I'm looking for someone to help out."

"I see," he said, slightly thrown. Had he and Mike even had the same conversation? "Do you mean you need someone to look after the animals? I've no experience with livestock."

"No, don't worry. Nothing like that. I do all that side. It's the place itself I need help with. Mike was saying you used to do maintenance at a factory?"

"That's right." He smiled at her and rested his chin on his hand and was pleased when she unconsciously mirrored the gesture.

"So you could do things like fix dodgy electricity supplies? There's a bit of fencing too. Drainage, guttering – that sort of thing."

"Doesn't sound too complicated."

"She hasn't told you the best bit yet." Gary put their drinks on the table, and although his voice was light, his body language told Finn a different story. Gary couldn't wait to get rid of him. He'd have thought he was interrupting a romantic date, had it not been for Ben's presence.

"What's the best bit?" Finn asked.

"You'll be working all hours and earning a pittance."

"Oh, don't put him off, Gary."

"He hasn't," Finn said, raising his eyebrows. "I was used to that at the factory." This wasn't quite true, but there was no way he was letting Maggie get away without at least arranging another meeting. Not that she seemed in any hurry to get away.

"Gary's right. I'm afraid I can't afford to pay you much. We're a charity, you see. I could throw in accommodation, though. Mike said you've just sold a cottage – so you're going to need somewhere to live."

Finn saw Gary give her a sharp look and he realised his earlier suspicions had been right on target. They weren't a couple, but Gary certainly wanted them to be, and he didn't want another bloke muscling in.

He sipped his pint and decided, for once, to throw caution to the winds. If fate decreed that the woman he hadn't been able to get off his mind for the last few months should offer him a job, he certainly wasn't going to turn her down out of hand.

"Maybe if I came and had a look round?" he said. "Tomorrow morning? Would that do?"

"That would be wonderful." Maggie looked pleased. She smiled at him, her whole face lighting up and Finn found himself thinking that he'd have worked for her for nothing as long as she smiled at him like that every day. No wonder Gary was smitten.

"You could see Candy's pups." Ben had been busy with another beer mat, but now he pushed the torn up pieces into a little pile on the table and rested his chin on his hands. "And Auntie Maggie's got a sick buzzard. And chickens. Millions of smelly chickens."

"Sounds wonderful," Finn said, turning to smile at the boy. He liked kids and this one was a right live wire. Gary didn't look at all pleased, though. He was staring into his drink, his intense face flushed.

Finn stood up. "Can I get anyone another?"

Maggie shook her head and Ben said, "No thanks."

Finn looked at Gary. "How about you, mate?"

"I've had enough." Gary didn't meet his eyes, but turned towards Maggie. "Are you ready to go now?"

"Yes, I think so." She didn't return his glance, but got gracefully to her feet and offered Finn her hand. "I'll see you tomorrow then, Finn. About ten?"

He took her hand, which felt cool and surprisingly smooth, considering her job. Nice nails – short, and painted with some clear shiny varnish. There was no sign of a wedding ring. "I'll look forward to it," he said.

She smiled again, and he returned the smile, acutely aware that beside her Gary was bristling with resentment. He wondered if she could feel the atmosphere. There was no sign of it in her face. So was she oblivious to the way Gary felt about her, or just playing it cool? He glanced back at Ben. "I'm looking forward to seeing those chickens."

He was rewarded with another delighted grin and a furious scowl from Gary. It would be an interesting meeting tomorrow, he thought, hoping Gary didn't have any say in whether he got the job or not. Not that he actually needed the job – but he'd like to get to know Maggie better.

58

His memory hadn't let him down. She was maybe a touch thinner than he remembered, but she was still just as attractive, and there was a very slight air of aloofness about her that made him want to know what went on behind those dark eyes. Why on earth had a woman like Maggie Clarke decided to bury herself in the wilds of Wiltshire looking after a bunch of animals that no one else wanted? He was intrigued. And he hadn't been intrigued by a woman for a very long time.

Chapter Seven

Sarah turned up to collect Ben just after nine the next morning and Maggie told her about her prospective employee as they stood outside reception.

"It sounds to me like you fancy the bloke," Sarah said, putting her head on one side. "How old is he and what does he look like?"

"Thirtyish, I'd guess, and I didn't really notice what he looked like," Maggie lied. "And of course I don't fancy him. I just need some help. It's not fair to keep asking Jack."

"Jack doesn't mind. And you know Ben loves it here. He'd far rather be with you, getting filthy, than at home doing boring stuff."

"It's the animals he likes, not me," Maggie protested, ruffling Ben's fair hair and brushing some flecks of dried mud off his back. She didn't know how he got so dirty; perhaps it was because he was closer to the ground than they were. "Isn't that right, young man?"

Ben gave her the full benefit of his gap-toothed smile and shook his head emphatically.

Maggie laughed. "You're a right smoothie, you are. So are you telling me you'd still come and stay with me if I didn't have all my waifs and strays?"

"Course, Auntie Maggie." Ben widened his eyes. "Anyway, I'm a big help, aren't I?"

'A big help' was his latest catch-phrase, which Gary had started off when Ben had helped him round up a litter of puppies that he needed to vaccinate.

"A big pest, more like," Sarah muttered. "Talking of which, are you still sure you don't mind having him next week?"

"Of course I'm sure." This was true, though Maggie was also terrified at the prospect of being responsible for Ben for a fortnight, especially as he wouldn't be at school for one of the weeks. Not that she had any intention of telling Sarah this because she knew how much Sarah wanted to meet Jack's parents and Ben was adamant that he didn't want to go with them. "I'm looking forward to having him all to myself. He'll have a lot more fun here than traipsing up to Scotland in the back of that minibus."

"Yes, that's what he said. He's nothing like me," Sarah added. "I'd have jumped at the chance to have an extra week off school when I was his age."

"Yes, I remember," Maggie said, smiling. "And your extra days off were usually strictly unauthorised from what I recall."

Sarah blushed. "Yes, well, I'm a responsible parent now, aren't I? And Ben loves school. I'm going to miss him, though," she added, the lightness of her words not concealing the ache of longing in her voice. "It's going to be really strange being childless for a fortnight."

"You can phone him every day," Maggie said. "And he can tell you what he's been up to, can't you, Ben?"

But Ben wasn't listening any more. He was in reception, trying to tempt a dove perched on the corner of Maggie's filing cabinet to land on his hand.

"Dawn's coming in every day next week, too," Maggie went on. "And with a bit of luck Finn will take the job, which will free some of my time up. Ben and I are going to have a lovely fortnight."

"What time is Finn coming? Maybe I should hang around and help you interview him."

"No, thank you. I'm quite capable of interviewing him myself," Maggie said firmly, because she knew Sarah

61

wouldn't be able to resist teasing Finn about sharing the cottage and she didn't want him frightened off.

They went eventually and Maggie breathed a sigh of relief. Finn probably wouldn't take the job anyway, she reflected. Not when he found out what she could afford to pay him – or, more accurately, not afford to pay him. And even if he did he wouldn't stay long, she decided, as she looked around the yard. He'd just stay until he got a better offer and then he'd be off again; but having someone around, even for a short while, would be a great help. She'd made light of it to Gary, but it did worry her that the place was falling down around her ears and she didn't have time to do anything about it.

A car drew into the yard just before ten and she saw Finn get out and stand in the muddy yard, looking around appraisingly. He'd probably only turned up because he didn't have anything better to do. In half an hour he'd be gone, shaking his head as he drove away, his impression of her as a batty animal-lover entrenched. A tale to tell in bars across the country. No, she mustn't pre-empt. He might be desperate enough to work for her. She took a deep breath and switched on the answer machine and fixed what she hoped was a welcoming smile on her face.

As she went out to meet him Maggie tried to imagine what The Ark must look like to a stranger. After all the rain they'd had lately, tracks of mud ran round the yard, and the ramshackle buildings looked dismal and run-down. No one in their right mind would want to work here.

"I'm afraid you're not seeing it at its best." She glanced at his unsmiling face, which told her nothing. His eyes were thoughtful. He was either very good at hiding his feelings or simply indifferent. She hoped it wasn't the latter. But at least he didn't look horrified, which was a good start.

"Shall we just walk round and you can see what you'd be letting yourself in for?"

"Sure."

She took him through the gate that led up past the cattery and the horses' paddock and on towards the kennels. This part of the sanctuary was on higher ground and wasn't as muddy as the reception end. Above their heads a weak spring sun was trying to push through the clouds.

"There's a lot to be done," Finn remarked, as they went past the tatty pink caravan where she kept bedding for the dogs. "That's not the accommodation you're offering, is it?"

She glanced at him sharply, before realising there was humour in his grey eyes. She was about to make an appropriate retort when Diesel, who had the uninterrupted run of the place, strolled around the side of the caravan, almost at their feet, with a large wriggling mouse in his mouth.

Maggie gasped and Finn looked at her. Swiftly, before she could react, he picked up Diesel by the scruff of his black neck. The cat was so surprised that he dropped the mouse and it scurried away across the yard.

Diesel yowled in disgust and Maggie burst out laughing. "You've just made an enemy for life. You realise that?"

"By the look on your face I figured that mouse must be one of the residents," Finn said, still holding the struggling Diesel in his arms.

"Not that I know of. But I'm glad you stopped him. Diesel's a cold-hearted monster. He's always murdering things and I'd rather he did it out of my sight. This is an animal sanctuary, after all."

As she spoke, Diesel gave another frantic wriggle, scratched Finn's hand and leapt to freedom.

Finn looked so affronted that Maggie started to laugh again. Then she remembered she was trying to get him to work for her and said solicitously, "He hasn't hurt you, has he?"

"It'll heal." Finn glanced at her. Then he smiled too, his grey eyes warming. It was in that moment that Maggie knew that it was going to be all right. He was going to take the job.

Finn drove back to the cottage, deep in thought. It wasn't like him to make impulsive decisions where women were concerned. Not since Shirley, anyway, and that impulse had cost him dearly. He frowned; charging in without thinking about the consequences always led to trouble. Was that was he was doing now?

By the time he'd got back to the cottage he'd convinced himself that he wasn't. Taking the job was sensible. It meant he could stay here longer than he'd planned and maybe give the painting a real go, too. Besides, he was hardly overloaded with options. If a job fell into his lap he'd be a fool not to take it. It was only a temporary position, Maggie had made that clear.

It would be interesting living in her house and although she hadn't offered him much money, free lodgings was a bonus. Finn had never needed much money.

He wandered around the empty rooms of his grandparents' cottage. Two or three more trips to the charity shop and one more trip to the tip should do it. The contracts had been exchanged and the completion date was next week. So he'd have a full week to paint. He had a feeling that he wouldn't have an awful lot of spare time once he started working for Maggie. He glanced at the faded oblong squares on the walls where the pictures had once hung and remembered he'd promised to show Mike his paintings. Deciding that he might as well have lunch at the Red Lion, he packed the canvasses into the car.

"Bit of a result that, eh, Finn?" Mike grinned at him across the bar. "Bet you didn't expect to find a job and a place to live so soon – eh?"

"Thanks very much for the introduction."

"She's a sweetie, Maggie Clarke," Mike continued. "She's had a tough time of it lately. She lost her mother eighteen months ago. Think it did something to her, that. She was all set on some high-flying veterinary career in Bristol. I don't think she'd have come back if she hadn't lost her Mum."

He paused, a frown crinkling his forehead. "She grew up round here, but she wasn't like the rest of the kids. She left as soon as she got the chance. Must have been hell coming back here and I must say I was surprised when she set up that animal rescue place. Got a bit of opposition when she first suggested it. There had been hopes in the village that a developer would buy the land and build some nice modern flats."

"The villagers have accepted her now, though, have they?" Finn enquired. Not that Maggie had struck him as the type to be put off by a bit of opposition.

Mike tapped his nose. "Let's just say they tolerate her. I've heard a few mutterings lately that the place is going to rack and ruin, becoming an eyesore. But that'll change now you're here. Mind you, you'll have your work cut out."

"Reckon I will," Finn said, sipping the half pint of Guinness Mike had put in front of him.

"So what's Gary like? Are they…?"

"God, no." Mike guffawed and slapped a hand down on the bar. "That's not to say Gary wouldn't like them to

65

be – but the bloke's a prune." He rested his elbows on the bar and lowered his voice with the air of one sharing a confidence. "For someone who has his hands up cows' 'you know whats' half his life, he's bloody uptight. He was married once, but she left him for the best man a week after the wedding. If you ask me, he's still a virgin."

"Right," Finn said, feeling a little sorry for Gary and deciding to be very careful what he said to Mike in future.

"Fancy a crack at her yourself, do you?" Mike asked, his eyes glinting at the prospect of gossip.

"She's not my type," Finn lied smoothly. "Besides, I don't believe in mixing business with pleasure. Always ends in tears."

Finn was just leaving the pub when Mike called after him. "Hold on a tick. Weren't you going to show me some paintings?"

He hesitated. Last night, fortified with Guinness, it had seemed a good idea, but now, in the cold light of day, he felt a bit vulnerable. He'd never shown his work to a stranger before.

"I'll come out and have a quick shufty," Mike continued. "You're not rushing off, are you?"

There was no way he could refuse without seeming rude. What was the worst that could happen? Mike could say he thought they were no good, which would only confirm his own suspicions. Painting was an odd thing, Finn mused. When he'd just finished a picture he was usually pleased with it. Still caught up in the fire of creation. It was only later, when he'd had time to study it and see all the imperfections, that the self-doubt would creep in. But there was the faintest chance that Mike might think they would sell. That was what he wanted to do. Sell his work to people who bought it because they liked it, not just because they were his mates and were doing him a favour.

A few moments later they were standing in the car park beneath a sky that looked heavy with rain. Hoping it would hold off, Finn hauled the two biggest canvasses off the back seat and propped them up against the tyres of the Toyota. One of them was of Stonehenge, the stones dark and brooding against a winter sky, and the other was of Bournemouth beach, which Finn had visited often with his grandparents. In the foreground, a small girl was building a sandcastle with a red plastic spade. The wind swept back her hair so that you could see the intense concentration on her face. Behind her, the sea was a moody grey.

Mike studied the paintings without speaking and Finn could feel his stomach turning over. He wiped his hands on his jeans and felt sick. He'd just taken a few steps away from the car, deciding he could stand the suspense no longer, when Mike said, "They're bloody brilliant, these are. Give us a hand to cart them inside and I'll find a place to put them up later."

"Do you think they might sell, then?" Finn asked cautiously.

"Don't know about that – depends on how flush the tourists are feeling. But it's worth a try."

Finn nodded, feeling deflated.

"Twenty-five per cent commission if they do," Mike said, as they walked back towards the pub with the canvasses.

"All right." They shook hands on the deal and Finn went back to the cottage. It was one twenty. By now Albert would be halfway through his second pint at the Sheaf of Arrows, having just ordered his Sunday lunch from Big Lil, the landlady. Roast of the day with as many potatoes as you could eat. Finn braked to miss a squirrel that had just darted out in front of him; his thoughts flicked back to Maggie and he had to suppress a sudden and unexpected surge of home-sickness.

Chapter Eight

"So, where is he?" Sarah asked, struggling into reception the following Friday evening with a small suitcase and a selection of bulging overnight bags, which she plonked on the wooden floor.

"If you mean Finn, he's not starting until tomorrow. He said he wanted to do some sketching this week. Apparently he's an artist."

"Should get on well with Ben, then. I'll just get the rest of his stuff."

"More stuff?" Maggie said in alarm. "What on earth is it all?"

"Clothes, computer games, school stuff, and that carrier bag is mostly stuffed with dog treats, he's been saving his breakfast sausages. I did tell him you fed them."

Maggie shook her head in amazement. "It's a good job I cleared out the spare room. What time are you off in the morning?"

"Hopefully about six. Jack's loading up the bus now." Sarah paced across the office and looked out of the window. "It's set to get really cold again, according to the weather forecast. I hope we don't drive into too much snow."

Maggie wondered if the minibus was in better shape than it had been the last time she'd seen it. Personally, she'd have thought Sarah would have been more worried about the chances of simply getting there than the possibility of snow when they did.

"I'm glad you've got some help," Sarah went on. "I don't feel so bad about you looking after Ben."

"Stop it, Sarah. You know I love having him. Where is he, anyway?"

"He went to see Candy's pups. He doesn't seem a bit bothered about me going off for a fortnight. I'm going to miss him like hell, it's the first time we've ever been apart."

"I expect he's more bothered than he's letting on," Maggie said, hearing the wistful note in Sarah's voice. "But it's good really, isn't it – the fact that he feels secure enough to want to stay here without you."

"Yes, I suppose so." Sarah's eyes were soft and Maggie saw the shine of tears in them.

"Oh, Sarah, come here." She hugged her friend tightly, breathing in the scent of apple shampoo mixed with the wild musk scent that Sarah always wore. "I won't let anything happen to him. He'll be fine."

"I know he will. I'm sorry. I'm being silly." Sarah sniffed and Maggie said softly, "Come on, I'll take his stuff inside and you go and see what he's doing. Two weeks will be gone in no time, I promise. And when you get back you can meet Finn. Maybe we could all go out together. I'll ask Gary, too," she added, before Sarah could jump to any wrong conclusions.

Ben reappeared just as Maggie was carrying in the last of his bags. His face was grimy and his eyes looked suspiciously glittery.

"Diesel scratched me," he said, with a distinct wobble in his voice. "Where's Mum?"

"Oh, darling. It's all right, she's just popped to the loo. Where did he scratch you?"

Ben sniffed and rolled up his sleeve and showed her the thin red weal on his arm and Maggie swallowed hard and wondered again if this was going to work. Yesterday she and Dawn, who was sensible and middle-aged and had several grandchildren of her own, had gone round the entire sanctuary and 'Ben-proofed' everything that they'd

70

thought might be a problem. There were padlocks on all the animal pens apart from the chickens, Maggie's medical supplies were out of reach as well as under lock and key, and Maggie was certain that the fencing around the paddocks was childproof.

But Diesel was a law unto himself. Maggie wondered if perhaps she should confine him to the cattery for a fortnight.

"I was only cuddling him," Ben mumbled. "Not tight, Auntie Maggie, honest, I wasn't."

"He's a grumpy old sod," Maggie said, realising belatedly that she probably shouldn't have said 'sod'. "You can cuddle Mickey in a minute. He likes a nice cuddle."

Ben stuck his thumb in his mouth and looked around for Maggie's dog, who was the only animal, apart from Diesel, who had the run of the place. Mickey was the 'rug on legs' that Sarah's neighbour had had to give up because of her asthmatic grandchildren and Maggie had decided with slightly irrational logic that the best way to avoid anyone rejecting him was to keep him herself.

Fortunately Sarah appeared at that moment and Ben ran into her arms, sniffing loudly.

Maggie chewed her lip as she watched Sarah kiss his fair head and wished she didn't feel quite so terrified at the prospect of being solely responsible for him for a whole fortnight.

"I'm really not trying to interfere, Maggie, but don't you think you ought to be more cautious? At least get some references. You don't know anything about the guy."

"I doubt if he's an axe murderer, Gary," she said, glancing at the vet's flushed face and wondering why he was so agitated.

71

It was Saturday morning and Ben was 'helping' Dawn clean out the chicken run, while she and Gary were standing in the hospital block beside the dog pen. Gary had declared that Tiny was coming along nicely, but didn't seem to be in any hurry to go. "I didn't say I thought he was dangerous. I just think you ought to be careful. Not rush into anything."

"I've already employed him. In fact, he should be here any minute."

"Don't you think you ought to find out more about him?" The vet's voice was rising in agitation. "After all, he's not just an ordinary employee. He's going to be living in your house."

Maggie blinked. She was pretty sure that Gary's sudden possessiveness stemmed from the fact that he wanted them to be more than friends, but it was difficult to tell him this wasn't what she wanted when he hadn't actually asked her out. If she was wrong she'd make a complete fool of herself and embarrass them both.

"He's hardly going to pinch the silver, because I haven't got any. In fact, I've got nothing worth the trouble of carrying out the front door."

"I didn't mean that." Gary's swarthy face was troubled and she regretted her sharpness.

"Look, I know you're only trying to help and I appreciate it." She touched his arm lightly. "But Finn's accepted the job despite the fact I'm paying him next to nothing, and to be honest, Gary, I can't afford to be too choosy. He seems nice enough."

"You will be careful, though, won't you? You'll let me know if he gives you any trouble?"

"He didn't strike me as being that kind of guy. Anyway, I'm a big girl. I can look after myself." She hoped that would be enough of a hint, but it seemed to go straight over Gary's head.

"I know you can look after yourself, but you can't tell about people, not from first impressions. He could be anyone."

There was a cough from behind them. Maggie spun round to see Finn standing there. She wondered how much of their conversation he'd heard.

"Sorry, I didn't realise you were here." She glanced at Gary, who seemed to have developed an all-consuming interest in something in Candy's pen.

Embarrassed, she fished a key out of her pocket and gave it to Finn. "Please go and get settled in and make yourself at home. Help yourself to coffee, whatever. I'll be over in a minute."

When he'd gone she turned back to Gary. "That wasn't a very nice welcome for him, was it?"

"He shouldn't have been sneaking about." Gary's voice was unrepentant. Then he grinned at her. "I won't say any more about it. As you say, we've got to give the bloke a chance."

"Let's hope he stays around to take it," Maggie murmured, not returning his smile. If she didn't know him better she'd have thought he'd set the whole thing up on purpose.

Finn went across to the cottage. So, he'd been right about Gary. The guy obviously wasn't at all happy about his presence. He wiped his feet on the doormat, which had a picture of a collie dog and the word 'Welcome' in black beneath it. Feeling like an intruder, he stepped inside. The place smelt faintly of dogs. He glanced around; he hadn't seen one when Maggie had shown him round. The hallway had two doors leading off it, both of which were open.

The left-hand one led into a lounge, which Maggie had shown him, but he hadn't really looked at properly. Now he stood in the doorway, his gaze travelling over a brown patterned settee and a matching armchair, both of which had seen better days. There was a bookcase, stuffed with books, and a coffee table scattered with papers. In the corner was a plastic dog basket with a tartan blanket in it. Behind the chair there was an open fireplace, which looked as if it had been recently used.

The other door led through to a tiny kitchen. He saw a pile of washing-up in the sink as he went past. He continued on up the uncarpeted stairs. On the first floor were two bedrooms, Maggie's and the spare, which she'd explained that Ben was staying in while his mum and dad were on a business trip.

"You can have it when he goes home in a couple of weeks – if you're still here then," she'd joked, but he'd said no, the attic room, which was at the top of a further winding staircase, would suit him fine.

He carried on up and pushed open the door to his room.

Light flooded through a large, oblong skylight, casting golden pools across the little single bed. There was a small wardrobe and a washbasin with two white towels folded on the rail. Maggie might not bother with the rest of the house, but this room was spotless, so she wasn't that oblivious, Finn thought, smiling as he dumped his stuff on the bed. There was a radiator behind the bed, which was on, he discovered, when he touched it.

He glanced out of the window and saw that Gary and Maggie were just coming out of the hospital block. Perhaps he'd unpack first and sort out a few things. He could catch up with Maggie later when Gary wasn't around.

"Sorry, I haven't had a chance to see much of you," Maggie called, as Finn came down the attic stairs later that evening.

"It's all right. I know you're busy."

She was standing in the open doorway of Ben's bedroom and when he reached her he could see that the boy was in bed. By the look of it there was a dog in there, too – although it was hard to tell it was a dog and not a hearth rug until it scrabbled a paw out of the covers.

Maggie followed his gaze and smiled.

"Mickey's not supposed to be up here, but he's keeping Ben company until he falls asleep."

"So I see," Finn said softly, wondering if Ben was missing his mum. "Mickey looks more fun than a bedtime story," he said.

"I have those too," Ben told him, sitting up gleefully. "Auntie Maggie's a betterer reader than Mum. We had a long story, didn't we, Auntie Maggie?"

"Yes and it's definitely bed time so I think you should snuggle back down." Maggie's voice was gentle and Finn felt the edge of a memory, a long-ago painful memory of his own mother, and the awful, aching emptiness he'd felt when she'd gone. He swallowed. "Sweet dreams then, mate," he said, stepping past Maggie and going downstairs.

He heard her say, "Don't leave the light on too long, sweetheart. I'll leave this open in case Mickey wants to come down."

Then she followed him downstairs and into the warmth of the little back room. A Chris De Burgh CD was playing – so she was a romantic at heart, then – and an open fire was snapping and crackling in the grate.

"Wow, I haven't seen one of those for years," he murmured, breathing in the scent of wood-smoke and stepping across the room to warm his hands. "Dad used to have a real fire when I was small, but then he got a grant from the local authority and had central heating put in."

"Not the same, is it?" she said, looking at him with pleasure and gesturing for him to sit on the chair beside it.

"Ben's a nice kiddie. Do you often look after him?"

"Not as often as I'd like to. Sarah and Jack usually take him with them on their trips – but they're not usually away for so long. They've gone to Scotland this time. They didn't want him to miss any school and, besides, it's a pretty long haul for a six year old."

"Yes," Finn murmured, watching her face, which was animated when she talked about Ben. There was so much he wanted to ask her, like why she ran this place all alone and why she didn't have any children of her own, when she so obviously loved them. It was an odd life for a young, attractive woman.

"I was brought up round here," she said, pre-empting him. "My mother owned four hotels. She wanted me to go into business with her – run one of the hotels – but I'm afraid I disappointed her. All I ever wanted to do was work with animals. So I persuaded her to let me go to vet school in Bristol."

He wondered if she still felt guilty about that; it was never easy to go against your parents' wishes. He'd never gone against Albert's, but then despite the fact that Albert wasn't very good at anything touchy-feely, Finn had always known his father loved him, in his gruff, no-nonsense way. There was something in Maggie's voice that told him she'd had a very different relationship with her mother.

"I should think it's very hard work being a vet," he prompted, resting his elbows on his knees and leaning forward.

"Yes." There was a hint of sadness in her eyes. "But I never got that far, in the end. Mum had a stroke, you see, and I came back to look after her. Then she had another stroke – a fatal one this time. It was a huge shock. By the time I'd sorted everything out, I'd realised that my life had moved on – I decided not to continue with studying."

Finn nodded slowly, remembering the first time he'd seen her at the cemetery. She'd been pretty cut up then, a year after she'd lost her mother. There was a part of her that was still grieving. He could see it in her eyes.

"Was your dad involved in the business as well?"

She shook her head. "No, Dad left when I was small. I don't remember him."

Her face was shadowed now, as though she was looking inside herself, at something she'd rather not see.

"That must have been tough," he said quietly, wondering if he should change the subject. He didn't want to push her. It was obvious that Maggie was deeply troubled about something in her past.

Then she turned back to him and said in a voice that was a little too bright. "Anyway, Finn, we're here to talk about you, not me. What's your background? Do both your parents live in Nottingham?"

Thrown by this swift change of subject, he hesitated. In some ways his background mirrored hers. Only it had been his mother who'd left, not his father. Finn could barely remember her. She'd left when he was six years old and he'd had nightmares about it for years. Albert had provided for him materially, but he'd never been an emotional man. Finn had spent many a childhood illness longing for the touch of his mother's hand, gentle on his forehead, the scent of her hair as she leaned over him in bed. Now and again he still had nightmares, waking up drenched in sweat and feeling an overwhelming sense of loss.

He coughed. He hated talking about his mother, but he felt obliged to say something.

"Er, no," he said. "My parents split up when I was young, too. My mum was from Dublin, hence my name, and she went back when they separated. I haven't seen her since and neither has Dad."

Maggie nodded, her eyes soft, and he thought with a stab of irony that it was a shame that the first thing they should find common ground on was painful memories.

"You don't have any other relatives in Nottingham? No other ties?"

"I was living with someone for a while," he said, guessing that this was what she wanted to know. "But things didn't work out so we decided to call it a day. That was a while ago, six or seven months."

She nodded, but he didn't elaborate. That was all he planned to tell her about Shirley. To say anything else would have been tantamount to telling her what an idiot he was with women.

"Then, I got made redundant at the end of January. I was lucky. I had a reasonable pay-off, and Dad needed someone to sort out the cottage, so I thought I'd take some time out. Plan what to do next with my life." He smiled at her. "Besides which, I've always liked it down here. I used to stay with my grandparents a lot when I was younger."

There was a small pause and then before either of them could say anything else, the lounge door swung open and Mickey appeared with something white and lacy dangling from his mouth. Before either Finn or Maggie could move, the dog trotted across to him and deposited what turned out to be a bra in his lap.

"Oh, I'm so sorry." Maggie was out of her chair, her face aflame with embarrassment. "He must have been in the washing basket again. He's a terrible thief."

Finn handed the bra to her, feeling almost as embarrassed as she was and deciding that he didn't know her well enough to make some light-hearted remark about women's underwear. "No worries. Er – I've a reference here for you from my previous employer. I can't give you any references on the house-sharing front, but I'm fully house trained…"

"Thanks." Maggie stuffed the envelope and the bra into the pocket of her fleece without looking at him and he knew she was aware of what he hadn't said: *Despite what your vet may think of me*.

She got up and went across the room and proceeded to remove half a dozen items of clothing, mostly socks from what he could see, from the dog basket.

"You'll have to keep your door shut, or everything will end up in his basket – or in the garden if you're unlucky, down some hole he's dug."

Finn smiled, relieved that they'd got off the subject of anything too personal. He listened while she outlined the routines of the sanctuary and how she saw him fitting into things.

"Sounds fine," he said, yawning. "I guess I'd better turn in if I'm going to be any use to you tomorrow."

He lay in the unfamiliar room looking at the scattering of stars beyond the skylight and thought about Shirley. If he did have any regrets about leaving Nottingham they were centred around her. Not because he thought there was any hope of them getting back together – she was married to his best mate, make that his former best mate – but because he was concerned about her welfare. He knew he would

79

always be concerned about Shirley. Peter might have made her all the promises in the world, but Finn knew he was too drunk most of the time to remember them. Still, he mused, shifting restlessly beneath the coolness of the duvet, at least Albert had promised to keep a discreet eye on things.

Albert would let him know if Shirley needed him. That would have to be good enough for now.

Chapter Nine

"Auntie Maggie, Diesel's got a mousey," Ben yelled from the direction of the chicken run. "Quick, come and see."

With visions of Ben getting upset if Diesel did his usual decapitating trick, Maggie hurried across to the child, who was standing on top of the chicken run, waving his arms about. It was fun having Ben around, but it was also exhausting. There was a part of her that would be heartily relieved when half-term was over. Trying to make sure he stayed out of trouble, was safe and kept reasonably clean, was a Herculean task. She'd abandoned the reasonably clean bit after the first couple of days and just piled all his clothes into the washing machine every night.

"Look, Auntie Maggie, he's very naughty."

Ben pointed and Maggie realised with a jolt of horror that Ben hadn't said mousey, he'd said Maisie, which was the name of one of the ex-battery hens. Diesel was inside the chicken run, black tail swishing furiously – although when she got closer she could see that he hadn't got Maisie, at all. It was more the other way round. The hens had surrounded the black cat and had edged him into a corner and every so often one of them darted in for an experimental peck.

"How did he get in there?" she gasped, swinging open the latch on the front of the run and trying to avoid the big cat's flailing claws as he fled past her, pursued by several hens.

"He wanted to go in," Ben said, widening his eyes innocently. "He was scratching on the door."

"So, you let him in. Oh, Ben, sweetie, I don't think that was a very good idea. He could have hurt them."

Although, right now, she had to admit the opposite was probably more likely. Diesel gave one last affronted yowl of annoyance, hurtled away from his pursuers, and shot up a tree and on to the stable block roof, where he sat glaring at her accusingly.

Maggie caught hold of Ben's hand. "How about we go and take a dog out together?"

"I'm bored of dogs. Can we go and see the buzzard? I want to paint him for school."

"How about painting some puppies?" Maggie suggested. "Bertie Buzzard's still not feeling too well – it's probably best if we leave him in peace and quiet today."

The pups were in reception where she could keep an eye on Ben and also answer the phone. Dawn had been doing it while she tore round in circles trying to keep Ben out of trouble and she was feeling guilty because Dawn – like everyone else who helped her out, apart from Finn – was an unpaid volunteer.

"He's not doing my blood pressure any good at all," she told Finn later that night when Ben was safely tucked up in bed, which was the only time she didn't worry about him. "I don't know how full-time mums cope."

"They haven't got full-time jobs as well," Finn said, raising his eyebrows and smiling at her from the armchair by the fire where he was reading the newspaper. "Kids that age are hard work."

He sounded as though he was speaking from experience and Maggie glanced at him curiously, but before she could ask him how he knew that, the smoke alarm went off in the kitchen and she remembered the tripe she'd put on for the dogs.

"What the hell is that stink?" Finn said, coming in behind her. "Christ, I don't know how you can go near that stuff, it's disgusting."

"I'm cooking it, not eating it," she said crossly, rescuing the smouldering pan from the cooker and dumping it in the sink.

"Burning it, more like." Finn shook his head in disbelief and stood on the kitchen table so he could reach the smoke alarm. By the time peace had been restored Maggie had forgotten his throwaway comment and she didn't remember it until the next morning when she moved a pile of paperwork off the kitchen table, and knocked Finn's wallet onto the floor.

He must have left it there last night, she realised, as a handful of pound coins, a mixture of business cards and some credit cards slid out of various compartments. She knelt to pick them up, glancing at them as she put them back. A couple of credit cards, a kidney donor card and a business card from a shop called Gedling Artwork. She was gathering up the pound coins when she found the photograph lying face down on the floor near the fridge.

It was a passport-sized photo of a child, she saw as she picked it up, a little boy with brown hair and blue eyes who didn't look much older than Ben.

Maggie felt her heart thud uncomfortably. Finn hadn't mentioned any younger relatives – not that there was any reason why he should, she supposed. She stared hard at the photo. The boy looked nothing like Finn, but that didn't mean they weren't related. Perhaps he was a nephew, although hadn't Finn said he didn't have any brothers or sisters? Well, whoever he was, Finn must be fond of him to carry his photo in his wallet. She slid it back, hoping she'd put it in the right place. She didn't want him to think she'd been nosing through his things. Despite Gary's clumsy warnings, she liked Finn. She certainly wasn't going to pry into his private life, however curious she was. Maggie decided to put the photo out of her head, which actually wasn't difficult, as worrying about Ben took up most of her thoughts.

She was counting down the hours to the end of half-term. There was just today and the weekend to get through and then he'd be back at school and for the first time Maggie knew exactly what the mothers who helped her out meant when they said they were mightily relieved when half-terms were over.

Maggie broke the ice on the water trough the next morning and watched Ashley with a growing sense of unease. She'd just turned the horses out and Ashley was ignoring the two geldings and circling Rowena, his tail swishing. The mare was going to have to go somewhere else, but Maggie didn't have the space. There was a farmer up the road who might be persuaded to let her use his field for a while. Maybe she should try him.

"Ben can come and give me a hand if you need to make some phone calls," Finn offered when he found out what she was worrying about. "I'm replacing the rotten fencing in the top field – it's nice and mucky, he'll love it, and I'll make sure he doesn't come to any harm."

"All right, thanks," she said, after a moment's hesitation. Ben liked Finn and Finn was brilliant with him, endlessly patient with Ben's endless questions about painting. She trusted Finn instinctively – she had since the first moment she'd met him, she realised, remembering when he'd stopped to offer his help with the red kite she was rescuing. It was weird; she hadn't trusted a man, not even Alex, whom she'd always known deep down was trouble, for a very long time.

Later that morning when she was on the phone doing her best to convince the farmer that he really didn't need to charge her much rent, if any, since she was running a charity, Gary's van drew into the yard. Remembering the lecture she'd got the last time she'd seen him, and seeing his serious face as he came into reception, she didn't hurry to finish her conversation, but eventually had to put down the phone.

"Hi, Gary."

"Morning." He smiled at her and she relaxed a bit. "I'm afraid this isn't a social call." He inclined his head towards his van. "Sorry to spring this on you, but I thought you might be able to squeeze in a little one."

"Always room for a little one," Maggie quipped, looking into his kind, brown eyes. "What have you got?"

"Jack Russell. Or to be more accurate, Jack Russell – ish."

They went out into the yard and Gary opened up his van. In the dog transporter Maggie could see the outline of a little dog, mostly white.

"Hello, sweetie," she murmured, holding out her hand.

The dog lunged at the bars, and Maggie glanced at Gary.

"Prosecution case," he said. "Sorry."

The bitch stared at them, her lip curled in warning. Maggie stared back, taking in the skeletal rib cage, the dark, circular marks on the dirty coat. "What happened to her?"

"You don't want to know. But she won't be going back. She's still young. I think she'll settle down in time. They have an enormous capacity for forgiveness, don't they?"

Maggie nodded, her irritation with Gary forgotten. This was the hardest part of her job and she didn't think she'd ever be able to harden up. She didn't know how Gary coped. If she'd had to meet the little dog's owners, then, prosecution or not, she knew she wouldn't have been responsible for her actions. She gestured for Gary to bring the transporter to the kennels and they walked up the yard in silence.

Diesel was sitting on top of the chicken run.

"I thought you'd gone off chickens since your close encounter," she said, pausing to stroke the big black cat.

He arched his back and spat at her and she withdrew her fingers just in time. "There's gratitude for you. Tell me why I'm doing this again, Gary."

"Because you couldn't bear to do anything else," he murmured, and she glanced at him in surprise.

"Is it that obvious?"

"It is to me."

"The only reason I keep Diesel is because no one else would put up with him," she said, which wasn't true, but was preferable to having Gary think she was soft.

He gave her a disbelieving look and they carried on up the yard. By the kennels a group of volunteer dog walkers were talking to some prospective owners. Some of them came from miles around to take the dogs out in their spare time. Without their help, life would be much harder. And they were all there for the love of it. She gestured Gary towards the quarantine block and went across to thank them, which she knew she didn't do nearly enough.

"No probs, love," said one of the younger mums, who usually came in at school holiday time. "Wears my kids out a treat, coming here. Don't hear a peep out of them when we get home. How you getting on with Ben?"

"I think he's wearing me out more than I'm wearing him out," Maggie confessed and they all laughed.

She caught up with Gary at the quarantine block, which was almost empty, opened up a run at the very end because she had a feeling this little dog ought to be kept as far away as possible from the general public, and tossed a handful of doggie treats towards the inner sleeping compartment. Gary unlatched the front of the transporter and put it inside the door.

"How's it going?" he asked her. "New employee settled in all right?"

"I don't see that much of him." This wasn't true either, but she didn't want to start Gary off on another lecture about the recklessness of sharing her cottage with a stranger.

"Do the RSPCA know you brought her to me?" she asked, as the Jack Russell, deciding it was worth the risk for a biscuit, crept out on her stomach.

"No." His face shadowed and he didn't elaborate. They both knew where the dog was supposed to be. In a black bag by now, having been painlessly destroyed at Gary's surgery – maybe the only pain-free thing that would have happened to her in her short life, Maggie thought with a shiver.

Gary edged the transporter back out again, but the dog ignored them. She was wolfing down another biscuit. They left her to it and went out into the brightness of the day once more.

"I'll pop in later and see how she is," Gary said. "She's not going to be easy, that one, and you've got enough to do."

That was the understatement of the year, Maggie thought, as she filled up Fang's water bowl from the safe side of the wire netting on Sunday morning. They'd nicknamed her Fang because she tried to bite everyone who went near her, which was a pain as it meant Maggie had to see to the little dog herself. She couldn't risk anyone getting bitten.

"How's she doing?" Gary asked, when he turned up mid-afternoon. "Settling down at all?"

"A little," Maggie lied, not wanting him to feel bad that he'd lumbered her with a dog that was three times as much work as the rest.

"I was thinking that maybe I could come in a couple of times a week, try and socialise her a bit," Gary said, stamping his feet on the ground and rubbing his hands together. "Christ, it's a cold one today."

"Come in whenever you like," Maggie said. "You can go in there now if you like, but I'd put some gauntlets on if you're planning on touching her. Or you won't have any fingers left."

"I've got a couple of calls, but I could pop in on my way back," Gary said, glancing at his watch. "I've got a few minutes now, though. Why don't I take over here. I'm sure you've got plenty of things you could be doing."

"Thanks." Maggie left him to it and went down to reception, where she'd left Ben finishing off his painting of the pups under Dawn's careful supervision.

"Is it all right if I take a dog out, Auntie Maggie?" he asked, as she went in, stamping the ice off her boots.

"What's wrong with Mickey?"

"We've been out already, but he doesn't like the frost on his paws. It makes him go all skiddy."

"Okay then, but not on your own. I'll come with you if you hold on a minute." As she spoke the phone rang and she glanced at Dawn and picked it up.

Ben went outside and cracked the ice on some puddles with the heel of his trainer while he waited, but by the look on Maggie's face it was going to be a long phone call. When he glanced back through the reception window she shrugged her shoulders at him and mouthed 'sorry' and then carried on talking.

He put his hands in his pockets. He'd taken a couple of leftover sausages out of the fridge, which he was going to feed to whichever dog he took out. Maggie was pretty cool most of the time, but she could be a bit of a fusser, like his mum. He didn't need her to tell him which dog to walk. It was easy enough to work out. He wandered up the yard and found Finn up a ladder in the yard.

"All right, mate?" Ben said, pausing to watch.

Finn stopped what he was doing and came down a couple of steps. "Hello there. How's it going?"

"Okay. Need any help?"

"Not just at the moment," Finn said, smiling. "Maybe later if you've got some time spare?"

"Might have." Ben scuffed his feet and blew on his hands, which were starting to go numb. He liked Finn. He didn't speak down to him or treat him like a kid and he'd said that his painting of Diesel was really good.

"See you later, then," he said, nodding seriously and heading up the yard. He stopped at the chicken run, tore off a bit of sausage and stuffed it through the wire. One of the birds came across and pecked at it, then dropped it again. Ben glanced back down the yard. Maggie wasn't coming and he was sure a minute had passed. Lots of minutes, probably. It wouldn't hurt to just nip up and have a quick look at the dogs. He mooched up and down outside the kennels, trying to decide which one to take first. He was still undecided when he saw Gary coming out of the quarantine block. He must have been with Fang, the new dog, he thought curiously. Maggie had told him that he wasn't to go near Fang, but it couldn't hurt just to look, could it? He wasn't going to go in.

He glanced back over his shoulder, but there was still no sign of Maggie. Shoving his hands deeper into his pockets he carried on through the last gate, which led to the quarantine block. There was a big notice on the door, which said, 'NO ADsomething' in spiky capital letters. Ben gave up trying to work out what it said, unbolted the door and stepped inside. There was a hot, crunchy feeling in his stomach as he headed up the walkway past the dogs' sleeping areas. Dogs smelt a lot better than chickens, he thought, peering into the first few runs, which were empty. At the end he found the run which contained Fang. She was in her basket, curled up. A white roly-poly ball of a dog on a blanket, except that when she heard him she stood up and he could see her ribs jutting through her coat. Her coat was a mess, Ben thought, crouching down for a better look. In some places the fur was missing altogether. He wondered if she was cold.

"Poor little sweetie," he said, putting his fingers through the wire door. She looked at him. She had a brown patch over one eye and pricky-up ears.

"Come on then, girl." He wriggled his fingers and looked at the bolt that held the gate in place. "You wouldn't bite me, would you?"

She gave a low growl and lifted her lip at him to show white teeth.

"Don't be scared," he said. "I'm not going to hurt you."

He gave the bolt an experimental tug and it shifted easily. He pulled it right back and opened the gate enough to squeeze through. "Look," he said, putting his hand in his pocket and retrieving one of the sausages. "Come and see what I've got here for you."

Gary drove to his next call, deep in thought. He wished he'd said more to Maggie. Tried harder to talk her out of sharing her house with a complete stranger. Except that it had already been too late by then, he thought, switching on

90

the demister to clear the windscreen, and wishing it was as easy to clear his mind of Maggie.

It was his own fault for being such a coward. He'd told himself that he hadn't asked Maggie out before because he didn't want to affect their working relationship, but deep down he knew he'd been kidding himself. There was only one reason he hadn't asked Maggie out. And that was Anita.

He'd steered clear of women since his disastrous marriage, although there were plenty in the village who'd made it clear they wouldn't mind a liaison. They stood in his surgery, fluttering their eyelashes over heavily made-up faces, and 'accidentally on purpose' brushing his fingers, while he examined their fat Labradors and their bad-tempered Persian cats.

He wasn't interested in any of them. Anita had put him off predatory women forever. Besides, he'd convinced himself that he was happy with his life as it was. He loved his work, which he was good at, and he spent most of his spare time gardening. The house he'd shared briefly with Anita was a touch small, but it was fine for him and it had one amazing saving grace: French windows led out on to a hundred foot back garden, which stretched down to a stream, beyond which there was nothing but fields. Gary tended the garden with the same careful precision with which he spayed cats and de-scaled canine teeth, and it was beautiful. Full of sweet-scented wild roses and climbing plants on artfully positioned trellises so that the garden was sectioned off into little private corners. This year's plan for it included the creation of a jasmine-scented bower. There would be a bench, where you could sit and sip wine on long summer evenings. Lately, he'd harboured the odd fantasy that one day he'd sit there with Maggie, his arm draped casually along the back of the bench behind her.

91

He sighed. There was no sense in beating himself up about it. Suggesting that he call in regularly to socialise Fang had been a stroke of genius. And if Maggie had suspected that his motives weren't entirely altruistic, she hadn't said anything.

At least it meant that he could keep a weather eye on that Finn chap. Maggie might think he was the best thing since sliced bread, but Gary had serious doubts. He wouldn't have been at all surprised if Finn were on the run from something or someone. Blokes like him didn't jack in well-paid jobs without good reason. The guy was definitely not all he seemed. Someone had to keep an eye out for her and Ben. They could get into all sorts of trouble.

Maggie suddenly remembered she was supposed to be getting a dog out for Ben, who, to her alarm, seemed to have disappeared. Grabbing her coat, she hurried up the yard and found Finn up a ladder

"You haven't seen Ben, have you?" she called up to him.

He climbed down, with difficulty, because his hands were full of bits of broken plastic, and stood next to her. "He was around a little while ago. Said he was going to give me a hand later."

Maggie smiled. "Let me know if he's a pest and I'll find him something else to do."

"He's not a pest."

As he spoke the phone began to ring again and Maggie sighed.

"Damn, I promised I'd get a dog out for him." She glanced up towards the kennels, her face anxious. "I hope he hasn't gone by himself."

"I'll go and check if you want to get the phone."

She nodded and ran back down the yard. "Tell him I'll be two ticks," she shouted over her shoulder. "He's probably in the chicken run."

Ben wasn't in the chicken run, so Finn walked on towards the kennels, setting the dogs off barking as he passed the first block. The kennels were full, Maggie had told him yesterday when she'd pointed out some guttering that needed doing, except for the very end section.

"It's where we put the newcomers," she'd said. "We use it as a quarantine block, or, in her case," she'd pointed out Fang. "if they're not too good, temperament wise. We don't want to take any risks."

As they'd passed, Fang had hurled herself at the wire door of her run and Finn had stepped back, alarmed.

"She's a cruelty case," Maggie had told him, her face darkening. She'd pointed out the circular marks on Fang's coat.

"Cigarette burns?" he'd said, horrified.

Maggie nodded. "She'll settle down. But, in the meantime, I don't want any unsuspecting members of the public wandering up here. If she bites someone I'll have to have her destroyed. And it hardly seems fair, does it? After what our kind has done to her."

Finn went past the main block. There was no sign of Ben and he was about to turn back when he noticed, with a jolt of unease, that the door of the quarantine block was open. Surely Ben wouldn't have gone in there? Yesterday the door had been padlocked and bolted, but it wasn't now. It wasn't shut at all, Finn realised, as it swung open beneath his touch.

"Ben," he called, stepping into the run and closing the door behind him.

There was no answer. He made his way past the first few kennels, which were empty, and then came to Fang's run. Through the wire mesh of the door he could see Ben sitting on the floor holding something out towards the small dog.

"Come on, girl," he was saying. "Don't be scared now. Come and have a bit of sausage."

Finn sucked in his breath. He knew very little about dogs, but this one didn't look happy. She'd backed away from Ben, almost into a corner. Her ears were flat against her head and her eyes were wary. As he hesitated, the door clanged at the other end of the run. In the same instant, Ben, who hadn't noticed he was no longer alone, began to edge towards the cornered dog.

Chapter Ten

Aware that Ben was in grave danger, Finn shoved back the door, which Ben hadn't re-bolted, and scooped the boy up in his arms. Fang snarled at him, but he swung away from her, kicking the door back in her face as she launched herself through the air. With Ben still in his arms he slammed the bolt back into place. He wasn't sure whether it was his own frantic heartbeat he could hear, or Ben's, as, on the other side of the mesh, the little dog bounced up and down barking furiously.

"Finn, what's going on?" He heard Maggie's voice at the end of the run. Ben was big for his age and too heavy to hold for long. Finn put him gently on the floor, feeling the adrenaline pumping round his body, but for a few moments he was too breathless to speak.

"I said, what's going on?" Maggie shouted and Finn could hear the panic in her voice as she hurried towards them.

Ben had begun to cry. "I wasn't doing nothing. I wasn't hurting her."

"It's all right." Finn knelt on the concrete floor beside him, feeling the dampness creep through the knees of his jeans. "It's okay. You're not in trouble."

"Oh yes, he is," Maggie contradicted, reaching them and crouching down beside the boy. "Ben, you're a naughty, naughty boy. What have I said about coming in here?"

"Didn't do nothing!" Ben yelled, and behind them Fang's barks grew ever more frantic.

Finn stood up, realising Maggie was close to tears too. "It's okay. He's fine. No harm done."

She didn't look at him, just hugged the sobbing child, and he suppressed the urge to put his arms around both of

95

them and hold them tightly. He was still a stranger, and he knew she hated appearing vulnerable in front of anyone. For reasons he hadn't yet fathomed, she'd spent a lifetime building walls. He knew because he'd done exactly the same himself.

He was tempted to tell her that it was Gary, not her, who'd left the kennel door unlocked, but, satisfying as it would have been, it wouldn't have helped, so he kept quiet, and escaped from the all-pervading smell of dogs out into the bitter, winter air.

Maggie was only vaguely aware that Finn had gone. She hugged Ben to her. "It's all right," she soothed. "It's all right. I'm sorry I shouted at you. I was scared, love. Scared you were going to get hurt, I'm sorry."

She held him in her arms until gradually his crying stopped. She'd never shouted at him before and she felt terrible. Especially as she knew she'd only shouted because she felt guilty. She'd promised Sarah she'd look after him and she'd let him walk straight into danger. She should have remembered he wanted her to come here with him. She should have made it more difficult for him to get into this block. She shouldn't have kept Fang in the first place. God knows what the little dog would have done if Finn hadn't pulled Ben out when he did.

"I only wanted to give her a sausage," Ben mumbled, and Maggie saw that he was clutching something.

"But you know what I told you about Fang, don't you, darling?" She tipped his face so that he was looking up at her with his huge, tear-washed eyes.

"You said some horrible people hurt her and now she doesn't like people any more."

That was exactly what she'd told him, she remembered, blinking a few times.

96

"But I wasn't going to hurt her. I just wanted to show her that not all people are horrible."

Maggie swallowed. Telling him the truth, or at least a watered-down version of it, had seemed a good idea. But Christ, how did she explain that Fang couldn't tell the difference between horrible and nice? That Fang would have bitten him anyway. She shuddered and glanced into the kennel. The dog was quiet enough now. But Ben had been in here, she'd seen Finn grab him and then kick the door back in Fang's face. What if he hadn't reacted so quickly? Things might have turned out so differently.

"Come on, sweetheart. Let's go outside now."

"What about Fang's sausage?" Ben muttered, uncurling his fingers and showing her the squashed brown lump.

"We'll leave it here for her to have later. Come on now." She held his hand and they went outside again into the clear, sharp air.

Finn kept out of Maggie's way for the rest of the day. Or maybe she was keeping out of his, he wasn't sure. When he finally went into the cottage there was no sign of her and he went straight to his room, exhausted. Starting work at dawn and being out in the fresh air was very different from doing nine to five in a warm factory.

He flopped on to the bed and promptly fell asleep. When he woke up the room was dark and he felt stiff and cold. For a moment he couldn't think where he was. He rolled over, used to a double bed, and found himself on the floor. Cursing, he got up and switched on the light and reality came flooding back. He felt as though he'd been asleep for hours, but it wasn't that late. Only just gone eight. Blinking, he stood still for a couple of moments to clear his head.

"Are you all right up there, Finn?" Maggie's voice came from the bottom of the staircase.

"I'm fine," he called, going out on to the landing so he could see her. "Is it okay if I have a bath?"

"Help yourself. Water's hot."

"Sorry, I haven't had a chance to see much of you," Maggie said, as he came down with a towel and change of clothes.

"It's all right. I know you're busy."

When he got downstairs, feeling slightly more human after his bath, she was sitting at the table in the back room, surrounded by dozens of pieces of paper.

"Still at it?"

"Yes. I had no idea there'd be so much paperwork when I started this place. I'm just catching up with some invoices. Most of my suppliers are great, they know I'm running a charity, and Gary's wonderful, he lets me have all the drugs at cost and doesn't charge too much for his labour, either."

Finn was pretty sure the vet would have liked to negotiate payment in kind if he'd thought he could get away with it, but he said nothing.

"The pet food supplier's the worst," Maggie went on. "If I'm a day or two over, Reg Arnold sends me these reminders with 'Overdue' stamped all over them in red. Bloody cheek. He's a horrible little man."

"Can't you use someone else?"

"I could, but he's closest and he's cheap. Besides, I might find I've jumped out of the frying pan into the fire. I'm a bit of a believer in better the devil you know."

She paused and glanced up at him, her dark eyes troubled, and he knew she was wittering on to avoid the subject that was uppermost in her mind. "Thanks for what you did earlier, Finn. I feel terrible about that. I'd never have forgiven myself if anything had happened to Ben."

"Nothing did," he pointed out gently.

"Yes, that's what Sarah said when I told her." She pressed her fingers to her forehead and he wondered if the pain was physical or emotional – probably a bit of both. "But that's thanks to you, not me. If you hadn't been there... I feel as though I should keep him locked in his bedroom for the next ten days, at least he'd be safe."

"It'll be easier when he's back at school." Finn sat on the sofa opposite her. "And it's probably a better idea to get a proper lock system sorted out for the quarantine kennels," he added, because it was the only thing he could say that would make her feel better without dumping on Gary. "I'll get on to it first thing tomorrow, if you like."

"That would be great. Thanks." She went back to her paperwork and he decided it would be best if he left her to it. He might not be comfortable about snitching on Gary, but he was damned sure he was going to say something to the vet next time he saw him.

Chapter Eleven

A couple of days later when Finn had got up before anyone else, which meant before six in this house, and was carrying his mug and a newspaper through to the lounge, there was an ear-splitting scream from upstairs. Spilling hot tea all over his hands and cursing under his breath, he abandoned the mug and took the stairs two at a time. He found Maggie dancing around on the landing, a white bath towel clutched around her and her face flushed from the shower.

Behind her, the bathroom door was open and steam was rolling out into the chilly air, but Maggie seemed oblivious to this. She was jumping about on the bare floorboards as if they were scalding the soles of her feet.

"What's the matter?" he said, trying not to look too interested as she lost part of the towel completely and he was treated to a view of one breast, jiggling tantalisingly as she jumped up and down.

"Don't just bloody stand there staring! Do something. Catch it."

"Catch what?" Finn asked, completely at a loss. He took a couple of anxious steps towards her. She'd got herself covered up again, but she was still dancing around like a mad woman. Then Ben's bedroom door opened and he came out yawning. Ben didn't seem at all disturbed by Maggie's antics. He was scanning the floor, which like the stairs was uncarpeted. Then, to Finn's utter amazement, Ben launched himself into the air and landed with both slippered feet on the same spot of floorboard.

"Got it," he yelled triumphantly, straightening up and inspecting the sole of his slipper. "Yuk, that was a biggie."

"I said catch it, not kill it." Maggie glared at him and pulled her towel tightly around herself, as if suddenly aware of her state of undress.

"She's scared of spiders," Ben told Finn with a glance at Maggie. "Have you finished? 'Cause I need a wee."

"Nearly." She did actually look quite embarrassed, Finn thought, as with another cautious look at the squashed, black object on the floorboards she fled back into the bathroom.

"Once when she was staying with me and my Mum a spider fell on her head when she was in the bath," Ben told Finn gleefully. "She didn't have a towel. She runned all round the house with no clothes on. It was gross." He screwed up his face and Finn suppressed a smile.

"Women, eh?" He shook his head and Ben shook his too and they exchanged a man-to-man smile. Ben scraped the rest of the spider off his slipper and poked it down a gap between the floorboards, then banged on the bathroom door. "Hurry up, Auntie Maggie. I'm wetting myself."

Finn went downstairs. Gross was the last word he'd have used to describe Maggie charging around with no clothes on. In fact, after what he'd just seen, the image was very appealing. He gave himself a mental shake. The more he got to know her, the more he liked her. He didn't want to blow it by making unwanted advances. He sensed that she would have to make the first move.

To Maggie's intense relief, there were no more dramas in the next day or two, or at least none she couldn't cope with. Ben went happily back to school, they re-homed four dogs and took in three more, and the farmer who had Rowena agreed to keep her until he needed his field.

Best of all, Ben didn't mention Fang again, although he took great delight in teasing Maggie about what he called her spider dance.

"They can't hurt, you know," he said, at every opportunity, but particularly when Finn was around. "They're only tinsy winsy little things."

"Actually they bite," Finn said in her defence, and she'd given him a grateful smile.

Ben was okay, that was the main thing, and she was pleased that Gary needed so little prompting to agree to come in and socialise Fang as often as he could. Finn had fixed a padlock to the kennel door and given Gary the spare key to it.

"I'll come in every night and take her out from now on," the vet had told Maggie, looking curiously guilty. "That should speed things up."

"Well, if you're sure. Don't get yourself bitten."

"I'll be fine." He'd given her a rueful smile. "Anyway, she didn't actually bite anyone, did she? Don't suppose she would have done. Finn was probably overreacting."

She'd glared at him and he'd changed the subject hastily.

Fortunately, his strategy seemed to be working. By the middle of the week Fang no longer tried to attack anyone who walked past her kennel, although Maggie still didn't let anyone else in with her. It would be a long time before she'd risk that.

Finn seemed to have settled in. She'd started off by telling him what needed doing, but soon realised this wasn't necessary, so she left him to get on with it. She tended to lock the main gates to the public at about six, but she often had paperwork to do at the end of the day, which she only took into the house if it got too cold in reception. Finn's days were governed by the light, or the lack of it. He spent the occasional evening at the Red Lion, which was within walking distance of the sanctuary, but he never came back roaring drunk. As Sarah had predicted, Ben and Finn were getting on well, their mutual interest in art drawing them together

Maggie was still curious about the photo that Finn carried around with him, but she put it to the back of her mind. She didn't want to pry into his personal life, although from the way he was with Ben, she guessed that he'd been close to a child once.

"Perhaps he's got one hidden away somewhere?" Sarah suggested during one of her nightly phone calls.

"Maybe," Maggie said, hoping he hadn't. She knew he must have some baggage – you couldn't get past thirty without it – but she hoped it wasn't a child. She didn't like the idea of him having a child he no longer saw. It didn't fit in with her impression of him, which was what, exactly? she mused, as she was pinning one of Ben's painting up on the wall of reception one morning after dropping him off at school.

A cough behind her made her turn and Finn came into the room, with what looked like another of Ben's paintings in his hands.

"Have you seen this, Maggie?" His face was serious as he laid the painting on the reception table and she looked at it, realising that she hadn't, and feeling a little twinge of jealousy that Ben had shown Finn before he'd shown her.

The picture was of a small white dog with a patch over one eye, crudely done, but unmistakably Fang. The dog was in a kennel. Above it Ben had painted blue sky and a big yellow sun, but the kennel itself was dark. The dog was crying giant tears that had made a large blue puddle at her feet.

"Ben said she's sad because everyone hates her," Finn said quietly.

"I didn't realise he was still thinking about her." Maggie could feel coldness spreading through her. "When did he do this?"

"Last night, I think. Maggie, to be honest, it's probably a good thing. It could be his way of dealing with it. Getting it out of his system. Painting can be very cathartic."

She frowned. "Do you think so?"

"Yes, I do. And I should know. I've been doing it for long enough."

Maggie wondered if he meant painting as a catharsis or just painting. She couldn't imagine Finn needing to paint to get something out of his system. He always seemed so comfortable with himself. He was one of the few men she'd met who exuded calm. She glanced at him curiously, dying to ask what he meant, but not sure if this would be misconstrued as prying.

He smiled at her as if he knew what she was thinking and went on, in a voice that was lighter, "On a technical level this painting is really good. Look how he's used the colours to reflect mood. Different blues for the tears in the dog's eyes, and the tears on the ground, and another shade for the sky. Most kids would use the same colour. Blue's blue, but he hasn't done that." As he spoke he pointed to the various bits of the picture, his grey eyes lit with enthusiasm.

Maggie stared at him, realising that in the last few careless sentences he'd told her more about himself than he had since he'd been there. She'd never seen him look so animated.

They were standing so close that their arms were touching and suddenly she was very aware of him. The fresh, outdoor scent of him, his hands smoothing out the painting on the desk. She hadn't noticed his hands before. Strong hands, with long fingers, which were grubby at the moment from whatever he'd been doing outside. She felt breathless. Involuntarily she stepped away from him. She couldn't remember the last time she'd felt like this. What was she feeling, anyway? Attraction? Lust? Yes, definitely both of those. She felt as though she could rip all her clothes off, and his, and make love to him, right here on the wooden floor.

Shocked at herself, she tried to concentrate on what Finn was saying.

"He should be taught. Properly, I mean. He could be really good one day." He glanced at her and she felt heat in her face, but Finn didn't seem to notice. He was too caught up in his enthusiasm for Ben's painting. "Do you think his mum would mind if I taught him properly? In my spare time, I mean. I don't want to affect his schoolwork or anything."

"I don't suppose she'd mind at all. I'll ask her when I speak to her later." To Maggie's surprise, her voice came out quite normally. "Thanks – I – er – just need to get something from the house."

Outside, she took deep gulps of fresh air and wished her heart would slow down. Fancying Finn McTaggart was a bad idea. A very bad idea. He'd not said anything about getting himself another job, but they'd agreed that this was a temporary arrangement for both of them. It was only a matter of time.

Besides, he was too much of a free spirit to stay in one place for long. When she'd first met him she'd thought him self-contained to the point of coolness. But every now and then it was as though he allowed his guard to drop and she saw great chunks of warmth in him. When he'd been talking about Ben's painting, there had been real passion in those grey eyes of his.

"Hi, Maggie." Dawn was just getting out of her car in the yard. "What's the matter? You look all hot and bothered."

"I've just been talking to Finn about Ben's painting. He's got hidden talents." She hadn't meant to say that at all. She'd meant to say, Finn said Ben's got hidden talents, but somehow it had come out wrong.

"I wouldn't say they're that hidden," Dawn said, grinning. "If I were twenty years younger, I'd be making a play for him myself." She arched her eyebrows, gave her blonde perm a little pat and glanced through the reception windows to where Finn was still standing by the desk. "What's he been doing to you in there?"

"Nothing," Maggie said, escaping to the cottage before she could dig herself in deeper.

Several miles away, Gary was sitting in his car eating a ham and pickle roll and thinking about Maggie. He couldn't believe he still hadn't had the nerve to ask her out. He was there most evenings. He'd felt certain that if he saw Maggie so often, it'd be easy. He could just slip it into conversation. 'Maggie, would you like to go out for a meal some time? Only there's this new Italian I've had recommended. I thought we could give it a try.' Or, 'Maggie, how about we go into Salisbury and catch a film one night?'

He didn't even know what type of films she liked, he thought gloomily, tearing the cellophane off another roll and frowning as a lump of pickle fell out on to his lap. Somehow, every time he got Maggie alone, all his carefully rehearsed lines seem to freeze in his throat. Finn being around didn't help. If Maggie did turn him down, the last thing Gary wanted was an audience. And Finn was like a shadow. You never knew when he was going to creep up behind you and make snide remarks.

Gary was still smarting over the bloke's accusation that he'd left Fang's door open. Finn had cornered him about it the previous day.

"All locked up in there, mate?" he'd murmured as Gary came out of the quarantine block, having just settled Fang for the night. "We don't want any more nasty incidents, do we?"

"Are you trying to say something?" Gary snapped, the tone of Finn's voice putting him instantly on the defensive.

"Maggie's worried about that dog biting someone, which isn't surprising after the fiasco with Ben. I was just checking that you'd locked the door." The words 'this time' were never actually said, but they hung in the air between them.

"I'm very well aware of Maggie's security arrangements, thank you," Gary had snapped, aware that he sounded rather pompous, but too angry to care. How dare Finn accuse him of not being careful? He'd only been here five minutes and already he was trying to throw his weight around.

"I'm sure you are." Finn's voice was mild. "But someone left that door unlocked."

"Well, it wasn't me," Gary said, bristling with anger. He was sure – well, almost sure – that he hadn't left the quarantine door unlocked, ever.

No doubt Finn had told Maggie that the blame lay with him, too, although she'd been nice enough not to say anything about it.

Gary tore his thoughts away from Finn before he got wound up all over again, ate the rest of the roll, and glanced at his watch. Ten past two. He'd best get on to his next call, which he wasn't looking forward to. He was doing a home visit to euthanase an elderly cat, which had kidney failure and no quality of life left.

Gary hated this part of his job. Mrs Heath was sensible and kind and would offer him cups of tea and home-made cherry cake, even while she was blinking back tears. And he'd have to stand and make polite conversation in her front room, made empty without the presence of Tiger who'd been her only companion since her husband had passed away.

Maybe after this call he'd do something positive and phone and book a table for two at the new Italian place. He could book a table for this evening and ask Maggie to come along with him – an impulsive romantic gesture that he was sure she'd love. It would also take his mind off Mrs Heath and her loneliness and, if he booked the table for tonight, he'd have to ask Maggie to go with him. It crossed his mind that she might already be busy, but then he decided that this was unlikely. Maggie never went out, except to the Red Lion now and then, and he was sure she'd rather go for a proper meal. He loved Italian food. He could almost smell the garlic. He imagined himself pouring Maggie a glass of red wine. She'd smile at him across the candlelight and say, 'This is nice. We ought to do it more often, Gary.'

'Yes, we should,' he'd reply, and he'd touch her hand ever so casually. It was a pleasing picture and one that warmed him all the way to Mrs Heath's pretty house.

At The Ark, Maggie, Ben and Finn were in the caravan looking at some of Ben's paintings. Ben was standing by the window. When they'd first come in Finn had turfed Diesel off the seat, so they could sit down. Diesel had stalked outside in disgust. Ben wished he could go outside too. The caravan was musty and too small for the three of them, but Maggie said she could keep an eye on things from here without too many distractions.

He watched Diesel cross the yard, carefully avoiding the puddles, and jump up on to the roof of the chicken run. The black cat didn't seem very interested in the chickens. He was watching a couple of magpies in a tree in the field next door. As if suddenly aware of the danger, one of the magpies rose up in the air, its wings flapping against the white sky.

Ben wished he could be a bird, flapping his wings in the sky. Since the trouble with Fang he hadn't been allowed to wander around on his own as he usually did. Maggie kept turning up to check what he was doing. He glanced back at the table where she was chatting to Finn. He didn't know whether to feel pleased or embarrassed at all the fuss they were making over his pictures. He knew his paintings were good. Or at least some of them were. He could tell which ones were the best because of the little shivery feeling he got in his stomach when he finished them. If you didn't get the feeling, then the painting was rubbish. Simple. He'd tried to explain it once to Miss Benson, his art teacher, but she'd just looked stern and told him he must never tell people something he'd done was good, but must wait for them to tell him.

He'd tried to explain it to his mum once, too. "All your paintings are wonderful, Ben," she'd said.

"No, they're not." He'd pressed his mouth into a straight line. "Some of them are rubbish."

"Don't be silly. They're all lovely." He'd given up then. He didn't have the words to tell her properly about the shivery feeling. But he knew, as he watched Finn smoothing out the pieces of paper, that he would understand. Definitely.

"Which are your favourites, then?" Finn was asking him.

Ben pointed to a picture in the top right hand corner of the table. It showed a tree bent over in the wind, with a lightning bolt in the dark sky behind it. Then he pointed to a small one of the chickens in their run. He'd spent ages getting the colours right for their feathers. "Those two are best, I think."

Finn grinned in delight. "He's right, you know. Those two are the best. Are either of his parents creative? It quite often runs in families."

Maggie frowned. "I don't think Sarah's ever tried to paint. I'm not sure about his dad."

Ben wondered if he should mention that his real dad was dead, but something stopped him. They never talked about his dad. There weren't even any photos of him in their house. And Mum didn't like talking about him either, she always changed the subject when he asked.

He stared out of the window. "Can I go and see Candy's puppies?" he asked, without much hope, because Maggie had been funny about him going near any dogs except Mickey lately.

"We'll go in a minute," she said. "Finn's got some paintings in the Red Lion, Ben."

"Mike reckons he can sell them," Finn said, and he had a funny, jokey sound to his voice and Ben knew suddenly that Finn wasn't sure if his own paintings were any good.

"I'd love to see them," Maggie added. "Perhaps we could all go up tonight. It'll save me cooking. Do you fancy that, Ben?"

Ben sighed. Grown-ups spent far too much time talking, and for some reason they seemed to be even worse when they were in pubs. Although sometimes talking could be good, because it meant he could slip off. He looked at

Finn. He was pretty sure that Finn would let him try his beer when Maggie wasn't looking. And he'd be able to stay up later if they went to the pub.

"Okay," he said, shoving his hands in his pockets.

Maggie turned back to Finn. "Shall I ask Gary if he wants to come as well? He's bound to be in soon."

"If you like." Finn didn't sound as though he was bothered one way or the other. Ben didn't blame him. He wasn't over-fussed on Gary either – he always seemed to be in a mood.

"So, can we go and see Candy's puppies now?" he begged.

Gary was whistling as he pulled into the entrance of The Ark, just after five. It was all arranged. He'd booked a table at Da Vinci's for eight thirty. That should give Maggie enough time to finish up here and get changed. He wondered what she'd wear. He'd never seen her in anything but jeans, worn with either a fleece or a tee-shirt, depending on the time of year. Thinking about it, he couldn't recall ever seeing her legs outside denim, although she had nice legs, from what he could make out. Not long, but slender and shapely. Maybe she'd wear a dress tonight, or at least a skirt. She probably wasn't the type to wear a very short skirt, he thought, with a little stab of disappointment.

His Anita had lived in short skirts, some of them practically indecent. But his Anita had also been the type who enjoyed having other men ogle her. And look where that had got him. No, it was just as well that Maggie wasn't a short skirt kind of girl.

He could see her through the reception window as he locked the van door. She was talking to a young couple, but she still glanced out and smiled at him. Gary slammed the car door and waved. He'd pop up and see Fang while she was busy. Then he'd come back and casually mention the Italian. His heart pounded as he walked up the yard. It had been a good idea booking a table. He couldn't chicken out now.

On the way he bumped into Dawn and Ben. They had Candy on a lead and were heading for the dog walk field. That was good. Since the incident with Fang, Maggie had been paranoid about Ben and dogs.

"She's looking well," he said, bending to stroke the lurcher's pretty golden head. "How are the pups?"

"They're really cute," Ben told him. "They're all playing now and Tiny's put on loads of weight."

Gary already knew this, but he nodded seriously. "Has he now?"

"We're going to the Red Lion later to see Finn's paintings," Ben added. "Auntie Maggie's going to ask you to come too."

Gary felt his mouth tightening. It had to be Finn, didn't it? The bloke was a complete pain in the neck. "What paintings?" he muttered.

"Pictures of fields," Ben told him. "And he's done some of people. He showed me one of Big Lil from the pub."

"I see."

"Maggie's looking forward to it," Dawn said, smiling at him. "She said there's no end to Finn's talents."

"Did she?" Gary stopped stroking Candy's head and straightened up. It didn't matter, he could still ask her. Surely she'd rather go for a meal with him than to the pub? But what if she said no? He knew he wouldn't ask her and as he walked up towards Fang's kennel he felt as though all the sun had gone out of the afternoon.

On the way he passed Finn carrying some tools. "All right, mate?" Finn said pleasantly.

Gary couldn't bring himself even to speak.

Chapter Twelve

Maggie was beginning to wish she hadn't suggested coming to the Red Lion. She was tired and tense, and the couple of glasses of wine she'd drunk too quickly, in an effort to relax, were making her light-headed. Finn and Ben were talking about painting, their heads close together.

Gary was sitting beside her. He'd hardly said a word since they'd arrived. Deciding she'd better make an effort to be sociable, she glanced at him. "Are you okay? You seem a bit quiet."

"I'm fine," he said, not sounding it.

"So, what have you been up to today? Anything exciting?"

"I had to euthanase a cat," Gary muttered. "Belonged to an old lady who only lost her husband three months ago."

"Oh, Gary, that's awful. No wonder you look so fed up." Instinctively she reached for his hand. "I don't envy you having to do that at all. Was she all right, poor soul?"

"Yes, she was gracious and dignified and a damn sight braver than I'd have been."

A part of her mind registered that his fingers had closed around hers. They felt slightly clammy, but it would have seemed churlish to snatch her hand away.

"Euthanasia's one of the worst parts of the job – even when you know it's for the best." She swallowed. She'd witnessed it enough times at the vets and it had never got any easier. Trying to console someone who'd just lost a much-loved pet was heartbreaking.

"Anyone fancy another drink?" Finn asked.

Maggie withdrew her hand from Gary's, aware that Finn had registered the movement. "I'm all right, thanks."

"Oh, go on, have another one," Gary pressed, shifting his chair a little closer so that his knee brushed hers. "You hardly ever get the chance to let your hair down and you're not driving."

Suddenly Maggie felt reckless. "Yes, why not," she said. Another glass of wine wasn't going to make much difference. It was still early and poor Gary wouldn't want to go back to his empty house just yet. Not after the day he'd had.

She watched Finn go up to bar, feeling a pang of emotion she couldn't identify.

"You don't find the cottage too cramped with him there?" Gary asked, with a little edge of hardness in his voice. And she saw that he'd followed her gaze and there were frown lines crinkling his forehead.

"No, I don't," she said, relieved to see Finn on his way back with the drinks, because Gary wouldn't be able to pursue this conversation in front of him.

"One for the boss," Finn said, leaning across to put the glass of wine in front of her.

"Thanks." She looked up at him and felt a little jolt. Then, aware of Gary's scrutiny, she hastily looked away.

Finn sat beside Ben again, and Gary said in a voice only loud enough for Maggie to hear, "They get on well don't they? Got kids of his own, has he?"

"No, I don't think he has."

"Bit of a dark horse, really." Gary glowered at Finn. Maggie, anxious to change the subject, said the first thing that came into her mind.

"Did you ever find out about those tests for Ashley? To check whether he's got an undescended testicle or not – I'd be interested to know."

She wasn't aware that her voice had been rising, but both Finn and Ben glanced across with identical expressions of surprise and she found herself thinking that they were very alike. They could be mistaken for father and son.

"No," Gary said, his voice, sharp. "My colleague hasn't rung back. I'll chase him up."

"Thanks." Maggie took another sip of wine to cover her embarrassment.

"Can we go in a minute?" Ben asked when she was halfway through it.

"Of course we can, darling." Maggie's head ached from trying to work out if the atmosphere around the table was real or imagined. Going home suddenly seemed like a very good idea. She gulped back the rest of her wine.

"I'll give you a lift, Maggie," Gary was saying.

"What?" She stared at him.

"A lift… home…" He left spaces between the words as if she were a child or someone who didn't speak the language.

"It would make more sense if I took them," Finn interrupted. "It'd save you going out of your way, Gary."

He stretched, seemingly oblivious to the annoyance in Gary's eyes.

For a moment there was a tight, awkward silence between them and then Maggie rushed on, "It's nice of you, Gary, but Finn's right, it would make more sense…" She let her words hang in the air like a question.

"Right," Gary said.

He really didn't have any choice, Maggie thought, as he turned back to her, blocking the others out with his body.

"See you tomorrow," she said quietly.

"Yes, I'll call by." And with a curt nod at Finn, he called good night to Mike, who was serving, and stomped out of the door.

"Ready then?" Finn said and Maggie nodded. His face was blank, but she had no doubt he was aware of what had just gone on.

As they got into his car, Ben said, "Gary wasn't in a very good mood, was he? What was the matter with him, Auntie Maggie?"

"He'd had a bad day, love, I think." She avoided Finn's eyes and climbed into the front seat of the car. They drove back in silence. Maggie rested her head against the coolness of the glass window and wished she didn't feel so dizzy.

Finn pulled up outside the cottage and Maggie got out of the car, swaying a little as the chill evening air hit her, amplifying the effects of the wine. He stood next to her as she fumbled with her key in the front door, his proximity making her even more nervous.

"Shall I do that?" he said at last, not waiting for a reply, but taking the key from her. The brush of his fingers sent electricity sweeping through her and she snatched away her hand. He opened the door and she stumbled through it.

"Are you okay, Maggie?"

"I'm fine," she said, realising, with sudden, intense embarrassment, that she wasn't fine at all. She was drunk and she was going to be sick. She made a dash for the bathroom and got there just in time. Afterwards, she sat on the edge of the bath, mortified.

About ten minutes later there was a knock on the door. "Er, Maggie, are you going to be much longer? Only I'm crossing my legs out here and Ben wants to clean his teeth."

When she went out, feeling deeply ashamed of herself, Finn was standing with one hand on the banisters.

Beside him, Ben looked interested. "You're a bit white, Auntie Maggie," he said, peering at her. "Have you been sick?"

"No, of course not." She lurched past them, feeling weak and dizzy. "I'm just going to get a glass of water."

"Make it a pint. And have some aspirin with it," Finn called after her. "That always does the trick for me."

"I'm fine now," she called back, ignoring the amusement in his voice. "Just not used to drinking."

All the same, once she'd tucked Ben up in bed, she did go back downstairs to get a pint of water and some aspirin, and a bucket, just in case.

She switched off the light and lay in the darkness and a few minutes later she heard Finn's footsteps go past her door and up the top stairs to his room.

She lay thinking about him in the tiny bed upstairs, until eventually she fell into a restless sleep filled with dreams of Finn McTaggart leaning over her and saying, "The best thing for hangovers is to take off all your clothes. Trust me, I used to be a vet, you know." Then his grey eyes slowly changed into Alex's mocking, dark ones and Maggie woke up, bathed from head to foot in sweat.

Rather to her surprise she didn't have a hangover the next day, although whether this was due to Finn's hangover cure or the fact that she'd sweated most of the alcohol out of her system in the night, Maggie wasn't sure.

It was a surprise, however, to find out about Gary's thwarted plans to take her to the Italian restaurant, which Mike took great delight in telling her about when she went into the Red Lion to drop off his order of free-range eggs.

"Poor chap was quite put out," Mike said, leaning on the bar and grinning. "He doesn't like Finn much, does he?"

"What's it got to do with Finn?" Maggie said. "He didn't know Gary was planning to take me out. Neither did I, come to that. Why on earth didn't he say?"

"Oh, you know what Gary's like. He might be a good vet, but he's a dead loss where women are concerned." Mike frowned. "Now let me see, I think Gary's exact words were, 'if it wasn't for that bloody bloke's paintings, Maggie and I could have been having a romantic meal for two.' It was after his fourth pint." He straightened the beer towel on the bar and looked pleased with himself. "Da Vinci's, apparently. That trendy new place in Salisbury. He'd got it all set up. Taxis there and back, so you wouldn't have to drive. Champagne. The works."

Maggie stared at him in shock. "But he knows I'm looking after Ben. What did he think I was going to do with him?"

"Ask Finn to babysit, I expect," Mike went on slyly. "Would you have gone then? If you'd known?"

"I don't know," Maggie said, aware that whatever she told him would be swiftly relayed to the entire village, with one or two embellishments of his own.

"He's quite a catch," Mike said. "Good looking. Bit of money. Be handy too, wouldn't it? Having a vet about the place. That's one of your biggest bills."

"Oh, stop it, Mike. That's no reason to go out with someone."

"So the answer would have been no, then would it? Poor Gary."

"The answer is none of your business," Maggie said, softening her words with a smile. "And don't you dare tell him you've told me. He'd be mortified."

"Mum's the word." Mike tapped his nose. Then he leaned forward and picked a bit of straw off her coat.

"What about your new employee, then Maggie? What would you say if Finn asked you out to a posh Italian?"

Completely unprepared for the question, Maggie could feel heat rising in her face.

"Thought so," Mike said, banging his hand on the bar in triumph so that several beer mats jumped an inch into the air. "Strikes me that Gary wasn't so wrong about Finn mucking up his plans, after all."

Chapter Thirteen

The next day, the day before Sarah and Jack were due back, Ben went to his friend, Darren's, for tea straight from school, and Maggie, feeling at a loose end, strolled up towards the quarantine kennels. It was gone six and Gary hadn't turned up to take out Fang. She decided to put the little Jack Russell in the dog-walk field for a run about. Then, restless to do something, she started to hose down the block.

A few minutes after she'd started she heard the door clang at the other end. "Watch the floor," she called, glancing up, expecting to see Gary, but it was Finn. "It's slippery," she mouthed over the noise of the water as he came along the run.

"What?"

"The floor." She gestured impatiently, and at the same moment felt her trainer skid beneath her. There was a second when she thought she would save herself, then a horrible stomach-wrenching instant when she knew she wouldn't. Her feet were sliding from beneath her and she was falling backwards. Her head hit the concrete and she was aware of flashing lights, then of not being able to breathe, then, more slowly, of pain and of wetness seeping through her sweatshirt.

"Maggie, are you okay? No – stupid question. You went down with a hell of a bang." Slowly, she became aware that Finn was crouching beside her in the run.

She struggled to sit up and he put his hand on her arm. "Give it a minute." There was concern in his eyes. "You hit your head, didn't you? What else hurts?"

"My back. I've grazed it." She glanced at the sharp edge of the drain that ran down the edge of the block. "And I'm getting soaking wet." She attempted to smile, but judging by the expression on his face she wasn't making a very good job of it.

"Take it slowly," he said. "Lean on me." He put his arm around her, supporting her.

She stood up, wincing. "Thanks. I'm all right. Can you turn off the hose. I feel such a fool."

"It's like a skating rink in here."

"That's what I was trying to tell you." Sickness was rising in her throat and she hesitated, then leaned forward, gripping hold of the wire netting, until the waves of dizziness passed.

"Just hold on a minute, Maggie." She was aware of him close behind her. "How are you feeling?"

"Dizzy, but that's probably just shock. And I feel like I've scraped several layers of skin off my back." She screwed up her face. She couldn't allow herself to be sick so soon after last night's performance.

"Take deep breaths," he advised.

She did as he said, but only because she didn't have much choice. Tears weren't far away. If she'd been alone she'd have let them out or at least done a great deal of swearing, but she didn't dare open her mouth in case she humiliated herself further.

"Now, slowly. Lean on me."

"I've got – to get Fang – lock up." The words were coming out in gasps.

"I can do that." He looked at her. "Hold my arm."

She did as he said. God, why did he have to be so damn calm and rational? Too bloody rational. He never seemed to get ruffled about anything. It was unnerving. And she knew it wasn't just his calmness that was unnerving. It was his proximity. But she felt too shaken up to do anything but lean on his arm as he led her along the ice-rink floor, because, if she didn't, she knew she would fall over and she was so, so scared of falling again.

Finn opened the door at the end of the run and they went out into the evening sunlight.

"You're as white as a ghost," he observed.

"I'm fine."

"Go and get showered off. I'll get Fang in and lock up."

"Careful she doesn't go for you."

"Relax, Maggie. I can handle a stroppy little dog."

In the end she had to let him go because he was right. She felt awful and sick and all she wanted to do was sit down. She limped down the yard, aware of him watching her. Hating her vulnerability. But it was all right when she got into the cottage. All right to breathe again in the cool, welcoming dimness. She went upstairs to the bathroom, where she stripped off and inspected the damage.

A jagged graze ran from her shoulder blade down her back to her hip and a purplish bruise was already forming at the base of her spine. Her shoulders ached where she'd wrenched them trying to stop herself falling. Tomorrow, the whole lot would stiffen up and she would hurt like hell. She stepped into the shower, wincing as the water hit her skin. She forced herself to stay under the spray as long as possible. It wasn't enough. She could see in the mirror that the edges of the graze were still bleeding, but it would have to do for now. She patted herself dry as gently as she could. Putting on a bra was out of the question. She pulled on an old, white tee-shirt, which was the softest thing she could find, and some leggings, and went downstairs.

Finn was in the lounge reading the paper and he glanced up as she came in. "Are you all right? Did you cut yourself?"

She shook her head. "Just a bit of a graze on my back. I'll survive."

"And you feel all right in yourself? You hit your head pretty hard."

"I'm fine, Finn, stop fussing."

"Sorry. I was a first-aider at my last job. Old habits die hard. You could probably do with a stiff drink. Good for shock, but I couldn't find any. Second thoughts, you shouldn't have alcohol if you've hit your head."

"I think I've had enough alcohol lately," she said bending to pick up one of her boots that Mickey must have stolen from their place by the back door.

Finn rested his chin in his hands and looked at her. "There's blood coming through your tee-shirt, Maggie. You ought to let someone have a look at it. I'll do it if you like. Or would you rather I ran you down to A&E?"

His grey eyes held hers and she sighed. "Yes, I suppose you're right. I don't want it getting infected."

"So do you trust me to do it? Or do you want to sit in A&E for an hour?"

Her hesitation stretched out between them and then she said, "I have to be here when Ben gets back. There's a first-aid kit in the kitchen cupboard. I'll get it in a minute."

"I'll get it."

The thought of him touching her made her come out in goose bumps. Not because she was attracted to him, she told herself, but because he was a stranger. But the thought of going to A&E was infinitely worse. She'd had enough of hospitals to last her a lifetime. She hadn't been in one since she'd lost her mother and she still had nightmares about that last, awful day.

When Finn came back he was carrying the first-aid kit, a packet of cotton-wool swabs and some antiseptic.

"I don't think you're supposed to put this on neat. Have you got a little bowl I can dilute some in?"

"There's one under the kitchen sink."

A few moments later he was back.

"Actually, I think I'm fine," she said again, her mouth dry. "I'm as tough as old boots. I'm sure it's clean enough."

"It won't take me a minute to check." His voice was quietly reasonable. "And it's better to be safe than sorry." He started to dilute the antiseptic and lined up a row of cotton-wool swabs on the coffee table. Then he came across and knelt by the settee where she sat. "Don't look so worried. I was doing this sort of thing at work for ten years."

"Dangerous place to work, was it?"

"You'd be amazed at the situations people got themselves into." He smiled at her. "Where did you hit your head, can I see?"

She indicated the spot and he parted her hair with gentle fingers. "You seem to have got away with that. Let's have a look at your back. It would be easiest if you lay on your front. You'll need to roll your top up."

She did as he said, conscious that she wasn't wearing a bra, tucking her elbows in tight to her breasts.

"It's a nasty graze, that. Can I roll this up a bit higher? Unless you want to take it right off."

She glanced sideways at him, echoes of her dream merging with reality. He grinned. "I'm joking about taking it off, but I will need to push it up a bit higher to get to the top of the graze. And I'm afraid you'll have to slip these down a bit, too. Don't worry, I can't see a thing."

The humour in his voice had the effect of relaxing her and she let him roll the tee-shirt up past her shoulder-

125

blades and slip the waistband of her leggings down a couple of inches.

"I'll just clean it up and then you can see how it is tomorrow. This might sting a bit."

He was right; it did sting. She clamped her teeth together as he dabbed at the graze, but his fingers were gentle. As he worked he asked her about the phone calls she'd taken that day and how the fund-raising was going, and she answered his questions, surprised. He wasn't much of a one for small talk. After a while she realised that he was only trying to take her mind off what he was doing, and she was grateful.

"That's better," he said, at last. "At least it's stopped bleeding and it's clean now. Dog kennels aren't the most hygienic of places to fall over in."

"Thank you, Doctor McTaggart." She pulled her top down and sat up. "From drain unblocker to first-aider, is there no end to your talents?"

"No need to take the mickey."

"I'm not." She touched his hand. "Thanks."

For a moment there was a softness in his eyes and she thought he was going to say something else. Then he blinked a couple of times and it passed and she wondered if it had ever been there at all.

"I've got a few phone calls to make," he said, and got up and went out into the hall.

Maggie stayed where she was on the settee, feeling more stirred up than she had in years. She didn't just want to go to bed with him, she realised, she wanted to get to know him. To discover everything about him, where he'd gone to school, who his friends were, what his deepest fears were, what he loved, what made him angry and what made him sad.

Startled by the force of her feelings, she giggled into the empty room and suddenly was afraid. It was the knock on the head, she told herself. Delayed shock. Sarah would laugh. Or maybe Sarah would understand. Maybe this was how she felt about Jack. She would ask her tomorrow.

Chapter Fourteen

"Hi, Maggie, we've just got back. Jack's unpacking now, then we'll be round to collect Ben's stuff."

Sarah sounded relaxed and happy and Maggie breathed a sigh of relief as she held the phone and glanced out of the reception window at the icy blue sky. She still hadn't forgiven herself for putting Ben in such danger, even though Sarah had played it down from the minute she'd told her.

"He shouldn't have been doing what you'd told him not to do," she'd muttered. "I'll have words with him when I get back."

"Oh, please don't, I think he's learnt his lesson," Maggie had said. She'd told Sarah about the painting of Fang Ben had done, too, when she'd asked if she minded if Finn gave him art lessons. Sarah had been of the same opinion as Finn; Ben was just getting things out of his system.

"So did Jack think it was a successful trip?" she asked now.

"Yes, I think so. Although it was really more pleasure than business, he sold enough to pay for the trip, which was good. Oh, and his parents are gorgeous. His dad looks just like him – but with more grey. They're really nice. I told them all about Ben and they can't wait to meet him."

Maggie smiled. "Are you sure you don't want me to pick him up from school? You must have lots to sort out."

"And you haven't? No, it's all right, Maggie, thanks. I can't wait to see him. I know we've chatted on the phone every night, but it's not the same. How's your handyman getting on?"

"He's great. I don't know how I ever managed without him." She gave Sarah a list of what Finn had done so far, not pausing for breath until she heard Sarah sigh.

"What? What have I said?"

"I've never heard you so excited about a bloke."

"He's not a bloke, he's an employee."

"He's a bloke as well, though, isn't he? Even you must have noticed that. So, what's he like to live with? Does he bring you tea in bed?"

"No, he does not," Maggie snapped. "He's never set foot in my bedroom." Not that the thought was unappealing, she realised, feeling her face colour and was glad that she was talking to Sarah on the phone and not face to face.

"I bet you that's only because Ben's been around," Sarah said archly. "It's like having a chaperone, isn't it?"

"Actually Ben gets on very well with him. They've been talking about painting – I feel quite left out sometimes."

"Loves kiddies too. Well, well. I shall look forward to meeting this paragon. Is he there now?"

"Yes, somewhere about."

"Well, make sure he doesn't disappear. We'll be round in ten minutes. We'll pick up his stuff first and collect him from school on the way back."

The phone rang as soon as Maggie put it down and she'd only just finished talking to a woman who wanted a kitten for her daughter when the minibus drew into the yard and parked outside reception.

Jack and Sarah came in together and Maggie looked at Jack's animated face and thought she'd never seen such a well-matched couple. She was surprised they hadn't decided to make their relationship more permanent. Maybe they had and Sarah hadn't told her yet. No, she thought, stepping over sacks of dog biscuits that had just been delivered, and kissing them both on the cheek. Sarah would never have kept something like that to herself.

"The kettle's just boiled," she told them. "You can make a brew while I go and find Finn. He takes his white with two sugars."

"Jack can make the tea, I'm coming with you," Sarah said. "I want to see all these miraculous transformations you told me about."

Maggie laughed, knowing that Sarah was far more interested in doing a spot of further interrogation than in Finn's handiwork, a fact that was confirmed as soon as they stepped outside into the sunlight.

"Now tell me the truth," she said, linking her arm through Maggie's. "You do like him, don't you? You can't keep something like this from me. I'm your best friend."

"All right," Maggie said, deciding that she might as well confess because Sarah wasn't going to give her a minute's peace until she did. And she did want to talk about Finn. She'd spent an uncomfortable night torn between thinking that she might be falling for him and wondering whether it was just the fact that he'd been so kind when she was vulnerable. She wasn't vulnerable very often. At least, not in front of people.

"Yes, I do like him. And there is chemistry. I'm pretty sure he feels it too. But he is working for me, and it's really early days, and I don't want to..."

"Rush into anything," Sarah finished for her. "Yes, I can see that. And I guess you don't need to, do you, seeing as you've got him exactly where you want him. I bet Gary hates his guts, doesn't he?"

"He's not over-fussed – how did you know that?"

"For someone who's so bright, you're amazingly dense where men are concerned," Sarah said glibly. "Gary's had the hots for you for months."

"I'm beginning to think you're right," Maggie said, and told her about the date that never was at Da Vinci's. "Don't you dare say anything to him, I'm not supposed to know. And if you say anything in front of Finn, I'm going to kill you."

"About Gary?"

"About anything. I don't want him frightened off. He's too useful."

"Don't worry. I won't. I can see you're smitten." Sarah gave her a quick, sidelong glance. "You're completely transparent, Maggie. Well, you are to me. I'm really pleased for you, it's about time you fell for something with fewer than four legs. Hey, is that him?" She paused and shielded her eyes and Maggie saw Finn up a ladder that was rested against the quarantine block.

"Yes. I think he said there were some tiles that needed replacing. I knew I should have bought new – it was false economy getting second-hand."

"Yes, well, you live and learn. He's got a nice bum, hasn't he?"

"Sarah!"

"He can't hear us."

They paused at the foot of the ladder and Finn acknowledged them with a nod and began to climb down.

"Sorry to interrupt," Maggie began, as he reached the ground and turned, smiling, towards her, "but I just wanted to introduce you to Ben's mum. Finn, this is my best friend, Sarah. Sarah, this is Finn, who's just started working for me."

There was a pause, which got longer and longer, and Maggie stood in the winter sunlight, feeling a rising sense of bewilderment.

It was hard to tell what Finn was thinking, it always was, but Sarah looked as if she'd just seen a ghost, complete with severed head clutched under arm and clanking chains.

It was Finn who broke the awkward silence. "We've already met," he said, glancing at Maggie. "Although I don't think we were on first name terms back then, were we?" He held out his hand, but Sarah didn't take it and after a few moments he nodded and let it drop back to his side. "It was a long time ago," he went on for Maggie's benefit. "It was a Christmas party, if my memory serves me right. And we'd both had way too much to drink."

"I can't remember much about that party," Sarah blurted out, seeming to find her voice at last. "After about nine o'clock it's a complete blank. I can't remember a thing." She raked her fingers through her long hair and glanced at Maggie. "Must have been a good party. We went to lots of parties in those days, didn't we, Maggie? You were probably there."

"Yes," Maggie murmured, even though she was sure she hadn't been. She'd never been much of a partygoer, she'd always preferred quiet pubs and restaurants where you could hear yourself speak.

"I can't remember much either," Finn said quietly, his eyes holding Sarah's and she nodded and went scarlet and looked vastly relieved, all at the same time. Maggie had the strangest feeling that Finn was letting her off the hook for something. But she had no idea what.

"Are you coming down for a cup of tea?" she asked Finn. "Jack's just making it. Or shall I bring it up here?"

"I'm all right for now." He smiled at her again, his grey eyes warm. "I had one not long ago. And I want to get these tiles done before it rains."

"Right," Maggie said, glancing distractedly into a cloudless sky, and hurrying to catch up with Sarah, who was already marching back down the yard.

"What on earth's going on?" she hissed, falling into step beside her friend.

"Nothing. Nothing's going on."

"Sarah, tell me. Oh, Christ." Realisation hit her like a bucket of ice. "It was that Christmas party. The one where you… Oh, my God, Sarah, Finn's Ben's father, isn't he?"

Chapter Fifteen

Sarah folded her arms and shook her head. "Don't be stupid. Of course he isn't. It's nothing like that." She tripped over a bit of uneven ground as she spoke and Maggie caught her arm, feeling pain shoot through her own wrenched muscles in the process.

"Don't lie to me, Sarah, please. You have to tell me. It's important. Is Finn Ben's father or isn't he?"

"Keep your voice down," Sarah pleaded, glancing over her shoulder. "Look, I can't talk about this now. I've got to go and get Ben from school."

"I'll come with you."

"No, you can't. What about the sanctuary? Someone might come in who wants an animal."

"I'll lock up reception and I'll put the answer machine on. Please, Sarah, we can't just leave it like this. You have to tell me the truth. Best friends – remember?"

By the time they got back to reception, Sarah was almost in control of herself again. The colour was back in her face and her eyes were calm. They found Jack sitting reading a dog-homing brochure and there were four mugs of steaming tea on Maggie's desk. He glanced up and smiled.

"Jack, I don't suppose you could do us an enormous favour and answer the phone for ten minutes while Maggie comes with me to collect Ben?"

"Course I can," he said peaceably, "if that's what you want."

"It'll be easier to park Maggie's Land Rover than the minibus," Sarah went on, somewhat irrationally. "And I'm sure Ben will want to say thanks to Maggie for having him. We'll come straight back."

He nodded and didn't question this change of plan and Maggie found herself thinking that it must make it a lot easier to lie if no one asked you any awkward questions. And then she berated herself for prejudging her closest friend, because she had said that Finn wasn't Ben's father. And although Maggie wasn't sure if she believed this, she was still clinging grimly to the last shreds of hope that he wasn't. Because if he was, then it changed everything. She couldn't have a relationship with the man who was Ben's father. She couldn't even employ him any more. Not when a secret like that hung between them. Sarah might be prepared to lie to him forever, but she wasn't. It wasn't fair.

Worry and fear made her drive faster than usual and Sarah clung on to her seat belt as she hurtled around a corner.

"You'll get us pulled over if you're not careful," she squealed. "Oh, Maggie, I'm so sorry. If I'd have known he was working here, I'd have told you. I'd never have let you fall for him."

"I haven't fallen for him. And you can't control how I feel."

"No, I know, I didn't mean that. Oh my God, he's met Ben, hasn't he?"

"You know he has. I told you. They get on really well."

"Well, he can't see him again. I don't want him in Ben's life. I don't want him to have anything to do with him."

"Listen to yourself, Sarah. For God's sake, be reasonable." Maggie yanked the Land Rover into a vacant space close to the school and switched off the ignition. "So, I take it Finn is Ben's father, then, and you were lying just now when you said he wasn't?"

135

Sarah hesitated. "I'm sorry. I was in shock. I never expected to see him again. Especially not here. Christ, he mustn't find out, Maggie, it'd ruin everything. You have to promise me you won't tell him."

"I can't promise you that. You know how I feel about it – how I've always felt about it." Maggie stared out at the blue sky beyond the window and remembered the arguments they'd had. Dozens and dozens of arguments over the identity of Ben's father. She'd never won any of them and she had a feeling she wasn't going to win this one, either.

"You're going to have to tell him," she went on. "It's not fair on either of them, not knowing. Not now they've met. They really like each other, Sarah. Besides, even if you didn't tell Ben, how are you going to explain that he's not allowed to see Finn any more? He spends most of his free time at The Ark."

"You could sack him. You don't even have to sack him, you could tell him that you can't afford him any more. He's done masses of the work already and I told you Jack doesn't mind helping out. We'll spend every weekend there. You won't lose out."

"No," Maggie said, meeting Sarah's blue eyes and seeing a mixture of fear and defiance in them. "I'm not throwing him out just because you can't face up to the truth. That's even less fair. He's only been working for me for two weeks."

They were still arguing when they got to the school playground, but Sarah broke off when she saw Ben coming across the tarmac, his school bag in one hand and a rolled-up tube of paper in the other.

Another painting, Maggie thought. Like father, like son. She remembered the night in the Red Lion, when they'd looked at her with identical expressions. It seemed so obvious now she knew.

"Mum!" yelled Ben, spotting them at the same moment. He broke into a run and Maggie saw Sarah's face soften as she looked at him. And then Sarah was bending down to hug her son, who submitted to being kissed for a few moments, before pulling impatiently away.

"Hello, Auntie Maggie. Where's Daddy Jack?"

"He's looking after the animals so that Auntie Maggie could come and pick you up with me. That's nice isn't it? Have you missed me?"

"A bit," Ben said, rolling his eyes and checking over his shoulder to see if any of his mates were looking. "But I like staying at Auntie Maggie's. I've been looking after the chickens. I've been a big help, haven't I, Auntie Maggie?"

"A very big help," she agreed.

"And I've been learning how to paint properly. Finn's been helping me. He's a proper artist. I'm going to be a proper artist when I grow up."

Maggie saw Sarah flinch and she felt a wave of compassion. What must it be like to have the past appear on your doorstep? The past that was going to threaten your entire future happiness. She might not approve of what Sarah had done, but she couldn't blame her for reacting like this.

"Do you want to see my picture of Candy's puppies?" Ben added, picking up the tube as if he'd suddenly remembered it. "I done it today. Miss Benson said it's the best thing I've done."

"I'll have a look at it when we get home, darling. Best keep it rolled up for now, or it'll get dirty."

"Can I show it to Finn when we get back to Auntie Maggie's?"

137

"I think he might be a bit busy at the moment. He won't want to be interrupted."

"He likes looking at my paintings," Ben said, his lips tightening mutinously. "He says he never gets too busy for that."

Sarah blinked a couple of times and Maggie swallowed a massive ache in her throat. How on earth had they got into this mess?

There was no sign of Finn when they got back to The Ark, much to Ben's obvious disappointment and Sarah's obvious relief.

"You'll have to leave it for Auntie Maggie to show him, sweetheart," Sarah told him, as they began to carry Ben's luggage out to the minibus. She gestured through the reception window for Jack to come out. "We need to get back. Anyway, don't you want to get home and see what we got you in Scotland?"

"Okay," Ben said, without enthusiasm.

Sarah met Maggie's eyes over his head. "Please don't say anything to him," she begged. "Give me a couple of days. I need to think things through. Otherwise the whole thing could be a nightmare. For both of them," she added, glancing at Ben. "You must know that."

"All right," Maggie agreed, feeling the beginnings of a headache starting at her temples. "I won't go blundering in – but you are going to deal with it, aren't you?"

"Of course." Sarah dipped her head and Maggie felt as though already there was a wall growing between them. An insurmountable wall. On the one side was her friendship with Sarah and she would never betray Sarah; but in order to protect her, she was going to have to lie through her teeth to Finn.

*   *   *

Finn came in early that evening, which was unusual. Maggie was washing up in the kitchen when she heard him taking his boots off in the hall and hanging his coat by the front door and she realised how used to his presence she had become, even after a fortnight. How much she liked him being around.

She thought he might go straight upstairs, but he came into the kitchen and asked her if she wanted a coffee. She nodded, moving out of his way so he could fill up the kettle, anxious that they didn't touch.

Finn spooned coffee into their mugs and Maggie sensed his gaze on the back of her neck, but she didn't turn round. This was madness. He was going to guess something was wrong. How could he not?

"How's your back now?" His voice was mild. "I bet you ache a bit today, don't you?"

"It's not too bad, thanks," she said, still without turning.

"It'll be quiet without Ben around," he remarked, at the same moment as the kettle switched itself off.

"Oh, he'll soon be back," Maggie murmured, emptying the washing-up bowl and rinsing it out and wondering what else she could do to avoid turning round and meeting his eyes.

"Did his parents have a good holiday?"

"Yes, I think they did." She found a teaspoon in the bottom of the sink and held it under the tap. At least that was one saving grace – Finn thought that Jack was Ben's father, so he wouldn't be putting two and two together and coming up with the right answer.

"Your coffee's ready," Finn said mildly. "Maggie, if that teaspoon's done, can you sit down a minute. I want to talk to you about something."

She turned around and even though he was standing at the furthest point away from her in the kitchen, she still felt threatened. If he started asking her questions about Sarah, she was going to have to lie and he was going to see straight through her. She'd always been hopeless at lying.

"Is it to do with work?" she asked, glancing at the kitchen clock and thinking frantically. "Because I've got to go out to do a home check in a minute, so I haven't got long. We've got a surplus of dogs at the moment, and I need the space."

"It's not to do with work. No," Finn replied, his voice casual. "Actually, it's a bit more personal than work. Perhaps it would be better to discuss it another time. When you're not so rushed."

"Much better," Maggie said, relief flooding through her as she hurried across the kitchen. "Blimey, is that the time?" She fled out of the door and then had to go back for the keys to the Land Rover, which she'd forgotten. She pulled back the main gates and locked them again behind her and wondered what on earth she was going to do for the next couple of hours.

Chapter Sixteen

Finn had gone to bed by the time she got home and she didn't see him first thing in the morning either, which was a relief. But she knew she wasn't going to be able to avoid him forever.

Seeing Reg Arnold's van pull through the gates just before lunch didn't improve her mood. He was another person she'd have dearly liked to avoid. But it was too late to hide from her most impatient supplier. He'd already seen her and was striding up the yard.

"Maggie." He gave her an ingratiating smile. "Long time no speak. I was just passing and as you never seem to return my phone calls, I thought I'd pop in and see how things were."

See if I could write you out a cheque, more likely, Maggie thought, with a surge of irritation. She couldn't be more than a couple of days late. She paused from sweeping the yard and waited for him to reach her. He was a stringy, wiry, grey-haired little man who reminded Maggie of a jockey.

He stopped in front of her, thrust his hands in his pockets and said, "This place is looking a bit more cared for than it used to. I heard you had some help."

"That's right." She glanced at Finn, who was just going past with a hammer in his hand. "I've got some temporary help." She waited for Reg to make some comment about being able to afford to hire people, but not to pay him on time, but it wasn't forthcoming.

"Mind if I take a look around?" he said. "I'm thinking of getting a dog myself, actually."

"Help yourself." She leaned on the broom and watched him heading up towards the kennels. He was probably just being nosy; he didn't strike her as the type who'd re-home from an animal sanctuary, even if he did want a dog.

"I'll pop in and see you on my way out," he called over his shoulder. "You never know, I might see something I like."

"Not that I'd let him have one of my dogs," Maggie told Finn in reception a few minutes later.

"Why not? I'd have thought being a pet food supplier would have made him quite a good proposition," Finn said, without looking up from the box of screws he was rummaging through. "At least it would never go hungry."

"He's mean-spirited and I don't like him," Maggie said, surprising herself. She hadn't realised she felt that strongly about him.

"That doesn't mean he won't be able to offer a dog a good home," Finn continued. "Some people are better at communicating with animals than they are with their own species." Now he did glance at her, raising his eyebrows and smiling slightly.

She flushed. "You are talking about Reg Arnold, I take it? Or was that a cheap dig at me?"

"All I'm saying, Maggie, is that for all you know he'd make a very good pet owner. Just because he's a bit short on the charm side you shouldn't write him off. You were saying yesterday that we could do with re-homing some dogs, so you ought to at least give him a chance." He stood up then, having presumably found what he wanted, grinned at her, and went out into the sunshine.

Maggie frowned. The irritating thing was that he was probably right. But it was all pure speculation and not worth getting wound up about. Reg Arnold might not even find a dog he liked. She didn't want to admit to herself that Finn's little dig about people who communicated better with animals than humans irked her. Sarah had said the same thing plenty of times, but it was different coming from Sarah. She was her closest friend. She snapped her thoughts away from Sarah, not wanting to think about yesterday and what was going to happen to their friendship now.

She'd almost forgotten about Reg Arnold when he came into reception about half an hour later, rested his hands on the desk in front of her and said, "I've found the perfect dog, Maggie. Little lurcher bitch – got puppies with her."

"Candy," Maggie said, looking at his lit-up face and thinking that she'd never seen him look so enthusiastic, with the possible exception of when he'd come in to collect a big cheque. "It'll be a while before she's ready to go to a home."

"I can wait. I just had a chat with someone called Dawn. She told me I could put a reserve on her if I came and spoke to you."

"We'd need to do a home check first," Maggie said, inwardly cursing Dawn.

"Home check? But you know me, Maggie."

"It's just a formality. I have to check your fencing, things like that. And Candy will need to be spayed, or at least have the arrangements made. Give me a ring in a couple of weeks if you're still keen. Then we can arrange a time for me to pop over and see you."

"Yes. All right, I suppose, if that's what you have to do." He looked disappointed. Straightening up, he ran a hand through his wispy hair and said, "You know I really miss having a dog around the place. We had Jackdaw for nearly eighteen years."

"Jackdaw?"

"He was a black Labrador. Had him from a scrap of a pup. Broke my heart when he went. Still, I suppose eighteen's not bad for a Lab."

"No," Maggie agreed, thinking that perhaps she had misjudged him. "Well, as I said, give me a ring when you've had a think."

"You're the boss." He hesitated. "You're doing a great job here, Maggie. I'm impressed. Maybe we could leave the cheque..." He screwed up his face, as if he were having some internal battle with himself, and Maggie held her breath. "Until you come and do the home visit." Another flash of that ingratiating smile. "That would help you out a bit, wouldn't it?"

"That's very thoughtful, Reg, thank you," she said, trying not to laugh at the magnanimous expression on his face.

"Up until that moment I was starting to think he was a decent human being," she told Dawn that afternoon as they walked dogs in the field. "A few weeks extra credit, whoopee do – he looked so pleased with himself."

"I thought you were looking stressed," Dawn said, glancing at her. "Are you sure it's just Reg Arnold? Or is there anything else on your mind?"

They paused in the corner of the field to let a dog walker with a greyhound go by and Maggie noticed a broken fence post by the road and made a mental note to tell Finn about it. There was a lot on her mind, but most of it was classified, she thought with a surge of weariness, aware that Dawn was waiting for her answer.

She shook her head. The older woman was kind and discreet and could be relied on to keep quiet, but none of what was on her mind was hers to share.

They'd reached the end of the field and paused to let the dogs sniff a patch of grass, before turning to retrace their steps. Then, before either of them could say anything else, a rabbit shot past them with the greyhound, minus its walker, in hot pursuit. The terriers started to dance and bark on the ends of their leads and, despite the fact that they were only small dogs, Maggie felt the sudden wrench on her shoulders, which until then had been healing nicely.

The rabbit reached the fencing and shot through the gap by the broken post. The greyhound, unable to stop, crashed into the wire and yelped, then withdrew limping and holding one dark paw in the air. The dog walker was running down the path towards them.

"Sorry," she panted. "Took me by surprise and I couldn't hold him."

"Don't worry." Maggie knelt by the dog, trying not to wince at the re-awakened pain in her shoulder. "He's probably just twisted it. No damage as far as I can see. Your rabbit-chasing days are over," she said to the greyhound, who blinked his liquid brown eyes and licked her hand.

"He looked like he could win a few races to me," Dawn remarked.

Maggie smiled and returned the greyhound to his walker, glad that the moment for confessions had passed. She and Dawn headed back towards the sanctuary.

She was about to shut the main gate that evening when Gary's van drew up outside. He wound down the window and beckoned her across.

"You're late tonight. I was just locking up."

"I got held up at work. Sorry. I had an urgent call last thing." He looked tired and there were lines of stress around his dark eyes.

Maggie crouched beside the van. "You don't have to come every night, you know," she said gently. "You should have left it. I can cope with Fang."

He brushed a hand through his hair, a curious gesture of vulnerability that touched her, and smiled. "I'm all right. Long day, that's all. Have you eaten, Maggie, only I was wondering if you'd like to come for a bit of tea?" He reddened a little, his dark eyes even more intense than usual.

Maggie hesitated. She was still aching like mad and all she really wanted to do was to lie in a bath and let the water soothe her wrenched muscles. Yet, she didn't want to turn him down flat. Not after what Mike had told her.

"Not tonight, Gary." She kept her voice gentle. "I need an early night. I'm really tired."

He looked so defeated that she heard herself adding, "I'd love to come another time, though."

His face brightened and before she could qualify this by suggesting they go to Mike's one evening, he said, "How about next Saturday? I could book somewhere. Do you like Italian?"

"Yes, why not." She wondered if the same restaurant would let him book another table. "But you'll be in before then to see Fang?"

"Of course." He switched off the ignition. "I could go up there now if you like?"

"I've just locked up. You'll disturb the others." As she spoke, Finn came down the yard, heading towards the cottage, and she saw Gary's face tighten.

"I'll see you tomorrow, then." He leaned out of the van and put his hand on her arm and Maggie had the horrible feeling that it wasn't for her benefit, but some signal of possession to Finn.

She stepped away. "See you tomorrow."

He gave her a quick smile, started the van, and pulled out of the yard. She watched him go with mixed feelings.

Dusk was already creeping through the air, bringing a chill dampness with it that promised yet more rain.

"Going to stand there all night, or are you coming in?" Finn's voice interrupted her thoughts.

"I'm coming now."

"Are you okay? You look shattered."

Shattered just about summed it up – if she hadn't been so tired and distracted, she was sure she wouldn't have agreed to go out with Gary. She glanced at Finn, longing for the easy rapport that had built up between them before Sarah had dropped her bombshell, but afraid to relax her guard. She wasn't like Sarah, she couldn't act as if nothing had happened and there was no way she could laugh and joke with Finn while she was also lying to him. She'd have been hard pushed to do it with a stranger, let alone someone she liked and trusted.

"I am tired," she said, jolting away from him as they took their coats off in the hallway of the cottage and their arms brushed accidentally.

"And jumpy," he added quietly. "What's on your mind, Maggie?"

"Nothing." She spoke too quickly, too sharply and she saw his face tighten even in the dim light of the hall. "What I mean is…"

"You don't need to explain." He cut her off mid-sentence. "I think I can probably work it out for myself."

That was pretty bloody unlikely, even for someone as perceptive as Finn, but Maggie knew there was nothing she could say to let him know that this wasn't what he thought. She wasn't judging him for something that had happened long before they met. Far from it.

Chapter Seventeen

There was no word from Sarah for the next few days and Maggie was saddened, but not surprised.

Finn said no more about wanting to talk to her either, which was a relief. He too seemed to be keeping out of her way. The prospect of going out for dinner with Gary loomed like a black cloud and she wished she could back out of it. But that would have been crueller than saying no in the first place. Why hadn't she said no? she thought, cursing herself for being such a wimp.

As she got ready on Saturday night, Maggie realised she hadn't told Finn that she was going out with Gary. Not that she normally filled him in on her activities. But then she didn't normally go anywhere. She looked at herself in the mirror critically and wondered if she'd subconsciously chosen an outfit that covered every bit of flesh. Coffee-coloured trousers, a cream silk shirt that she'd bought for interviews and boots with no heels because she was out of practice at walking in heels and there might be a walk between car park and restaurant.

She looked smart, but casual, she decided, and there was no way Gary could get the impression they were going on a hot date. She checked there was no lipstick on her teeth and opened the bedroom door to meet Finn coming out of the bathroom.

"You look nice," he said, a mixture of surprise and appreciation on his face. She didn't know whether to feel insulted or flattered. Before she could make up her mind he added, "I take it you're going somewhere more interesting than the Red Lion?"

"Just for a pizza with Gary," Maggie said, feeling awkward at the knowing look in his eyes. "You up to anything?"

"I thought I might head down to the pub and see if Mike's sold any of my paintings yet."

"I'll keep my fingers crossed for you."

A few minutes later the doorbell rang and Gary strolled into the cottage. He made a big thing about giving her a bunch of flowers and whistling his appreciation of the effort she'd gone to. By the time she'd got him out of the door her face was flaming. This had been a mad idea. She was never in a million years going to be able to let Gary down gently.

Gary was torn between worrying about whether Maggie would like the restaurant he'd chosen and delight that their long-awaited date was finally happening. The Italian had been fully booked, so he'd picked an English restaurant that hadn't been open very long. She didn't seem particularly excited about coming out with him, but there was bound to be a certain adjustment period. This was new territory for them both. He'd decided to drive her himself and not have anything to drink. That way he could fully enjoy the evening. Unglazed by alcohol, he could also make sure he didn't commit any faux pas. This evening had to be perfect.

A waiter took their drinks orders and left them with leather-bound menus. Rather to his chagrin, Maggie had asked for a diet coke. But nothing really mattered, he thought, as he watched her scanning the menu. The main thing was that she was here with him; his woman, at least for the evening. He tried to suppress the little feeling of satisfaction that Finn would be sitting in the Red Lion on his own. It wasn't charitable and he could afford to be magnanimous now.

Knowing that Maggie was vegetarian, Gary had decided to forfeit his usual rare steak and go for sea bass.

But the sea bass was sold out, so he'd picked guinea fowl, which seemed the most innocuous of the remaining choices, with prawns to start.

"Soup all right?" he asked Maggie, picking up a prawn and deftly snapping off the head.

"It's lovely, thank you, Gary." She dabbed her mouth with her napkin and Gary looked around for a finger bowl and saw that there wasn't one. Unable to catch a waiter's eye he had to resort to wiping his fingers on his own napkin. Preoccupied with this he didn't notice until Maggie was halfway through her soup that although they had butter on the table there was no bread.

"Would you like some bread with that?" he asked belatedly.

"No, I'm fine, Gary, thanks."

"Are you sure? I can get you some." He stood up, knocking his fork on to the floor with the edge of his jacket.

Maggie bent to pick it up. Fortunately, at that moment their main courses arrived. Or at least Gary's did.

"Yours will be two minutes," the waiter informed her.

Two minutes passed, during which Maggie tried to ignore the guinea fowl on Gary's plate. A piece of bone, presumably its leg, stuck out at an angle, the end of it trussed in white paper. Was the paper meant to be a disguise or decoration, Maggie wondered, reminded of the buzzard she was currently nursing back to health, and feeling a pang of sympathy for the guinea fowl, which had not only had to die, but had been made to look so undignified afterwards.

"Please start, Gary, don't wait for me," she urged, seeing that his gravy was beginning to congeal on his plate.

He ate as slowly as he could, she saw, which was sweet of him, but he was still almost finished by the time her main course arrived.

"So sorry," the waiter said, putting it on the table with a flourish.

Maggie thanked him absently and he swept away, his nose in the air. She wondered what Sarah would have made of all this. She'd have probably said Gary was a stuffed shirt with a chip the size of Wiltshire on his shoulder. Except Sarah wouldn't have been as polite as that. And suddenly she felt overwhelmingly sad that Sarah felt she couldn't phone her for a chat, even if she wasn't ready to confess all to Finn. Even when she'd been away in Bristol they'd always kept in close contact, more like sisters than friends. It was impossible to believe that a space had come between them so swiftly. Maggie turned down dessert, and they drove back to the cottage in silence. A strained silence, Maggie thought, or maybe it was just her. Gary seemed okay. He'd hummed all the way back to the car. Now she glanced at him and tried to work out the most diplomatic way of telling him that she'd had a lovely evening, but had no desire to repeat the experience. He'd refused to let her pay any of the bill, which made it all worse.

Gary parked his car outside the main gates, switched off the ignition, and reached across to release her seat belt at the same moment as she pressed the button.

"It sticks a bit sometimes," he said apologetically, as their hands knocked against each other.

"It seems to be all right tonight," she muttered, pulling her hand away.

Gary leapt out of the car and came round to open the door for her.

"Thanks."

"My pleasure." What a pity she wasn't wearing a skirt, he thought, as she uncrossed her legs and got out gracefully. He was wondering whether he should risk a goodnight kiss. The evening hadn't quite lived up to his expectations. Maggie hadn't seemed as relaxed with him as she usually was.

She clutched her handbag to her. "That was a lovely evening, Gary."

They stood with a little gap between them below the sign for The Ark. It was a beautiful night, clear and crisp, the stars coldly bright above them. A perfect evening for romance, Gary thought, taking a step closer to her.

She looked beautiful in the moonlight, her eyes wide and dark. He had an urge to put his arms around her, but he still wasn't sure. Eventually, cursing himself for his shyness, he bent and gave her a peck on the cheek. "See you tomorrow, then."

"Okay. Goodnight and thanks again." She made no move to invite him in and after a moment of awkwardness, he stepped back, still looking at her and tripped over a tree stump. He put his hands out to save himself, then overbalanced completely and fell backwards into the hedge that ran alongside the cottage.

"Are you all right?" Her voice was all concern and she bent to help him up, which didn't help his ego one bit.

He scrambled to his feet, brushing dead leaves and bits of grass off his trousers and feeling like a complete idiot.

"I hope you're not driving in that condition."

They both glanced up to see Finn coming round the corner, presumably on his way back from the Red Lion.

"I'm not drunk," Gary snarled, wondering if the bloke did it on purpose.

"Hey – take it easy – I was joking." Finn put up his hands in mock defence. "You just didn't look too steady there for a minute."

Maggie, Gary saw to his embarrassment, was pressing her fingers to her head and looking as if she'd rather be somewhere else, anywhere else. Some romantic finale that had been, he thought bitterly. "I'll be off then," he said, and, giving Finn a curt nod, he got into his car. When he looked in his rear-view mirror, Finn was saying something to Maggie as he opened the gate for her. He felt a little twist of jealousy. He hated the thought of them going into the cottage and sharing coffee and perhaps a laugh at his expense. Still, she'd chosen to go out with him tonight, not Finn, he consoled himself. It was just a matter of time. They could go out a few more times and then maybe she'd decide she didn't want Finn living in the cottage. After all, you didn't go out with one man and live with another, did you?

"Nice evening?" Finn asked, looking at Maggie, eyebrows raised, as they got inside the cottage.

"Lovely, thanks," she said. It was a minor lie in the big scheme of things. "You?"

"Not bad. You stopping up for coffee?"

"I'll just have a glass of water, I think. I've got a bit of a headache."

"Side effect from landing on it last week, probably." He looked at her and she smiled.

"Yeah, I expect you're right," she said, although she knew her headache had nothing at all to do with last week, but more to do with the feeling that she shouldn't have gone out with Gary. At the very least she should have said something, but she hadn't been able to. Not after he'd

153

landed in the bush in front of Finn. It would have been like kicking him when he was down.

Now it was going to be twice as difficult to persuade him that she wasn't interested in him. Water splashed over her hands as she filled up her glass and she realised Finn was still standing in the kitchen.

"So, has Mike sold any of your paintings yet?"

"No, I think he's right. I'll have to do more local landscapes."

"You could do more of Stonehenge. It's beautiful in spring."

"Yes, maybe I will." As she passed him he handed her a foil-wrapped blister of tablets. "Pain killers."

"Thanks."

Upstairs, Maggie lay in bed, feeling curiously depressed. She and Gary had a lot in common. It would have been nice if she'd fallen for him, but there was no spark, none of the electricity that flared between her and Finn and left her disconcertingly breathless at the most inappropriate moments.

She blinked away the thought. Fantasising about Finn was both stupid and painful. In a few months time he'd be a distant memory because, despite what she'd told Sarah, she knew that when it came to it, her loyalty was to her best friend. If she had to choose between friendship and a crush on a man she barely knew, there was no contest.

Chapter Eighteen

Finn walked around Stonehenge, trying to find an angle where the barbed wire perimeter fence least interfered with his line of sight. But even when he'd found a spot and set up his easel, he still couldn't concentrate.

He'd got up early and, realising Maggie hadn't surfaced, gone and knocked on her door. When she hadn't responded he'd been gripped by a sudden fear that she might not be all right. She never overslept and last night she'd complained of a headache. What if it was a delayed effect of the bang on the head when she'd slipped in the run? Deciding he couldn't take the risk that she might be unconscious, he'd poked his head around her bedroom door.

She'd been lying on her front, one arm tucked beneath her head, her breasts crushed against the bottom sheet. The duvet had been at the foot of the bed and he hadn't been able to stop his gaze from travelling down her naked body. As well as the graze on her back, which looked as though it was healing nicely, there was a large bruise at the base of her spine, just above the gentle curve of her buttocks. There was another bruise at the top of one smooth thigh. Her face was peaceful, though, and she was breathing steadily. As he watched her, she stirred and murmured something. Finn closed the door, his heart beating too fast, and he'd had to go outside to cool down.

Since he'd realised that Maggie's best friend was also his long-ago one-night stand, he'd been tearing himself apart over what to do for the best. Maggie obviously knew about it. He knew enough about women to know they'd have discussed it in detail, and, even if he hadn't, he'd have guessed by her attitude towards him. She'd begun to be relaxed around him, but that had gone now. He was torn between telling her that he wasn't in the habit of having one-night stands, and saying nothing at all. Least said, soonest mended, his father would have said, and perhaps he was right.

Not that Maggie had given him much chance to discuss the subject, even if he'd wanted to. When he'd tried, she'd run a mile. He sighed. He sensed that it would be counterproductive to push her into a corner. The best thing he could do was to give her as much space as possible, which meant that at the moment she was off-limits, but telling himself this did nothing to make the memory of her nakedness less evocative.

He was bound to feel aroused, he decided. He'd been celibate since Shirley and he was living in the same house as a gorgeous woman whom he'd wanted to take to bed from the moment he'd seen her. Sharing her routines, using the same bathroom, knowing she was sleeping in the room just below him. He'd have to be a eunuch not to be affected.

His thoughts drifted to Gary. He'd been surprised when Maggie had gone out for dinner with the bumbling vet, but perhaps he'd underestimated him. She must have had some reason to go; perhaps she'd hoped to negotiate better discounts. Or perhaps it was some sort of signal to him that she wasn't available. He didn't think she was the type to play games, but then he still knew hardly anything about her.

Dismissing Gary, he shook his head and forced himself to concentrate on the ancient stones he was trying to sketch. Beyond them, the sky was a backdrop of blue with only the occasional cloud to break it, but despite the glorious weather there weren't many people about. Maggie had told him that in another couple of weeks the place would be flooded with tourists. Today was a good day to come.

He worked for another couple of hours, the air soft on his face, the peace of the countryside slowly seeping into his mind. Then he got up and stretched and walked around a bit. Time to find himself a pub lunch.

It was after six when he got back to The Ark. Gary's van wasn't around, he saw with relief. He had a feeling he'd seen quite a bit more of Maggie this morning than Gary ever had and he was not anxious to bump into him for a while. He wasn't keen on bumping into Maggie either, come to that. What if some half-formed memory of him opening her door had been sharpening in her mind during the day? Perhaps she'd already packed his bags and was about to tell him he was sacked?

He parked his car and opened the boot to get his painting things out. When he straightened, he saw Maggie coming down the yard. Seeing him, she frowned and came hurrying across.

"Hi, Finn, I'm glad you're back. Have you got a minute? I'd like a quick word."

Finn looked guilty, Maggie noticed, as they went into the cottage. He'd jumped out of his skin when she'd spoken.

"Did you have a productive day?" she asked. "Get much done?"

"Yeah, not bad, thanks. Very relaxing."

He didn't look at all relaxed. She smiled at him. "If you're rushing off somewhere it can wait. It's not important."

"I'm not rushing off." He leaned on the door frame of the lounge. "Fire away."

"There's a broken fence post in the dog-walking field and there's a little gap that leads out on to the road. I

157

noticed it the other day, but I forgot to tell you. I'm worried that a dog might get loose and go through there."

"That's what you wanted to talk to me about?"

"Yes. Oh, and I also wanted to say that you really must have a day off in the week too. You must think I'm a slave driver."

"Not at all. You're not exactly a slacker yourself, are you?"

She flushed. "But I'm doing it for the love of it, Finn. You don't have to work such long hours. I probably don't tell you enough, but I really appreciate having you around." She paused and flicked him an anxious glance. "Wasn't there something you wanted to talk to me about?"

He hesitated. Would now be a good time? She looked on edge and he decided that it would be better to wait. He wanted her to listen to him, to trust him and she had to be relaxed for that.

"It'll keep," he murmured, knowing instantly from the relief on her face that he'd said the right thing.

Maggie waited until she was sure he'd gone to bed, then closed the lounge door and phoned Sarah, who rarely went to bed before midnight.

"Have you decided what you're going to do about Finn?" she said, launching straight in. "Because he's been acting really strangely today and I think he might have guessed. I asked him what was on his mind just now, but he didn't want to discuss it."

"He can't have guessed," Sarah said stubbornly. "Why on earth would he connect Ben with himself? Anyway, he said he couldn't remember what had happened."

"I think he was lying. So as not to embarrass you, he's that type of bloke."

"So as not to embarrass himself, more like," Sarah snapped. "It takes two, you know. I didn't drag him into that field."

Maggie flinched. She knew she was torturing herself, but she couldn't get the image of Sarah and Finn, backed up against a tree, or wherever it had happened, out of her head. She knew they'd been drunk and very young, but they'd still wanted each other, hadn't they? And they'd still produced Ben, so she couldn't even kid herself that it had just been a desperate fumbling where not much had really happened.

"Maggie, please give me a bit longer." A note of fear had crept into Sarah's voice and Maggie sighed.

"How much longer? A week, a few weeks, a few months? I hate this. I hate seeing him every day and knowing something like this. He's a nice bloke. He's going to be really hurt."

"Yes, I know, but I've got to think of Ben. And there's Jack. I've got to find the right time to tell him, too. I love him, Maggie. I'm scared of buggering things up between us."

"But isn't sooner going to be better than later?" Maggie paused. "And Jack loves you. It's not as though he thinks Ben's his child, is it?"

"No, but he does think that Ben's father didn't want to know. I told him I'd had a relationship with this guy who was much older than me and he left when I got pregnant. Well, I was hardly going to tell him what really happened, was I?"

Her voice was getting lower with each sentence, but Maggie heard the message loud and clear. Of course Sarah wouldn't have told Jack about something of which she was deeply ashamed. She wanted him to think she was an independent, single mother who'd been abandoned by the

159

father of her child – just as she'd been abandoned by everyone else in her life. That she'd come through it all by her own strength of character. She didn't want the man she loved to see the flaws, the desperate insecurity that had been behind her decision not to contact a man whose name she hadn't even known.

In some ways Maggie couldn't blame her. Perhaps she'd have done the same in her place.

"And Maggie, there's been a development I haven't told you about. Jack has asked me to marry him and I've said yes. If I tell him the truth, the whole thing will be off. I can't risk it."

"Congratulations," Maggie whispered, feeling a deep sadness welling up in her because once she wouldn't have had to call Sarah to find out what must have been one of the most important decisions of her life. A few weeks ago Sarah would have been straight on the phone.

"We're coming over at the weekend to tell you officially so pretend you don't know. And, Maggie, please don't say anything to Finn. Let me do this, my way."

Chapter Nineteen

Blossom the colour of pink candy floss was everywhere and new grass had sprung up in the fields. There were hundreds of lambs, too, and Maggie could never see them skipping after their mothers without feeling a pang of bittersweet poignancy, knowing they were destined for the table. Despite the fact that Maggie had been a vegetarian since she was fifteen, she turned a blind eye to Finn cooking bacon and sausages in her kitchen, although the subject had come up a few times.

"I won't do it if it bothers you," he'd said one morning, when he saw her wrinkling up her nose.

"I'm not standing in judgement on you," she said huffily. "Do what you like. Just make sure you don't use my best non-stick pan, you'll wreck it."

"Wouldn't dream of it. Doesn't the smell of frying bacon get your taste buds going even a bit?"

"No, it doesn't." She glared at him and he hadn't pushed it any further.

Later that day, when they'd gone to collect some new fence panels, a rabbit ran across the road in front of the car and he'd only just missed it.

"Why don't you try driving a bit slower?" she snapped.

On the return journey he'd insisted that she drive and when she'd slammed on the brakes to avoid something else in the road and a fence post had nearly skewered him in the back, he'd said crossly, "For God's sake, Maggie, was that really bloody necessary?"

"I didn't want to hit it. What was it anyway?"

He glanced out of the window and said, "Can't tell, you've flattened it. Poor little thing." Then, seeing her shocked expression, he'd leaned over and patted her knee and said, "You just killed a defenceless plastic bag, Maggie."

For a moment he'd thought she was going to slap him, then she'd smiled and they'd both ended up in fits of laughter.

Apart from the lambs, spring was Maggie's favourite season. Even the air smelt new, crisp and lemony with a hint of the summer that was to come. Rowena was back from the farmer and Maggie was hoping that someone would respond to her advert about Ashley before the mare came into season again.

Candy's pups had all gone to new homes, apart from Tiny. Maggie told everyone that he needed a bit longer than the rest of the litter, being the weakest, but the truth was she didn't want to let him go. It was stupid, she knew. You couldn't afford to get sentimental about one perfectly re-homable puppy. Not when you had a whole kennel full of other dogs; but there was something special about Tiny. In her mind Tiny's progress was tied up with the sanctuary's future and, in some strange way, her own.

It was superstitious nonsense, she knew, not far removed from the challenges she'd set herself when she was a child. If she could get down the whole street without treading on the cracks in the pavement then she'd have a good day at school. If she got top marks in maths, which she hated, then her mother would pick her up instead of sending the childminder. Life wasn't like that. You couldn't make bargains with some deity. But, however irrational it was, she couldn't shake off the feeling that Tiny's survival was tied up with the future of The Ark. If she kept him safe, The Ark would survive too. And the only way she could keep him safe was to keep him here with her.

Candy, though, would be going soon. Finn had asked Maggie if he could go with her to do Reg Arnold's home check.

"Why?" she'd asked, curious. It was the first time he'd shown an interest in anything directly concerned with an animal.

"I just want to see what excuse you're going to find to say he can't have her," he'd replied with a wry smile. "Or are you going to be more professional than that and put Candy's welfare first?"

"I always put the animal's welfare first," she'd said, "not that it's got anything to do with you."

"So can I come, then? You can take me for a drink afterwards if you like."

She'd been so taken aback that she'd agreed and they'd driven round to Reg Arnold's house in her Land Rover. Despite what she'd said to Finn, she had been thinking of saying Reg couldn't have Candy. Not because she didn't like the man, but because anyone as tight-fisted as he was might skimp on looking after an animal. What would happen if she needed expensive veterinary treatment? She parked outside the address that Reg had given her and they both got out of the car and looked at the house.

"Bit posh," Finn said, echoing her thoughts. He peered over the fence that surrounded an impressively large garden. "Nice lot of space for a dog to run around. Candy would love it."

She stood beside him. The garden was what an estate agent would have referred to as 'mature'. A long, sloping lawn flanked with bushes and trees led up to a big conservatory. The house itself was encircled by a gravel driveway, where Reg's delivery van and a five-year-old Jaguar XJS were parked.

"Blimey, so that's what he does with his money," Maggie said. "He could afford to wait weeks longer for his accounts, the miserable sod."

"Ah, but then he probably wouldn't be able to afford this lot," Finn said, grinning at her. "Made up your mind, then, have you, Maggie?"

Ignoring him, she let them through the five bar gate and they walked towards the house.

"Gary's got a nice garden too," Maggie commented, as they waited on the front door step. She glanced at Finn. "How are you getting on with him, these days?"

"I don't think we're ever going to be best buddies," he replied, but was saved from having to make further comment when Reg opened the door.

"Come in, come in. Nice to see you both." He ushered them into a country farmhouse kitchen, which wouldn't have looked out of place in a glossy magazine, and made them both coffee.

Supermarket own brand, Maggie thought uncharitably, as he showed them the place next to the Aga where he planned to put Candy's basket.

"I just need to check your garden's secure," she said, aware of Finn's eyes on her, but despite walking all the way round the quarter acre plot, she couldn't find anywhere the little lurcher could possibly squeeze through.

"Can I have her, then?" Reg asked when they got back to the house again. "Have I passed the test?"

"With flying colours," she said, not looking at Finn. "Just one question. Why do you want to take on a rescue dog? Why don't you just go out and buy a Labrador puppy?"

Reg rubbed his hands together. "I like to do my bit," he said, "as you know, Maggie. Now, about your latest account. Maybe a little discount would help?"

"That's very generous, Reg. Thank you." She smiled at him. "There's an adoption fee payable when you come to collect Candy. Her inoculations are all up to date, but she'll still need to be spayed. Either you can go through your own vet, or ours might be cheaper. If money was an issue, I mean?"

He cleared his throat. "Of course. I'll – er – pop in next week and we'll discuss it."

Afterwards, Maggie drove Finn to the Red Lion and bought him a drink, as agreed.

"Satisfied yourself about my professional abilities?" she said, as she put the glass down in front of him.

"Perfectly. I was very impressed." He grinned at her and said, "So, you see, you can't always judge people from what you see on the surface, can you?"

"And what's that supposed to mean?"

"Well, you thought Reg was an old skinflint who'd be a totally unsuitable dog owner, didn't you? But closer inspection proved that not to be the case. Am I right?"

She didn't answer and he sipped his pint of Guinness and went on idly, "And I thought you were a mad, idealistic animal-lover, but there's a lot more to you than that, isn't there?"

"I should hope so," she said, meeting his steady gaze. "If I was just a mad, idealistic animal-lover I probably wouldn't have got this far. I would have given up after the first three months when I found out that running an animal sanctuary is damn hard work. Anyway, Finn McTaggart, enough about me, what about you?"

"What about me?" His voice was soft. "What would you like to know, Maggie?"

She wouldn't ask him about Sarah, she decided. Or about whether it was a regular thing for him to jump into bed with women he didn't know. Partly because she didn't want to spoil the easiness of the moment – she'd missed this easiness so much – and partly because she wasn't sure if she'd like his answer. Besides, what business was it of hers what he'd done in the past? She thought about the photo of the little boy in his wallet. She wanted to ask him about that, but she couldn't do that either, since she wasn't supposed to know it was there.

She stared into her orange juice, aware that he was waiting for her to respond and kept her voice deliberately light.

"I don't know. Stuff. Like, have you got any brothers and sisters? What your dad does, that sort of thing."

He smiled. "No brothers and sisters, and Dad's retired now, but he was a miner until the pit closed down. How's that?"

Maggie would have liked to ask more about his mother, but she sensed that he'd clam up completely if she did, so she said, "Are you close to your dad? You could ask him down for a holiday some time, if you like. You said he liked dogs, didn't you?"

"Yes, he does like dogs. Thanks, I might do that."

"I promise I won't interrogate him too much. What's his name?"

"Albert," Finn said. "And he'd probably enjoy being interrogated by you, Maggie. Do you want another drink?"

She shook her head and then before she could lose her nerve, went on softly, "So why did you really move down from Nottingham, Finn? It must be quite a culture shock living here."

He met her eyes steadily. "I've always liked it here. I was down every summer when I was a kid. I was close to my grandparents. And there was nothing really to tie me to Nottingham when I lost my job. Apart from Dad, of course, but he's got quite a full social life. He belongs to a working men's club and he's got his old cronies from mining. Although there aren't as many as there used to be. They're all getting on a bit – and not many miners live to a great old age."

Maggie picked up a beer mat and twiddled it nervously. "The girl you lived with in Nottingham – did she have any children? You don't have to tell me. If it's private, you know…"

He smiled. "It's not private. Yes, Shirley had a little boy." He rummaged for his wallet and Maggie felt her face burn as he slipped out the photo she'd seen and slid it across the table. "This is Stewart. You've seen this photo already, though, haven't you?"

"It fell out of your wallet when you first started working for me," she murmured, knowing how unlikely that must sound. "I wasn't prying, truly. But yes, I did see it."

"Shirley was married to my best friend, Peter," Finn went on with a wry smile so she wasn't sure whether he believed her or not. "I was best man at their wedding. I was close to both of them, but then Peter started drinking heavily. It was soon after Stewart was born – I don't think he could handle the responsibility of being a parent." His face clouded and Maggie felt a tug of guilt because the one thing she was sure about was that Finn would make an excellent father.

"Peter started knocking her about," Finn continued quietly. "One evening he broke her arm because the carrots in his stew weren't cooked properly. She told me about it. She didn't want to tell me – she was desperately ashamed that it was somehow her fault – but she was terrified that he might start on Stewart."

"My God," Maggie whispered. "That's awful. What happened?"

"She left him. She and Stewart came to live with me for a while because she didn't have anywhere else to go. I cared about them both."

He hesitated. "Peter found out where they were, turned up one night and gave me a good hiding. I pressed charges and he ended up in prison. Which was actually the best thing that could have happened in some ways, because he got treatment for his drink problem."

"And you ended up with Shirley?" Maggie asked, fascinated.

"We were never a proper couple," Finn told her, raising his eyebrows and Maggie wondered whether he meant they didn't sleep together, but his next words shattered this. "Basically, she needed someone and I was there. We sort of drifted together, but I was a lot more involved with Shirley than she was with me. She still loved Peter, you see. When he came out of prison she went back to him. I think I always knew she would."

He sipped his pint, his eyes serious. "I shouldn't have got involved – in any sense of the word, I guess. But it's difficult not to in a situation like that."

"And are they okay now?" Maggie asked, wanting more than anything to take his hand, but not sure if he'd want her to. He certainly didn't want her sympathy, she could see that in his face.

"Yes, I think so. Dad keeps a discreet eye on them both. He lives quite close to them. Dad would let me know if they needed me. He adores Stewart, he takes the lad fishing. He's the grandson he never had."

His eyes held hers and eventually she had to drop her gaze. Finn had a son and Albert had a grandson and they should be sharing his life, but they didn't even know he existed. Maggie ached with the deceit of it all.

"It's okay," he murmured, catching her stricken look. "I'm over Shirley. I just got a little more involved than I should have done. I knew deep down that she was always going to go back to Peter and I'm glad that they're happy. Even if I did lose a mate. Are you sure you don't want another drink?"

She couldn't sit here any more, listening to him opening his heart, when she could never do the same. She forced lightness into her voice and managed a smile. "No, I guess we should get back. Getting out of the sanctuary for a while feels a bit like playing truant from school."

His eyes warmed. "I've never met anyone who works as hard as you do."

"Is that supposed to be a compliment?"

"Yeah, I guess it is." He leaned across and picked up their glasses and for a second he was very close to her. She could smell the faint citrus smell of something he wore and she felt a little shiver of excitement run through her. She glanced at him and their eyes held and Maggie knew he was as conscious of her as she was of him. Supercharged with awareness, she couldn't breathe. He dropped his gaze and got up to take their empty glasses across to the bar. Maggie hugged her arms around herself and tried to get the bittersweet ache of longing out of her throat. By the time he came back, loping in that casual, easy way he had, she was in charge of her breathing again; well, almost.

They drove back to the sanctuary in companionable silence and Maggie thought once again about Sarah. Since she and Jack had come over to announce their engagement, they'd been rushing around organising things and hadn't been over to the sanctuary much. And although Maggie knew the real reason why Sarah kept away, she'd tried to put it to the back of her mind.

Let Sarah have her happiness. Until this conversation with Finn, she'd even begun to think Sarah might be right. What Finn didn't know couldn't hurt him. But now the doubts that had nagged at the corners of her mind came crowding back. Finn wasn't just some faceless stranger any more. He was the sort of person who cared – he'd put himself in danger to protect someone else's wife and child. Maggie was very aware that he must have known exactly what he was risking when he'd taken in Shirley and Stewart, but he'd done it anyway.

She sighed as Finn pulled up outside the Ark and he looked at her quizzically.

"Penny for them."

"I was just thinking about what you said in the pub."

"Ah – my murky past," he said dryly. "You must tell me yours some time, Maggie."

"Yes," she gulped, leaping out of the car and hurrying towards the house. Fleetingly she hated Sarah for putting her in this position, but she hated herself more. What would Finn do when he found out the truth and the part she'd played in keeping it from him?

Chapter Twenty

Prompted by an advert that she had seen in a magazine, Maggie had set up an animal sponsorship scheme. Dawn had said she'd take photographs of their most photogenic animals, while Maggie wrote a piece about each one. The idea was that prospective sponsors paid a set annual fee and received an adoption pack, which included a photograph and information about their chosen animal.

When Finn saw their photographs, he offered to do some sketches.

"It would be a bit different," he said. "Might help to drum up business."

"All right, but you must let me pay you for doing them. You work enough hours already."

"Don't be ridiculous, Maggie, I enjoy it. It's a pity Ben doesn't come over so much, these days. He could help. How's he getting on with his painting?"

"Great," Maggie muttered, aware of his curious gaze and feeling heat in her face despite herself. "But they've got masses on at the moment, what with organising the wedding."

"I'm sure they have." Finn's voice was ultra-casual and, anxious to get off the subject of Ben, Maggie said, "How's your dad now? Is he over his flu bug yet? Did he say when he wants to come down?"

"He's still coughing. But he sounds a lot better than he was. I spoke to him last night. If it's still okay with you, he'll probably come for a week in May."

"Yes, that'll be great," Maggie said, hearing the phone ringing at the other end of the yard and making her escape. The caller turned out to be Sarah wanting to know if she fancied a drink at the Red Lion that night to discuss wedding plans.

"Of course, I'd love to come. Will it just be the two of us?"

"Yes, Jack's baby-sitting and we haven't had a girlie night for ages, have we?"

"No," Maggie said pointedly, but if Sarah heard the irony in her voice she didn't comment. As she got ready to go out that night she decided to make a supreme effort to keep the talk on weddings.

Sarah was already there when she arrived, sitting at a table with two large glasses of wine and a pile of glossy wedding magazines in front of her.

She waved as Maggie came in and Maggie flew across to hug her and then sat down opposite.

"So how's it all going? I haven't seen much of you lately." She tried to keep her voice neutral. It was like treading on eggshells talking to Sarah, these days.

"We're getting there. We've booked the church and we'll have the reception at home. Just a few friends and Jack's family, we don't want a big fuss. Dawn said she'll do the photographs for us. I was wondering if you fancied coming along to help me choose a dress some time?"

She looked so happy that Maggie felt herself softening; how could she not be happy for her?

"I'd love to. You know I would." She caught Sarah's hand across the table. "I'm so pleased for you. Jack's lovely, isn't he."

"I know." Sarah's smile was radiant. There was a little pause and Maggie let go of Sarah's fingers and wished things were different. Wished that Ben's father were some unknown stranger, far away from here, and not someone she cared about so much. And she did care. It was rapidly becoming pointless to try and deny it – even to herself. She dropped her gaze, but Sarah didn't miss the look.

"Please don't be angry with me, Maggie. I am going to sort things out with Finn. But just not yet."

"I'm not angry, just worried. I don't want all this to backfire on you."

"How can it?" Sarah pursed her lips. "You're the only other person in the world who knows the truth about Ben's father."

"Yes," Maggie murmured, wondering whether she should tell Sarah how she felt about Finn. Not that she was a hundred per cent sure herself. She seemed to go through the whole range of emotions when he was around. Lust, fear, warmth, tenderness, guilt. Guilt had been the main one lately. But then she'd always been plagued with that. It was part of her genetic make-up, she sometimes thought.

She sipped her wine and decided to change the subject to safer ground. "Gary asked me out again last week."

"What did you say?"

"No, of course. He didn't take it very well. I felt as if I was whipping a cowed dog." She paused, deciding it would probably be better not to tell Sarah what else Gary had said.

"It's him, isn't it? Finn." He'd spat the word as if he didn't want it in his mouth. 'I knew this would happen.' Then he'd reached for her hands and she'd drawn back from him, horrified at the bitterness on his face.

"It's got nothing to do with anyone else. Honestly, Gary. I just don't want a relationship. Not with you. Not with anyone."

And though finally he'd seemed to accept it, she still felt uneasy. He was still coming every day to socialise Fang. Fortunately, so far, Finn had kept out of his way.

"Gary will get over you sooner or later," Sarah murmured, taking a gulp of wine and not meeting Maggie's eyes. "It's a shame you don't fancy him, because..."

"Then you'd be off the hook," Maggie finished, regretting the words as soon as she'd said them.

"No, I didn't mean that. I just meant that you deserve someone nice, and he is nice, isn't he? I want you to be happy, Maggie. I want you to feel what I'm feeling."

There was an awkward little silence, which was broken by Mike striding over to their table, rubbing his hands together. "Evening, ladies. Is Finn coming in tonight by any chance? Only I've got some good news for him. I've just sold one of his paintings."

They glanced up at his happy, bearded face.

"Er, I'm not sure." Maggie smiled back at him. "Which one? Stonehenge?"

"No. It was the one of the little girl on the beach. To the woman in the twin-set and pearls over there. Said it reminds her of her granddaughter."

The woman, who was sitting on a bar stool, raised her glass to them.

"She said she'd like to meet the artist. Could you give him a ring on his mobile, Maggie?"

"Of course," Maggie said, glancing at Sarah.

"My cue to go, I think." She stood up. "Don't worry, Maggie, I've got to get back anyway. I can't drink any more, I'm driving. Thanks for tonight."

"Something I said?" Mike asked, raising his eyebrows as Sarah hurried towards the door.

"She's got a lot to do, wedding things," Maggie told him, glancing at her watch and deciding that she'd have to wait for Finn. She couldn't just phone him and disappear. He'd be hurt.

He arrived surprisingly promptly. He was wearing his smartest jeans and he was freshly shaven. He looked nervous, she saw with a little tug of tenderness. When he saw her, he headed across and pulled out a chair.

"So is she still here then, this woman? Or are you going to tell me this is a wind-up?"

"Of course it's not a wind-up. You should have more faith in yourself. You're really good."

He reddened a little and Maggie touched his arm. "I'm serious, Finn. She's sitting at the bar. Go over and Mike will introduce you."

"I'll get you a drink."

"I'm up to my limit already."

"Oh, go on," Finn pressed. "You're not driving and you can't celebrate with me unless you've got a drink."

"She wanted me to write on the back of it for her," Finn said, when he finally came back with their drinks. "I didn't like to just rush off."

"Don't worry. It gave me the chance to sober up." Maggie smiled at him. "Congratulations. Is that your first sale?"

"To a stranger, yes." His grey eyes were warm. "A few people back home have bought them, but I was never sure if they were just being nice."

"Here's to many more," Maggie said and they clinked glasses. Then they chatted for a while longer about art and the sanctuary until eventually Maggie stood up. "I'd better get back. Are you staying?"

"No, I'll walk with you."

It was relaxing walking back with the darkness settling around them and the odd nocturnal rustle in the hedgerows reminding them they weren't the only living creatures out in the still night. The hawthorn was in flower, its sweetness scenting the air and there was a new lemon sliver of a moon. Above their heads thousands of stars speckled the clear sky.

"Have you ever tried to count them?" Finn asked, tilting back his head and standing still for a moment in the middle of the country road.

"No." Maggie looked at him, surprised.

"Sometimes, if I can't sleep, I count the ones I can see out of my skylight. Twenty-three's the record so far. Might just beat it tonight."

"Do you often have problems sleeping?"

"Not really. But I'm definitely going to have problems tonight." He grinned at her. "You must think I'm mad, getting all excited over a painting."

"I don't think that at all. But then maybe I'm not a very good person to judge the sanity of others – being a bit mad and idealistic myself."

"Ouch," he said. "And there was me thinking you'd forgotten that conversation."

"I don't forget much, Mr McTaggart." She went across and stood next to him in the middle of the road. It must be the wine. Maybe she wasn't as sober as she'd thought. Or maybe it was the fact that tonight his face was unguarded and happy and his enthusiasm was infectious.

"Your dad's going to be pleased too, isn't he? Do you get your artistic side from him?"

"He reckons I do, cheeky sod. Not that he's ever painted anything in his life. He'll be made up when I tell him."

Impulsively, she caught hold of his hands. "You've got artist's fingers," she said, lifting them up and studying them. "Did you get those from your dad?"

"I'm not sure. I'll have to check." There was a moment's silence, as if each of them had suddenly become aware that they were holding hands. And in the silence Maggie realised her heart was thumping far more quickly than was necessary. She daren't look at him for fear he'd

176

read her expression and guess that she could have stood here all night, just holding hands with him, it felt so right.

Shocked at the strength of her feelings, and still without looking at him, she said, "So what's the plan, then – with your dad, I mean?" because suddenly words were ambiguous.

"He's a lot better. I said I'd phone him tomorrow to firm up dates. He'll come down by coach." He drew his fingers from hers. "We'd better get going, we'll get run over, standing in the middle of the road."

They walked back with a little space between them, although Maggie wasn't sure who was creating it.

When they reached the cottage, he went ahead of her into the kitchen and she watched him make coffee.

"Shall we drink these in the other room?" They went through and sat where they usually sat, Maggie on the settee and Finn on the armchair opposite. "It's very peaceful here, isn't it?" he said, after a few moments silence. "Perhaps that's why I couldn't sleep when I first came here. I was so used to the noise of the traffic. My flat in Nottingham was quite close to a main road and there was always traffic. Even in the early hours of the morning."

"Yes, I found the same thing when I first came back from Bristol. Although to be honest I don't think I'd have slept wherever I was. I felt too guilty about Mum. If I'd have taken over Arleston Court like she wanted me to, she wouldn't have been so stressed. Maybe she wouldn't have had a stroke. I was so selfish." Where had all that come from? She definitely shouldn't have had that last glass of wine. She shifted uncomfortably, aware of Finn's eyes on her.

"You came back when she needed you. You gave up your dreams of being a vet." His eyes were soft. "I don't call that selfish."

"It was too little, too late," she whispered, feeling the familiar ache of grief inside her and for once putting how she felt into words because it was easy to talk to Finn in the peace of this little room. "She might not have died if I'd been a better daughter – if I'd done what she wanted."

He leaned forward in his chair, chin on hands, his eyes serious. "Don't torture yourself, Maggie. Everything's easy with the benefit of hindsight. You did what you thought was right at the time." He paused. "So why this place? Why an animal sanctuary?"

"Because by then I'd realised that a vets is a silly place to work anyway if you really love animals." She gave him a bittersweet smile. "People used to bring them in and ask us to put them down. For all sorts of reasons. They were moving house, having babies, changing jobs. It used to break my heart." She sipped her coffee and looked at him. "Am I being boring?"

"Not at all, I'm interested."

So she carried on – telling him how the vets almost always became philosophical across the years. It was better for a dog to be humanely destroyed than dumped on a motorway.

"I knew that they were right, well, the logical part of me did, but I wanted to do something concrete," she went on. "When I was at the practice where I did day-release, I felt so helpless about all those unwanted animals. I set up a mini-rescue scheme there, but I used to dream about having a place like this. Then, when I lost Mum, well, I thought it was a good time. I had the money from Arleston Court and I wanted to do something with it. Something all-consuming. Something that would help me get over her death."

She glanced at him. "I got dumped by my boyfriend, too. He was a couple of years older than me – he was a vet at the practice in Bristol. We used to work together – but what I didn't realise was that he didn't restrict himself to one woman at a time. He had three of us on the go."

"Tosser," Finn said and she smiled at him.

"You don't approve, then? Some men would."

"I'd say that one woman at a time was more than enough trouble." His eyes were warm. "It's gone midnight, Maggie."

"I know. I suppose we'd better go up. Although I can't say I feel particularly tired." She took their mugs back out into the kitchen. When she came back he was waiting for her at the foot of the stairs.

"Would you like to come and count stars?" he said.

For a moment she just stared at him. "I'm not propositioning you, Maggie." He smiled at her. "I'm serious. I bet you've never looked out of that skylight at night, have you?"

"I don't think I've looked out of it in the daytime, either."

He started up the stairs and she followed him. On the landing by her bedroom door he glanced at her, the hint of challenge on his face, and she amazed herself by going straight past her room and following him up the rickety staircase to his. He opened the door and gestured her ahead of him, but he didn't put on the light, and she had to stand for a few seconds to let her eyes adjust.

"There's a perfect view if you lie on the bed," he said, "but to prove my intentions are honourable, you can probably see just as well if you sit on the end of it."

She giggled and sat down and he came and sat beside her, the bed dipping under his weight. They were not touching, but close.

"We should have more or less the same angle," he said, tilting his head back. "Let's see if we can beat twenty-three."

They sat in silence and Maggie began to count. At first she could only see six, but then she realised he was right, there were a lot more. Much fainter, but just discernible. She still couldn't get past sixteen, though. Disappointed, she told him, "I'm sure I could see more if I cleaned the skylight. It's got bird droppings all over it."

"I can see twenty-seven," he said, with obvious satisfaction. "Try looking harder."

They sat a bit longer. It was odd how comfortable she felt sitting on Finn's bed in the dark. She sneaked a glance at him. His head was still tilted back, his strong face in profile, but he had his eyes closed.

"You're asleep," she accused.

"No, I'm not." He opened his eyes and gave her a sideways glance. "I was just thinking how peaceful it was." He held her gaze for a few seconds, his eyes soft in the half-light. She stared back at him. It was like being on the edge of a precipice. One more step and she'd be lost. The moment stretched out and she knew he was aware of it too.

"Still not tired?" he murmured.

"No, but we've got to get up early in the morning." She felt so short of breath she could hardly speak. Dragging her gaze away from his, she said, "I'm sorry, I'm keeping you up."

"I'd be happy if you kept me up all night, Maggie." He touched her face with his fingers, the most fleeting, the most gentle of touches. "But we'd probably regret that tomorrow."

"Yes." She ached for him to touch her again, but she made herself stand up, wondering exactly what they might regret. Then he stood up too, slightly taller than her. They were still facing each other, but they weren't as close as they'd been on the bed. It was easier to get things in perspective standing up. Easier to control her breathing and the frantic thumping of her heart.

"Night, Finn." She forced herself to move across the room. When she reached the door she looked back at him. He was still standing beneath the skylight, his face in shadow so it was impossible to tell what he was thinking.

"Night, Maggie. Sweet dreams."

It was only as she closed her own bedroom door that she realised tension was tightening her muscles. Tension because she'd ached for him to touch her, or because she was terrified that he would? It was impossible to tell, she felt so weak and giddy. She undressed and got into bed, shivering slightly as the duvet touched her over-sensitised skin.

"Get a grip, Maggie," she told herself. But when she closed her eyes all she could see was his face. And she knew she'd been kidding herself thinking that it didn't matter that a huge lie stood between them. She wanted nothing between them. She wanted him totally and utterly and she thought of Sarah's words. 'I want you to be as happy as I am, Maggie'. And she thought how ironic it was that the one man she knew she could be happy with was as out of her reach as the stars.

Chapter Twenty-one

"I hear Finn's sold a painting," Gary said. "Clever bloke, isn't he?" He'd just arrived to take Fang out and caught Maggie in reception.

"News travels fast." She paused from the list she was making on her 'Things To Do' pad and glanced up at him. There were tight lines of stress around his eyes and his mouth was drawn into a thin line.

"I went into Mike's for a drink last night and he said you'd all been in together on Saturday."

"It was just me and Sarah, actually," she said, wondering why she felt the need to explain herself. "Mike asked us to call Finn because the woman who was buying his painting wanted to meet him."

"So what's she like then, this woman?" His voice was conversational, but there was a hint of something else in his eyes. Something she couldn't quite put her finger on.

"In her fifties, fairly posh. Why do you ask?"

"Mike said she was quite taken with 'The Artist'. I thought she might want to whisk him off to do some special commissions for her."

"I doubt it. She's just an ordinary tourist, Gary. She's staying in the village in a B&B with her daughter. I think the painting only caught her eye because it reminded her of her granddaughter."

He came across to the desk, sat heavily in the swivel chair opposite her and twisted it from side to side so it squeaked. "Pity."

"He's not a bad guy. I don't know why you dislike him so much."

"I don't dislike him, but I thought this was only going to be a temporary arrangement. I thought he was just working here while he looked for another job. One more suited to his many talents."

There was that edge to his voice again. It was beginning to annoy her. "Maybe he just hasn't found one yet. There's not a lot going round here."

"There was the perfect job for him in the *Farming Times*. Maintenance Engineer at Jacob's pig farm. That's what he does, isn't it – maintenance?" Gary produced a slip of paper from his pocket and pushed it across the desk towards her. "I cut it out for him. Just in case he'd missed it."

"That's nice of you, Gary," she said evenly, folding up the paper without looking at it. "I'll make sure he gets it."

His dark eyes flashed and he stood up. "There's a skittles match at The Crown and Anchor next Friday. Don't suppose you fancy coming along for a basket meal with me, do you?"

"I can't, Gary, no. Finn's dad is coming on Friday. They've asked me to go to Mike's with them in the evening for something to eat."

He didn't reply, just gave her a curt nod, and the momentary pang she felt at not inviting him along passed. Besides, she was sure he knew Finn's dad was coming on Friday. Mike would no doubt have passed that on, too.

She watched him stalk out of reception, his shoulders stiff with annoyance. Then the phone rang again and she found herself speaking to a nurse who said she'd seen Maggie's advert and was interested in re-homing Ashley. In her excitement, Maggie forgot all about Gary.

"Are you staying there all night?" Finn came into reception just as dusk was beginning to creep across the yard. "Only I was just going to lock up."

She yawned. "I've been immersed in paperwork. Time flies when you're enjoying yourself, doesn't it! Anyway, isn't Gary still here?" She glanced out of the window and answered her own question. "That's strange, he didn't say goodbye."

"I don't think he was in a very good mood," Finn said. Actually, that was the understatement of the year, but he didn't intend to tell Maggie about the little exchange they'd had earlier.

"He brought this in for you." She handed him a slip of paper and he scanned it.

"Pig farm assistant, eh?"

"Is that what it says?" She looked startled. "He told me it was a maintenance engineer job."

"His idea of a joke, I expect." Finn crunched the paper into a ball and tossed it into the wastepaper basket by the desk. "He doesn't like me very much, does he?"

"He can be a bit funny at times. He'll get over it."

Finn doubted that. Gary was besotted with Maggie. It didn't take a genius to work out that he thought Finn stood between him and the object of his affections. Some hope, he thought wryly, when she was still keeping her distance from him. It had to be because of Sarah. He was sure she had feelings for him and he could think of no other reason for her reticence. Perhaps she was waiting for him to bring up the subject, but it was a hard subject to raise. He could hardly just say, 'oh, about that one-night stand with your friend, it didn't mean anything, we were both too drunk to know what we were doing.' Well, he supposed he could, but it wouldn't be very tactful. Maggie and Sarah were close. He didn't want to say anything that would put Sarah in a bad light. And the only other way to do it was to say he'd taken advantage of her – which would be worse. It was a Catch-22 situation.

"So are you looking for another job, then?" She was watching him, her dark eyes serious.

"Why? Had enough of me?"

"No. No, of course not." She smiled and his stomach twisted. Why was it so difficult to just walk across the room and tell her that he really cared about her? He'd never been so hesitant with a woman before. But then he'd never cared so much before about the possibility of being rejected.

"I keep an eye on the papers, but there isn't a lot around. You'll say though, won't you, if it gets tricky to pay me?"

"I think I can afford you for another couple of months," she said lightly.

They went into the cottage and Finn found himself checking over his shoulder, just in case Gary had decided to make a re-appearance. Crazy, he knew, but then there'd been craziness in the guy's eyes earlier when he'd cornered him up at the kennels.

"Think you've got your feet right under the table now, don't you, mate?" had been his opening sentence.

"I'm not with you," Finn said, playing for time.

"Maggie's not interested in you, you know. So don't start getting any ideas."

Finn had met Gary's furious eyes with a calmness he didn't feel. "Look, whatever problem you've got, it's in your own head. I work for her. That's it. Not that it's got anything to do with you."

"You think you've got a right cushy number, don't you?" Gary had been almost dancing around in his anger. "You might share the same house, but you'll never get any further than that with her. Not while I'm around. Got it?"

If it had come to a fight, Finn had no doubt that he could handle Gary, but he knew that flattening him in the middle of the animal sanctuary, however tempting, wasn't the answer. Maggie was not going to be impressed if she had to scrape her vet off the concrete yard and he didn't fancy getting sacked over Gary. With a huge effort of will, he'd turned away from the almost palpable anger in the other man's face.

"I'm not interested. So just leave it, will you."

Eventually his words had seemed to sink in and Gary had stalked away towards the kennels. It could have been nasty, though, he thought now. And he couldn't see the situation improving. Not while Gary was still pursuing Maggie.

"You look miles away." Maggie's voice interrupted his thoughts. "Did you have anything to eat earlier, or would you like some tea? I've got some quiche if you fancy it."

"No, I'm all right, thanks. I grabbed a sandwich earlier. Think I might just finish that painting I started."

"The one of the magpies?"

"Yeah. All right if I shower first?"

"Feel free." She was frowning now. "Did Gary say anything to you earlier?"

"Not much. See you in the morning."

Maggie spent the days prior to Albert's visit cleaning the cottage from top to bottom.

"There's really no need," Finn told her when he caught her on her knees, scrubbing out the kitchen cupboards at eleven thirty one night. "He'll take us as he finds us."

"I don't want him to think you're living with a complete slob," she said, smiling at him. "Anyway, you're just as bad. I've hardly seen you this week, there can't be anything else that needs doing outside."

186

"I've been painting. The light's perfect in the evenings at the moment and Mike wants me to fill the space on his wall."

"What about all those little signs you've been putting up everywhere? I notice you've renamed the quarantine block, New Arrivals."

"It's so Dad can find his way around. He hasn't got a very good sense of direction."

Maggie looked puzzled, but Finn didn't tell her the real reason he'd been carving and painting the wooden signs was because it kept him outside for longer hours. If he were out of Maggie's way he wouldn't be tempted to touch her. As soon as Albert's visit was over, he decided he would sit her down and talk to her about Sarah. Then he would tell her how he felt about her and if she threw it back in his face, well, he'd have to deal with it. It had to be better than carrying on like this. Being so close to her and yet so far away – it was agonising.

Chapter Twenty-two

The day before Albert's visit, the nurse who was interested in re-homing Ashley came to see him. Maggie didn't know what she'd expected, but it wasn't the stunningly attractive girl who came rather uncertainly into reception and introduced herself as Jane Turner. She had long, coppery-gold hair and intense dark eyes and she was younger than she'd sounded on the phone. She looked as though she'd be more at home on a catwalk than a hospital ward, Maggie decided, feeling dowdy in comparison. She found herself hoping, somewhat irrationally, that Finn wouldn't materialise while they were talking.

Jane was wearing jodhpurs and she was carrying a riding hat and obviously expected to ride Ashley, which threw Maggie a bit because the horse was still in his field. She'd groomed him, first thing, but she hadn't thought to bring him in.

"How come Ashley ended up in an animal sanctuary?" Jane asked, as they walked up to see him.

Maggie hesitated. Jane was a nurse, for goodness sake, so why did she suddenly feel embarrassed at bringing up the subject of Ashley's overdeveloped sex drive?

She was saved from having to answer straight away by Jane's exclamation of delight. "Oh, wow, is that him?"

They'd reached the paddock and Ashley, spotting the bearer of Polo mints and other such interesting treats, pricked his ears and came trotting across to greet them. His summer coat was coming through and it gleamed chestnut in the morning sunshine. He looked the picture of health, his head and tail high, as he wheeled to a halt by the gate. Compared with the other horses in the paddock he looked a prince, Maggie thought, with a little rush of pride.

"Yes, this is Ashley." She stroked the horse's nose and fed him a Polo.

Jane patted his neck, her face animated. "He's very handsome. I never expected him to look like this. How high is he? He's obviously easy to catch."

"About fifteen two, I think. And yes, he's never been a problem that way."

"But he is a problem in other ways?" Jane's voice was doubtful as she picked up on Maggie's tension. "Does he buck or something? I don't want to take on a dangerous horse."

"He's not dangerous," Maggie rushed on, annoyed with herself. She was going to blow this if she didn't get her act together. "He's just..." Why on earth couldn't she bring herself to say the words? She could see Finn heading towards them. God, she was going to have to say something before he reached them.

"He's rather fonder of the ladies than he should be. Actually, well, to put it bluntly, he's a bit of a sex maniac."

"He's a sex maniac!" Jane repeated loudly and Maggie realised, with intense embarrassment, that she'd followed her gaze and was looking at Finn as she spoke. "Haven't you had him gelded, then?"

"Sounds like an interesting conversation," Finn said, shooting a sideways look at Maggie. "She'd have everything neutered round here if she had the chance." He grinned at Jane and added, "But I haven't let her catch me yet."

Maggie glared at him. "Did you want anything in particular, Finn?"

"I was just going into town for bits and pieces. Need anything picking up? I hear they've got some DIY gelding kits on special offer. I could get probably get discount on a bulk buy."

189

"No, we don't need anything. Thank you."

Finn, completely unfazed by the sharpness of her voice, just nodded. Then, with another grin at Jane, he loped off down the yard.

Maggie turned back to Jane, who was looking puzzled at this exchange. "He's got a strange sense of humour," she explained. "Anyway, as I was saying, Ashley's here because he embarrassed his previous owner by – er – mounting a mare in the show ring. Unfortunately the mare already had a little girl on her back."

Jane clapped a hand over her mouth, her eyes widening.

That's it, Maggie thought. She's never going to go for him, now. But, to her surprise, Jane seemed more amused than anything else.

"Is it all right for me to have a ride on him? Or perhaps I should rephrase that?" She giggled and Maggie found herself warming to her.

"I'll nip and get his tack for you. It's in the house."

Finn was getting into his car as she passed. He winked at her and drove off before she could say anything.

Twenty minutes later, Maggie leaned on the fence and watched Jane trot Ashley round the field. He tossed his head and high-stepped and generally looked very full of himself, which wasn't surprising, Maggie thought, as no one had ridden him since he'd been here. She'd meant to take him out herself, but she never had time to do much that wasn't essential and she'd also worried in case she'd fallen off and hurt herself. She couldn't afford to be injured.

Jane could ride, though, she observed, pleased. She looked good on him, her auburn hair streaming in the sunshine, her back very straight.

Rowena, who was grazing with Conker and Sparky on the other side of the field, lifted her head to watch and Maggie started to feel optimistic. It would be such a relief if Jane took Ashley on. She wondered if she should mention his escapist tendencies. Perhaps not. It wasn't as if he'd jumped out of the field lately, or undone any bolts, but then he hadn't had any reason to.

Jane trotted the horse over to the fence where Maggie stood. "He's lovely," she said, when she'd got her breath back. "Just what I'm looking for. I've always wanted a horse, but I never thought I'd be able to afford one."

"They're not cheap to keep," Maggie cautioned.

"I know, but I'm lucky there. My Uncle Arthur owns Willett's stud farm on the other side of Salisbury. It's where I'm planning to keep Ashley. That shouldn't be a problem, should it? It's not as though he's going to be able to get in with any mares."

Maggie looked up into her enthusiastic face and her conscience got the better of her. "Ah," she said. "I'm afraid that might be more of a problem than you think."

Gary arrived just as Jane and Maggie were carrying Ashley's tack back towards the cottage. Maggie felt herself tensing as he parked the van, but all he did was give her a cursory nod and go into reception.

He was sitting in a chair when she went back in with Jane.

"I've just brought in a couple of invoices. Is there any particular reason why your post box is taped up?"

"There's a pair of great tits nesting in it, I didn't like to turf them out."

Gary shook his head in mock exasperation, but he didn't smile and Maggie had a horrible feeling he was going to have another go at her about Finn.

"Jane's thinking of having Ashley," she said, deciding that at least he'd be pleased about that. "We've just been chatting about his problems."

"Yes, it's a shame because I really like him." Jane smiled her friendly, open smile at Gary. "But I'm going to have to rethink my stabling arrangements. I was going to keep him at Willett's stud farm, you see, but in view of his, er – tendencies, Maggie thinks that wouldn't be a good idea."

"It'd be torture for the poor sod." Gary gave Maggie a pointed look. "I'd go so far as to say, cruel."

Maggie flushed and wondered if Jane was aware of the atmosphere, but she didn't seem to be. She turned back to Maggie, her eyes warm. "I'll have to try and find some cheap alternative stabling. I'll be in touch – and I'll pay for that test to be done. Like we discussed. Perhaps you could give me a ring once it's organised."

"Of course." They shook hands and Jane nodded at Gary and went out into the yard. Maggie watched her through the window.

"Pity about that," she said to Gary. "She'd have been ideal."

"You'd better keep your fingers crossed that something can be done about his urges, then," he remarked, giving her another black look. "Is it all right if I nip up and see Fang?"

Maggie nodded. It was on the tip of her tongue to say something, but Finn would be back any minute. There was no way she could start a 'clearing the air' conversation if there was a risk of him walking in on them. She took the invoices from him. Their talk would have to wait. With a bit of luck, in another week or two it might not even be necessary. And if it was, then she was going to have to seriously think about getting another vet.

She told Finn about Jane's stabling problem later that night as she washed up the plates from their tea. "It's such a shame," she said, frowning. "It was going so well. Although I could have done without your smart remarks about DIY gelding kits."

He picked up a tea towel and grinned at her. "Touch a nerve, did I?"

"No, you did not touch a nerve."

"You mean you don't want to neuter all the males in the vicinity? How about Gary?" His grey eyes challenged hers.

Was he insinuating that she'd led Gary on? She was already regretting that she'd ever gone out for that meal.

"Why don't you mind your own business?" she said, more abruptly than she'd meant to.

He put the tea-towel down and raised his hands in self-defence. "Oooh, I have touched a nerve, haven't I?"

"Don't be ridiculous." Forcing indifference into her voice, she met his eyes and hoped he wouldn't be able to read her expression and see how close he was to the mark. Though it wasn't Gary she was wary of. She was sorry he'd read more into their friendship than there was. But time would sort things out between them.

Finn, however, was a different matter. He unnerved her. Made her feel as though she could break apart under his gaze. Especially the way he was looking at her now. Half quizzical, half knowing. Sarah had a lot to answer for, she thought, blinking and turning away from him to study a damp patch on the wall just above the kettle.

It was a huge effort to keep her voice casual. "I'm just disappointed that Jane's not taking Ashley. They'd have been good for each other. I feel as though I've failed him."

"You haven't failed him." Finn's tone changed completely and he came across the kitchen. "No one could work harder than you do, Maggie. You go well beyond the call of duty for this lot. At the risk of you telling me to mind my own business again, I'd like to recommend that now and again you spare a thought for yourself. There's a world out there, you know."

She looked at him. His eyes were soft. All traces of mockery had gone from his face now and she felt choked.

"I'll bear that in mind," she said and fled before he could take advantage of her shattered defences.

The following morning Maggie walked round the sanctuary, checking that all was as it should be. Finn had left half an hour ago to pick up his father from the coach drop-off point. They'd be back soon. At least the sun was out, she thought with relief. Everything looked better when it was sunny. Diesel was lying on top of the chicken run, eyes closed, the tip of his black tail flicking.

"Monster," she said, as she passed, and he blinked sleepy golden eyes at her.

Satisfied that all was as it should be, Maggie headed back towards reception. She planned to close the sanctuary up as soon as Finn's dad arrived. Anyone with a dire emergency could park outside the cottage and ring the bell.

She was just writing a note to put on the front gate when Finn's car drew into the yard. White hair and a tweedy jacket were Maggie's first impressions of his father. She waited while Finn switched off the engine and went round to open the passenger door, and then she went into the yard to greet them.

194

"So this is that slave driver boss of yours. Albert McTaggart at your service," the old man said, as Finn introduced them.

Maggie added a gravelly voice, a firm handshake and a direct gaze to her first impressions. "Slave driver, eh? Is that what he's told you?"

White eyebrows arched above grey eyes that were very similar to Finn's, and to Ben's, and Maggie was struck, once more, with the painful realisation that it wasn't just Finn she was deceiving.

Albert pumped her hand. Deep lines etched his face and he was older than she'd expected.

For a moment he looked quite stern and then his face cracked into a smile. "It's grand to meet you at last, my dear. Hope he's not been causing you too much trouble."

"None I can't handle." She glanced at Finn as she spoke, aware of his amusement. "Well, would you like coffee before you start your grand tour?"

"I'd like a rollie," Albert said "But I don't suppose that's allowed with all the straw an' stuff round here, is it?"

"You can smoke in there if you like." Maggie indicated reception. "Or in the cottage if you open the windows. I don't mind."

"Don't encourage him," Finn said. "I've told him this is a strictly smoke-free zone."

The phone rang and Maggie apologised. "You'll have to excuse me a minute. I'll put the answer machine on and then I'll catch up with you."

By the time she'd dealt with the phone, locked up the main gate and got into the cottage, they were installed in her lounge, talking animatedly. Albert had obviously thought better of smoking, despite the fact that Finn had produced an ashtray from somewhere and opened all the windows that weren't painted shut.

"So, did you have a good journey?" She sat next to Finn on the settee and addressed his dad, who was in the armchair opposite. "How long did it take?"

"Not bad and too long." Albert winked at her. "But that's coaches for you. At least they've got conveniences on them these days."

"And coffee, Dad. You said that was quite good."

"Aye, I suppose it wasn't bad. Not as good as yours, though. Or maybe it's the company." He shot a glance at his son and Maggie was struck by the pride on his face. Struck too, by the warmth in Finn's eyes. Neither of them were the type for big declarations of emotion, she thought, but there was a lot of love there.

She smiled at both of them. "So, what are your plans for today?"

"First of all I'm going to go and pick out the dog I'd most like to take home," Albert said. "Not that they're allowed on coaches, I shouldn't think. And then…" He was overtaken by a fit of coughing that seemed to rack his whole body. It was painful to listen to and when he finally stopped, Finn said, "That's why he shouldn't be smoking." There was a mixture of crossness and sadness in his voice.

"Stop fussing, lad. And then, I'm going to check out Finn's local – see if they've got any decent paintings on the walls." He winked at Maggie. "After that, we're going for a little drive around."

"And tonight we're all going to Mike's," Finn added. "You are still joining us, I take it?"

"I'm looking forward to it. Now, how about I show you around?"

As they went past the locked reception Maggie heard Finn say, "That flu took a while to get over. What did Doctor Jenkins say about it?"

"Not much," Albert muttered. "Seeing as I didn't tell him I had it. What's the point? Can't do 'owt, can they?"

Maggie was following a couple of steps behind them, feeling a little surplus to requirements, when Albert suddenly turned. "Now then, young lady, when does the grand tour begin?" He raised his eyebrows. "I want to know all the ins and outs of the place."

He wasn't joking either, she realised, as they went round the sanctuary. At the hospital block he wanted to know all the details of the animals that had recently been treated there. Maggie told him about the buzzard with the broken wing, about Candy's pups and about the cat with an injured paw someone had brought in the previous week.

Then he wanted to know all about the current residents of the cattery and how come that black beggar had escaped and was sitting on the chicken run, looking like he owned the place.

"Diesel," Finn explained, repeating the story of how the big black cat had had much of his fur burnt off when he'd been trapped under the bonnet of a diesel car.

And why did they have chickens anyway? What did they need rescuing from?

"They're ex-battery hens," Maggie said. "They don't have very long lives in battery farms. It's too intensive and as soon as egg production goes down, they're for the chop. But once they get back to something resembling a normal life, they start laying again. We sell the eggs to raise funds."

Eventually they went up towards the kennels, stopping short of the gate that led to the first two kennel blocks.

"Once we go in here we won't be able to hear ourselves think, let alone speak," Maggie told Albert. "So I'll tell you about the dogs out here, then you can have a wander round. I'll sit in the sun and wait for you."

They weren't gone long, five minutes or so, and Maggie sat at the wooden picnic bench, with her face turned up to the sun, and felt very relaxed. Two magpies had just flown into the tree in the field next door. Two for joy, she thought, remembering the old rhyme. A good omen for today.

Then the gate clanged and Finn called, "Is it all right if I take Dad up to New Arrivals? He wants to see Fang."

"You carry on. You can take her out if you like. She doesn't normally get a walk at this time of day."

Albert and Finn reappeared with Fang on a lead. The small dog was wagging her stubby tail and looking very pleased with herself.

"Gary's done wonders with that dog," Maggie called out to them. "A couple of months ago and she'd have had your hand off. Mind you, I still wouldn't trust her with a child."

"Would you trust her with an old man?" Albert asked. "She's my type of dog, she is." He bent to fondle the Jack Russell's head and she pricked her ears.

Finn came across to where she sat and put his hand on Maggie's arm. A casual little gesture, but as she glanced at his fingers she was reminded of the night when she'd held them and asked him if he'd inherited them from his father.

He smiled at her. "Dad could have a dog, you know. He's got a lovely little garden. And no cats for her to terrorise. She'd have a nice life with him."

Maggie smiled up at him. He'd had his hair cut for his father's visit and his face was tanned from being outside and she was very aware of his touch.

198

"Well, she's up for re-homing like all the rest of them," she murmured. "Why doesn't he take her for a walk round the field? See how he gets on."

Chapter Twenty-three

Gary frowned as he parked outside the cottage, read Maggie's note and unbolted the side gate. He was sure Maggie had said they were going out this evening, not out to lunch. She never closed the place up in the day. What if there was an emergency?

Then something else struck him. She'd been offish with him all week. Perhaps she'd just said they were going out this evening so she didn't have to go out with him. He wandered up the yard, opened the little gate that led to the upper part of the sanctuary, and froze.

Ahead of him by the picnic table an old guy, presumably Finn's father, was bending down and petting Fang. The little Jack Russell, far from snapping and growling, had rolled over on to her back and appeared to be enjoying the attention. For weeks, Gary had been the only one allowed near her, yet, as soon as his back was turned, Maggie had let some unqualified bystander take her out without so much as a by-your-leave.

Maggie was sitting at the table and Finn stood just beside her, one hand on her arm. She was looking up into his eyes and smiling that beautiful smile. Jealousy so sharp it was a physical pain cramped Gary's abdomen and he could feel a pulse beating in his head. He clenched his fists into balls. Finn had been sniffing around Maggie ever since he'd arrived and not content with stealing her, he was after the little dog too. Something snapped inside Gary's head and he stormed up the yard towards the group. It was high time Finn got what was coming to him.

Maggie was the first to notice Gary heading towards them. Even before he reached them she could tell from his body language that he was furious, although she didn't have a clue why. She stood up uneasily, aware that at the same moment Finn had taken a step back from the table. "Hi, Gary. How's it going?"

But if he heard her he didn't react. He just marched straight up to Finn and threw a punch at him.

Finn, who'd sensed what was about to happen just before it did, dodged. He didn't get the full fury of Gary's fist, which was just as well or it would probably have broken his nose, but the blow still knocked him off balance.

"Good God." Albert, reacting more quickly than any of them, dashed to his son's side, elbowing Gary to one side in the process. "Are you all right, lad?"

"What the hell do you think you're doing?" Maggie yelled at Gary at more or less the same moment. "Have you gone completely mad?"

Gary stood blinking in the sunlight, as if he wasn't quite aware of what he had just done. On his right, Finn held a hand to his bloody nose and straightened up slowly.

"Well, let's hope that's finally got it out of your system," he said, his voice icy.

Maggie could feel herself trembling. "I think you'd better leave, Gary. Before Finn takes it into his head to press charges. Or I do."

Gary looked at her, confusion in his eyes. "But what about Fang?"

"You've scared the life out of her." Maggie crouched down and held out her hand to the little dog, who was hiding beneath the picnic table, her whole body trembling violently. "Get out of my sanctuary, Gary. Before I call the police and have you thrown out."

He turned, his shoulders round with defeat, and retraced his steps slowly down the yard.

For a few seconds no one spoke and then Finn said quietly, "I think that if he's definitely gone, I'll just go and clean this up before I bleed all over my clean tee-shirt."

"I'll come with you and make sure." Maggie glanced apologetically at Albert. "I'm so sorry about that. He's normally such a mild-tempered chap. I'll be back in two minutes." She went with Finn down the yard. "Are you okay?"

"I'll survive." He gave her a wry smile. "It's just a pity he had to pick today to stake his claim."

"What claim? What are you talking about?" Maggie went across to the main gate and saw to her relief that the van was gone. Finn didn't say anything else until they were standing inside the front door of the cottage.

"What all that was about," he said looking at her, "is that Gary is in love with you. And he thinks I'm the reason you don't return his affections."

She stared at him, confused. "But you're not. I mean, we've never even – well…"

"It's not about us." Finn's voice was unusually sharp. "It's what's inside Gary's head that counts." He frowned and touched his face. "Can I borrow your first-aid box? I think I'll sort this out in the bathroom. Come up a minute."

"What about your dad?"

"He'll be fine. I expect he's having a sneaky rollie to calm his nerves."

Upstairs, she sat on the edge of the bath while Finn sponged the blood off his nose. There was a small cut just above his lip.

"Does that hurt?"

"Yes, it does a bit." He met her eyes in the mirror. "But not half as much as it would have if I hadn't ducked at the last minute."

"I'm really sorry. I mean, I know he had a bit of a crush, but I'd no idea he was going to get violent about it. Or take it out on you."

"It's not your fault. He's been getting crosser and crosser for a while. He had a go at me the other day when he brought the advert for that pig-farming job in. Perhaps I should have mentioned it, but I honestly didn't think it would come to this."

"What did he say?"

"He warned me off you. That was about it. I certainly didn't wind him up. At least I don't think I did." He dabbed at the cut. "Mind you, having Fang out probably didn't help. His dog and his woman. He just exploded, didn't he?"

She nodded, clenching her hands in her lap. "What do you think I should do? About him hitting you, I mean. I can't let him think he's got away with it."

"I don't think you should do anything. He's not going to do it again, is he? I think he shocked himself as much as he shocked us. I'd be willing to bet that he's already regretting it." He sat beside her on the edge of the bath. "Don't upset yourself over Gary. I'm not. I just wish he hadn't done it in front of Dad."

She reached out and touched his face just above the cut. "That won't do much for your love life, will it?"

"You don't think so?" There was a softness in his eyes that belied the facetiousness of his voice. Then he caught her hand and kissed the tips of her fingers very gently. She looked at him, trembling slightly.

"Are you cold? Or just shocked?" Letting go of her fingers, he cupped her face in his hands and kissed her mouth and she found she was trembling again, not for either of the reasons he'd suggested, but because she was filled with a sudden, desperate longing for him. She kissed him back, scared of hurting his mouth, but never wanting it to stop. At some point, as if by tacit agreement, they stood up, but even when they finally drew apart they were still holding hands.

"Seems to have done wonders for my love life," Finn remarked. "Maybe I should get myself thumped more often."

"We're steaming up the mirror," Maggie whispered, looking up into his grey eyes, half enjoying the frantic flutterings inside her and half afraid of them.

"You're such a romantic."

"Do you think we'd better go downstairs?"

"I can think of lots of things I'd much rather be doing, but yes, I think we'd better." He searched her face. "I wanted to do that the other night. You did too, didn't you?"

She hesitated, battling with the urge to tell him he was right and inwardly cursing Sarah because she couldn't let this go further. If she told him how she felt she'd have no excuse to keep the distance between them. Finn could crash through her barriers and she wouldn't be able to stop him.

"Are you two all right up there?" Albert's voice came up the stairs. "Only I reckon we should all go and have a stiff drink. Good for shock. And the pubs'll be closed if we don't get our skates on."

Finn smiled at Maggie. "He never misses a trick."

"No." She pulled her hand from his, rubbed a patch in the mirror and glanced at her flushed face. "Can we talk about this later?"

"Sure. You go down." He indicated the first aid-box still open on the loo seat. "I'll just clear up and I'll be with you."

Half an hour later they were at a table in the Red Lion.

"Are you sure you don't mind me gate-crashing your lunch?" Maggie asked Albert again. Lunching at the Red Lion hadn't been a part of the day's plan and she could hardly believe they were sitting here, but then the whole day was beginning to take on an unreal quality.

"Course not, lassie." He'd lit a rollie as soon as they'd arrived and was now making another. "I figured you might want to get away for a bit in case that maniac turned up again. What'll you do, Finn?"

"I'm not going to do anything. I'm sure it was a one-off." Finn waved a curl of smoke away from Maggie's face. "Gary's not normally prone to violent mood swings. He must have had a bad morning. He's Maggie's vet, Dad."

"Is he now?" Albert puffed thoughtfully. "Not a very James Herriot thing to do, is it? Going around punching your customers. He could probably get struck off for that, couldn't he?"

"I'm not sure if vets do get struck off, as such," Maggie said, frowning.

"Well, I certainly won't be complaining," Finn said. "Least said, soonest mended, I'd say."

"Yeah, you're probably right. And there was me thinking the countryside was a nice, peaceful place where nothing ever happened. Still, there's nothing like a bit of excitement to work up an appetite. Now then, what are you two having to eat?"

Maggie glanced at Finn. He was smiling, but he looked awfully tense. She wondered if he was regretting kissing her. And what had he meant about wanting to do it the other night? She'd wanted to do a lot more than kiss him on the night they'd counted stars. She'd wanted him to take her to bed. She'd ached to feel his body pressed against hers. She still did. But the image of him with Sarah haunted her. And what if they did go to bed? Wouldn't that just make things worse? While she kept the distance between them, the fact that she was keeping Sarah's secret

205

didn't seem so traitorous. She wasn't sure if she could sleep with him and still lie to him. She sighed, and then aware that Albert was waiting for her to order, she fixed on her professional smile and turned her attention to the menu.

Chapter Twenty-four

Gary drove away from the sanctuary, his head throbbing. There was no way he could go back to the practice. They'd have to cancel the rest of the afternoon's calls. He dialled the number on his mobile, his hands shaking so much that it took four attempts. Then he headed towards home. He pulled up in his driveway, switched off the ignition and put his head in his hands. What the hell had he done? He wasn't aware of the tapping on the driver's window until it became a frantic knocking.

"Mr Collins. Excuse me. Are you all right there?"

Emily, his next-door neighbour, he realised with a start. He unwound the window.

"I took a parcel in for you, this morning," she said, her face wrinkling up into a frown. "It was too big to go through your letter box. Are you all right? You don't look very well."

Gary got out of the van. He was about to say that he was fine, but somehow the concern in her face made him feel even worse. He stood swaying in his driveway.

Emily put a hand on his arm. "You're not all right, are you?" Her voice softened. "Come on now. Come and sit in my kitchen and I'll make you a nice cup of tea and you can tell me what's happened. Was it a bad case you've been to?"

He didn't have the energy to argue so he followed her through her blue-painted front door into a hallway that smelt of lavender furniture polish. Despite being well past seventy, she trotted ahead of him and pushed open the kitchen door.

"Now, sit yourself down," she bossed, indicating a stool alongside a modern breakfast bar.

Her kitchen wasn't what he expected. It wasn't an old lady's kitchen at all, but a modern affair, with yellow sunflower wallpaper, wooden cupboard doors and a top-of-the-range dishwasher and microwave. On the breakfast bar was a flat white parcel with his name on it.

"There you are." She put a mug of tea beside him and nudged the sugar bowl across. "Your colour's coming back now. You looked right poorly out there for a minute."

Gary smiled, despite himself. Emily reminded him of his own gran. She had the same inquisitive, chocolate-button eyes and thought tea was the answer to everything. Unlike his gran, though, who'd had short cropped white hair, which she'd said was befitting when you got to a certain age, Emily had a long grey plait, which was coiled on top of her head in a sort of bun. It must take her ages to do that, he thought, as she sat on a stool opposite him.

"What do you think of the kitchen, then? Jane, she's my youngest granddaughter, designed it for me."

"It's very nice."

"Yes, she's got good taste. Takes after me, see. Only I wanted something modern and I wouldn't have known where to start. Are you going to open that?" She glanced at the parcel, which had a label in one corner with the name Perfect Pooches emblazoned in gold across it.

"I already know what it is. It's a designer dog collar."

"I didn't know you were getting a dog."

"I'm not. It's for one of the dogs at The Ark." Gary closed his eyes and thought: what lousy timing. The dog collar was for Fang. But she'd never see it now. He'd probably never see her again. Never see any of Maggie's animals, come to that. She was hardly going to let a half-crazed vet back on to her premises. He'd be lucky if she didn't put in an official complaint. Christ, how could he have been so bloody stupid?

"Anyway." Emily regarded him over her mug, her head on one side like a bird. "Tell me what's been happening to you this morning. Cruelty case, was it?"

He sighed. She knew what he did because of the van and once, when he'd come back from a particularly bad case, he'd confided how much he hated that part of the job.

Since then she'd taken a keen interest in what he was up to and often timed her outings to coincide with him getting into his van so she could interrogate him. To Gary's shame, he'd taken to avoiding her. Not because she wasn't a sweet old dear, but he was normally running late and didn't have time for the long, in-depth conversations she was fond of.

"I've done something really stupid," he said, sipping his tea and meeting her eyes. "I'm not sure if I can even bring myself to tell you."

"I've done plenty of stupid things in my time," she said, her eyes brightening with interest. "Nine times out of ten, we think they're a lot more stupid than anyone else does."

"Not this time." He fiddled with the sugar spoon and lowered his eyes. "I've screwed up big time. I'm in love with this woman and I've just blown any chance I ever had with her."

"It can't be all that bad." Emily's voice was gentle. "If she loves you too, you'll soon sort it out."

"That's the trouble," Gary said bleakly, putting the sugar spoon down with a small clink on the breakfast bar. "I don't think she's ever seen me as anything other than her vet. And after this morning, I'll be lucky if she ever speaks to me again."

"The best thing you can do is to go round there and tell her you're desperately sorry," Emily said after Gary had

209

poured out the whole story to her. "Explain that you'd had a bad day, a moment of temporary insanity – whatever. If she's half the woman you say she is, I think she'll forgive you. Maybe not straight away, but in time."

"Should I take flowers?"

"No, I don't think you should, love. Just take yourself and convince her you mean it. And don't forget to apologise to the lodger, too. However much you dislike him. The sooner the better."

Gary thought about this conversation all afternoon. Emily was right. It wasn't just his professional reputation that was on the line, although that was reason enough to go back as soon as possible, it was his friendship with Maggie. In every quiet moment he could hear her voice shouting, "Have you gone completely mad?" Every time he closed his eyes he could see her shocked dark eyes. And then the coldness in her face when she'd told him to get out before she called the police.

Finn had looked pretty shocked, too. In that moment, just after his fist had connected, he'd been sure Finn would hit him back. Sure he'd see his own furious anger reflected. Yet there had been no anger in the bloke's eyes, just a kind of resigned acceptance. It was that expression, as well as Maggie's horror, that was tormenting him.

It was the first time Gary had ever punched anyone. Violence sickened him. It had done ever since school when he'd been bullied by Terry Bradshaw and his gang: held face down in the mud one sunny, winter afternoon because he'd come top in English, Biology and Maths.

"Filthy little swot," Terry had snarled, tipping his books into the puddle, too, and then stamping on them for good measure.

When his mum had asked him what had happened, he'd told her and she'd gone straight to the headmaster, demanding action.

All the boys had been disciplined and after that he'd been beaten up regularly. Except that now the gang were careful where they put the bruises. Nowhere that showed. His groin or his lower back.

"Grass again and you're dead," Terry had told him one terrifying night. "And don't think we don't know how."

Gary had believed them. He'd done his best to keep his head down after that. He still worked hard, but he was careful not to come top in anything again. Academic subjects were a doddle to him. It was easy enough to put in the odd wrong answer, which would keep Terry off his back. When it came to the real thing he could just fill in the papers properly, secure in the knowledge that none of his classmates would ever know his final exam grades.

In some strange way, though, it was Terry's bullying that shaped his future career. Gary had left school with twelve GCSEs and four 'A' Levels and a burning passion to do something that would enable him to protect the vulnerable. He wasn't sure exactly what. Something in the social services possibly. He knew social workers got a bad press, but he'd be different. Idealistic and desperately shy, he'd got as far as doing the first year of the course. The academic side was a breeze, but he'd found it difficult to form relationships with the other students. He was too insular, too inward-looking, his tutors said. He should lighten up a bit. In the end Gary decided that working with people wasn't for him and left. Then a friend suggested that with his academic background he ought to try and get into veterinary college. Within a month of beginning, he knew he had found his vocation.

But now he'd been the perpetrator of exactly the sort of violence he'd always sworn to oppose. He sat at his kitchen table, which was a lot scruffier and less modern than Emily's breakfast bar, buried his head in his hands and felt sick. It was just after eight and he hadn't eaten all day. Maybe that was the cause of the hollow dizziness in his stomach. Or maybe it was as Emily had said. He wouldn't feel better until he'd put things right. He couldn't go up there now because Maggie had said they were all going to the Red Lion. On the other hand he couldn't wait until tomorrow because, if he did, he'd never get any sleep. He decided he'd have to go tonight. Later, when they were back from the pub. They wouldn't be that late. They had an early start the next day. Saturday was one of the sanctuary's busiest days.

"I don't know about you youngsters, but I think it's time I headed for bed," Albert said, draining the last of his Guinness and dropping the butt of his rollie into the ashtray. "Quite an eventful day, one way or another."

Finn glanced across at Maggie. "Are you ready?"

She nodded. She looked strained, but then she had all evening. Earlier, when he'd kissed her, she'd been soft, almost vulnerably open. Now she seemed to be deliberately blocking him out again. Was she regretting it? Or was he being over-sensitive?

He took their empty glasses to the bar and walked back to the table, rubbing his eyes. He was tired and his face was sore where Gary had hit him. Maggie stood up as he reached them. She looked a bit lost and he had an urge to put his arm around her, tell her that everything was going to be fine. Maybe when Albert had gone to bed, they'd get the chance to talk. Really talk this time. He'd put off this conversation for long enough.

They walked in silence for the first part of the journey back. There was none of the easiness they'd shared the last time they'd walked home. There were no stars tonight either; clouds covered the sky and the air felt hot and oppressive.

"How's your face?" Maggie asked him.

"Fine now."

"I still think you should report the maniac to the police," Albert muttered gruffly.

The lights of the cottage came into view as they reached the final stretch of the lane. What had gone wrong? Maggie thought. How could he be so gentle and warm one moment and so distant the next? Maybe it was because Albert was with them. Maybe this was some sort of macho pretence that he was okay for his father's benefit.

She wondered what would happen when they got back. Would they just go in this awful, stiff silence to their respective rooms? It was probably best if they did. It was obvious that Finn was finding the prospect of talking to her a huge ordeal, which, she decided, meant he was regretting kissing her earlier. Tonight, she'd touched his arm and he'd jumped away as though he'd been stung. She didn't need him to spell things out.

As they reached the hedge that surrounded the cottage, a shadow detached itself and materialised into a figure and Maggie, already edgy, jumped out of her skin.

"Gary!"

She heard Albert's sharp intake of breath and she could feel Finn's sudden tension beside her. "What are you doing here?"

Gary raised both hands, palms facing them. "It's okay. I'm not here to cause trouble. I've come to apologise." He hesitated, his face shadowy in the moonless night. "To all of you. I'm so very sorry about earlier. I just wanted you to know."

Maggie didn't reply. She glanced at Finn, who'd gone very still as soon as Gary had stepped out in front of them. Now, he cleared his throat, but he didn't say anything. There was tension in his shoulders, though, and she noticed he was keeping his distance from Gary, as if he was worried the vet might suddenly change his tune.

"That's all I came to say," Gary went on quietly. "I won't hold you up. I just wanted you to know how sorry I was. I couldn't have slept otherwise. Of course I appreciate that you'll be employing another vet. If you still want to use the practice, I'll make sure someone else responds to your calls."

He looked diminished and Maggie stepped forward so that she was facing him. "It's all right," she said, looking into his dark, troubled eyes. "We know it was out of character. I'm glad you came. We both are." Half turning, she included Finn in the conversation and he gave the slightest of nods.

"Perhaps it would be best if you didn't come to the sanctuary for a while, though," she said, hating to kick him when he was down, but knowing she owed that much at least to Finn.

"Of course. Good night." He took a few steps away, and then, as if suddenly remembering something, he hesitated. "I hope you don't mind, but I got this for Fang."

He thrust a package into her hands and then turned and went to his van, which was parked out of sight, just beyond the entrance to The Ark. Only when she'd watched his taillights disappear around the bend in the road did Maggie feel herself relax.

"You okay?" Finn was standing behind her.

"Yes. You?" She turned to look at him, but once again his eyes were unreadable.

"I'm glad I don't have to keep looking over my shoulder any more. Come on, let's go in."

"Did you still want to have that talk later?" Finn asked, once Albert had headed, yawning, for bed.

"No, I'm too tired," she said quietly. "Like you said earlier, least said, soonest mended."

"I was talking about Gary."

"Goodnight, Finn," she said, without looking at him. "And thanks for the meal, I enjoyed tonight."

He murmured something unintelligible and slammed the lounge door, and it took every bit of self-control she had not to race after him.

Chapter Twenty-five

Finn came into reception one morning looking worried. Maggie steeled herself. Finn hardly ever looked worried, but there had been an awkwardness between them since Albert's visit.

"I've just been talking to Dad on the phone."

He had a piece of paper in his hand. He must be going to hand in his notice, show her the details of some new exciting job. "Yes," she said, a lot more tersely than she'd intended. "Is he all right?"

"He's fine, Maggie. Thanks for asking." There was surprise in his voice and she felt a little stab. Had they got so far apart that he thought she didn't care?

He smoothed out the paper, which was creased, as though it had previously been screwed up. It looked innocuous enough. There was a phone number scrawled on it with a code she didn't recognise. Finn retrieved another piece of paper from the pocket of his jeans and unfolded it so she could see. "I wasn't going to show you, but the interfering old bugger said if I didn't mention it he'd phone you himself."

It was a news item about three donkeys that had been abandoned on Skegness Beach. They were being looked after by a local woman, who was appealing for someone to re-home them by the end of the week because she didn't have the space or money to keep them for longer. The newspaper was asking for information that might lead to tracing the donkeys' former owner, but so far no one had come forward.

"I'm not surprised," Maggie said, looking at the picture of the donkeys. "They're not exactly in tip-top condition, are they? The RSPCA would probably prosecute."

"Dad saw it in a free newspaper when he went to visit a mate at Skeggy. He's got it into his head that you might want to bring them here." Finn sounded apologetic. "Like you haven't got enough to do without trekking up there and getting yourself another load of trouble."

"Donkeys aren't much trouble," she said, reading through the report and feeling her insides turning over. "Poor loves. Sound like they've had a hard time of it."

"Going up to get them would be a fair bit of trouble," Finn said, quietly reasonable. "Especially as you haven't got a horse box."

"I could hire one."

"That's an expense you could do without."

"It's the reason I do fund-raising, so I can do things like that."

"There's a time limit," Finn pointed out. "And who's going to look after the sanctuary if you go gallivanting off on a donkey rescue at the other end of the country?"

"Sarah and Jack would probably do it if I asked them. And Dawn would help out, I'm sure."

"It's going to take you longer than a couple of hours to drive up to Skegness."

Maggie sighed. His quiet logic was gradually overriding the impulse she had to go up there now, this minute, but he was right. It would take some organising. Thinking quickly, she said, "I'll phone Sarah. I'm sure she'll say yes. If I went up in the evening, I'd only be away for a day and a half."

Finn sighed and Maggie felt touched, knowing he was only trying to protect her. So perhaps he did still care a bit. "It's what we're here for, Finn," she murmured.

"It's a bloody long trek there and back in a day."

"I won't do it in one day." She was determined not to be deflected now she'd made up her mind. "I'll book into one of those travel lodge places the night before. That'll be cheap enough. Then I can pick up the donkeys in the morning and drive them back here."

"A small hotel would be cheaper and probably nicer. There'll be plenty of room this time of year. I'll come with you. I can drive. It's the least I can do, seeing as it's my fault that you've got to go in the first place." He smiled at her. "Don't worry, I'll pay for my room."

In the end Maggie agreed because sharing the driving was sensible. And the prospect of spending some time away from the sanctuary with Finn was appealing. Maybe, once they were away, she could get a different perspective on the situation. Maybe she'd even realise she didn't like him so much, after all.

A week later it was arranged. Maggie had talked to the woman who was looking after the donkeys. "She's got them in her back garden," she said to Sarah, shaking her head. "Are you sure you don't mind looking after this place?"

"Of course we don't," Sarah said. She'd agreed instantly once she'd known Finn wasn't going to be around. "It's the least I can do and Ben's in his element."

They left mid-afternoon on Tuesday, having given Sarah a long list of instructions.

"Just get going or you'll hit the rush hour at Newbury. I'll phone you if there's the slightest problem."

It was strange driving away from the sanctuary. Maggie hadn't left it for more than a few hours since the day she'd opened it. This is how it must feel if you were a new mother leaving your baby with someone else for the very first time, she thought idly. It was strange being alone with Finn, too. She sneaked a glance at him. He looked very at home driving the horsebox and she found herself

218

wondering if there was any situation he wouldn't look at home in.

"What?" he said.

"Pity we haven't got time to pop in and see your dad."

"If he'd have kept quiet you wouldn't be having to drive two hundred and fifty miles to pick up another load of expense and hassle," Finn grumbled.

"I'm not driving, you are. And anyway I don't look upon them as a load of expense and hassle. Poor loves."

He shot her a look of exasperation and then shook his head.

"And don't think I'm falling for that hard man, I wouldn't care if they ended up in French stew, act, either. You're as worried as I am about them."

"I'm not worried about them in the slightest. They'll be living the life of Riley once you get them back to the sanctuary. Why should I worry about them?"

He raised his eyebrows and looked at her and she smiled. She and Finn were good like this. Light-hearted banter. She could cope with this.

They reached Newbury just ahead of the rush hour and hit Oxford and Milton Keynes without any hold-ups either. They didn't talk much, but it was an easy silence. She felt safe and cocooned by the darkness and the rumbling rhythm of the engine. The road snaked ahead of them, the headlights and tail-lights of the rest of the traffic like bright strings of rubies and diamonds. All the same, she didn't realise she'd fallen asleep until she woke up with a start, aware that they were no longer moving.

"Are we in a traffic jam?" she asked, sitting up and feeling groggy.

"No, we're here." Finn yawned. "I'm just going to see if they've got any rooms. The car park's a bit full. I guess we should have booked, after all."

"I'll come with you. God, I must have been asleep for ages. What time is it?"

"Just gone nine. We ought to think about getting something to eat. There's a nice-looking Italian around the corner."

They went into the little reception and were greeted by a harassed hotelier, who shook her head when Finn asked for a room.

"Normally you'd be fine mid-week, but we've got a writers' conference here at the moment. Romantic novelists. Sorry, I think we're fully booked."

"Completely fully booked?" Maggie asked, dismayed.

The hotelier frowned and opened a book in front of her. "Hang on a sec. It doesn't look as if they've got number seventeen. I'll just go and check."

She came back smiling. "You're in luck. I'm afraid it's only a twin and it's not en suite, but I could do you a discount. Is it just for one night?"

Maggie glanced at Finn and he said, "Your call. We can try somewhere else if you like."

She looked at his tired face and knew she couldn't ask him to drive any further. "No, it's all right. A twin will be fine."

They followed the hotelier up a creaking staircase and then a further, even creakier one at the top of the hotel, where she opened the door on to a sloping-ceiling attic room with a skylight.

"Home from home," Finn said, bending his head as he put their bags on to one of the single beds.

"Actually it's not bad," Maggie said when they were alone. She looked around. There was a pine wardrobe and dressing table and the wallpaper was pale pink to match the bedspreads. On one wall was a print of a girl with a straw hat. "Quite Barbara Cartlandish. I wonder why the romantic novelists didn't want it."

Finn sat next to the bags on the bed. "Who knows? Shall I see if we can get a table in the Italian, or don't you want to bother?"

"Yes, let's go out. I've never been to Skegness. Anyway, you haven't eaten all day. You ought to eat something after all that driving."

Half an hour later they were sitting in La Mamma's, which had a friendly, busy atmosphere, smelt delicious, and was surprisingly full for nearly ten o'clock on a Tuesday. There was a Courvoisier bottle candle on their table, the wax of countless evenings forming a waterfall of colour down the glass.

"If I fall asleep halfway through my pizza give me a prod," Maggie said, putting down her menu and yawning.

"Am I that boring?"

She shot him a look and saw humour in his grey eyes. "Stop fishing for compliments."

"Heaven forbid that I should need to do that. Fancy some wine to go with your pizza?"

"I don't know if the budget can stretch to that."

"Well, we've saved on the room." He raised his eyebrows. It was the first time either of them had mentioned it, but before she could respond, he added, "Besides, this is my treat. What would you like, red or white?"

"I don't mind. You choose."

"There's one here called Bugger," Finn said, looking down the menu. "Made of classic Bordeaux grapes, apparently." He pointed it out to her. "Perfect with pasta and pizza according to this."

"It says Boeger, pronounced with a soft J," Maggie said, trying not to sound smug. "But yes, let's give it a go. Are you having pizza, then?"

"The biggest they do with as many extras as they can cram on to it."

"I think I'll join you."

"Ah, you like one bottle of the bugger," the waiter said when he came to take their order a few minutes later. "Good choice." As he swept away, his order pad in hand, Finn glanced at Maggie and she laughed.

"Okay, Mr McTaggart, you win."

"I don't suppose that's really how you pronounce it. I think it's more likely that the waiter shares my warped sense of humour," he said, and she thought how different this evening was from the one she'd spent with Gary.

The waiter came back with their wine and uncorked it at the table.

"You like to try?"

"I'm sure it will be fine," Finn said, smiling at him and indicating that he should pour for them both.

When he'd gone again, Finn picked up his glass. "Perhaps we should have a toast. What do you think?"

"How about to a successful donkey rescue mission tomorrow?"

They clinked glasses and Maggie smiled and thought that the last time she'd felt this easy around him was the night they'd counted stars in his room. It seemed like an eternity ago, a night imbued with magic, and as the evening wore on and they ate and laughed and drank the wine, which was smooth and velvety, it was as though some of that magic had found its way here to this little restaurant in Skegness.

*   *   *

"Are you too tired to walk back?" Finn asked, when they finally rolled out of the door at half past eleven. "I could call us a taxi."

"No, let's walk. I'm just getting my second wind. What's the night life like here?"

"You never stop surprising me." He shook his head. "I haven't a clue. But if you're not tired I could give you the grand tour. Dad brought me here quite a bit when I was a kid. It was the closest beach."

"Will we be able to get back into the hotel?"

"I've got a front door key. It's not like the old days of seaside landladies, you know. They don't lock you out if you're not back by eleven."

She smiled. "Lead on, McTaggart."

They went past a theme park and he pointed out the big wheel and the roller-coaster, which were shadowed and silent, like great, hulking monsters, asleep until daylight.

"We used to come for the day quite often," Finn said. "And a day was a whole day. No messing about. We'd catch the train, get here about eight and then walk around shivering in our shorts and tee-shirts until the sun warmed us up. Dad always insisted that we wore our shorts because we were at the beach and it was bound to be sunny."

"And was it?" Maggie asked, fascinated. "I thought Skegness had a reputation for bracing winds."

"It does, but whatever the weather we had a strict routine. Breakfast in a beach café, slot machines until lunch time and then the theme park. That was always Dad's favourite."

"He liked going on rides?"

"Oh, he didn't go on anything. He liked watching me clinging on for dear life. He used to stand on the ground slapping his leg every time my carriage came past and

223

roaring with laughter. I bet he didn't strike you as sadistic, did he? I was terrified most of the time."

"You weren't, were you? I can't imagine you being terrified of anything."

"You'd be surprised." His face darkened and then he grinned. "I'm winding you up, Maggie. It was a good sort of terror. The sort that gets your heart thumping, even though you know you're quite safe, really."

She nodded, aware that her own heart was thumping a bit. She couldn't decide whether it was his proximity, or simply because they were in an unfamiliar town at night.

They went past a closed-up ice-cream kiosk with red-and-white striped shutters, a shop that sold buckets and spades and a variety of inflatable animals in garish colours, and then finally he led her along a dark street that went past a golf course.

"Where are we going?"

"Wait and see."

At the end of the street, the tarmac gave way to a track and then to sand and there was a new, salt freshness in the air. Finn gestured her down some steps ahead of him and she realised they were on the beach. The tide was out, leaving a great expanse of sand stretching towards the dark sea. A moon path lay across the water, a strip of silver glitter on a piece of black paper. Like a child's drawing, Maggie thought, reminded of Ben and his pictures, as she followed Finn towards the hard sand at the water's edge.

She was amazed how easy she felt in his company. Or maybe it was the alcohol relaxing her. They'd followed up their pizzas with espressos and amarettos on ice, which Finn said was the only way to finish a meal, but rather to Maggie's surprise, she didn't feel tired or particularly drunk. She just felt warm and happy.

"Your turn," Finn said as they listened to the soft swish of the waves. "Tell me about your childhood."

"It was great. I had a pony and a dog and a cat. I was really lucky."

"No brothers or sisters?"

"No. Mum was a career woman. She didn't really want any children. Neither did my dad. I was a mistake. She told me once that's why he left."

"I'm sure that wasn't true," Finn murmured, his eyes narrowing. "Parents say a lot of stupid things."

"Mum didn't have time for children anyway. She was too busy building up her business empire."

"And your dad didn't stay in touch with you?"

"No." She glanced at his face. "The same thing happened to you, didn't it? Only it was your mum."

"We're talking about you, not me," he said and his voice was light, but his eyes darkened. If she wasn't mistaken, Finn was still hurting over that, Maggie thought. So he wasn't as indifferent as he liked people to think.

"So, come on, what else?" he went on.

"I spent most of my time living a life of luxury," she said flippantly. "I was utterly spoilt."

She gazed into the frill of the tide, remembering, and Finn reached for her hand and said, "Then why do you look so sad? What are you thinking?" And she wished for the hundredth time that he couldn't read her so easily.

"I'm not sad," she said, leaving her hand where it was, but not looking at him. "This is a lovely beach, isn't it? Did you have animals when you were little?"

"We had the odd dog, but not 'til I was older. Dad worked long hours at the pit and I was at school and he didn't think it was fair to leave a dog on its own all day."

"I spent more time with animals than with people," Maggie said dreamily. "It was easier for us because we

225

lived in the country. Right out in the sticks with no other houses within walking distance. I suppose Mum thought it would give me something to do. She wasn't around very much." She paused, aware that he was looking at her, his face soft in the light of the moon.

"What have I said?"

"Nothing that surprises me. Is that really why you didn't go into the family business, Maggie? Because you resented the hotels for keeping your mum from you?"

His eyes were gentle and she shook her head and then decided it was pointless denying what he'd already worked out and added, "Partly, I suppose. I did feel that the business came before me. Well, with hindsight, I guess it had to. It was what supported us."

"Is that why you sold the hotels?"

"Yes, I think it was." She met his gaze and said, "She only owned one of them outright, Arleston Court, where I was brought up. The rest were mortgaged to the hilt. I sold Arleston Court to a developer. I went and watched it being demolished. I thought it would make me feel better seeing it razed to the ground. But it just made me feel even more awful than I already did."

"And so now you bury yourself in work." He touched her face. "Just like your mother did."

"But I don't have children," she said sharply. "So it's hardly the same thing. Come on. Let's walk."

For a while he didn't say anything else. They were still holding hands and it felt so natural to walk along the beach with him, listening to the lap of the waves and fanned by the faint sea breeze. Every so often they climbed over groynes that were barnacled and frilled with seaweed. At one of them, she'd just put her feet on the ground when she spotted something on the sand ahead of them, a dark shape. As they got closer, she realised that it was a crab on its back, its legs paddling the air, but slowly, as if it had been there a long time and had given up hope of ever righting itself.

"Let's take it back to the sea," she said.

"Never off duty, are you?" His voice was teasing, but it was he who picked up the crab and who got his feet wet when he misjudged the waves to put it back.

"You're a big softie at heart, aren't you, Finn?"

"No way. I just know better than to argue with my boss. Anyway I seem to remember you're scared of spiders. I thought you might not want to pick it up. All those legs wriggling about. Not so different, are they."

"I'm not that scared of spiders," Maggie protested.

"You could have fooled me. I've heard of rain dances, but never a spider dance." He sounded amused and she felt a prickle of embarrassment.

As though sensing her discomfort, he changed the subject and said, "How long have you known Sarah, Maggie?"

"Since we were small," she murmured, deciding that she wanted to talk about Sarah even less than she wanted to talk about the spider dance.

But for once Finn was oblivious to her thoughts.

"Have you always been close?"

She hesitated, knowing where this was leading, but not knowing how to stop it and then she realised they'd come to a halt on the shoreline and that Finn was holding her hand once more, so there was no escape.

"She was the sister I never had," she said quietly. "Actually, I think we were probably closer than sisters. We were soul mates. When she got pregnant with Ben she asked me to be his godmother because…" She came to an abrupt halt, realising that she'd almost given herself away.

"Because what?"

"Because we were close, I guess."

"Ben's a great kid. It's a pity we haven't seen so much of him, lately."

"Yes." She didn't meet his eyes, suddenly terribly afraid that he'd already guessed. And he'd brought her here to ask her for the truth. She was going to have to lie and he'd know she was lying.

"Maggie. Do you trust me?"

"Of course I do. What sort of a question's that?" She could hear the bleakness in her voice. Here it came.

"Then why do you keep me at arm's length? Is it because of Sarah? Because of what happened at that party?"

"No." She met his eyes, glad of the darkness.

"Then why?"

"I don't know. I'm...."

"Scared?" he asked quietly. "I'm not going to hurt you. I'm not in the habit of having one-night stands. That time with Sarah was a one-off. A mistake that I've regretted ever since, not because she wasn't a lovely girl, but just because it wasn't something I did. Not even then, and certainly not now." He paused, his eyes gentle. "Do you believe me?"

She nodded, not trusting herself to speak, and he stroked her hair. It was agonising, being so close to him. She felt dizzy with wanting him. All she had to do to stop this was to tell him the truth. Then he wouldn't look at her like that, as if he wanted her, too, and was waiting for her to reciprocate. But she couldn't find the words. And he was still looking.

"I wanted you to know that," he said, "in case it made a difference."

"It doesn't." She forced brightness into her voice. "It was a long time ago."

"Then I assume there's some other reason you don't want things to go any further between us," he said lightly. "Or have I misinterpreted the situation completely? Have I just made a complete fool of myself?"

Chapter Twenty-six

All she had to do was nod and she'd be off the hook, but she couldn't bring herself to do it. Not even for Sarah.

In a voice that didn't sound like hers at all, she said, "No. No you haven't done that, Finn."

He smiled and let go of her hand. "Good. I'm glad we've got that sorted out."

She felt so weak with disappointment and relief she thought she might collapse at his feet. Then it struck her that perhaps he meant they could spent the night together now. This night. She was going to have to think of some way of stopping it. She shivered. The effects of the alcohol were beginning to wear off, and it was starting to get cold. A stiff breeze had come up since they'd been walking, turning the breakers milky white and whisking up the top layer of sand.

He glanced at her. "It's nearly one o'clock, Maggie. We ought to get back soon, or we'll never get up in the morning."

The hotel bar was still open when they got back and as they hesitated outside the door they could hear a lot of rather slurred talk about plots and agents and six-figure advances.

"Different world," Finn remarked, as he followed her up the creaky staircase to their room. He wished fervently that they weren't sharing. The barriers between them had crashed down again tonight, but he wasn't going to push her. She had to come to him. He didn't know how much longer he could stand it if she didn't.

She went to get undressed and clean her teeth in the bathroom on the landing and Finn sat on his bed. He felt ragged. When he'd suggested bringing her up here his motives hadn't been entirely altruistic. He'd thought that if

230

he got her away from the sanctuary for a couple of days, it would be easier to tell her about Sarah. Easier to find out how she felt, and now he had a clue that she did feel the same as he did, he wasn't sure what to do about it. He'd shot himself in the foot telling her about Sarah tonight. If he made the first move now, she might think he'd just been saying that to get her into bed.

He frowned. She'd opened up to him for the first time, let him see a little of what was behind the wall, and in doing so she'd been enormously vulnerable. He'd have been taking advantage of the situation if he'd done what he really wanted to do and made love to her right there on the beach.

Maggie came back into the room, her dressing gown belted loosely around her. There was a sprinkling of talc on her toes, he saw. He tore his eyes away, the intimacy of the moment catching in his throat.

"Forgot my slippers," she said, following his gaze. "Bathroom's free."

"Thanks."

As he cleaned his teeth, he wondered if anyone would notice if it wasn't free for the rest of the night. He could sleep in the bath. It would be a damn sight easier than sleeping in the same room as Maggie. He shook his head. It was a stupid idea. He had to get a grip on himself. He'd waited all this time, he could hold on a bit longer.

When he went back into their room she'd put the bedside light off and was curled away from him, the bedspread moulding around her slender figure. He could hear her quiet breathing and realised with a little stab of irony that she was oblivious to the effect the evening had had on him. She was already asleep. He got into his own bed, swallowing an unfamiliar tenderness that was somehow metamorphosing into pain in his throat.

*   *   *

They had breakfast in a pink and white dining room, amidst dozens of romantic novelists who didn't look in the least hungover.

"Hardened drinkers, obviously," Finn said, pouring Maggie's tea. "How are you feeling?"

"I'm all right." She glanced at him. The truth was that she was feeling quite edgy. She should have told him she wasn't interested in him, made some excuse about not mixing business with pleasure and, now she hadn't, it was only a matter of time. So close and yet so far, she thought, hating herself for her weakness.

"You look tired, Finn," she said briskly. "Wasn't the bed comfy?"

"It was fine. What time did you say we were seeing this woman?"

"Ten o'clock." He seemed tense too and he was having trouble meeting her eyes. Perhaps he was as embarrassed as she was. Perhaps she'd read more into what he'd said last night than had been there. Maybe he just wanted her to know that he wasn't a one-night stand kind of man. Wanted the slur on his character gone.

"I'll just go and settle up then," she said, getting up. "I don't think I can manage a full breakfast at this time in the morning. Anyway, I'm still stuffed from last night."

"I've already done it."

"But you can't pay for the room, that's not fair."

"I was going to pay for mine so it makes no difference." He frowned at her as she got up anyway.

"I'll go and get the bags, then."

232

"Whatever." He made no move to follow her. "If it's all the same to you, I think I'll have some breakfast. I doubt if we'll have time to stop for lunch."

They found the address of the woman with the donkeys easily, despite the fact that it was in the middle of a housing estate.

"No wonder she can't keep them here," Maggie said, looking over the wall into what looked like a back garden, but was obviously the right place because three donkeys were tethered to the fence. One of them was white and the other two a more traditional grey, but all were thin, their heads lowered in resignation as if nothing much surprised them any more.

"I shouldn't think the neighbours are too impressed," Finn remarked, opening the gate to let them in. "Do donkeys kick?"

"They might. Best keep away from their rear ends." They walked cautiously past, but they needn't have worried about kicking. All three of the donkeys cowered away from them, particularly from Finn.

"Poor little sods," he muttered. "Doesn't look like they've been much-loved pets, does it?"

"I thought you didn't care."

"I didn't say I didn't care." He glared at her and Maggie felt almost as cowed as the donkeys.

"Blimey, you did get out of bed the wrong side, didn't you," she muttered, but Finn didn't answer and she decided that he was the most contrary man she'd ever met. Last night on the beach he'd been so warm, tender almost. And now he couldn't be more different. Was it any wonder that she preferred animals? She stormed ahead of him and rapped on the back door. At least animals were consistent. You knew where you were with them.

Gary was thinking exactly the same thing. He'd just been treating a goat for mastitis and her owner, Jimmy Stanton, had been issuing dire warnings from the moment he'd got there.

"Molly's a mean-tempered bugger," he'd said, as he'd introduced Gary to his patient. "Mind you stay out of the way of her back legs and her teeth, or she'll 'ave you."

Molly had flicked her ears nonchalantly, as if attacking vets was the last thing on her mind and she'd submitted patiently to Gary's examination so that he'd wondered what on earth the man was talking about.

"Watch yerself," Jimmy yelled excitedly as Gary had moved around the goat, with apparent disregard for his warnings.

"I'm pretty nifty on my feet," Gary reassured him.

"Not as nifty as Molly. She had my boy the other day. Sunk her teeth right into his hand. Little bitch."

Gary wondered what exactly the boy had been doing. Molly was one of the quietest patients he'd ever come across. But he'd decided it was best not to say anything. Animals were always fine with him. Like little Fang at the sanctuary, he thought with a pang of regret. She was supposed to be a raving lunatic, but she'd never so much as lifted her lip at him. It was about how you treated them, he thought. Animals weren't like humans. They didn't make unprovoked attacks. He frowned, remembering Finn. How stupid that had been. He wondered how much longer he would need to leave it before he did as Emily suggested and called by the sanctuary – just to see how things were going. He finished his examination of Molly and she glanced at him, a benign look on her whiskery face.

"You can put her back in her field," he told Jimmy, as he packed away his visiting case and opened up the back of his van to put it away.

He was just about to close the back doors when he heard a shout of warning and, almost at the same time, felt a stabbing pain in the back of his thigh.

"What the hell?" Jerking away from the pain he half turned and saw Molly, head down, lining herself up for another attack. Without stopping to think he hurled himself into the back of the van, bashing his head on the open door in the process, and landed in a heap amid a couple of cat baskets and some old blankets that smelt of dogs. Molly skidded to a halt in a cloud of dust.

"You little bitch. You cow!" Through the series of lights shooting in front of his eyes, Gary was vaguely aware of Jimmy Stanton, dancing around in a fury outside the van. Then he passed out. He couldn't have been out for more than a few seconds because when he came to very much the same scene was going on outside, only now someone else had joined in. A younger version of Jimmy, presumably his boy, was also dancing around with what looked like a rope lasso in his hands. Molly had turned from the picture of docility to a raving nutter and was charging about the yard like a beast possessed. They'd never catch her like that, Gary thought groggily. He put a hand up to his head and felt stickiness. Blood, he saw, lowering his hand and gazing at it. Or at least he thought it was blood. Everything kept going in and out of focus. Deciding that he was no longer interested in Molly's welfare he lay back down again. His right buttock was on fire and a hot pain was spreading down the back of his leg. He shifted gingerly, turned his head to look, and saw that there was a hole in his trousers and, more worryingly, a gash in his leg. Groaning, he stayed where he was in the van, partly because it didn't sound as if they'd caught Molly yet and partly because he felt too sick to move.

"Are you sure you don't want me to drive?" Maggie asked Finn again. They'd just been into a service station to give him a break and refuel and he looked worn out, his grey eyes shadowed and a little sad. Where was the sadness coming from? "I shouldn't have kept you up so late," she added, biting her lip. "It was all right for me, I slept in the lorry yesterday, but you've been on the go the whole time."

"I'm all right, Maggie, really." Finn leaned into the driver's section of the box and opened a little hatch so they could check on their charges. The donkeys hadn't minded going into the horse box at all and they looked peaceful enough now. They were standing with their heads down. The white one, nearest to them, flicked her ears nervously.

"I wish I knew what had happened to them," Maggie said.

"I don't suppose we ever will." He softened his voice and looked at her. "They're going to be fine. It's the future that counts, not the past."

"Yes." She searched his face, but couldn't read his eyes. With a small sigh she climbed back into the van beside him.

"Not regretting bringing them back, are you?"

"I'm not regretting a thing," she lied.

They got back late afternoon and were met by an anxious Sarah as they drove through the gates.

"What's happened?" Maggie asked, leaning through the window. "Is Ben okay?"

"Everything's fine," Sarah said, but her smile looked forced. "How are the donkeys? Not too het up from the journey?"

"I think they're less stressed than we are." Finn jumped down from the driving seat.

"Oh?"

"Take no notice," Maggie said. "We're fine. How are things here?"

"Like I said, everything's hunky-dory."

"But?" Maggie said, feeling a thread of unease run through her because she could tell by the anxiety in Sarah's unusually serious eyes that she wasn't telling the full story. Perhaps she suspected that away from the sanctuary Maggie had caved in and told Finn the truth.

"It's okay, I haven't said anything," she murmured so only Sarah could hear. "If that's what you're worried about."

"What? Oh no, it's not that. Actually, it's Gary." She shot a look at Finn. "That new vet, Paul, came by earlier to drop off some antibiotics and he said Gary had just been taken to hospital. He was attacked by one of his patients this morning. I know you've fallen out with him, but I thought you'd want to know."

"Is it serious? What happened? Not a dog, surely?" Maggie asked, concerned.

"No, it was a goat. It – er – charged him from behind, apparently, and took a chunk out of his rear end and he knocked himself out trying to get away from it."

Finn snorted and Maggie glared at him. "It's not funny, Finn."

"Paul seemed to think it was quite funny too." Sarah's smile was rueful. "Poor Gary does seem to get himself into trouble, doesn't he?"

"It couldn't happen to a nicer chap," Finn said, ignoring Maggie's furious glare and going round to the back of the horse box to let down the tail-gate. "Are you dashing up to the hospital to play Florence Nightingale,

Maggie, or shall we get these poor donkeys settled in first?"

"What did happen in Skegness?" Sarah asked, as soon as they'd put the donkeys away and she'd got Maggie on her own again.

"Nothing," Maggie said shortly. "Nothing at all."

Sarah coloured up. "Sorry. That was insensitive. You still like him, don't you?"

"It doesn't matter how I feel about him, does it? Tell me about Gary. It must have been pretty nasty if he had to go to hospital. Did Paul say which hospital it was?"

"Why? You're not going to visit him, are you? I thought you wanted to keep out of his way."

"Yes, you're right. I suppose it would be best not to go," Maggie agreed.

But later that day when Sarah had left and Finn had disappeared, in that way he often did, she decided that perhaps she would go and see Gary. The poor bloke was bound to be feeling pretty sorry for himself and she'd never intended to bar him from the sanctuary forever, just for long enough to make him realise that she wouldn't tolerate any more of his antagonism towards Finn.

It was only later, as she walked through the main entrance of the hospital, that she began to wonder at the wisdom of her decision. The last time she'd been to the hospital had been on the day her mother had died. She felt herself tense as she walked past Neurology. It was true what she'd told Finn, work had eased the grief, but the guilt would never go away.

Just after her mother's first stroke, she'd rushed back from Bristol, terrified after an emergency call from the hospital.

"Bed four," the registrar had told Maggie, his eyes compassionate, when she'd raced in. "Don't stay too long. She gets very tired."

Maggie had approached the bed warily. Her mother was lying down and her eyes were closed. She looked startlingly pale, her usually immaculate dark hair disarrayed, and her face even more lined and tired than normal. As Maggie got closer she could smell her mother's familiar scent, but faded a little, which seemed somehow appropriate in the circumstances. Maggie wasn't sure whether she should speak softly, or wait for her to wake up. She was still trying to decide when Elizabeth's eyes flicked open and she saw a mixture of emotions: recognition, surprise, vulnerability and something more alarming: defeat.

"Hi, Mum," she said, hoping her voice didn't give her away. Her mother had always seemed invincible; it was a shock seeing her like this.

"Magg…ie." The word was obviously an effort and Maggie realised something that had not been apparent until she tried to speak. Only one side of her mother's face was working. The left-hand side of her mouth drooped and there was a tiny dribble of spittle in the corner, which increased as she tried to speak again. "Maggie."

Shocked to the core, she moved closer to the bed. "Don't try to say anything, Mum. I've brought you some things. Some overnight stuff. I picked them up from the hotel on the way here." To cover her turmoil, she turned her back on the bed and plonked the bag on the floor alongside the regulation bedside cabinet.

"Urghh." The sharp note of distress had Maggie swinging round swiftly. "What is it, Mum? Shall I call someone?"

On impulse, she caught hold of her mother's hand and was startled when it was yanked out of her grip. Maybe that was a side effect of the stroke, maybe she couldn't control her movements properly.

Biting back tears, she looked into her mother's eyes and saw frustration there, which turned gradually into bewilderment.

"You're going to get better, okay. This is just temporary, a side effect of the stroke. That's what the doctors have said. It's not going to last." She could hear her own voice shaking, not just from upset, but from anger, because this was so unfair. This was the worst thing, the very worst thing that could have happened to someone who had always been so strong, so much in control. Now lying as helpless as a new-born, desperately trying to communicate, but unable to do so.

"Do you understand, Mum? Do you understand what I'm saying? You're not to worry. I'm going to take care of everything. I'll look after Arleston Court for you and I'll get in touch with the other managers, too, and I'll let them know what's happening. You're not to worry."

She wasn't sure if her words had registered. There was no sign that they had. She shifted uneasily from one foot to the other, feeling like a child, as she always did around her mother, but also feeling as if she'd suddenly grown up. As if she'd just been shot several years into the future into a scene which should have been taking place in thirty years time. And then only if they were really unlucky. Mum was only fifty-four. She wasn't ready for this. Neither of them was ready. Maggie longed desperately for Sarah to be there, with her down-to-earth wisdom and her warmth.

In the next bed another patient was coughing and she could hear the murmur of distant voices and the far-off drone of a Hoover. She folded her arms and took a step forward.

Elizabeth's eyes shut again, as if the effort of keeping them open was too much, and Maggie waited. She had no idea how temporary these side-effects were, but it was obvious this wasn't going to be a short-term thing.

"Don't you worry about a thing," she said again, more softly, the urge to touch strong. Yet she didn't think she could bear the risk of another rebuff. She wasn't going to cry. No way was she going to cry. "I'll sort everything out. I'll keep things ticking over until you're better. Is that what you want me to do?"

There was no response and Maggie stayed where she was for another five minutes before she realised that her mother was asleep.

A few minutes later she had found Sarah, who'd taken her to the hospital, in a visitor's room, pacing restlessly. "The nurse told me to wait here. Are you all right? How is she?"

"Not good," Maggie said, thrusting her hands into the pockets of her jacket to stop them trembling. "I spoke to a registrar and she's going to be here a little while. I'm going to have to move into Arleston Court and oversee things until she's better."

"But you'll hate it," Sarah said, her blue eyes worried and her voice edged with doubt. "Are you sure that's a good idea? Can't you get a manager in?"

"I don't want to," Maggie murmured, glancing at a child who was sifting through a box of toys in the corner of the room while his mother smiled at him indulgently.

Not that she was really surprised at Sarah's reaction. Having spent her whole life adamant that she was never going to work in one of her mother's hotels – no matter what happened – it must be hard for Sarah to understand such a complete turnaround.

But then she hadn't told Sarah how awful it had been seeing her mother in such a state. She would tell her, but not yet, because it was still too raw in her head. And also because she felt guilty. Perhaps if she hadn't been so stubborn, so single-minded about doing her own thing, then her mother wouldn't have had to work so hard. Stress had undoubtedly contributed to the stroke – the doctor had told her that. So perhaps she was partly responsible.

Maggie knew Finn was right about everything being easy with hindsight. But knowing that did nothing to ease the awful guilt she still felt. Remembering why she was here, she took a deep breath, straightened her shoulders, and headed towards Men's Surgical.

Chapter Twenty-seven

"Third on the right, love," said a sweet-faced nurse, in answer to her query.

She found Gary sitting up in bed, reading a veterinary journal, which he put down as soon as he saw her.

"Maggie, hi!" He sounded so pleased to see her that she felt terrible.

"Hello, Gary. How are you feeling?"

"All the better for seeing you." He smiled and his whole face lit up. Then he shifted in the bed and winced, and the journal slipped off his lap on to the floor.

"Are you very sore?" she asked, reaching to pick it up.

"No, not really. It was my own stupid fault for thinking I knew best. Molly – she's the goat who put me in here – gave me the impression that butter wouldn't melt in her mouth, although her owner did try to warn me."

"What happened?"

"Basically, she head butted me with her very sharp horns. And while I was trying to get out of her way I knocked myself senseless on the van door. Didn't take a lot of doing. I was halfway there already."

He looked at her as he spoke and she wondered if he was referring to hitting Finn. Not sure how to respond, she glanced around the room. There was a vase of lilies on the bedside table – their sweet scent filled the room – and a card, although she couldn't see who it was from. She moved across to the bed and gave him the box of chocolates she'd bought in the hospital shop.

"Thanks. How are things at The Ark? How's Fang? Is she still there?"

Maggie nodded, relieved that Albert had decided against having Fang in the end. She'd have hated to have to tell Gary that he wouldn't see the little dog again. "She's fine. She misses you. We all do," she added impulsively. "You'll have to pop in and see us some time. If you want to, I mean."

"If you're sure, then I'd like that very much." He turned towards her and Maggie saw the bruise and a small cut on the side of his head.

"That looks nasty. Is that why they're keeping you in?"

"Yes. Just for the night, with a bit of luck. I can hobble about all right, but they don't like to take any risks when you've knocked yourself out. How did you know I was here?"

"Paul popped in this morning and told us."

"I bet he was laughing his socks off, wasn't he?"

"No, I don't think so. I wasn't there, as it happens. He told Sarah. I was in Skegness rescuing some donkeys."

"That's a long way to drive – did Finn go with you?"

"Yes," she murmured.

"Things are working out all right with Finn, then?" There was a hint of resignation in his voice and Maggie nodded, reminded suddenly of the donkeys.

Compassion rose in her and she said, "On a work basis, yes. I shouldn't think he'll stay around much past the end of the summer. He'll want to get something better."

"I'm glad. That things are working out with him, I mean." Gary smiled. "I guess I ought to prepare myself for being the butt of a few jokes when I get out of here. Literally, in my case."

They both laughed and the tension left the room.

They talked for a bit longer about the animals she'd taken in and re-homed and then Maggie said, "I'd better get off. It's later than I thought."

"I really appreciate you taking the trouble to come, and I'd love to call by and see Fang some time. That's if you're really sure?" He lifted his hand but at the last minute seemed to think better of it and dropped it back on to the bed.

"I wouldn't have said it if I weren't." She hesitated and added, "See you soon then. Give me a call when you're feeling up to coming over and I'll make sure I'm there."

And she'd make sure Finn wasn't, she decided, as she drove back to the sanctuary. Perhaps asking Gary back hadn't been such a good idea. It had seemed the right thing to do, but she knew she'd have to tell Finn and she wasn't at all sure how he was going to take the news.

"It's up to you, Maggie," Finn said, not looking up from the crossword he was doing. "As long as the bloke doesn't decide to have another pop at me. I might hit him back next time."

"I'm sure he won't. I think it'll be a while before he can even work again."

Finn didn't answer and she sat down on the settee. He might say he didn't mind her inviting Gary back, but the temperature in the room had definitely dropped since she'd told him.

"Thanks for coming to Skegness," she added, anxious to get things back on an even footing.

"Like I said, it was my fault you had to go there in the first place. It was the least I could do." His voice was cold and suddenly she was angry.

"What is the matter with you?" she demanded, getting up from the settee and storming across to him. Before he had time to react, she snatched the paper from his lap and flung it on to the floor. He looked startled. Then he stood up so they were facing each other.

"I just can't work you out," she snapped, aware that her voice was rising. "One minute you act as if you're a normal human being. Quite a decent person, in fact. And the next you're a bloody iceberg."

For a moment he didn't say anything, just looked at her with an expression she couldn't fathom. Then he grabbed hold of her arms, pulled her roughly against him and kissed her. It was such a shock that she felt her legs melting beneath her. Or maybe it was the passion in his kiss. Iceberg-like, it was not. There was no tenderness there, either. Not like the last time they'd kissed, at all.

When she'd recovered the use of her legs she tried to pull away from him, but he wouldn't let her go. His tongue explored every corner of her mouth, probing and invasive, causing ribbons of fire to flicker inside her, and to her dismay Maggie found herself responding. She hated herself, but she never wanted him to stop. When he did, she felt too weak even to slap him.

"Was that bloody normal enough for you?" he growled, and she saw that his grey eyes were blazing. And then he spun around and slammed out of the room.

Maggie sank on to the settee, so shocked that she could hardly believe it had happened. Perhaps she should go after him. She dismissed the idea immediately. She'd provoked him quite enough for one evening. Best to let the dust settle.

She touched her lips, which still tingled from the roughness of his kiss. She wanted to cry and laugh at the same time. She took a few deep breaths until the hysteria subsided. Well, it had certainly proved one thing, she thought wryly. Indifferent to her he was not. And then her mind leapt ahead to work and the normality she'd been trying to recapture. Christ. What on earth were they going to say to each other tomorrow?

*   *   *

Fortunately they didn't have to say anything because when she got up the next day he was already out working. Deciding that there was a better chance of them resuming a professional relationship if as much time as possible passed before they saw each other again, she threw herself into the routines of the morning.

Finn kept out of her way for most of the day. Around teatime he called across the yard that he was going to creosote some fences and that he'd probably be a while.

Maggie locked up and took her paperwork into the cottage. He'd have to come in sooner or later.

It was dusk and she was sitting in the lounge, showered and changed and having extreme difficulty concentrating on a batch of invoices, when the front door banged.

"Is that you, Finn?"

"No, it's a burglar." His footsteps slowed outside the lounge door, but he didn't come in.

Maggie got up and went into the hall. "I want to talk to you."

"I'll get changed first. I'm covered in creosote. Is there any hot water left?"

When he came down his hair was still damp. "I'm all yours," he said, stepping into the room, his face guarded.

She'd been going to hedge round the issue, but, now she was facing him, she couldn't, so she just launched straight in. "Why did you kiss me last night? And I want a straight answer. I've had enough of your games."

"I'm not playing games." He gave her a direct look. "I thought we'd got that clear in Skegness."

"Just tell me why you kissed me."

He looked uncomfortable. His gaze flicked around the room and he took a step away from her. Then he brushed a

247

hand through his hair, leaving a spike of it sticking up so that Maggie had a sudden impulsive urge to go across and flatten it down for him. "I guess because I couldn't help myself. I'm sorry. It shouldn't have happened. Do you want me to go?"

"No, of course I don't want you to go." She watched his face. He rarely looked unsure of himself, he hardly ever looked vulnerable, but she could see he was both, now. She wanted to make him feel better and she'd had enough of keeping this forced distance between them. She was tired of pretending and she was worn out with lying – not just to him, but to herself.

"I enjoyed it," she murmured. "Didn't you?" She'd surprised him, she saw, but then she'd surprised herself, too. In for a penny, in for a pound. She took a step towards him. "Am I embarrassing you?"

"No." He stayed where he was.

Just two more steps to the point of no return, Maggie thought, wondering who would be the one to take them. Or were they going to turn away from each other again? Keep pretending that there was nothing between them? She could feel the electricity sparking, but had a feeling that if they stopped now they'd never reach this point again. Making a decision she knew she would live to regret, she took another step. But it was he who took the final one. He put his arms around her and gave a small moan.

"Christ, Maggie." His arms tightened and he buried his face in her hair and then his lips found hers and she knew that he wanted her as much as she wanted him, and that this time they weren't going to stop.

She forced herself to break the kiss and he looked at her, his eyes quizzical, but before he could speak, she grabbed his hand and led him out of the room.

Her bedroom door was open and they went inside wordlessly.

She sat on the bed and he knelt on the carpet in front of her. "Are you sure this is what you want?" His voice was little more than a whisper, his eyes smoky with desire, and in answer she kissed him again and drew him up on to the bed beside her.

He undid the buttons of her blouse with infinite gentleness and she watched his face in the light of the moon shining through the window. Then, tired of being forever passive, she tugged his tee-shirt over his head and swore when she discovered his jeans had buttons instead of a zip.

Smiling, he helped her with them and she tugged them over his hips and off completely. When they were both naked he took her in his arms again and they lay on top of the duvet, side by side. He ran his fingers down her back, pausing as he reached the curve of her hip. Then he gave another soft moan and pulled her against him so that she could feel the entire hard warmth of his body. And there was no hesitation in him now.

She lay beneath him, every part of her leaping in response to his touch. She dug her fingers into the hard muscles of his shoulders and drank in the scent of his skin and she knew they should have done this long ago. She had never felt so on fire, so much at one with another person. She gazed up at the outline of his face. His eyes, dark with passion, were totally unguarded. It was like looking into his soul. In that moment none of the past mattered. She felt as though she was exactly where she was meant to be. As if her whole life had been leading up to this point and if there was no more time left to her afterwards, it wouldn't matter.

*   *   *

In the morning, when Maggie woke up, there was an empty space beside her and she thought for a moment that it had all been a wonderful dream. But she could still feel the effects of his body on hers, a delicious soreness that was replaced by a quiver of lust when she thought about what they'd spent the night doing. So the love gene hadn't been missing in her, as she'd always suspected; just buried, she reflected, rolling over and burying her face in his pillow. What a pity she hadn't discovered it before. She'd been missing out.

So where was he now?

Chapter Twenty-eight

Concerned, she sat up, and then the door opened and he stood there with two mugs of tea. He hadn't bothered dressing to make it, she saw, but suddenly shy of her own nakedness she hugged the duvet around her breasts. He smiled, and to cover her confusion she said flippantly, "You'll frighten the post lady walking around like that."

"So, I'm frightening now, am I? Don't worry, it's too early for the post lady. It's only just gone six."

"Is it? It feels much later."

"Well, it's not." He put the mugs of tea on her dressing table. "Am I allowed back in, then? I'm feeling at something of a disadvantage."

She turned back the corner of the duvet and he climbed in beside her. Then he propped his head on his elbow and looked at her. "I was going to make some toast as well, but I wasn't sure how hungry you'd be."

"Not hungry in the slightest."

"Maybe you need to work up an appetite." He pulled the duvet away from her and without taking his eyes from her face he traced the curve of her breast with his fingers.

"You're a tease, Finn McTaggart."

"Shall I stop?"

"Don't you dare."

By the time they had worked up enough of an appetite for their toast, the tea Finn had made was too cold to drink.

Maggie spent the morning in a haze of happiness, which was only slightly marred by the fact that nothing had really changed. One night of passion, amazing as it had been, did not alter the fact that Finn was Ben's father and that she and Sarah had been deceiving him for the past four months. Bathed, as she was, in the afterglow, she managed to put

251

this out of her mind, more or less. Jack and Sarah's wedding was July 24th, still a month away. Sarah certainly wasn't going to tell him before then, and she'd promised Sarah she wouldn't. Maybe when the time came, they could somehow work things out. Maybe he'd be involved enough with her to forgive her for not being honest.

She was midway through cleaning out the chickens when this thought struck her. Crouched there, amidst the smell and the soft flutter of the birds, she knew for sure that she was kidding herself. What did she think he'd do? Forget he had a son? Walk away? Finn wasn't the type of man to do either. All she'd done by sleeping with him had been to complicate things further.

But she'd known that, deep down, hadn't she? She stretched out her fingers to stroke Maisie, who was the tamest of the ex-batteries and had strutted across to see what she was doing.

"You wouldn't be so silly, would you?" she murmured, the bird's feathers downy-soft beneath her fingers. "Life isn't so complicated in Little Red Hen land, is it?"

Maisie blinked and leaned into her touch.

"Having fun?" Finn's voice made her jump and she banged her head on a jutting-out bit of wood.

"Ouch."

"Sorry, didn't mean to take you by surprise. Are you okay?" His voice was solicitous.

She rubbed her head. "It wasn't your fault, I was miles away."

"Somewhere nice, I hope."

She glanced at him and reflected that they couldn't be in more unromantic surroundings, yet all she wanted to do was go to bed with him again. One night hadn't been

252

nearly enough. She wanted to spend every night in bed with him.

"I was thinking about what to get Sarah and Jack for their wedding present," she improvised hastily. "I managed to prise the list off her the other day."

"Maybe we could get them something together," Finn suggested. "Or am I being too forward here?"

"No, of course you're not." She smiled at him. "Good idea. We'll catch up later."

Halfway through the morning, Gary phoned to say he'd been let out of hospital, but was off work for a while and would call in and see Fang when he felt more up to it.

"I'll look forward to it," she said, meaning it. Hopefully, he'd come on Sunday when Finn wasn't around. She didn't think Gary would be in any hurry to bump into Finn.

By six o'clock, Maggie felt as if she'd spent the whole day with the phone pressed to her ear. She was just about to lock up reception when the phone rang again.

"Could I speak to Finn McTaggart?" said a woman's voice.

"He's not about at the moment. Can I take a message and get him to call you back?"

There was the faintest of pauses on the other end and the woman said, "To be honest, it's quite urgent. Is that Maggie?"

"Yes," Maggie said, suddenly apprehensive.

"I'm Shirley Brewer. I'm a friend of his from Nottingham. I hope you don't mind me calling, but I can't seem to get Finn on his mobile."

"We're not in a very good area," Maggie murmured, feeling a small flicker of jealousy, which she knew was irrational. Why shouldn't Shirley call Finn — they'd obviously been close once. "I can take a message if you like," she offered.

"Thanks. I wanted to speak to Finn about Albert, actually. He was supposed to take Stewart, my son, fishing last night, but he didn't turn up. He's not answering his door and I've checked at the pub and he hasn't been in. I just wondered if he was all right. He's had this awful cough, but he won't go to the doctors, stubborn old bugger. I don't like to think of him holed up in that house on his own."

"No," Maggie said, concern instantly replacing the jealousy. "Thanks very much for phoning, I'll get Finn to give you a ring."

"Oh, no, don't worry, I just thought I'd better pass it on. It might be that Albert's gone away for a few days, but he didn't mention it."

Maggie hung up, worried, and switched on the answer machine. She was about to go and find Finn when she saw him coming down the yard.

He wiped his hands on his jeans and came across smiling. "God, it's still hot, isn't it?"

"Finn, I just had a phone call for you, from Shirley – in Nottingham."

His smile vanished and concern leapt into his eyes. Maggie had to swallow more jealousy.

"Shirley? What on earth did she want?"

Maggie told him and his face grew even more serious.

"Well, he's certainly stupid enough not to go to the doctor's. And, thinking about it, he didn't answer his phone earlier, when I tried to ring. I'll try him again on his mobile. I should speak to Shirley, too. Is it all right if I use the reception phone?"

"Of course it is. I'll just lock up the other end." She rushed away, not wanting to hear Finn on the phone to his ex-girlfriend. When she came back down the yard, Finn was shaking his head. "I can't get any answer from his mobile or his land line, and Shirley seems really worried. I know it's short notice, but would it cause you a problem if I took a couple of days off and drove up there?"

"No, of course not. Will you go in the morning?"

"Actually, I think I might go now. If I put my foot down I'll be there before ten." He hesitated. "I'm sorry, this is really bad timing, but I am a bit worried."

"Don't be silly. Of course you must go. You will phone and let me know how he is, won't you?"

"Sure." His eyes were distant, as if he'd already left. Maggie felt chilled despite the balmy air. She'd liked Albert, too, and she hated the thought of him being ill and alone. Though she wasn't keen on Finn driving up to Nottingham, not when he was worried sick. Her feelings had nothing to do with the fact that she wasn't keen on the idea of him spending time with Shirley, she told herself. But as she waved him off she found herself regretting, for the first time, her decision to run a business that you couldn't leave.

Despite putting his foot down wherever he could, Finn didn't get to Nottingham until gone eleven. The whole country was obviously heading in the same direction. He'd tried ringing his father on his mobile a couple more times on the way, but still got no answer and he grew more and more worried. Even if Dad had nipped out, which didn't seem very likely from what Shirley had said, he'd surely be back by now.

He couldn't find a parking space anywhere near the little end-terrace house, so eventually he had to park in the next street and walk. Dad's house, like the one next to it, was in darkness. He banged on the door and wondered what he'd do if he couldn't get in. After about five minutes with no response from either knocking or carefully aimed stones at his father's bedroom window, he climbed over the side gate, which was locked, and went round the back.

The back door was locked, too. He supposed he could smash the glass and let himself in that way, but if Albert had just unplugged the phone and gone to bed for an early night, he'd scare the life out of him. Somewhere under one of the numerous flowerpots in the garden there was probably a spare back door key, but finding it in the dark was going to be tricky. Why the hell hadn't he thought to bring a torch?

He decided to work his way methodically through all the likely hiding places and struck gold in the sixth flowerpot, when his hand closed over an old baccy tin that rattled when he shook it. When he managed to prise the lid off, he found a key on a bit of frayed string which fell apart in his fingers, so that the key tinged on to the path. Cursing, Finn fumbled around for it.

Twenty minutes after he'd arrived, he let himself into his father's tiny kitchen and switched on the light. Tidy, as always, he saw, when his eyes adjusted, but there was something missing. He frowned. Tobacco smoke. Conspicuous by its absence. He couldn't remember ever walking into this kitchen without noticing its pungent smell.

Alarmed now, he went through to the back room, which was where his father ate his tea, watched telly, had his after-dinner Scotch, did practically everything, in fact. The room was empty. Finn closed the door quietly and stood at the bottom of the stairs. "Dad!" he shouted up. "Dad, can you hear me?"

No answering cry greeted him. Suddenly Finn didn't want to go up there. Didn't want to walk into a room and find his father collapsed unconscious on the floor. Or worse, still and unmoving in bed. How long did it take for the smell of tobacco to vanish so completely from a house? Surely, by now, it would have seeped into the very walls themselves. He put his foot on the first brown-carpeted stair and it creaked beneath his weight. "Dad?" he called again. It was no good. He was going to have to go up.

On the landing he hesitated. His father's bedroom door was ajar. He pushed it open and stuck his head around the door. Even in the dim light he could see that the bed was neatly covered with its usual white bedspread and that his father wasn't in it. He didn't realise he'd been holding his breath until he started to breathe again.

Without much hope, he checked the rest of the house. This was all very strange. According to Shirley, his father had been at death's door the last time she'd seen him. Certainly too ill to go out. It didn't make sense. Not only was he obviously not here now, but Finn would have laid bets that he hadn't been here for days.

Finn was rudely awoken from one of the deepest and most exhaustion-fuelled sleeps he could remember. Someone was prodding him with a stick, the wrong end of a broom, he saw, as he opened his eyes and tried to remember whose settee he was lying on.

He'd been covered by an eiderdown he'd found in the hall cupboard, but his assailant, a white-haired, seventy-something old lady with cross blue eyes, had removed it, presumably with the broom, which she was still jabbing around. The eiderdown was now lying in a crumpled heap on the floor and Finn, wearing only his boxer shorts, felt rather vulnerable.

"And who exactly might you be?" she demanded. "Come on – get up and explain yourself."

Finn sat up and glared at her. "I might ask you the same thing," he said. "This is my father's house. What are you doing here?"

"Oh, you're Albert's son, are you?" Her face broke into a smile. "Why didn't you say so?"

He resisted the urge to point out that she'd attacked him before he'd had the chance and said coolly, "So, where is my father? I thought he was ill."

"Ill…? Albert…?" She sounded so incredulous that, for a minute, Finn felt as if he must have tumbled into some alternative reality.

"Well, isn't he ill, then?" he said irritably.

"No, dear." She gave him a look that he'd have described as coquettish in someone a few decades younger. "He's a little tired, but that's probably because he's not used to all the exercise."

Finn, deciding that he was losing the plot, said, "I'll just get dressed and you can explain what you're talking about."

"Now tell me what you'd like to know?" she said a few minutes later, as they sat at opposite ends of the settee he'd just vacated, sipping the coffee she'd made them. "I'm Dorinda, by the way."

Finn shook his head, not entirely sure he wasn't still dreaming. "Where Dad is now would be a good start."

"That's easy. He's at my place. Three doors down," she added, as if this explained everything.

"And he's definitely not ill?"

"No, dear."

"He's never mentioned you."

"No, well, we haven't known each other long." She fluttered her eyelashes, which looked too long and black to be her own. "He's mentioned you a lot. Said you were a fine-looking young man, but you can't always tell.

258

Sometimes it's parental pride. Not in your case, though."
She giggled and Finn felt heartily relieved that he hadn't
been sleeping in the nude as he usually did.

"Do you want to tell him I'm here? Or shall I come to
your house and see him?"

Dorinda glanced at her watch. "He'll be along in a
minute, he was having a shave when I left. Then he was
popping up to get a paper and a pint of milk. We haven't
been here for a while and he didn't think he had any in. I
said I'd come and put the coffee pot on. Open a few
windows and such like."

"You're living together?" Finn felt his eyebrows rising
in amazement.

"Don't look so shocked. You youngsters don't have
the monopoly on living in sin, you know. Us oldies could
show you a thing or two, I can tell you."

Finn had no doubt whatsoever about that. It was just
that his father hadn't lived with anyone since his disastrous
relationship with Finn's mother. He'd always been dead set
against the idea, so why change his mind now he was in his
early seventies? To his huge relief, the door banged at that
moment and he heard his father's voice.

"I'm back, Dorrie, love. Where are you?"

"In here, Pumpkin. You've got a visitor."

Finn had never in his life imagined he'd hear his father
called Pumpkin. He stood up wearily as Albert came into
the room. "Hi, Dad. Sorry to barge in on you like this, but I
came up last night and when you weren't here I crashed on
your settee. Hope you don't mind."

"No, lad. Course I don't mind. I see you've – er – met
Dorrie, then."

"Yes, we're well acquainted," Dorrie interrupted. "I'll
leave you two boys to catch up. Will you be stopping to

dinner tonight, Finn? Because if you are I'll phone up and book another seat at the Cock and Bottle."

She rose gracefully without waiting for an answer and left the room. Finn and his father stared at each other.

"You could have warned me you were coming," said his father, looking sheepish.

"I didn't know I was until the last minute. Shirley phoned and said you were ill. And when you didn't answer your phone, well, I didn't know what else to do."

"Shirley said I was ill?"

"Yes. She said you were supposed to take Stewart fishing and you didn't turn up."

Albert clapped his hand over his mouth. "Bugger – I'd forgotten all about that. I'll have to phone the little lad and say I'm sorry."

"And you haven't been in the pub either, have you? Shirley said your cough was so bad she was worried it was bronchitis again. She told me that's what you had last time, not flu at all."

"Ah, yes… well, same difference."

"It's not the same thing at all," Finn said, exasperated. "So why haven't you been in the pub? It's usually your second home."

"If you must know, I've given up the dreaded weed and I can't go in the pub because it makes me cough."

"You've given up smoking!"

"Aye. Dorrie made me."

"Well, good for you. But, Dad, how long's this been going on? Dorrie, I mean. You never said anything about her when you came down. Or when you phoned up about the donkeys, which are, you'll be pleased to hear, now happily installed at The Ark."

"No – no, I didn't, did I?"

"Why not, for God's sake? I nearly had a heart attack when I woke up and saw a strange woman standing over me this morning."

"If I'd known you'd be on the settee, I would have mentioned it, lad. But I didn't. Strikes me we've both not been mentioning things."

This argument was so devoid of logic that for a few seconds Finn was speechless.

"Besides – I wasn't sure you'd approve," Albert added. "It was a bit of a whirlwind romance, Dorrie and me."

He narrowed his eyes. "So how's the gorgeous Maggie? Have you asked her out yet?"

Chapter Twenty-nine

Gary woke up late on his first morning home. He hadn't set the alarm and the painkillers he'd taken the previous evening must have knocked him out. He got out of bed and limped across to the window to see what sort of day it was. Christ, he felt sore. He drew back the curtains and saw bright sunlight. Beyond his garden he could see mist curling off the fields that led down to the river. So far July was as blazing as June had been.

He thought about Maggie's visit. It had been good to see her. Not that he was kidding himself any more that Maggie would ever feel the same about him as he felt about her. But he longed for them to be friends again. Also, she'd mentioned that Finn would be gone by the end of the summer. That was good news, too. He knew he'd never feel comfortable around Finn.

When he went to get his milk in, bending with difficulty to pick it up, Emily was just getting hers.

"Gary, how are you, love?"

He straightened and smiled at her. "I'm getting there. Thanks for the flowers. They were lovely. How did you know I was in hospital?"

"That nice young vet told me when he brought your van back. Now, you are going to take it easy for a few days, aren't you? No dashing about."

"I don't think I'll be dashing anywhere for a while."

"Poor lamb. It'll do you good to slow down. You work far too hard." She put her head on one side so that he could see the coil of her grey plait and added casually. "You could pop by the animal sanctuary, couldn't you, dear? See how young Maggie is."

He grinned. "Young Maggie came to see me in hospital."

"That sounds promising."

"Don't get too excited. I don't think there'll be any more candlelit meals, somehow."

"Maybe there wouldn't have been even if you hadn't thumped her lodger," Emily said. She smiled. "My Jane's coming over to see me later. She likes animals. Talking about getting a horse, she is. Maybe you could take her along to the sanctuary with you."

"Maybe," Gary said, although he knew it was the last thing he'd do. Women were not top of his agenda, right now. "I might see if I can bring Fang home for a while," he went on. "Seeing as I'm going to be here a few days. It would do her good."

"Jane likes dogs, too."

"Does she." Gary gave her another quick smile and closed the door. He made himself breakfast and got dressed with difficulty. The doctor at the hospital had advised him to take at least a week off work, not least because it would be difficult to drive. Getting to the sanctuary was going to be tricky, but Gary was firmly of the opinion that anything was possible if you wanted it enough, and Maggie had invited him. If he waited, she might have second thoughts and tell him not to come.

He got there just after eleven and found a very harassed Maggie trying to do several things at once.

"Where is everyone?" he asked, as she fielded phone calls and advised various walkers which dogs could be walked together without a fight.

"Dawn's looking after her grandchildren today and Finn's gone up to see his dad. He's not well."

"I'm sorry to hear that," Gary said, although he certainly wasn't sorry that Finn wasn't around. "Let me answer the phone for you. I can't do much else at the moment, but I can sit in here, no problem."

"Are you sure, Gary?"

"Course I'm sure. Go on, you get up the yard and do whatever needs doing. I'll be fine." He eased himself into the chair and, with a grateful glance at him, Maggie disappeared out of the door.

He watched her go, deciding that fate moved in mysterious ways. When she'd banned him from the sanctuary he'd hit rock bottom and when that blasted goat had attacked him he'd thought things couldn't get any worse. But now it all seemed rather fortuitous. It was a shame about Finn's dad, but apart from that, he thought with a sigh of contentment, the timing was absolutely perfect.

Maggie was shattered. It had been one of the busiest Saturdays she could remember. They'd had an influx of dogs, which often happened in the holiday season. It amazed her how many people would rather re-home their dogs than pay out kennel fees for them.

Finn hadn't yet phoned and she was worried about that, too, although it was possible he'd tried and hadn't been able to get through. The phone had been ringing non-stop.

Gary grinned at her as she went into reception. "You look worn out, Maggie. Do you fancy coming for a pint and a pie up the road? Save cooking?"

What she really wanted to do was to collapse in exhaustion but she couldn't because she had a home check in Salisbury. She looked at Gary doubtfully.

Misreading her expression, he said, "I mean as friends, Maggie. No strings attached. I admit I used to hope it could be more, but those days are gone. Truly."

"I could meet you there later, if you like. I must owe you several drinks after today. How about eight o'clock?"

264

"Great. See you there."

As she drove to Salisbury, Maggie wondered if she should have agreed, but Gary had seemed genuine enough and she was tired of looking for ulterior motives where probably none existed. They'd have their own cars and she wouldn't stop long. Besides, going out had to be better than being alone in the cottage and jumping out of her skin every time the phone rang in case it was Finn.

The home check took longer than she expected. The woman, a sweet old lady whom Dawn had recommended, wanted to chat, and Maggie didn't want to rush her, but she finally got away. At this rate she was going to be at least half an hour behind Gary. She hoped he wouldn't think she'd stood him up.

It wasn't until Gary was home and trying to shower without getting any water on his stitches that he remembered he hadn't asked Maggie about Fang. He'd mention it later, he decided, wincing as he moved too quickly. Rather to his consternation, the prospect of meeting Maggie at the Red Lion, with no Finn around to muck things up, did not give him the pleasure he'd thought it might. True, he'd told her there were no strings attached, but he hadn't realised he'd meant it quite so unequivocally.

It had been great to see her again, but some of the bittersweet pain he'd always felt when he was around her, that 'so near, so far' feeling, had been missing. It was as if somehow the time they'd spent apart had dulled some of his feelings, taken the edge off his passion, and it hadn't really sunk in until today. A self-defence mechanism, maybe, now that he knew they were never going to be more than friends. He wiped the mirror clean of steam and shaved. Perhaps it was just a temporary feeling because he was too sore to fantasise about jumping on Maggie. He gazed at his reflection. Or perhaps Emily was right and he was finally acknowledging the truth. Maggie wouldn't have ended up declaring undying love to him, even if he hadn't thumped Finn.

He was rinsing out his mouth with Listerine when the doorbell rang. Deciding to ignore it he spat into the sink and dabbed his mouth dry, but the caller was persistent. Frowning in irritation, he pulled his bathrobe from the back of the door and, twisting the cord around his waist, limped along the landing and went carefully downstairs.

Pulling open the front door, words of annoyance half-formed on his lips, he stopped dead in his tracks. An amazing-looking redhead was standing on his doorstep. She looked familiar and he frowned, trying to remember where he'd seen her before.

"Sorry, have I called at a bad time?" she murmured, her smile uncertain. "I'm Jane, Emily's granddaughter. She said you wouldn't mind if I called round and saw your new dog. I know you from somewhere, don't I?"

"Jane." Gary's mind was spinning. It was something to do with horses, something to do with Maggie. "Come in," he said, deciding now was not the time to tell her that Fang wasn't actually in residence. If he didn't let her in now, he might never see her again. "Go through to the lounge and make yourself at home. I'll just go and get dressed. Won't be two minutes."

She smiled again and walked ahead of him and he allowed himself a quick glance at her petite rear, which was encased in a tight, black skirt, beneath which he could see long, tanned legs.

"In here?" She turned at the door of the lounge and caught him looking at her and Gary felt heat creeping up his neck.

He nodded. "Make yourself at home."

Upstairs again, he dressed as quickly as he could, splashed liberal amounts of *Pour Homme* over himself and went out on to the landing. Deep breaths, he told himself. No need to get flustered, she was just Emily's granddaughter. Why hadn't Emily told him how gorgeous she was? Come to think of it, Emily had probably been pretty gorgeous herself in her younger days. She had the high cheekbones of timeless beauty and she still had long hair, albeit grey and plaited and coiled up on top of her head. He should have guessed that Jane would be lovely too. He wished he could remember where he'd seen her.

Outside the lounge door, which Jane had closed behind her, he took more deep breaths and then went casually into the room. She was standing by the French windows, her back to him, her long hair cascading like a mane of gold in the evening sunlight.

"What a beautiful garden you have," she said, turning and smiling at him. "You must spend hours on it."

"It's a hobby," he murmured, moving to stand beside her.

"And now you're going to have a little dog racing about digging up the flower beds. Won't that be an awful pain?"

"I love dogs and she'll soon learn where she's not supposed to go."

"I love dogs too. Where is she, then?"

The jigsaw pieces came together in his head. "That's where I've seen you before. At The Ark, Maggie Clarke's place."

"Wow, you've got a good memory." She was looking at him with those amazing eyes. They were the colour of Bournville, flecked with gold. "That's right. I was going to have a horse from her, but it didn't work out."

"It's where my dog's coming from, but I'm not picking her up until tomorrow." He was lost in her eyes. "Can I get you a drink of anything? Coffee? Or perhaps a glass of wine?"

"Wine would be lovely," she said, showing no signs of wanting to dash off. "Is it all right if I go outside and have a look? I love gardens."

Enchanted, Gary unlocked the French windows for her.

"I'm always telling Gran she should get someone to do her garden," Jane said, stepping out on to the immaculate lawn. "Is it all right to walk on this? I don't want to leave heel marks. How do you get it to look so perfect?"

"It is hard work," Gary admitted, forgetting about the wine and following her outside. "Maybe I could give your gran a hand. I didn't realise she needed someone."

"I'm sure she'd like that." Jane bent and slipped off her strappy sandals. She had slender, brown feet with some sort of sparkly pink varnish on her toenails. "Oh, it feels just like walking on luxurious carpet, only cooler."

"Does it?"

She glanced at him. "Gran likes you, you know. She often mentions you when I visit. Strange we've never bumped into each other here before."

"I'm out working a lot." He followed her across the lawn to a rose bush where she dipped her head to the pink blooms. "These smell gorgeous. Most of the roses in florists don't smell these days. I think it's a dreadful shame."

"Me too. I'll – er – just go and get your wine."

When he came back with a bottle and two glasses she was sitting on the little wooden bench that he'd picked up from an antique shop and restored to its former glory.

"Shall we have it out here? It's such a beautiful night."

"Why not?" He sat beside her awkwardly and saw the concern spring into her eyes.

"Gran said you'd had a problem with an ungrateful patient."

"I got savaged by a goat." He gave her an embarrassed grin. "Not very romantic, I'm afraid. It's a bit uncomfortable." He was suddenly aware that his soreness was not the reason he no longer fancied Maggie. Not if his reaction to this girl was anything to go by. He held the wine bottle in front of him and for a few moments neither of them spoke.

Then she reached across and took the bottle and the corkscrew from his hands. "Here, let me do that. Can't have you straining yourself."

He watched her remove the cork with ease and pour out two glasses.

"Thanks." Putting his down for a moment, he got up and went across to the rose bush and snipped off the most perfect bloom with the secateurs he'd brought with him from the kitchen. Then he took it back and handed it to her.

"Thank you, Gary." Again, she dipped her head and breathed in the scent of the rose, her eyes half closed. She had freckles on her nose, Gary saw wonderingly. And long eyelashes and full lips the colour of palest pink that turned up at the corners, even when her mouth was in repose. Why hadn't he noticed how gorgeous she was when he'd seen her at the sanctuary?

When she looked back at him, she was smiling again, her eyes soft. That was the moment that he fell finally and irrevocably in love.

Maggie got to the Red Lion at twenty to nine. She'd been stuck behind a tractor most of the way back. What the hell was a tractor doing on the road on a Saturday night? She hoped Gary hadn't got fed up with waiting. After parking the Land Rover she tore into the Red Lion, glanced around the crowded bar and felt her heart sink. There was no sign of him. Waving over the head of a man in a deerstalker hat at the bar, she tried to get Mike's attention. "Has Gary been in at all?"

"Haven't seen him, Maggie. Hey, didn't the silly bugger have some run-in with a goat?" He smirked. "Are you sure he's not still in hospital having some cute nurse give him a bed bath?"

"Positive, he's been at the sanctuary today." She felt annoyance rising in her at the amusement on Mike's face. Why couldn't he ever take anything seriously?

"You're looking a bit stressed yourself, love." He studied her and his expression changed to concern. "Want your usual?"

She nodded. "Finn's dad isn't well. And I've had a nightmare of a day." She took the glass he gave her and carried it to a table by the window that a giggling couple had just vacated. It was the table where she'd first seen Finn. He'd been staring out of the window, a pensive expression on his face. She hoped he was okay – she was tempted to phone him and ask, but if Albert was really ill, she didn't want to be a nuisance. She knew it was stupid, but she couldn't shake off the feeling that he might regret their night together once he saw Shirley again. And even though she knew it shouldn't have happened because it made everything a hundred times more complicated, she didn't think she could bear it if he regretted it.

She glanced at her watch and saw that it was almost ten to nine. It was beginning to look as though Gary wasn't coming. She finished her drink, waited another ten minutes, then got up to go.

"Tell Gary I was here, if you see him," she called to Mike, who was collecting glasses. "But I've got to go. I've got a bit of a headache."

He abandoned the glasses and came over and patted her arm and the gesture of kindness brought tears to her eyes. She must be more tired than she'd realised, she thought, turning away so he couldn't see.

"Take it easy, Maggie. And I hope Albert's okay. Nice bloke."

"Yes, he is. Thanks, Mike." She left the pub before she gave herself away, shivering as the coolness of the evening hit her. It was another clear night. Thousands of stars studded the velvet sky. The night when she and Finn had sat and counted them seemed a long time ago. As distant and as untouchable as the pale moon that hung in the sky above her.

The cottage seemed curiously empty because she knew that Finn wasn't in it. Even Mickey didn't bother getting up from his basket, just gave her a cursory wag and went back to chewing what looked like one of Finn's boots.

"Bad dog," Maggie chided half-heartedly, prising it out of his mouth. When she straightened she saw, with a little jolt, that the answer machine light was flashing.

The first message was from a farmer wanting to know if she'd take a litter of puppies. His best working bitch had escaped during her season for a romp with the local stray and the resulting brood was no use to him at all. His voice was so accusing that he sounded as if he held Maggie personally responsible for the dalliance.

The second message was from Finn. He was somewhere noisy; it sounded like a busy restaurant. Maggie could hear laughter and the clatter of cutlery on plates in the background. "Sorry I missed you, Maggie, but just to let you know Dad's fine. A case of crossed wires. See you in a couple of days. Bye."

She replayed the message over and over. His voice was curt. Finn's pet hate was leaving messages on answer machines. Or maybe he just hadn't wanted to phone her. Maybe he was out with Shirley, comforting her because her husband had left her again.

Cursing herself for her overactive imagination, she rubbed her eyes, which felt gritty with tiredness, and picked up the phone to call Sarah. She was halfway through dialling the number when she realised that she had no idea what she would say. She didn't want to tell Sarah that her relationship with Finn had moved up a gear – that they'd slept together now and that it had felt so right, so gloriously, painfully right.

She replaced the receiver. The worst thing was that Finn couldn't be anywhere near as keen as she was to repeat the experience. Or he'd have come back tonight and not just left her a message. And, as she stood there, staring into space, all the old, old insecurities came flooding back. She wasn't a nice enough person to interest anyone for long. She would always come second, never first in anyone's life. Except for the animals, who depended on her.

She took Finn's boot back out to the front door and in a sudden burst of frustration hurled it at the wall. Feeling sadder and more alone than she had for years, she went upstairs.

Chapter Thirty

Gary woke up on Sunday morning feeling hung over, but also deliriously happy. For a few moments in the hazy gap between sleep and wakefulness he couldn't remember why. And then it all came flooding back. Sitting in the garden with Jane. The bottle of wine they'd drunk, then the other bottle in his lounge when they'd been forced indoors by the midges.

They'd talked and talked. She'd told him all about her job as a nurse at Odstock Hospital, and she'd listened, enthralled, by his version of 'it shouldn't happen to a vet'. The wine and her enthusiasm had melted away his usual shyness. As the evening stretched on, they'd gone further back into each other's pasts. He'd even told her about being bullied at school, he remembered with a quiver of embarrassment, but she hadn't laughed, she'd put her slim hand over his, empathy shining out of her beautiful eyes. "So that's why you're so passionate about animals, they're so vulnerable, aren't they?" she'd murmured and he'd looked at her wonderingly. He'd never felt so at ease with anyone in his life.

At the end of the evening, when she'd said reluctantly that she ought to go back or Emily would worry, they'd stood at his front door, Jane holding the pink rose he'd given her, and he'd kissed her. Then, having extracted a promise that she'd come and collect Fang with him the next day, he'd climbed upstairs, the pain and stiffness forgotten, and collapsed on his bed, ecstatic with happiness. It was only as he was dropping off to sleep that he remembered with horror that he'd been supposed to meet Maggie at the Red Lion at eight.

Now, he went downstairs and mixed himself a sachet of morning-after cure. He'd arranged to give Jane a knock

273

just before ten. Plenty of time to recover from his hangover. He hoped Maggie wouldn't be too upset. Perhaps she'd been relieved when he hadn't turned up. She hadn't exactly looked thrilled at the prospect of meeting him in the first place. But no, that was unfair. Maggie had just been tired; she'd probably be cursing him for dragging her out for nothing. Maybe he ought to pick her some flowers as a peace offering. No, not flowers. He'd decided last night that, from now on, the only woman he was ever going to give flowers to was Jane.

He went into the lounge. Two glasses and an empty bottle of Merlot sat on the coffee table where he'd left them. He smiled to himself. So it had happened. It hadn't just been a beautiful fantasy. As he crossed the room to get the glasses, he noticed something pink on the floor. A rose petal, he saw, bending with difficulty to pick it up. He held it to his face and breathed in its delicate scent. Then, leaving the glasses where they were, he carried it back into the kitchen and laid it on the Formica work top. Last night had been the start of something wonderful. The beginning of a new era in his life.

When Gary's van drew into the yard just after ten thirty, Maggie was on the phone to the farmer with the collie-cross pups. She glanced up and saw Gary go round to open the passenger door to let out an attractive, vaguely familiar girl. His movements were almost reverent, she noticed with a mixture of affection and amusement. She wasn't the betting type, but she'd have put money on it that the flame-haired beauty had something to do with him standing her up last night.

Gary came into reception and put a box of Quality Street on the desk in front of her. "I'm really, really sorry, Maggie. I – er – completely forgot we said we'd meet."

"And that's a peace offering, is it?"

He nodded. The girl, who was standing behind him and a little to his left, stepped forward.

"Jane," Maggie gasped, recognising her. "I didn't know you two knew each other."

"My gran lives next door to Gary. Small world, isn't it?"

Maggie smiled at them both. "Don't worry about last night, Gary. I was tired anyway."

"You looked it. I was wondering if it would be okay if I took Fang home for a week or so. Just while I'm off."

"Of course it is. I could do with freeing up some space. I've just agreed to take in another eight pups."

"Oh, how cute. What kind?" Jane's eyes were shining with enthusiasm.

"Collie something," Maggie said, just as the phone started to ring again.

"Hi, Maggie, it's Dawn. Sorry about yesterday. How did the home check go?"

Maggie told her.

"I'll be over later to give you a hand. You sound like you could do with it. Oh, and before I forget, my next-door neighbour's after a puppy for her grandchild. Do you have any in at the moment?"

Maggie told her about the collie-crosses.

"Sounds perfect. I'll bring her with me to have a look. See you in a bit."

Maggie put the phone down and went out into the yard. Ahead of her Jane and Gary were standing by the cattery, hand in hand. Small world indeed, she thought, wondering how long Gary had been seeing Jane. It must have happened recently, or surely he'd have said something. Didn't that prove that miracles could happen? So maybe one would happen for her and Finn, although she

275

had the horrid feeling they might need rather more than a miracle.

Dawn's neighbour, who was plump and kindly and wore her glasses on a gold chain around her neck, came in to tell Maggie that she'd found the perfect pup.

"He'll do us better than a collie-cross," she said, her eyes sparkling with excitement. "They do a lot of chewing, collies, don't they?"

"All pups chew," Maggie said, thinking of Mickey, who was at the moment lying in the sun outside reception, looking like butter wouldn't melt in his mouth. "Some of them never grow out of it."

"This one's ready to go now, too. Dawn said we just need to have a home check, is that right?"

"Yes," Maggie said, realising with a small jolt that she was talking about Tiny, the last of the litter. She walked with the woman back up the yard to the main block.

"Are you really sure she'd like this one?" Maggie said, bending to pick him up and resting her face against his soft baby fur. She loved the smell of puppy fur. Why couldn't she suppress the stupid and irrational feeling that if she let Tiny go, things would start to fall apart?

"Yes, he's the one for us." The woman smiled and Maggie forced herself to smile back. She kissed Tiny's head and he blinked sleepily at her. "I'll come and do a home check tonight," she promised.

Chapter Thirty-one

Finn left his dad's about eleven, although both his father and Dorinda had pressed him to stay longer. But, much as they made him welcome, he still felt as though he were playing gooseberry – and an uninvited gooseberry at that. He kissed them both goodbye and promised he'd drive up and see them again soon.

Before he left Nottingham, Finn phoned Shirley, deciding that the least he could do was to reassure her that his father was not, as she'd feared, at death's door.

"Pop in if you've got time, Finn. Stewart would love to see you."

"And Peter?"

"He won't be back until three."

Even so, now he was here, Finn hesitated outside the familiar front door, not at all sure he wanted to re-awaken painful memories that he'd at last managed to put out of his mind. He'd brought four framed sketches of the animals at The Ark, a present for Stewart, and now he clutched the gift-wrapped package and rang the doorbell.

"Hi, Finn." She stood there for a moment, her blue eyes anxious and then she flicked back her blonde hair a little self-consciously and smiled at him. "Come in. I'm so glad your dad's all right. Sneaky old bugger, shacking up with a woman at his age and not saying a word about it."

"Perhaps he thought no one would approve." It was odd being back in the familiar narrow hallway with its bare banisters and brown patterned wallpaper. It still all looked exactly the same, but changed somehow. It took him a few moments to realise that the change was in himself. He was seeing it all through different eyes.

"Stewart!" Shirley called up the stairs. "Come and see who's here."

A fair head appeared over the banisters. "Finn!" Stewart came tearing down the stairs. At least there was no doubting his welcome.

"You haven't been to see me for ages. Why not?"

"I've been working a long way away," Finn said, aware of Shirley's anxious glance. "It's a great place, it's a rescue centre for unwanted animals."

"Like the ones on telly?"

"Just like those." He handed Stewart the oblong package and Stewart ripped off the paper with enthusiasm.

Finn and Shirley watched as he studied each sketch, his head on one side. "Are these all the animals that no one wants?"

"A few of them."

"But they'll get good homes in the end? Families who'll look after them."

"With a bit of luck. Yes."

"We're a family again now, aren't we, Mum?" Stewart looked at his mother for confirmation, and she shifted in her chair. "Yes, love, we are."

"I'm glad," Finn said. "And I hear you've been looking after my dad, too."

"We've been fishing lots. I normally catch more than he does. He coughs so loudly he frightens all the fish away."

"Does he now?"

"It's nice to see you, Finn." Shirley smiled at him over her son's head. "I'll make us a cup of tea."

He sat at the kitchen table, feeling out of place. "And Peter's still all right, is he?"

"If you mean is he drinking, then no he's not. He hasn't got a job, mind, but then, no change there."

"But you're managing okay?"

"Course."

She looked happy. It didn't matter to her that Peter wasn't working. He could have done whatever he liked, with the possible exception of turning back to drink again, and she'd still have loved him. It shone out of her face and Finn realised that he really was glad she was happy. She'd never felt about him the way she felt about Peter. He sipped his tea, surprised that this knowledge didn't hurt.

"Will you stay in Wiltshire now, do you think?" Her voice was soft.

"For a while longer, yes. Maggie might not be able to afford me forever. It was meant to be a temporary arrangement. But I expect I'll find something else."

"She sounded nice. I suppose you'd have to be to run a place like that."

"Yes, she is nice."

Shirley looked as though she'd have liked to say something else, but thought better of it. He refused a second cup of tea, anxious not to outstay his welcome, and not quite ready to meet Peter. He hugged Stewart goodbye and at the door he pecked Shirley's cheek.

"Take care of yourself."

"You too, Finn."

"And thanks again for keeping an eye on Dad."

"Obviously not a close enough one." She laughed. "I'm sorry I dragged you up here on false pretences."

"I'm glad you did."

For a lot of reasons, he thought, as he drove away. Not so long ago he'd thought he loved Shirley, but now he knew that he'd never felt the same about her as he felt about Maggie. It was a revelation.

He wanted to get back and talk to Maggie. Get everything sorted out between them. After their meal at the pub the previous evening, he and his father had talked long into the night. Something that was almost unheard of in the

McTaggart family, especially when the talk was about relationships.

He didn't know what sort of spell Dorinda had woven over his 'oh so reserved' old man, but as well as persuading him to give up smoking, which Finn had been trying to do for years, Albert seemed more open than Finn had ever seen him.

"I think you should stop mucking about, Finn, and tell Maggie how you feel. Life's too short to faff about waiting for the right moment. She's a nice lassie. She's not going to hold some ancient misdemeanour against you, I'm sure."

"No," Finn had murmured, hoping desperately that his father was right. At least he'd got one thing clear in his mind. Being away from Maggie had made him realise just how strong his feelings were. He couldn't stop thinking about the night they'd spent together. The way that she'd been with him, so giving, so honest and uninhibited. But it wasn't just a physical thing, he knew that now. Seeing Shirley had confirmed it. He loved Maggie. He'd never felt like this in his life.

To his intense relief, the unaccustomed exercise Dorinda had mentioned his father was taking had turned out to be long walks and nothing more dubious. She'd persuaded Albert to join her rambling club and Finn had met several of the members when they'd gone out to the Cock and Bottle. Not that Finn was against his father having a few wild nights of passion, but he wasn't sure if Albert's heart was up to it.

All in all it had been a weekend full of shocks. Starting with Dorinda and ending with the realisation that he was in love with Maggie. And, in between, Albert's U-turn when it came to discussing matters of the heart. Finn thought ruefully that perhaps he should have taken more advantage of it and asked him about his mother.

He'd been six years old when she'd walked out on them. It had been a Friday evening, an ordinary evening. He'd just gone to bed and she'd come up to tuck him in as she always did. He had a vivid memory of her leaning over him, her blonde hair stiff with hairspray and her eyelashes black and spidery. She'd stroked his forehead with a slender white hand, her fingers soft. Then she'd hugged him so tight he was half suffocated with her scent.

"Night, baby."

"Night, Mum."

Usually she turned out the light, but tonight she didn't. Just stood there looking down at him. Then she brushed something from her face and he realised she was crying. He'd never seen her cry before. For a moment he'd been so surprised that he hadn't been able to speak. Then he'd said, his voice hesitant, "What's the matter, Mum?"

"Nothing, Poppet. I got something in my eye downstairs, that's all. Nothing for you to worry about."

"Can't you get it out?"

"Yes, I expect I'll be able to get it out in a minute. I just wanted to catch you before you fell asleep."

He'd nodded, only partly reassured. "Maybe Dad can help you get it out."

"Maybe."

In the morning when he got up for breakfast she was gone.

"She's staying with a friend for a few days," his father had told him. "Nothing for you to worry about."

"Did she get that thing out of her eye?"

His father looked at him, but Finn could tell he wasn't really listening. His father never said much anyway.

Finn couldn't remember how much time had gone by before he'd realised that his mother wasn't coming back. Time had blurred in his mind. The one thing he could remember was that about the same time he'd read a fairy tale at school in which a beautiful princess got a piece of glass in her eye and it made her see the world differently. For a long time he'd wondered if that was what had happened to his mother. She was a bit like a beautiful princess, but no one seemed to want to tell him. No one seemed to want to talk about his mother at all.

It wasn't until years later that he'd pieced together what had happened. There'd been a big age gap between his parents. Almost twenty-two years. The general consensus amongst his aunts, who were all from his father's side, and who he rarely saw, was that poor Bridie had been too young to cope with the responsibility of having a child. She was still so much a child herself and had fled back to Ireland to her family who'd never approved of her relationship with Albert anyway. This disclosure, which was said kindly and designed to make him feel better, had only served to make him feel that it was somehow his fault. If he hadn't been around she'd never have left. If he could have somehow helped her to get that piece of glass from her eye that night, then maybe things would have been different.

It was even later that he'd discovered that his parents had never actually been married.

"She never wanted to marry me, lad," his dad had said one drunken Christmas when Finn had been about fifteen. "Her family never approved of me. Far too old – and the wrong religion, amongst other things. She never told them about you. She didn't dare."

It explained why he'd never seen her again. And why his father had never tried to track her down.

"There'd have been no point. The family would have closed ranks if I'd gone over there. Anyway, I still had you."

282

"But didn't you still love her, Dad?"

His father hadn't answered this. Even full of Christmas whisky, he hadn't been able to bring himself to talk about such things. He'd never married or lived with anyone else, although Finn did remember there being a few women around in his childhood. Some of them were kind to him, some indifferent. Finn didn't dare let himself like any of them too much in case they went away, like his mother had done.

He'd grown up craving the security that he was sure love must bring, but not at all sure how to go about finding it, or even if he would recognise it when it appeared. He never had any problems attracting girls, but as soon as they dropped hints about taking things further he backed off. And it had been like this until now, he reflected, as he drove past the 'Welcome To Wiltshire' sign. Maggie had got inside his head, and inside his heart, too. Before he'd met her, he hadn't really known what love was.

At sunset, he stopped the car on the boundaries of Maggie's land and got out, reluctant to finish his journey. What if she didn't feel the same? What if his father was wrong and he just ended up pushing her away from him by rushing her? Coward, he berated himself.

Dusk was stealing over the fields and he watched bats swooping out of the line of trees that bordered The Ark. He imagined Maggie in the cottage, sitting in the little back room, going through the reams of paperwork she always seemed to have. Or maybe she'd gone out somewhere with Gary, whom she'd obviously forgiven. No doubt the vet would have taken full advantage of his absence. His stomach churned at the thought. What on earth was the matter with him? He didn't even know if Gary still had designs on Maggie. He'd certainly seemed genuinely apologetic about hitting him. Much more bothered about it than Finn had been, for some reason. Anyway, Maggie rarely went out on Sundays.

Eventually, when the darkness had grown so deep that the trees were just a blurred outline in front of his tired eyes, and the bats were just passing shadows, no more substantial, he decided, than his fears that Maggie might not feel the same as he did, he got back in his car and drove the last few hundred yards to the sanctuary. The gates were locked so he parked the car outside, got his bag from the boot and, feeling oddly nervous, let himself into the cottage.

Mickey came to greet him, but there was no one else about. Maggie must be out somewhere.

He went into the lounge and sat in the armchair where he'd sat so many nights talking to Maggie. Even though she wasn't there the room didn't feel empty, but full of her presence. It was very peaceful. At his father's he'd had to get used to the traffic sounds all over again. He'd been surprised at how difficult it had been to adjust to the constant buzz that was Nottingham. He closed his eyes, luxuriating in the silence. It was strange how quickly this place had begun to feel like home.

Chapter Thirty-two

"He's back then," Dawn remarked, as she drew up outside Maggie's cottage just after ten. She indicated the outline of Finn's Toyota parked on the verge outside. "Couldn't have had that much to detain him in Nottingham."

"No," Maggie said, feeling excitement tighten her stomach. It felt like he'd been gone forever. How had he got into her heart like this? How had she let him when she knew nothing could ever come of it?

"Go on, then," Dawn prompted. "If you don't mind me saying, you look knackered. You could probably do with a decent night's sleep."

"I am a bit tired." That was the understatement of the year, Maggie thought. She was shattered. Not just because of working flat out, but because she was so torn apart with wanting to go to bed with Finn again, and worrying about what would happen if she did.

"And thanks for coming to do that home check tonight," Dawn added, smiling at her. "Chloe's going to be thrilled to bits when she sees Tiny. I was worried for a while that you were going to change your mind about them having him."

"No, he's much better off with them than here. He'll make a lovely family pet. They can come and get him tomorrow. Any time after nine." Maggie got out of the car and stood in the darkness, gathering herself before she went in.

Her stomach was fluttering as she went into the lounge, which was also in darkness. Finn must be in bed. She didn't know whether to be relieved or disappointed. She was just reaching for the light switch when Finn said, "Hi, Maggie."

She jumped and spun round to face him.

"Sorry – I didn't mean to startle you. I must've fallen asleep in the chair." He stood up, his words slowing and he came across the room towards her. "Is everything okay? I've missed you."

"Everything's fine," she said, looking into his tired eyes and knowing that now he was here, it was. "You should be in bed."

"Is that a proposition?"

"No," she said, feeling a contradictory clench of lust in her groin.

"What a shame. In that case, Maggie, perhaps we could talk."

"What about?"

She looked wary and Finn felt his resolve weakening, but only for an instant.

"Don't look so worried, it's nothing bad." Taking her hand, he drew her on to the settee beside him. He had no experience of this, no preparation; he'd never told anyone he loved them before. He hoped he wasn't going to cock it up. Every sense felt heightened. He could hear the beating of his heart, smell the apple-scented shampoo Maggie used and he could feel the warmth of her denim-clad knee against his. There was a mixture of emotions in her dark eyes and as he looked at her, Finn knew she was fighting her own internal battle. She was scared, too. They'd had similar upbringings in some ways. Both of them desperate for their mother's love and not having it. He'd been luckier than she because he'd had Albert, whom he'd always known had loved him, in his gruff, down-to-earth way, and she'd had no one.

"I don't want to rush you, Maggie, I just want you to know how I feel," he began.

Maggie felt light-headed. This was what she wanted. This was what she'd wanted for a long time now. To hear him say he cared about her, to be able to tell him how she felt, but as she looked into his serious grey eyes all she felt was a tearing pain. If being away from him these past forty-eight hours had taught her anything it was that she couldn't carry on lying to him. Couldn't let him bare his soul to her, without knowing that she hadn't been honest with him.

"Finn, wait a minute." She put her hand on his arm and he hesitated. "Before you say anything else there are things you should know."

"I know everything I need to know about you." His eyes were soft.

"No, you don't." She stood up abruptly. This would be easier if they weren't touching each other. She didn't want to feel his recoil. She paced to the window and looked out at the dark night.

It was two weeks until Sarah's wedding day, but this couldn't wait. Every second she spent in Finn's company would make it harder to tell him the truth. And a great deal more painful when she did. Was she being utterly selfish? She wasn't sure any more. Betraying her best friend was something she'd sworn she'd never do, but living with this lie was worse.

"It's about Sarah," she whispered, turning around at last to face him.

He stayed where he was, frowning slightly, his long legs stretched out in front of him. "I thought we'd already sorted that out, Maggie. It was a long time ago. I thought you understood that I wished it had never happened. And by the way she avoids me at every possible opportunity, I'd say she feels the same."

"No, you don't understand." She'd always known this wouldn't be easy, but it was ten times worse than she'd anticipated.

"Finn. That night that you and Sarah made love…"

"I wouldn't have called it that."

Best to spit it out – just say the words that she knew could never be taken back. The words that were going to end her relationship with him and very likely her friendship with Sarah, too.

"Sarah got pregnant that night, Finn. She got pregnant with Ben."

For a moment he didn't react. Then his face went very still. Maggie swallowed and backed up against the window and folded her arms in a little gesture of self-defence.

"Are you saying that Ben's my son?" He still didn't get up, but she could see tension in every line of his body, from the straightness of his arms to the rigid planes of his face.

She nodded, and now he did get to his feet and came slowly across towards her. Very self-contained, every movement controlled. When he was a step or so away he put his hands on her arms. His touch was light and his voice was icy calm.

"How long have you known this, Maggie?"

She looked into his eyes, wanting to lie. Wanting to say, 'just a few days. Sarah told me when you were in Nottingham, which is why I'm telling you now.' Because then the lie wouldn't be so long-lived, so treacherous.

"I've always known," she whispered.

"I see." He let go of her arms, went across the room, still at the same unhurried pace, and picked up his jacket and car keys.

"What are you going to do?"

"I should think that's pretty obvious."

"You can't go round there. Ben doesn't know. He thinks his father's dead. And Jack – well, Jack thinks he left when he found out she was pregnant." So many lies, she thought. Lies that she'd helped to perpetuate. And she'd have given all that she owned for things to be different. Not to be the one standing here delivering the death blows.

"Well, maybe you'd better phone and warn her then, Maggie." His voice was clipped and he turned and looked at her, and for the first time she could see the icy fury in his face. "What the fuck did you expect me to do?"

For a few moments after the door slammed behind him, she stayed where she was at the window. But when his tail-lights drew away and she knew it was real she was galvanised into movement. She hadn't thought Finn knew where Sarah and Jack lived, but then she realised she was being naïve. He could have seen it on Ben's school bag, or Ben could even have told him. She felt a twist of pain at the thought of Ben and the chaos this could bring into his safe little world. Oh, God, what had she done? She should have kept her mouth shut, she should have just told Finn she didn't want a relationship with him. Made him walk away. She hadn't done that because she cared about him too much, she realised, as she dialled Sarah's number with unsteady fingers. You couldn't lie to and cheat someone you cared about. Not forever. A decent person wouldn't have done it for this long.

Finn had a little trouble finding the road where Sarah lived, but no trouble at all finding the house because it was the only one with lights on at the front. It was eleven thirty – the other residents of Arleston must be tucked up in bed – but Sarah was obviously prepared for him, he thought, slamming the car door and striding up the garden path.

She opened the door before he could ring the bell. Her face was white and her blonde hair all fuzzed up, as if she'd just got out of bed. Her tee-shirt was on inside out. And back to front too, by the look of it, the label sticking up at her throat.

She gestured silently towards the lounge door and he strode past her. He half expected Jack to be waiting in there, but there was no sign of him. He stood in the middle of an untidy room, letting his gaze travel over gilt-framed photographs of Sarah, Ben and Jack on the walls and on top of the television. The child he had never known was his, so clearly a part of someone else's life. The settee was littered with soft toys. Sarah bent to move them, but he shook his head.

"I'm not stopping. You've spoken to Maggie, I take it."

She nodded. Her blue eyes were wide and afraid. "What are you going to do?"

"It's more a case of what you're going to do," he said, his voice quiet. "I want Ben to know I'm his father. I want to be involved in his life. I've missed far too much of it already."

"I can't." She took a couple of small steps away from him. "He thinks his dad's dead and Jack thinks something else."

"Then you'd better find a way of telling them the truth. I've had enough lying to last me a lifetime. From you and from Maggie." He could hear the bitterness in his voice, but he couldn't hide it. He couldn't believe that he'd spent so long playing softly softly with Maggie, doing all that he could to earn her trust, and she'd been deceiving him all this time.

"Finn, please – you have to give me some time. We're getting married in a fortnight."

"You've had the best part of seven years already, I think that's plenty of time, don't you?" He strode across the room towards the door. "Oh, and Sarah..." He paused and looked back at her. "I shan't say anything to Ben because I think it should come from you. But that doesn't apply to Jack. Bear that in mind."

He could hear her sobbing as he let himself out of the front door, but he was too angry to care.

Chapter Thirty-three

Maggie hardly slept that night. She kept hearing Sarah's stricken voice in her head.

"Why did you have to tell him, Maggie? Why couldn't you have waited like you promised? What difference would another two weeks make?"

She'd half expected Sarah to phone her back. Jack wasn't there, he was away on some sales trip, earning cash for a wedding that might now never happen. But the phone remained silent. Finn didn't come back either. Maggie tortured herself with how he must be feeling. But however much she wished she'd kept quiet, she knew that if she'd had the choice to make again, she'd still have told him.

But this didn't make her feel any better. She'd managed to devastate both Finn and Sarah with a few sentences. She'd probably never see Finn again – well, she'd survive that, she'd have to. But she couldn't bear to lose Sarah, too.

Maggie got through the following morning on autopilot. She felt drained and numb and she didn't feel too brilliant physically, either. Her head kept spinning – lack of sleep, probably – and her throat was on fire. She'd just popped into the cottage at lunch time to see if she could find some painkillers and a Lemsip when she heard the front door bang.

Thinking it was Dawn or one of the other volunteers she called out that she was just coming, but when she turned, having finally found what she was looking for, Finn was standing in the kitchen doorway.

"I've come to get my things," he said, his voice cold. "I'm going to stay at the Red Lion for a while."

She swallowed and regretted it. Her throat felt as though it were full of hot knives, and she didn't know whether it was the shock of seeing him, but Finn seemed to be standing at the wrong end of a telescope. Very distant and not really a part of her world. He came a few steps closer and she felt herself wobbling and grabbed hold of the table for support.

"Maggie, are you all right? You look terrible."

"Thanks very much."

Now he was right beside her and she could see the strain in his face and smell the citrus maleness of him. She frowned. Before she could stop him, Finn rested a hand on her forehead. "You're very hot. I'm going to take your temperature."

"No, I'm fine. You get going."

He ignored her and got the thermometer from the kitchen cupboard.

"I've got a sore throat, that's all."

"It looks more like flu to me. Put this in your mouth and we'll see."

She snatched it out of his hands and did as he said, too weak to argue. His concern was worse than his anger and she wished she didn't feel so giddy. There were all sorts of coloured lights on the edges of her vision and hot and cold shivers were sliding up and down her back.

"You've got a temperature of 101," Finn remarked. "Hardly all right. I think you'd be better off in bed."

There was no disputing that. She had a horrible feeling she was going to fall over if she didn't lie down soon. She moved to go past him and he stepped aside. Why did her legs feel so wobbly? It was a bit like being drunk. She hesitated and Finn, with an impatient shake of his head, put his arm around her waist. "I'm going to help you upstairs," he muttered. "Because otherwise you aren't going to make it."

"I don't need any help," she snapped, but it wasn't true. She'd had flu like this once before – it had washed over her with the same ruthless speed and left her flat on her back for a week. God, she couldn't afford to be out of action for that long.

They took the stairs, step by wooden step, Finn's arm supporting her, but she still felt exhausted and breathless when they got to the top. She paused on the landing outside her bedroom door.

"I'll be fine now. You can let go of me."

He let go, but only to open the door. Then he propelled her inside. "Get in bed. I'm going to nip out and get you something from the pharmacist. Do you feel sick at all? Shall I get you a bucket?"

"No, I'm perfectly fine now," she lied, and he frowned and shut the door. And then, suddenly, to Maggie's very great dismay, she was sick all over the floor.

When she woke up Finn was standing beside her bed, a glass of something opaque in his hands. Sleep hadn't been restful, but filled with nightmares, strange and garish and so vivid that she wasn't sure which were reality and which were dreams. She glanced at the floor, and decided she must have dreamed the vomiting. At least that was something.

He followed her gaze, but all he said was, "Drink this. The pharmacist recommended it."

She pushed herself up on the pillows, which seemed to take a lot more energy than the small movement warranted. And then she realised she wasn't wearing anything. So she hadn't dreamed it and he'd undressed her, too. Humiliated, she pulled the duvet up to her neck and glared at him.

"Your clothes are in the wash. You wouldn't have wanted to wake up in them, I can promise you." She saw a flash of something in his eyes – wry humour. Perhaps after yesterday when she knew she'd hurt him beyond belief, he was enjoying seeing her discomfort.

"Drink this," he said again, holding out the glass.

She took it warily. "How long have I been asleep?"

"A couple of hours."

"God, this tastes foul. I think I've got flu."

"Yes." He knelt beside the bed and she felt a snatch of pain because the last time he'd done that had been in such different circumstances. "Can I get you anything else?"

"No, I'll be fine by tonight. You can go to the Red Lion."

He raised his eyebrows. "Much as I'd like to get out of here, Maggie, I'm not that much of a bastard. I'm not leaving you in this state. Besides, you need me to look after the animals."

"No, I don't. Dawn will help if I ask her."

"Dawn's got a sore throat too. Which reminds me. The pharmacist recommended these pastilles as well. They'll help numb it a bit."

"Thanks." She took the packet from him, wishing fleetingly for something that would numb her heart, which she could feel breaking all over again. He was here, but he hated her, she could see it in his eyes and she couldn't blame him.

"I'm so sorry I didn't tell you about Ben before," she whispered, putting down the glass and lying back on the pillows.

"Not half as sorry as I am, I can assure you."

It was four days before she felt well enough to get back on her feet. Sarah came to see her on her first day up.

"Florence Nightingale wouldn't let me in before," she grumbled, coming into the back room where Maggie was curled up on the settee under a duvet. "He said you weren't up to having visitors."

"I wouldn't come too near," Maggie warned, gesturing Sarah towards Finn's armchair. "You don't want to catch this, believe me. Not when you're getting married in ten days."

"I'm not," Sarah said quietly. "I've told Jack the wedding's off. I told him last night and he's going back to Scotland."

"What do you mean, the wedding's off? Sarah, you can't do that. You love him."

"I adore him, but he's going to hate me once I tell him about Finn. I couldn't bear him to hate me. I'd rather he just thought I'd changed my mind." She blinked and Maggie saw tears in her eyes. She wanted to cry too – she'd never been able to bear seeing Sarah upset. Before she could argue with her, Sarah came across and knelt in front of her.

"I've done nothing but think these past few days, Maggie. I don't do it very often, do I – thinking. But I've decided you were right. I shouldn't have lied to everyone. Especially not to Ben – and I shouldn't have made you lie for me, either. I put you in an impossible situation, didn't I?"

"I had a choice," Maggie said, swallowing. It was a relief to be able to do it without pain. "We always have a choice."

"No, you didn't. You're my friend. You lied because I asked you to. Even though you knew it would mean the end for you and Finn. You love him, don't you?"

"I don't know."

"Yes, you do. That's why you told him. I'd have done the same thing in your place. If someone had been keeping something from Jack, I'd have told him what it was." She

296

sighed and drummed her fingers on the arm of the settee. "Anyway, I've done what I can to put things right. I've had a long chat with Finn and I've agreed that he can see Ben – have him some weekends if he wants, once we've made things official.

"I'm going to get his name put on the birth certificate. It's what he wants and it's only fair. All I have to do now is to tell Ben, but I can't see him minding. He's always asking about Finn. We've already arranged that Finn is coming to the results of Ben's art competition at school on Friday."

Maggie blinked. The world had moved on without her in the last few days. "I'm glad about Finn and Ben," she murmured, suppressing the urge to hug Sarah because she really didn't want to give her flu. "But I'm really sorry about Jack. You two are made for each other."

Sarah shook her head. "I should have done some thinking before, Maggie, shouldn't I? Proper thinking, instead of just burying my head in the sand and hoping the problem would go away. Finn's going back to Nottingham to live, isn't he?"

Maggie nodded, even though she hadn't known that. For the last few days he'd looked after the sanctuary and he'd looked after her, but they hadn't talked beyond trivia. Knowing he must be desperate to get away from her hurt badly. He would have to keep in touch with Sarah because he wanted to see Ben, she thought with a tug of pain. He'd probably forgive Sarah, in time, for lying to him. He would understand why she had; he was that sort of man. But he didn't have to forgive her.

Chapter Thirty-four

"Fang's really cute, isn't she?" Jane, who was sitting on Gary's lounge carpet, tickled the dog's tummy as she spoke and the Jack Russell wriggled ecstatically beneath her touch. "Are you going to call her Fang forever or change her name now she's a reformed character?"

"I suppose we ought to change it," Gary said thoughtfully. "Got any ideas?"

"How about Lucky? She is, isn't she, considering that she had a death sentence hanging over her head when you first found her."

"I suppose she is." He smiled. It was Thursday evening and they had the French windows open to let in the last of the evening sun. Jane's hair gleamed gold in its light.

"It's all down to you," she told him. "If you hadn't persevered she wouldn't be here."

"To be honest, a lot of it's down to Maggie. She was the one who took her in. I'm really glad she's feeling better. That flu was nasty. I've never known Maggie to be ill before."

"Was there ever anything between you two?" Jane asked idly, glancing up at him.

He knelt beside her on the carpet. "Why? Would you mind?"

"No," she said. "Well, maybe a bit."

"How much of a bit?"

"Stop teasing me, Gary."

"I'm sorry. And the answer's no, there's never been anything between us."

"Truth?"

"Okay, once I hoped there might be. But not any more." He smiled at her. "If you really want the truth, Jane, these last few weeks have been the happiest of my life."

298

"Mine too," she said.

"Really?"

"Yes, really." She stopped stroking Fang and reached out a hand to him so that her long hair fell forward. "My only regret is that Gran's been living next to you all this time and we didn't meet sooner."

He thought about the first time he'd seen her in the sanctuary when he'd been all screwed up with bitterness over Finn and he shook his head. "No sense regretting what's past," he murmured. "We'll just have to make up for lost time." He kissed her hand and thought again how beautiful she was. And how amazing it was that she seemed to feel the same way about him as he did about her.

He'd never in a million years have thought that he'd be pleased he'd punched someone. Not that he was planning to repeat the experience. But if he hadn't hit Finn that day, he'd probably never have got talking to Emily. And he very likely wouldn't be sitting here now, feeling happier than he'd ever done in his life. He got up slowly and went across to his jacket, which was hung across the back of a dining table chair.

"Jane, shall we go outside for a while, I want to ask you something."

She got up, her face curious, and followed him.

"I was going to do this properly," he murmured, sitting her down on the bench in the rose bower. "Slap up meal in a posh restaurant, champagne, the works, but I can't wait another second."

He knelt in front of her, his knees sinking into the damp grass, and his wound with its recently removed stitches still sore, and took both her hands in his. "Jane, will you do me the very great honour of agreeing to become my wife?"

"Oh, Gary." Her eyes were sparkling brighter than the solitaire that he'd now slipped from its box. "Yes, please. And, for what it's worth," she threw back her head and breathed in the sweet scent of summer roses, "I don't think you could have chosen a more romantic place on earth if you'd tried."

Chapter Thirty-five

"You've got to come, Auntie Maggie. EVERYONE'S coming and Miss Benson says I might win a prize." Ben, who was hunched over a computer game in Sarah's lounge, gazed across at her with Finn's eyes. The likeness between them caught at her heart and Maggie knew she'd never again be able to look at Ben without seeing Finn. She swallowed down a bittersweet ache of longing.

EVERYONE meant Finn and Sarah, Maggie guessed, and she hated the idea of trailing behind them like a spare part at Ben's school. But that was her problem, not Ben's.

"Of course I'll come, darling. What time is it?"

"Seven o'clock kick off," Sarah said, coming back into the lounge with two mugs of coffee and meeting Maggie's eyes over Ben's head. "Are you sure you won't be too busy, Maggie?"

Sarah was trying to let her off the hook and she was grateful, but she didn't see why Ben should be disappointed to spare her feelings.

"I won't be too busy. Which painting have you entered?"

"The one of Ashley. Daddy Finn says it's the best."

She blinked. It was hard to get used to him saying Daddy Finn, but the words tripped off his tongue as easily as he'd once said Daddy Jack. Perhaps children of his age did adjust more easily to change. He'd accepted Sarah's explanation that she'd made a mistake about his father being dead and he'd seemed happy to accept that not all fathers lived with you. That probably applied to half his class, Maggie reflected.

"I've got a grandad Albert who lives in Nottingham and he's going to take me to see Robin Hood and he's going to teach me how to fire proper arrows," Ben carried on happily.

"Is he, sweetheart." She wondered what Albert made of it all. She guessed he'd be thrilled to bits, once he'd got over the shock. Finn was pleased. He hadn't said as much, he was barely speaking to her, but for some reason now that she didn't need to read him, she could. He and Ben had renewed their friendship as if there had never been a gap.

Finn was still living with her – or rather he was living in the same house. But he was going back to Nottingham straight after the art competition.

She was worried about Sarah, though. She'd lost weight over the last couple of weeks. Her usual flippant manner had all but disappeared and although Maggie had tried to get her to talk, she had said very little about Jack.

"If I talk about him, I'll fall apart," she'd told Maggie the previous night. "And I can't afford to fall apart. It's not fair on Ben."

The judging of the art competition was taking place in the assembly hall of Ben's school. Sarah, Finn and Maggie wandered around, looking at dozens of paintings displayed on the walls and on several big green screens. The paintings were divided by the age groups of the children. Ben had temporarily abandoned them to chat to some mates across the other side of the room.

They paused, yet again, to admire Ben's painting of Ashley trotting across the field. Ben had got the chestnut shine on Ashley's coat very close to the original and there was a sense of movement running through the picture.

"It's very hard to draw horses, but he's got the perspective just right," said a voice from behind them and they turned to see Miss Benson.

Sarah smiled at her. "I'm so proud of him."

"Do you paint?" Miss Benson went on. "It often runs in families."

"He gets it from his father," Sarah explained, touching Finn's arm, and Maggie saw pride leap into his eyes.

"I dabble a bit, that's all," he murmured, flushing, and he and Sarah exchanged a 'proud parents' glance. Maggie knew it was irrational and stupid, but their shared closeness made her feel as though someone had stuck a dagger into her heart.

"Well, I'll wish you good luck for later," Miss Benson went on. "He's up against some stiff competition, but I'd certainly give him a prize if it were up to me."

"Are you all right, Maggie?" Sarah glanced at her with anxious eyes. "You've gone ever so pale."

Maggie became aware that Finn was looking at her, too, and avoiding his eyes, she said, "I'm fine. A little hot, that's all."

"We could go outside for a minute. It doesn't look as though the judging's going to be for a while."

But just as Sarah spoke, a crackly voice on the microphone informed them that if they'd like to start taking seats at the front of the hall, the results of the competition were about to be announced.

Ben ran across towards them. "Miss Benson thinks I should sit on the end of a row in case I win a prize." He frowned.

"Well, don't look so worried," Sarah told him. "I thought the idea of entering was to win a prize."

"Yes, but if I don't I'll feel stupid. I think I'll sit in the middle."

Sarah and Finn exchanged glances, and they compromised and took the last four seats of a row, Ben on the third one between Finn and Sarah, so he'd only disturb them if he did have to get up.

As they waited for the rest of the seats to fill up, Maggie wished she was anywhere but here. She scanned the faces of the other parents. Right at the back of the hall she saw a flash of red hair as someone sat down. Not Jack, surely? Before she could be sure, someone sat in front of him, blocking her view. She must be mistaken. Jack was in Scotland, six hundred miles away.

Ben won a prize, as Miss Benson had predicted. Not first prize, but runner-up, which he was thrilled with. He ran back to them with the trophy, a silver-plated affair in the shape of an artist's palette, his face shining with excitement. Sarah hugged him, but he wriggled out of her grasp so he could show Finn the trophy. "I wouldn't have winned it if you didn't help me."

"Sure you would. You're really talented." Finn hugged him too and Maggie noticed that Ben didn't pull away from his father. Their bond was apparent, even now. She saw Finn wiping something that looked suspiciously like tears from his eyes and she looked away, not wanting to intrude.

It was as they filed out of the main hall that Maggie saw Sarah, who was walking ahead of her and Finn, come to a sudden halt.

"What is it?" she asked, catching up, and then she could see for herself.

Jack was standing by Sarah's car, his face serious, as he waited for them to reach him.

Finn glanced at Maggie. "Do you think we should disappear?"

"I think we should see what he wants first," she murmured, worry coiling in her stomach. "He doesn't look very happy, does he?"

"Hello, Daddy Jack," Ben said, oblivious to the adults' tension. "Did you see I winned a prize?"

"Yes, mate, I saw you." Jack hunkered down to Ben's level and took the trophy from him and studied it. "Congratulations – and may it be the first of many." Then he glanced up at Sarah and added softly. "I came because he phoned and asked me to."

"You came all the way back from Scotland?" Sarah's face was apprehensive.

"Well, to be truthful, I was only halfway there. The minibus broke down." He gave her a rueful smile. "I left it in the Lake District and caught the train back."

He handed the trophy to Ben and stood up. "Ben told me that there'd been a mistake about his dad being dead. He said you'd found him." He glanced sideways at Finn and then he looked back into Sarah's eyes. "He also said that he wasn't the kind of dad who lived with you. But the kind he'd just see at weekends. Is that true, Sarah?"

Sarah chewed her lip and nodded and wiped her face with the back of her hand.

Maggie touched Finn's arm. "I think we could leave them to it now," she whispered.

When they got back to the cottage Finn went upstairs to pack and now his bags were piled up by the front door. Maggie heard him going up and down the stairs and cried silently over the washing-up bowl, her tears plopping into the water. She was dreading him going, but she also knew she couldn't carry on like this. Living in the same house as him, but having him act like a polite stranger, was torture.

She wiped her eyes, splashed cold water on to her face and went into the lounge to do some paperwork. She'd barely begun when he came in, but instead of just saying goodnight and vanishing to bed, which was what he'd taken to doing lately, he sat in the chair opposite her.

"Do you think they'll get back together?" he asked idly.

"Yes, I think they will. They're besotted with each other. They'll have talked everything through and Jack will forgive her for sending him away and for lying to him about you."

Finn raised his eyebrows. "Sometimes we can't forgive until we understand what's going on."

She stared at him. It was the first thing he'd said in days that was any more than polite conversation.

"What do you mean?"

"Sarah told me that you didn't say anything to me about Ben because she'd made you promise you wouldn't."

"That's right," she said quietly, wondering where he was heading. "Why else do you think I'd have kept it from you?"

"I want to know why you told me when you did. Was it because you didn't want us to become more involved? Did you tell me because you knew that was the one thing you could say that would stop things going any further?"

Maggie gasped. "Of course not."

He got up and came across the room and the settee dipped as he sat next to her. She glanced at him, torn between the desperate need to touch him and the fear that she'd be rejected if she did.

"Your timing was spectacular. Why then, Maggie?"

"I..."

"You can't say it, can you?" His eyes held hers. "You're afraid to let go, Maggie, aren't you? You're terrified to love anyone in case you get hurt. I think you'd rather push me away than let me get close. In case I hurt you."

She shook her head, but he carried on talking.

306

"You probably don't even realise it yourself. These things go back to childhood. You once told me you felt you came second in your mother's life."

"I did."

"I don't think it's as simple as that. Things are never black and white – but we think they are when we're children."

"You don't understand. You can't. You weren't there."

"I understand that she was a single parent and that she wanted you to have the things she never had so she worked hard so that you could. Okay, maybe she was a little blinkered and she thought material things would make up for not spending time with you, but I'll bet if you'd ever told her how you felt, she'd have been amazed. Did you ever tell her how you felt?"

"No."

He put his arms around her and she trembled beneath his touch. Something was tearing deep inside her. Something breaking and shattering and the pain was so deep that she wanted to die. She remembered how she'd stood and watched the first bulldozer moving towards her childhood home. The way the dust had flared out into the summer air, as Arleston Court had collapsed with a groan of protest. How she'd thought that once it no longer existed neither would the pain she still carried within her. The agony of thinking she wasn't loved, because she wasn't worthy of it. But it hadn't worked. You couldn't wipe out memories, however hard you tried.

She covered her face with her hands, not wanting him to see, even though she knew it was too late to hide from him, far too late. "The longest time I ever held her hand was when she was dead," she whispered through interlinked fingers. "Every time I tried to touch her – even

307

when she was ill, she shoved me away. She would never let me get close. Not even when she was dying, Finn."

Very gently he pulled her hands away. "You have to let it go. Look at me, Maggie." And because she had no choice, she looked into his eyes and his expression was so tender that she wanted to weep.

"You're not the only one," he went on, his voice gruff. "I'm the same, which is how I know about you. I'm going to tell you something I've never told anyone before. It's about my mother."

He started to talk, haltingly at first, his eyes clouded with pain. He told her about the night his mother had come to his room to say goodbye. About the fairy tale where the princess had something bad in her eye and how he'd been sure that the same thing had happened to his mother. How he'd always thought that if he'd been able to help her get it out, she wouldn't have left him. He talked of the wall of silence his relatives had put up to protect him. About the terrible conflict he had between wanting love and being unsure that he really knew what it was. And although his words were sometimes rambling, the emotions were so eloquent that Maggie wanted to cry her heart out with him.

When he finally lapsed into silence she realised that her fingers were entwined in her lap and her shoulders were stiff with tension, because she wanted to hold Finn, to comfort him, and she couldn't, because if she touched him she'd be lost again. She knew he was right. She was afraid of love.

"The fairy tale you're talking about was called The Snow Queen," she said, struggling for control. "I remember it too. My mother used to read it to me in bed. It was to do with a magic mirror that reflected only bad things. And then one day it got broken and the glass smashed into a million pieces and it was said that if you got one of the pieces in your eye you would never see anything beautiful again. The whole world would become ugly and distorted."

For a while she didn't think he'd heard her, but then he gave a deep sigh. "Oh, Maggie. All these years I've thought Mum had something in her eye, but it's been me, all along. I've been the one who hasn't been able to see anything clearly."

"It's just a fairy tale," she murmured.

"But aren't all fairy tales based on the tiniest grain of truth? I don't think I even knew what love was, until…" He looked at her and broke off. "How do you feel about me? I need to know."

His eyes were mesmerising. She didn't think she'd ever be able to look away. But she felt so exposed, so afraid. Emotions spun and churned inside her and all she knew was that she never wanted him to go. Never wanted him to stop holding her.

"Tell me, Maggie." Still she couldn't speak and the room around them seemed to draw in, holding its breath, waiting for her answer.

"I can't bear the thought of spending a second away from you," she whispered. "I'm terrified of you leaving and I'm terrified of you staying. Is that love?"

"I think it is." He smiled. That wry little smile she knew so well. Then he let go of her for long enough to hold his hands out in front of him and she could see that his fingers were trembling.

"I'm terrified too," he said. "For all the same reasons as you. And I'm not going anywhere. Unless you want me to go. Do you?"

Chapter Thirty-six

Gary and Jane arrived at the cottage on Saturday evening.

"We've got some news," Gary said. "And we wanted you to be the first to know." He grabbed Jane's hand and pulled her forward. "We've just got engaged. We know it's a bit quick, but we're both surer about this than we've ever been about anything."

"Congratulations." Maggie looked at the diamond ring on Jane's finger. Then, impulsively, she stepped forward and kissed her. "I'm very, very pleased for you both. When's the big day?"

"We haven't set a date yet." Gary was grinning so broadly that it was impossible not to smile with him. "One step at a time, eh, Maggie?"

"Absolutely. Finn's around somewhere. Shall I tell him?"

"Tell me what?" Finn said, coming through the door.

Maggie told him and watched with some amusement as he shook Gary's hand and then couldn't decide whether to shake Jane's too, or to kiss her cheek. In the end he did both.

"We're going to the Red Lion later for a celebratory jar," Gary said. "Would you like to join us? I thought I might ring Sarah and Jack, too. Or would that be insensitive, do you think?"

"Well, yesterday I'd have said it might be," Maggie said. "But you should be okay now." She'd spoken to Sarah the previous evening and for someone who'd just had to cancel a wedding, she'd sounded amazingly happy.

"We don't need a piece of paper to prove anything, Maggie. We can always get married some time in the future, there's no rush. He's here, that's all I care about.

And he's forgiven me. And I know I don't deserve it. I don't deserve you either, do I?"

"Don't be ridiculous," Maggie had replied. Ridiculous was one of her mother's words, she'd thought. She must drop it. She was going to have to drop a lot of things. The future had opened up before her, a yawning chasm filled with darkness and butterflies. Finn had a lot to answer for, asking her to jump into it. To make this leap of faith.

"We'd be glad to come," Finn said. "Perhaps we ought to make it a double celebration." He moved across to the mantelpiece and picked up Ben's trophy. "Have you seen this? Young Ben's going to be very famous one day. Better than me, I reckon."

Finn and Maggie exchanged glances and they talked about some of the other successes at the sanctuary, like the Skegness donkeys, one of which Maggie had re-homed the previous week.

"Oh, and I almost forgot, I've got some other news for you," Gary said, pulling a piece of paper out of his pocket. "I had Ashley's test results through yesterday. The bad news is that he's definitely a gelding, so the chances of doing anything about his overdeveloped sex drive are minimal. The good news is that Jane knows some people who are interested in taking him on. She's told them all about his problems and they're not bothered in the least. They want to use him for driving and they seem to think that he'll be working far too hard to worry about chasing after mares."

"Will you still get a horse, then, Jane?" Maggie asked.

"Actually we thought we might get one between us." Gary shot her a smile. "A nice little thoroughbred crossed with something heavier. We thought we might do a few working hunter classes."

"I didn't know you rode."

He tapped his nose in a way that made Maggie think he'd been spending far too much time with Mike. "I've been riding since I was six," he said, and then with a sly glance at Jane, he lowered his voice. "There's a lot you don't know about me, Maggie Clarke."

After the two of them had left, Maggie wandered up the yard to check that everywhere was locked up and found to her relief that Ashley seemed to be more interested in the Polos she'd brought him than Rowena.

The sanctuary was a far cry from the ramshackle collection of buildings it had been before Finn had arrived, she thought, as she leant on the paddock railings. She couldn't have justified employing him for much longer, even if things hadn't turned out the way they had.

"What are you thinking?" he said, coming to stand beside her. She told him and he nodded.

"As we seem to have the place to ourselves for once there's something I'd like to talk to you about."

"Talk away."

"Not here," he said, taking her hand and leading her up the yard and Maggie thought about the first time she'd seen him here. It was only a few months since that wet February day. Yet it felt as though he'd been in her life forever.

They went past the dog-walking field, which looked pink in the afternoon sun. There was a track around the outside worn down by dozens of walkers, but in the middle of the field the grass grew long and wild. It may have been a trick of the light, but the feathery tops of the stems had the faintest of rosy tints, giving the impression of a field of pink grass. A scattering of bright poppies added to the illusion. It was like seeing the field through rose-tinted glasses, Maggie thought. She knew there were thistles in the middle, but you couldn't see them from here. Perhaps there were always thistles in life, an irritating but essential part of the journey.

"I had a phone call from Mike this morning," Finn said, pausing by the gate.

"And?"

"He's got an art dealer staying at the pub who's interested in my work. He wants to meet me with a view to putting on an exhibition. I know it's early days, but I think I might be able to make a living out of painting, eventually."

"That's brilliant. It's what you want to do, isn't it?"

"One of the things I want to do." He smiled at her. "I don't mind what I do for a living. People are more important than anything else. Do you know, I love this place almost as much as I love you. I thought I'd miss Nottingham, but I don't. So maybe it's true what they say about home being where the heart is."

"Is that what you wanted to talk to me about?"

"Not exactly, no." He swung a leg over the five-bar gate. "You'll have to humour me for a while, I'm building up to it."

It wasn't until the sun was beginning to set and the field was bathed in honey-gold light that he pulled her into his arms.

He had a bit of trouble getting out the words. He skirted round what he wanted to say for a few minutes, talking about things like commitment and finding out the truth about your emotions.

Then, as the sun slipped below the line of trees, turning the field to a gloriously deep pink, he finally said, "Oh hell, Maggie, I'm hopeless at this, but what I'm trying to say is, would you consider marrying me? Some day in the future when you're ready?"

313

"Is that your idea of a romantic proposal?" she teased, and he looked so affronted that the effort of keeping a straight face eluded her.

"Laugh at me, would you?" He pulled her down on to the grass and kissed her so thoroughly that she had to pull away from him, breathless.

"Finn, we'll get arrested. And there are thistles."

"I can't see any. It's your bloody field. Why shouldn't we make mad, passionate love in it if we want to?"

"Because the farmer next door is baling hay," she pointed out, pulling away from him and thinking fleetingly of another long-ago field, not far from here. Of him and Sarah starting Ben, starting all of this, and a shadow passed through her and she hesitated.

"I thought, Maggie, that we were going to let the past go," he said softly, his grey eyes on hers, reading her face, as always. "But if you're still not sure of me, then I'll wait."

"I don't want you to wait. I'd love to marry you, Finn. Any day in the future. Tomorrow, if you like."

There was a look of such delighted surprise on his face that she added, "Did you seriously think I'd say no?"

"I hoped you wouldn't." He propped himself on one elbow, and said, his voice more serious, "I wasn't sure if you'd forgiven me yet for bullying you into admitting you loved me."

"Well I have. Anyway, you're not the only one who needs forgiving around here. I lied to you for far too long. I'm so sorry."

"We'll call it quits." He kissed her again, and for a long while they forgot all about the farmer in the next field.

They decided to keep their news to themselves for a while, though, because tonight was Gary and Jane's celebration and they didn't want to take anything away from them.

Much later, they sat in the Red Lion: Gary and Jane, Maggie and Finn and Sarah, Jack and Ben. At the bar, Mike was deep in conversation with the holidaying art dealer, who turned out to be a friend of the woman who'd bought the painting of the girl on the beach. "He's practising his negotiating skills," Finn told Maggie. "He keeps trying to persuade me I need an agent."

"He'd make a good one," she muttered. "That's what he's best at – negotiating."

"Who's for another drink, then?" Mike asked, coming across to them smiling. "This one's on the house."

"We've all had far too much already," Sarah said, clutching her head and rolling her eyes dramatically.

"I'll have one," Ben said, who'd been cashing in on the fact that they were all squiffy and had helped himself to a few sips of Finn's Guinness when no one was looking.

"But we can't turn down an offer like that," Gary pointed out. "It's never happened before and it might never come again."

So the drinks came and they toasted Gary and Jane yet again, and Ben's competition success and Finn's future career as an artist. And then, when each of them had just a sip or so left in their glasses, Finn stood up. "I'd like to make one more toast."

"Better be quick, mate," Gary said, his glass poised at his lips.

Finn grinned, looked at Maggie and raised his glass high. "Here's to second chances."

Epilogue

The sunlight was bright after the dimness of the church and they stood blinking in the ivy-covered archway while their guests tumbled out of the old oak doors, full of laughter and congratulations.

Finn grabbed Maggie's hand and kissed her again. "Cream really suits you, you look amazing."

"You don't scrub up so bad yourself."

"Mind you, you look beautiful, whatever you wear."

"You, Mr McTaggart, are a big smoothie."

"And you, Mrs McTaggart, shouldn't argue so much. I mean it. You should accept compliments in the spirit they're given and say thank you."

"Thank you. Now shut up and smile, people are trying to take photos."

"Can I get a picture of you both with the horses?" Sarah called, waving her camera at them. "While they're being so well behaved."

"That's a miracle in itself," Maggie whispered to Finn. "I was worried that when we came out Ashley might have extricated himself and Rowena from that harness and be off up the road up to goodness knows what."

"Perhaps his new owners were right about hard work taking his mind off sex," Finn murmured, kissing Maggie's neck, when they were finally allowed to climb back into the carriage. "God, you smell gorgeous."

"It didn't work for you, though, did it? Work taking your mind off sex."

"Do you mind?"

"I suppose I could get used to it."

316

"I think you'll have to because I have conjugal rights now." He grinned at her. "Shall we skip the reception and tell the driver to take us straight to the hotel? No one would miss us, would they?"

"I think Albert would have a thing or two to say about it. Dorinda was telling me she had the devil's own job getting him into a suit."

"They'll be next, I reckon. Living in sin at their age is shocking, don't you think?"

"I thought you approved of sex before marriage." Maggie curved her hands across her stomach. "Or are you going to tell me that this is the result of too many romantic meals?"

"Well, it is in a way." He laughed and placed his hand over hers. "You've made me so happy, Maggie. You, and meeting Ben, and having our own little one on the way, what more could I possibly want?"

She smiled and glanced out of the window at a sky so blue it could have been painted especially for them. They were passing the village green and daffodils filled the beds, their bright yellow heads lit up with sunlight.

"Are you as happy as I am, Maggie?" he whispered, taking her hand and touching her fingers to his lips. He did it every day, but it still made her shiver as much as it had the very first time, and he knew it.

"Once, I thought the only thing that would make me happy was knowing that I'd come first in my mother's life, but I think you were probably right. I think that perhaps I haven't always seen things as clearly as I've thought."

"Another bit of that magic mirror, I expect."

She smiled at him. "But we don't believe in fairy tales, do we?"

"Only ones with happy endings," he said, and kissed her.

317

About The Author

Della Galton lives in a 16th century cottage in Dorset with her husband and four dogs. Since she gave up her management career in 2000 she's had ten serials and hundreds of short stories published. This is her first novel.

Find out more about Della Galton and her work by visiting her website **www.dellagalton.com**

ONE GLASS IS NEVER ENOUGH
By Jane Wenham Jones

*"Delightfully sparkling, like champagne,
with the deep undertones of a fine claret."*

Three women, one bar and three different reasons for buying
it. Single mother Sarah needs a home for her children;
Claire's an ambitious business woman. For wealthy Gaynor,
Greens Wine Bar is just one more amusement. Or is it?

On the surface, Gaynor has it all – money, looks, a beautiful
home in the picturesque seaside town of Broadstairs, and
Victor – her generous, successful husband. But while Sarah
longs for love and Claire is making money, Gaynor wants
answers. Why is Victor behaving strangely and who does he
see on his frequent trips away? What's behind the threatening
phone-calls? As the bar takes off, Gaynor's life starts to fall
apart.

Into her turmoil comes Sam – strong and silent with a hidden
past. Theirs is an unlikely friendship but then nobody is quite
what they seem in this tale of love, loss and betrayal set
against the middle-class dream of owning a wine bar. As
Gaynor's confusion grows, events unfold that will change all
of their lives forever…

ISBN 1905170106   Price: £6.99

THE BOY I LOVE
By Marion Husband

"Compelling & sensual. Well written…"

Set in the aftermath of World War One. Paul Harris, still frail from shellshock, returns to his father's home and to the arms of his secret lover, Adam. He discovers that Margot, the fiancée of his dead brother, is pregnant and marries her through a sense of loyalty. Through Adam he finds work as a schoolteacher; while setting up a home with Margot he continues to see Adam.

Pat Morgan who was a sergeant in Paul's platoon, runs a butcher's shop in town and cares for his twin brother, Mick who lost both legs in the war. Pat yearns for the closeness he experienced with Paul in the trenches.

Set in a time when homosexuality was 'the love that dare not speak it's name' the story develops against the backdrop of the strict moral code of the period. Paul has to decide where his loyalty and his heart lies as all the characters search hungrily for the love and security denied them during the war.

ISBN 1905170009   Price £6.99

PAPER MOON
By Marion Husband

*"This is an extraordinary novel. Beautifully controlled
pacy prose carefully orchestrates the relationships of many
well drawn characters and elegantly captures the atmosphere
of England in 1946...This novel is perfect."* Margaret
Wilkinson, Novelist

The passionate love affair between Spitfire pilot Bobby Harris
and photographer's model Nina Tate lasts through the turmoil
of World War Two, but is tested when his plane is shot down.
Disfigured and wanting to hide from the world, Bobby
retreats from Bohemian Soho to the empty house his
grandfather has left him, a house haunted by the secrets of
Bobby's childhood, where the mysteries of his past are
gradually unravelled.

Following on from The Boy I Love, Marion Husband's highly
acclaimed debut novel, Paper Moon explores the complexities
of love and loyalty against a backdrop of a world transformed
by war.

ISBN 1905170149   Price £6.99

BAREFOOT IN THE DARK
By Lynne Barrett-Lee

A modern twist on Cinderella

Radio Wales DJ Jack Valentine finds a lost trainer on a station
platform. With echoes of Cinderella, he appeals on his show
for its owner, Hope Shepherd, to come forward.

Hope handles publicity for a Cardiff based charity, Heartbeat.
Encouraged by colleagues to secure Jack Valentine to raise
the profile of an upcoming fun run, she reluctantly heads for
the studios.

The attraction between Hope and Jack is immediate but, bruised
and battered by their recent divorces, they are reluctant to risk
romance again.

Barefoot In The Dark is a bitter-sweet novel about taking the
first steps towards trusting again. But when love at first sight
is the last thing you're after, is a fairytale ending an
impossible dream?

ISBN 1905170378   Price £6.99

MURDER IN STEEPLE MARTIN
By Lesley Cookman

"With fascinating characters and an intriguing plot, this is a real page turner" - Katie Fforde

Artist Libby Sarjeant's fresh start in a picturesque Kent village includes an exciting new venture – the Oast House Theatre. She never expects it to include a new romance in the form of Ben, but who's complaining? She just isn't expecting ingredients three, four and five: mystery, intrigue, and the shadow of old murder...

This is a tale of engaging misfits and muddlers in a Kent village, whose theatrical endeavours rouse the long arm of the past with murderous consequences.

ISBN 1905170157   Price £6.99

BY ANY NAME
By Katherine John

A bloodstained man runs half naked down a motorway at night dodging high-speed traffic - and worse. Cornered by police, admitted to a psychiatric ward suffering from trauma-induced amnesia, all he can recall is a detailed knowledge of sophisticated weaponry and military techniques that indicates a background in terrorism.

When two armed soldiers guarding his room are murdered and Dr Elizabeth Santer, the psychiatrist assigned to his case, is abducted at gunpoint a desperate hunt begins for a dangerous killer.

Terrorist - murderer - kidnapper - thief whatever he is, he remembers a town in Wales and it is to Brecon he drags Elizabeth Santer with the security forces in all-out pursuit. There, a violent and bloody confrontation exposes a horrifying story of treachery and political cover-up. Is Elizabeth in the hands of a homicidal terrorist or an innocent pawn? Her life depends on the right answer.

ISBN 1905170254   Price £6.99

WITHOUT TRACE
By Katherine John

A Trevor Joseph Mystery

In the chilly half-light of dawn a bizarre Pierrot figure waits in the shadows of a deserted stretch of motorway. The costumed hitchhiker's victim is a passing motorist. The murder, cold-blooded, brutal.

Without motive.

Doctors at the local hospital Tim and Daisy Sherringham are blissfully happy. The perfect couple.
When an emergency call rouses Tim early one morning, he vanishes on the way from their flat to the hospital.

And Daisy is plunged into a nightmare of terror and doubt . . .

ISBN 1905170262   Price £6.99

MIDNIGHT MURDERS
By Katherine John

A Trevor Joseph Mystery

Compton Castle is a Victorian psychiatric hospital long overdue for demolition. Its warrens of rooms and acres of grounds, originally designed as a sanctuary for the mentally ill, now provide the ideal stalking ground for a serial killer.

Physically and mentally battered after his last case (Without Trace), Sergeant Trevor Joseph is a temporary inmate – but the hospital loses all therapeutic benefit when a corpse is dug out of a flowerbed. Then more bodies are found; young, female and both linked to the hospital.

Everyone within the mouldering walls is in danger while a highly unpredictable malevolence remains at large. And, as patients and staff are interrogated by the police, the apparently motiveless killer watches and waits for the opportunity to strike again . . .

ISBN 1905170270   Price £6.99

MURDER OF A DEAD MAN
By Katherine John

A Trevor Joseph Mystery

Jubilee Street – the haunt of addicts and vagrants is a part of town to avoid at all costs, especially when it becomes the stalking ground of a brutal and ruthless murderer.

A drunken down and out is the first casualty, mutilated and burned alive but his grisly death raises even more problems for the investigating officers, Sergeants Trevor Joseph and Peter Collins.

They discover that their victim died two years earlier. So who is the dead man? And what was the motive for the bizarre crime?

While they seek a killer in the dark urban underworld, the tally of corpses grows and the only certainty is that they can trust no man's face as his own.

ISBN 1905170289   Price £6.99